PAMELA COOK
OUT OF THE ASHES

BOOKS

By Pamela Cook

The Blackwattle Lake Series

Blackwattle Lake
Out of the Ashes
A Place of Her Own

The Homecoming Collection

All We Dream
Cross My Heart
The Crossroads
Close to Home

Vinci Books

vinci-books.com

Published by Vinci Books Ltd in 2025

1

Copyright © Pamela Cook 2024

The author has asserted their moral right to be identified as the author of this work in accordance with the Copyright, Designs and Patents Act 1988.
This work is a work of fiction. Names, characters, places and incidents are the product of the author's imagination or are used fictitiously. Any resemblance to actual persons, living or dead, places and incidents is entirely coincidental.
All rights reserved. No part of this publication may be copied, reproduced, distributed, stored in any retrieval system, or transmitted in any form or by any means, including photocopying, recording, or other electronic or mechanical methods, nor used as a source for any form of machine learning including AI datasets, without the prior written permission of the publisher.
The publisher and the author have made every effort to obtain permissions for any third party material used in this book and to comply with copyright law. Any queries in this respect should be brought to the attention of the publisher and any omissions will be corrected in future editions.
A CIP catalogue record for this book is available from the British Library.
Paperback ISBN: 9781036704339

Printed and bound in Great Britain by Clays Ltd, Elcograf S.p.A.

Author's Note

Some of the events described in this story have been drawn from my family's experience with the 2019-2020 bushfires on the south coast of New South Wales. I also found inspiration in *Currowan*, by Bronwyn Aldcock. However, all people and events in *Out of the Ashes* are fictional and any resemblance to individuals is purely coincidental.

Prologue

South Coast Fires: An Act of Nature or Something More Sinister?
Special Feature by Emily Winters

The recent fires on the south coast of NSW have been a devastating experience for so many. It's been a time of reckoning as we come face to face with the effects of the long-running drought. But was there another cause that's yet to be uncovered?

It's a dull Tuesday afternoon, and I'm driving the familiar route south on the Princes Highway. The fall of rain on the windscreen is barely there, yet still annoying enough to need the wipers. Adele sings something mournful on the radio. The dreary weather matches my mood and the landscape as I leave the industrial fringe of Nowra behind me. The tension in my neck and shoulders travels to my grip on the steering wheel.

My destination is Yarrabee, a town very close to where my parents owned a holiday house at Blackwattle Lake when I was growing up. Many of my happiest memories spring from lazy days and summer weekends, blissfully endless school breaks spent in our weatherboard house nestled at the end of the lake. It's the place where my brothers and I learnt to swim, where we caught prawns in nets from the end of the wharf and tossed them brutishly into pots of boiling water before gobbling them back like baby birds – their high-pitched squeaks as they met their ends already forgotten as we chewed on their salty flesh.

As a young freckle-faced kid, the youngest of three and the only girl, I'd spend hours and days beachcombing and floating lazily on my airbed in the blistering summer sun while my brothers tried to impress the local girls, eating Jaffas at the open-air picture theatre where we all watched movies under the stars. Every trip to the cottage was a homecoming: a long, slow exhale as the busyness of life in Sydney gave way to the soothing calm of the bush and the mesmerising whispers of the ocean.

Those days have long since gone, my parents having sold the house and retired north to the warmer climes of Crescent Head. But the memories remain: holiday snapshots fixed firmly in my mind's eye, overlaid now with television images from the recent fires. People packing as many belongings as they could into their cars, watching from a distance as their homes went up in flames. Roads blocked as the fires spread. Communications out: no petrol, no power, no way of contacting loved ones to check on their safety.

In television images more suited to a post-apocalyptic movie, people queued outside supermarkets, waiting to be led into the store by a shop assistant with a torch to choose a maximum of six items while low-lying clouds of smoke suffocated the town. Thousands of hectares of bushland burned, closing roads and businesses. Lives lost. Wildlife decimated. The toll unimaginable.

I keep driving but switch the music off. Silence seems a more appropriate soundtrack to the view outside my window. The white trunks of the towering gums flanking the highway soon give way to long stretches of sepia-toned forest, its undergrowth stripped bare, the earth beneath the trees charred and barren.

By the time I reach the Sussex Inlet turnoff, I'm driving through a wasteland. News reels of a policeman screaming at motorists to turn back as the flames around him fly skyward flicker in my head. I stare at the remains of trees. Here, everything is black. Leafless branches claw the sky. Houses ordinarily out of sight from the road now sit exposed, naked. I pass the well-loved local nursery, reduced to rubble, where the eighty-year-old owners lost their beloved dog, their home and a business they will probably never rebuild. As I inch closer to Yarrabee impossible patches of green, broader sections of paddocks and the familiar sight of grazing cows are salves for my wounded spirit.

The dragon's hot breath spewed out at random, devouring everything in one pocket, leaving the next patch unscathed. Dead leaves line the verge – if this was autumn and they weren't gum leaves, the sight would be quite beautiful.

Unable to focus on driving, I've pulled over to record this introduction. These once-familiar surroundings are a foreign landscape: hectare after hectare of scorched bush that surely cannot sustain life.

How much wildlife has been lost?

How will the bushland ever regenerate?

How will the people who live here – the people who have lost so much – ever recover?

And with rumours of arson rife, is there a more sinister cause for these fires than we have so far uncovered?

Chapter One

For the second time in a matter of months, Eve Nicholls stared down the driveway of her childhood home, trying to picture the house where she once lived. A sign spelt out its name on the gate: *Mossy Creek Farm*. White rail fences, paint blistered and peeling, remained on either side of the gravel driveway. Horses dotted the paddocks, their tails swishing at invisible flies as they tugged at surprisingly green blades of grass. But there was one startling difference: the cottage that had stood on the far side of the dressage arena only a short time ago was no more than a pile of rubble.

Eve sat frozen in the passenger seat of Hugh's work van, her breath trapped inside her chest. Even if she could move the appropriate muscles, there was no way she could form the words swirling in her brain. It was …

'You okay?' Hugh's hand rested on her arm. Her good arm, the one that still worked. 'It must be a shock seeing it like this for the first time.'

She turned her head ever so slightly in his direction. His

green eyes locked onto hers, concern swimming in their depths.

She gave him a nod – all she could manage – and returned her attention to the ruins.

Charred stumps.

Scorched chimney bricks.

Sheets of corrugated iron burnt and warped – on the ground when they should be on the roof.

Bit by bit, Eve catalogued the seemingly incomprehensible damage, not daring to look at Hugh in case his scrutiny made her crack.

Silence rattled between them like a mute third passenger.

A sudden high-pitched bark pierced her brain. 'Enough, Banjo.' She turned, batting a hand in the Kelpie's direction, and he lay down, whimpering on the back seat. Her rebuke was too sharp, too stern. Poor boy. He was just happy to be home. Or at least the place he'd come to think of as home. Reaching towards him, her fingers grazed the soft fur between his ears, and he licked the underside of her wrist. 'Sorry, matey.'

'How do you think he'll like living in a caravan?' Hugh's question was tentative, as if he was unsure it should even be asked.

'Well, he spent plenty of time in the Kombi in our nomadic days. At least a caravan is a little roomier.' She forced a smile. God, what she wouldn't do for a cigarette right now. Funny how the urge never really left you, patches or not.

Hugh pulled up beside the caravan. A 1974 Viscount, its yellow panels tarnished and showing a few rust spots but solid enough to keep out the rain. Apparently, Harry had even added a shower and connected solar power, so the van had hot water. All the mod cons. Positively luxurious.

'I know you already declined …' Hugh glanced from the caravan to Eve and back again. 'But you're more than welcome to stay on at the back of my surgery.'

She reached out and touched his arm, and that damned tingling started up again. Definitely not something she could act on right now. Or ever.

'I really appreciate the offer, Hugh, but I think me taking up a longer residence might make your office space a little cramped. It's a vet surgery not a motel. Besides, I want to be here to look after the horses.'

The neighbours had rallied while Eve had been in hospital and rehab, but it was time she stepped up and managed her own responsibilities.

His mouth quirked. 'One-handed?'

Ouch! 'You really know how to burst a girl's bubble, don't you?' She flashed him a grin to let him know she wasn't too offended. 'You'd be surprised what I can do with one hand.'

A blush bloomed across his cheeks, and he shifted his focus back to the driveway.

Poor Hugh. It had taken him a while to get used to her slightly risqué comebacks, but in general he seemed to be coping. A week's worth of his hospital visits and another two camping out on his office sofa while the graft healed had given them a chance to become better acquainted. Probably even made them friends rather than a couple of strangers who'd survived a life-threatening fire together.

'And look,' she raised her left elbow, flapping her arm as if she was doing a chicken dance, 'almost perfect working order.'

Moving the arm was one thing. Getting it to actually do anything useful wasn't going to happen anytime soon, thanks to the nerve damage. Then of course, there were the scars. For now, the compression bandage was keeping it all under cover.

A whine from the back seat.

'Okay, I get the message.' Hugh stepped out and released Banjo from his automotive prison. Nose to the ground, the dog ran around in circles, taking in the myriad scents of grass, horse manure and whatever else he could pick up with those crazy canine receptors. Could he still smell the ash, despite the recent rains? Probably not.

Maybe Eve's imagination was conjuring that scent. Or maybe it lived on in her cellular memory. Could it be debrided the same way a physical burn could be? Could the damage it had done heal as miraculously? She stared down at her arm, and a wave rippled through her: ice cold, head to toe. Another place she was definitely not going.

Bags in hand, Hugh rounded the van to stand in front of her. 'Shall we?'

Even as she opened the door, the roar of a hot raging wind exploded in her ears. She splayed her palm against the side of the van and drew in a long, deep inhalation.

'You okay, Eve?'

Swallowing, she licked her lips. 'Yeah.'

Hugh scoffed, but clearly knew better by now than to argue.

Leading the way, she opened the caravan and stepped inside. The distinct aroma of fresh paint stopped her in her tracks, along with the perfume from the bunch of pink roses and yellow daisies in the vase by the sink. The interior was nothing like the outside. Painted in easy-on-the-eye cream, the windows dressed in mint-green gingham, with sunshine-yellow cushions on the orange upholstery of the seats, it was like stepping into a citrus orchard. Margo had been busy decorating.

'Wow. It's bright.' Hugh nodded his head. 'I like it.'

'Me too.' The tangy colours gave the caravan a summery feel. Breezy and light.

'Perfect.'

A golf ball-sized lump formed at the base of Eve's throat. Everyone had been so kind since the fires, even though she'd kept them all at a distance when she'd come back after her mother's death. Not at all what she'd expected.

Hugh hoisted the bags slightly higher. 'So where would you like these?'

'Well, in the absence of a mezzanine level, how about right here.' She pointed to the space between their feet, and Hugh plonked the bags down on the black-and-white lino flooring. Her entire life was contained inside one small suitcase and one duffle bag– and those few photos and mementoes she'd managed to rescue before the whole place went up in flames.

'I'll grab the groceries.'

'Thanks, Hugh.'

He took the two steps down and headed for the back of his van, his feet making an uneven shuffling noise across the gravel. Sometimes it was easy to forget his limp, but that tell-tale irregularity to his gait came into sharper focus from behind. Her fingers itched but refused to curl. Would her own scars become a forgotten part of who she was at some point? Or would they always be an unwelcome – and ugly – reminder?

Eve shook her head, rattling the thought away. Hashing it over all the time was stupid. She needed to forget about it and move on, the same way she'd banished all her other heartache. It wasn't like she'd never had practice.

Banjo's bark put an end to her musing. The silly goose was out in the paddock, chasing a plover attempting to dive-bomb him. It probably had a nest out there somewhere and didn't want a nosey Kelpie anywhere near the eggs. They'd sort out their respective territories eventually, or the plover would be victorious.

Hugh was back. He deposited the box of groceries on the table. Enough to keep her going for the next few days. Not being able to drive was a bitch, but managing the gearstick in the Kombi was impossible, and there was no way her bank balance would extend to car hire.

Hugh pulled his cap off and scratched his head. 'Are you sure you'll be alright out here by yourself?' That lovely Irish brogue never got old, unlike his worry-wort tendencies. Was it fatherly, an extension of his fabulous single parenting to his twins, or was the fussing for an entirely different reason? Hard to tell, but either way it wasn't necessary.

'I'm a big girl, Hugh. I left home when I was seventeen. I'm turning thirty-eight. And I've spent all the years in between looking after myself, so yes, I will be fine.'

Glancing out the door, his eyes narrowed. Eve followed his gaze to the wreck that used to be her mother's home. Her own home for the earlier years of her life, and again, for the briefest period before it turned to ashes.

'I know you're perfectly capable but …' He shook his head. 'Being out here on your own, after everything that happened, might be harder than you think.'

'Well, we'll soon find out.' She punctuated the statement with a smile.

Hugh's face fell, and Eve gave herself an internal kick.

Would she ever learn to reel in her flippant, smart-arse comments?

He glanced at his watch. 'I've got an 11 a.m. appointment, so I'd better get back to the clinic.'

'Of course.' She followed him out to the car.

From the driver's seat, he looked at her through the open window, his eyes the colour of sea glass. 'You know where I am if you need anything.'

Pins and needles dimpled the bare skin of her arms as he started the ignition. She'd spent years on her own. Loved her independence. So why was she going soft now?

She held onto the window frame but could so easily have touched his cheek instead. 'Hugh, I'm so grateful. Thank you for everything. I don't know what I would have done without you.'

His mouth twitched. 'That's what friends do: look after each other.'

Eve smiled back. 'Right.'

Before returning to Yarrabee, she could count the people she called friends on one hand. Now she most definitely needed two hands, even if one of those was currently out of action.

'I'll be seeing you.' Dust hovered above the driveway as Hugh drove towards the gate and out onto the road.

She kept her back to the remains of the house, but even so, the heat of the flames burned in her memory, licking the sky, turning it into a dense black cloud, sucking the oxygen from her lungs.

Horses whinnied and wheeled in the paddocks, charging in circles, crowding together as they tried to avoid the falling embers, escape the thunderous roar of the firestorm.

Banjo's rough tongue licked at Eve's cheek. She lifted her head, dragged her hands away from her knees and straightened. Without even realising, she'd dropped to her haunches and curled into a ball, her neck and shoulders tight as a freshly strung fence wire. Banjo whined and stepped back, looking up at her, tail whipping from side to side. Her crazy little man, checking in on her, always right here beside her.

She leaned towards him and drew him into a hug, taking one slow breath after another as she steadied herself. Not that she went in for all that meditation-in-the-moment crap, but the techniques the hospital psychologist had insisted on showing her did actually work. There were a whole lot of people out there doing it a lot tougher, and she'd survived worse herself.

'We'll be all right, won't we, Banj?'

Even as the words left her mouth, a gaping hole opened inside Eve's chest as the empty space where the house used to be swam in her peripheral vision. She twisted her hair into a knot and spun back towards the caravan. The cold goods needed unpacking. No time like the present to set up home. Even if it was temporary. Even though the thought of staying made everything inside her turn to water.

What had Margo said the caravan's name was again? Dora? No. Something to do with the colour. Something floral. Daisy! That was it.

'Well, Daisy, looks like it's just the three of us for the next little while. Let's see if we can make this work, eh?'

Eve shoved her underwear into the small drawer in the bedside cupboard and zipped up her pack; the whole thing emptied in less than ten minutes. One advantage of everything going up in smoke: an instant declutter. She turned in one direction and then the other, spotted a handle under the bed and pulled it out to reveal a nifty storage space.

Bags tucked away, she wiped her palms down the side of her jeans and perused her new home. Compact, but not too shabby. Better than getting under Margo and Harry's feet while he recovered from the heart attack, and they got their own place back on track. And better than staying at Hugh's surgery. Waking to the whiff of disinfectant or listening to Anne Patterson wax lyrical about her Shi Tzu's anal glands. Not to mention the proximity to Hugh.

Anyway, once the insurance money came through, she would be on the road again. With so many claims all happening at once, they'd already notified her that it would take some time but hopefully sooner rather than later.

Now, where was Banj?

She stuck her head through the doorway and peered across the paddocks. It was eye-blindingly green, almost fluorescent. Ash certainly did a good job as fertiliser: all that potassium. All the horses seemed safe and sound. She scanned the herd. There was Rain. Head down, nibbling at the grass, that beautiful chestnut coat almost iridescent in the morning sunlight. Such a survivor. First the injured leg and then the fires. They'd all need re-homing when Eve left, but leaving that mare was going to hurt.

A horn tooted from the other end of the drive. She shaded her eyes with her hand and peered into the soft autumn sunshine. As the car came closer, a woman with cropped grey hair came into view.

Margo. No doubt loaded with food.

Banjo appeared out of nowhere and ran alongside the car, barking and grinning from ear to ear. One of these days, the goofball was going to get himself run over.

'Banj. That's enough.' Oblivious to her call, the dog

picked up speed, racing ahead of the car as it pulled to a stop. Tongue lolling, he flopped down beside the caravan.

'Good boy. Sort of.' Eve leaned down to rub his forehead, her fingers finding a bunch of burrs turning the hair on his head into a mohawk. 'Nice one, mate. Not even here an hour and you're finding all the worst spots.'

He looked up at her as if she'd just offered him a giant, juicy bone. Was there anything better than the unconditional adoration of a dog?

'Hello there.' Margo climbed out of the car, opened the back door and pulled out two Tupperware containers.

'Margo, you—'

'Don't tell me I didn't have to. It's what I do, you know that. And since you're so pigheaded and insist on staying here on your own, you can expect a regular delivery service.'

Taking the top container, Eve balanced it on her hip and peered through the opaque plastic.

'Carrot cake.' Margo nodded towards the caravan door. 'Put the kettle on.'

The same warm fuzzy feeling Eve always got around Margo purred beneath her skin. Sure, her godmother was bossy, but in a more motherly way than Nell had ever managed. Margo's sass was tongue-in-cheek and well-meaning, whereas her own mother had been— no, Eve was being too tough. Nell had her maternal moments, even though they were few and far between.

Inside the caravan, Margo was already busy with morning tea. 'How's the hand?'

She dropped teabags into two mugs. 'Fine. It's feeling fine.'

'Pft,' Margo scoffed. 'You're not fooling me, you know.

I've been watching you since I got out of the car, and you haven't used it once.'

The kettle whirred to a crescendo and clicked off. Margo pursed her lips. 'Cut me a bit of that cake while I pour.'

The square container sat on the table, lid shut tight. Heat prickled behind Eve's ears. There was no way she could open that container with one hand. It was a test, and they both knew it. Focusing all her energy on her left hand, she silently implored it to work as she steadied the container against her palm. The fingers twitched but refused to budge.

Eve's shoulders drooped. 'Okay, so maybe it's not quite there yet. The doctor did say it would take some time.'

'You been doing the physio?'

Eve bit down on her bottom lip, willing away the colour she knew was rising in her cheeks.

Margo plonked the two full cups on the table, tucked the container against her middle and peeled the lid away. Soft peaks of cream cheese and the nutty smell of freshly baked carrot cake filled the van. 'It's not going to get better by itself, you know, and you're going to need help managing the horses and everything else out here.'

Eve took the slice of cake Margo served up on a piece of paper towel, placed it on the table and cut a piece off with a fork. Margo slid into the seat opposite. There was no point arguing with the woman. She was the original force of nature.

'Well, I did have your grandson working here, if you remember, before he up and left. Any news on Luke?'

Margo shook her head. 'Nope. Left a note saying he was going south to get some farming work but hasn't bothered getting in touch since. Not with us or his parents. I don't know what's got into the boy.'

'A shame. He did a great job with the horse feeds before the …' The word stuck in Eve's throat, a piece of gristle she couldn't swallow or bring herself to spit out. 'Would have been great to have him back on the payroll.'

Margo nodded, her gaze well and truly averted. 'I know.'

Whether that was in reply to the conversation about her grandson or a reference to their shared experience of the fires was hard to tell.

'How's Harry?'

The circles around Margo's eyes darkened, as the sallow colour of her skin paled to an even lighter shade. 'Frustrated. There's so much that needs to be done, but the doctor said he has to take it easy. I don't think we're going to be able to manage, and it will kill Harry if we have to sell.' Her voice wavered. She pulled a tissue from her pocket and dabbed at her eyes. 'As much as I love the old fool, he's not an easy man to live with when things aren't going his way.'

Eve reached out and grasped the back of her old friend's hand. A lifetime of lines, rough beneath her palm. Knobbly knuckles cold beneath her fingers. 'You have Dean and Michelle, and Luke and his brother. And me. We'll get through it.'

'Luke.' Margo scoffed. 'Little bugger. Couldn't have gone at a worse time. He doesn't know what he's doing to his parents, or he never would have taken off like that.' She didn't need to say, *What he's doing to me,* as it was written all over her face.

'Well, sometimes people have reasons for disappearing.' As soon as the words were out, Eve wanted to swallow them whole. Bringing back memories of her own vanishing act was not exactly going to lighten the mood.

'I hope it doesn't take twenty years for him to come back.' A wry grin lit Margo's face, her sense of humour kicking in just at the right time. 'You made any decision yet about the rebuild?'

The roar of flames whooshed through Eve's ears. Fire blazed inside her brain, and smoke stung her nostrils. As if she was back there in that dam, suffocating alongside Margo all over again. Margo's face blurred.

'You alright, love?' The voice came from far, far away. From the other side of the inferno. 'Eve, can you hear me?' Closer now, standing over her. A hand on her arm, shaking her free.

She sucked in a mouthful of air. Concentrated as it passed in through her nose, down her throat, filling her lungs – as the counsellor had taught her. And then the process in reverse.

Margo waited patiently beside her, looking down, frowning.

'Sorry.' Eve swallowed. 'Sometimes it hits me out of nowhere. Is it the same for you?'

Margo gave a barely-there nod. 'Nights are the worst, when the light goes off. Sometimes I feel like I'll never be able to sleep properly again.' Margo's shoulders rose as her chest expanded. 'But life goes on. And I've got enough to worry about with Harry thinking he's invincible. No time for me to fall apart.'

'Well, you're so busy looking after everybody else, Aunty Margo, you make sure you look after yourself.'

'I will. Now I'd better be off home and make sure bugalugs isn't trying to scale a ladder and clean the gutters.' Margo lowered herself down the steps. 'It's not making my sleep any easier knowing you're here on your own. Are you sure you're okay by yourself? With no car?'

'Perfectly. I like my solitude, and as much as I appreciate all the offers of a bed, I do need the space.'

Eve blew a kiss, and Banjo thumped his tail on the ground as they watched Margo's car disappear. She closed her eyes, inhaling the quiet. Not a sound. Not even birdsong. Even though the paddocks were greening and the trees starting to sprout those weird tufts of leaves, the bush itself had taken a beating. Nothing but black tree skeletons as far as the eye could see. Nothing to sustain the local wildlife – or the human inhabitants.

Sooner or later, she'd have to brave reality, so it might as well be now. Turning, she stared directly at the space where the house once stood. Old memories flickered through her mind like light dancing through treetops. Her grandfather's saddle propped up on its stand on the veranda, she and Bec climbing on top, squealing with delight, pretending to ride. Water fights on the front lawn with Jack back in their teens, her insides tingling as much as her skin at the splash of cold water and the hot touch of his hands against her waist. Her mother gazing out at the paddocks, rain dripping from the hood of her Driza-Bone, after losing her youngest daughter. And then that surreal vision of Nell, dead weeks before but standing in the midst of the fire, waving goodbye the night the place burned to the ground.

Banjo licked at Eve's shin and a smile flitted across her lips. Coming back the first time had been a necessity – getting the house ready to sell – and had helped her resolve unfinished business. With others, but more importantly with herself. Laying Bec's ghost to rest; coming to terms with her sister's drowning and accepting it had all been a horrible accident. That she herself hadn't been to blame. Finding some sort of forgiveness when she'd read Nell's letter. For both of them. But what was left here for her now?

Certainly not a house. Not a family. No work other than the part-time hours she'd been offered in the bookstore café. No real reason to stay.

Her damaged hand throbbed. She gave it a shake. Mentally moved the muscles in her fingers, but the patched-up skin was so tight after the graft, they only budged a few millimetres.

Keep working on it. It takes time. The physio's advice rang in her head like an annoying door-chime. One she'd like to shove a screwdriver under and rip off its rusty hinges. Almost three weeks since the operation, and despite the doctor's claim that the burns were healing well, her hand was still pretty much useless thanks to the nerve damage.

'Urgh.' She kicked at the tyre of the caravan, and slammed her good hand against its aluminium exterior, the force of the blow reverberating up the right side of her body. And with it, an overwhelming thirst for something she hadn't craved for quite some time.

Stepping inside, she pulled out her pack, unzipped the side pocket and dug down into its depths. The cool touch of metal kissed her fingertips. She pulled out the hip flask Marcus had given her for her birthday last year – at least something good had come out of that relationship. Clamping it between the inside of her forearm and her chest, she unscrewed the lid and inhaled the sweet scent of fine Kentucky bourbon.

Her last binge had been here with Marcus himself, their final farewell. It seemed so long ago now, that night he'd arrived unexpectedly, chasing her down and begging her to give him another chance. Before the fires, before the burns, before she once again became homeless.

Eve plonked herself down on the step and chugged back a mouthful, the sharp bite of the whisky dousing the sugary remnants of Margo's cake. So much for continuing the detox now she was out of hospital. Still, this was purely medicinal.

A blowfly buzzed around Banjo's face. He lifted his head and snapped it away, flopping back down onto his side, eyes closed, perfectly content.

Eve's gaze rose again to the empty space where her childhood home once stood. She slugged back another draught of liquid, licked the residue from her lips and savoured the taste on her tongue alongside the question that had been haunting her dreams for weeks.

Where to next?

Chapter Two

The shrill ring of a phone jack-hammered through Eve's skull. One of these days she'd learn some self-discipline. Stop at one drink. Or none. Cracking her eyes open, she reached down and retrieved the offending object. She squinted, zeroing in on the caller ID. Mel. What was she doing calling this early? Head back on the pillow, she pressed the green accept button.

'Hello?'

At the end of the bed, Banjo blinked and groaned.

'Evie, girl. What's happening?'

'What's happening? Are you serious? It's 8 a.m. and I'm in bed.' *With a pounding head.* 'Why are you calling at this God-forsaken hour?'

'You're missing the best part of the day, my friend. I have news.' Mel always had been an early bird. Preferred the first shifts at the Marrickville café where they both worked, which had suited Eve just fine. Starting at midday and working through into the evening was so much better for her body clock. 'Guess where I am?' Mel chirped.

Eve pinched the bridge of her nose to stave off the banging in her head. 'No idea.'

'I'll give you a clue. Beautiful one day. Perfect the next.'

'Argh, gee, let me think …' Even with a hangover, it was hard to stay annoyed with Mel, especially with the playful tone bouncing down the phone line. 'You're not in Queensland, by any chance?'

'You got it, sista. And guess what I'm holding in my hand?'

'Oh, come on, Mel, it's way too early for a game of twenty questions.' Eve shuffled further down the bed.

'Okay. I'll tell you. But I hope you're sitting down.'

Eve let out a very audible sigh. 'Go ahead.'

'I am holding in my hand the rental agreement for an absolutely perfect beachside café on the outskirts of Noosa. Exactly like the one we daydreamed about. I'm telling you, Eve, we manifested this baby into existence.'

A smile crept onto Eve's face, despite her mood. Mel was all about signs from the universe and stars aligning. It had been so much fun taking the mickey out of her when they'd worked together, but her enthusiasm was always infectious.

'You're there right now? In Noosa?'

'Yes! This place is everything we talked about. Our own little piece of paradise. It's going off up here and I've been through the accounts. Totally solid with major room for improvement. We could turn it into one of the coolest cafés on the coast. When can you get here?'

Eve sat upright, switching the phone off speaker mode and pressing it to her ear. 'Hang on a minute, Mel. That plan was purely small talk.'

'But that's because you never thought you could afford it. Once you sell your mum's place, you'll be cashed up.'

Cashed up. Something she'd never been in her entire life. Not that she cared. As long as she had enough to keep a roof over her head and Banjo in dog treats, they were both happy. 'You do know the house is no longer standing?'

'Well, yeah, but you're still selling, aren't you?'

Eve pulled back the curtain and peered out at the ruins. Her chest constricted, as if an invisible hand had inserted a ratchet into the centre of her diaphragm and was winding it tighter and tighter. 'Yeah, I am.'

'Perfect! Like I said, the universe has spoken. My sister finally paid back the loan I'd given her, and you've got your inheritance money. It's a no brainer, Eve.'

Banjo lurched to his feet and wandered to the door, giving the 'Please let me out' look. Eve threw back the sheets and a current ran through her arm, as if she'd just connected with a hot-wire. Drawing in a sharp breath, she rested against the edge of the bed, the pain colliding with Mel's proposition and creating a brewing explosion right between her temples.

'Sorry, Mel, I'm not feeling too good. I have to go.'

'Okay. But think about it. Like I said, babe, it's a no-brainer. I'll send through some pics. You'll love this place. Sunshine, ocean and good vibes. Everything we wanted.'

'Great. Talk soon.'

Eve ended the call, took the five steps to the door and pushed it open. Brilliant, blinding light burst into the caravan as Banjo jumped down the steps and raced to the paddock.

'Knock yourself out, matey.' Oh, to have that kind of energy in the mornings, even when she hadn't hit the booze too hard.

Craving coffee, she flicked on the kettle and squeezed into the seat behind the table. Her phone pinged: once, twice, three times. Photos coming through from Mel. She clicked on the first image and swiped to the others. A gorgeous weatherboard café painted in shades of pink, yellow and orange, outdoor tables covered with funky umbrellas, views of the beach right across the road. A real seventies vibe.

Wow. It really was everything they'd talked about, and more. They'd spent hours discussing the details while they worked, even though they both knew it was pie in the sky. And she'd spent nights wide awake, dreaming of sun-soaked days, managing her own business instead of slaving away for somebody else, filling the boss's pockets while hers remained threadbare.

An email notification came through. Subject: *Dream Business Rental*. And in the body: *Hi Hon, Details attached. I've told the agent we're interested. Honestly Eve, this is the one! Let me know asap.*

The kettle screamed, and she dropped the phone onto the table. Mel might be onto something, but caffeine was the current priority.

Sitting on the floor in the caravan doorway, she sipped the black brew and let the exquisite aroma soothe her headache. Out in the paddock, Banjo was nose-down tail-up, taking in the scents, plover-chasing.

Exactly like the one we daydreamed about. Everything we talked about.

Mel was so right. They'd both contributed to the vision, spent hours talking about their ideal life, living up north, running a business together. Mel would supervise the kitchen, and Eve would do front of house. They'd have acoustic sessions on weekends, do one-off dinners and events. Be their own bosses. Work to live, as the saying went, rather than live to work. And here it was, the whole shebang being handed to Eve on a glittering gelato-coloured platter.

And yet the buzz of the real possibility came nowhere near the daydream. If she'd still been in Sydney, still with Marcus – if Nell had never died –if she'd never come back to Mossy Creek, would she even think twice about jumping at Mel's offer? About living the life she'd always imagined but never really believed she could have.

Eve stepped through the door into *Something Brewing*, Banjo glued to her heels like a leech after heavy rains, closed her eyes and inhaled. Was there anything better than the mingled scent of coffee and books? She'd had plenty of bar and barista jobs over the years, but none where she got to put her feet up in the breaks to read.

This was an offer she couldn't resist, along with a regular pay-packet. Clive and Fran were probably being kind offering her this job but hey, you had to take what you could get, and it beat being on social security.

The Noosa idea simmered on Eve's mental back-burner. At some stage she'd have to reply to Mel's texts. In the forty-eight hours since they'd spoken, there'd been over a dozen messages, all extolling the virtues of life in the north and how much money they could make if they took on the business. Not to mention the ridiculous number of seriously hot men frequenting the esplanade out front of the café. Mel was five years younger and a total piranha when it came to dating. In fact, when it came to anything. At some point, she'd start calling and demanding an answer.

Reaching into her pocket, Eve switched her phone to silent and flipped the sign on the door to *Open*.

'Thanks again for the lift, Clive.' Having her boss drive all the way off the main road to collect her was problematic, even though it had been his idea.

'All good. I don't mind the drive out to yours. And we do get to gossip in the car.' He grinned and waggled his eyebrows Groucho Marx-style as he poured another bag of beans into the grinder.

Such a lovely man. A 'blow-in' as locals liked to call the tree-changers who'd moved into town over the last few years. Exactly what she'd be if she took the leap and moved north.

Time to set up: open the blinds, wipe down the bench, check the fridge for supplies. It was early days in terms of working together, but already she and Clive were into a solid routine. He manned the machine during the morning rush before taking off to help Fran at the gallery, while she manned the counter, serving the customers and tolerating the chit-chat, all perfectly doable one-handed. After lunch Eve was left to her own devices, dusting the shelves, flipping open the odd book or two, having only to decide which title to settle on for the quiet hours before closing.

'What does a girl have to do to get a coffee around here?'

The voice was instantly recognisable. She closed the fridge and stepped up to the counter. 'A cartwheel would be acceptable.'

Cat laughed, her freckled skin glowing in the morning light. 'God, remember the competitions we used to have?'

'Sure do. And you beat me every time. Think your record was thirteen in a row, wasn't it?'

'Doubt I could even do one now. Probably break a limb.'

'You and me both.' Eve leant on the counter and tucked a loose hair back behind her ear. 'And I'd be doing mine one-handed.'

'The usual, Cat?' Clive's question floated out from the kitchen along with the easy-listening playlist.

'Yes, please.' Cat's attention shifted to Eve's bandaged arm. 'So, how's it going?'

'Pretty good.' Eve clutched the cleaning cloth in her right hand, moving it in circles on the countertop.

'You managing alright?'

'Friend question or doctor question?'

They seemed to have sorted out their issues, dealt with the demons from their past, but Cat was always so work obsessed it was probably the latter. Then there was the whole Jack situation. Things had been more than complicated when Eve had returned and discovered he'd married her former best friend. Her reconciliation with Cat had almost imploded before it could start.

'Friend first, doctor second.'

Warmth radiated from deep in Eve's core like rays of internal sunshine. 'Well, thank you on both counts, and the answer is yes.'

'Graft healing okay?' Now Cat was most definitely wearing her doctor hat.

'You know it is, Cat. You saw me in the surgery last week, said I was fine to go home.'

'Just checking. You need to make sure you keep up the physio.'

'You also told me that.'

The whirring of the milk-frothing machine signalled that Cat's order was almost ready. It was still so fresh, this reconnection between the two of them, so fragile. Navigating the boundaries was tricky.

'Tell me about your weekend. How's Lilly?'

'She's good. She had a little friend over for a playdate. I did a bit of gardening. Nothing special.' Ever since the fires, there was a sad, lost look about Cat – but then she wasn't alone: a lot of people in town carried the same expression. No one had emerged unscathed, and the emotional toll was huge for the firefighters and their families.

'How's Jack?'

Cat shrugged. 'The same. Keeping to himself. Spending a lot of time in front of the TV, zoning out.'

'Is he working back at the produce store?'

'Nope.' Cat pursed her lips. 'Says he doesn't want to go back. Doesn't want to deal with people. Grant has hired someone to fill his spot, which is a drain on the business. To be honest, we could do with the money. I know my doctor wage is pretty good, but we have the mortgage and things are a little tight.'

Clive appeared, pushing Cat's order across the bench. 'One mochaccino. Just what the doctor ordered.'

'Thanks.' Cat's lips quirked at what had become a standard line. She picked up her coffee, and Clive returned to the kitchen. 'Did you have any luck finding a builder?'

Eve shook her head. 'No.' Not that she'd looked but telling Cat she'd be leaving once the insurance money was through wasn't a bridge she wanted to cross right now. For some reason, Cat seemed to assume she'd be sticking around. Maybe she'd mumbled something along those lines in the hospital while she was dosed to the eyeballs on painkillers. Luckily, demand for builders was so high there was no chance of finding a local, and that might buy her some time until she worked out how to break the news she wasn't staying.

'There must be someone around who'd be willing to do the rebuild.' Cat poured a sachet of sugar into her cup and gave it a stir. She lifted her head, her eyes glittering like a disco ball. 'Maybe Jack could do it?'

'Your Jack?' Eve's voice made a weird hiccupping sound. She'd long ago stopped thinking of him as *her* Jack – he was most definitely Cat's – but the idea of him back at Mossy Creek day in day out set her insides trembling. 'I'm not sure that's a great idea.'

Cat flicked her hand in the air as if shooing away an annoying fly. 'Eve, I know I was a little wary when you first arrived back in town, but that's all in the past. I have absolutely no issue with Jack working at your place. It's the ideal solution. You need a builder. Jack doesn't want to return to The Shed. He still has his builder's licence, and he could do a lot of the work himself, bring in tradies when needed.'

You could almost see the neurons firing inside Cat's gorgeous head. A surprise, given the complicated history between the three of them.

'Leave it with me. I'll talk to him tonight.' Cat gave a hurried glance down at her watch. 'Better get going. I've got some calls to make before the appointments start. Thanks for the coffee – can you pop it on my tab?' She whirled out the door, her long ponytail of red curls bouncing across her back.

Eve stared into the vacant space left in Cat's wake. How had that whole conversation happened? At what point had she agreed that it was a good idea for Jack to do the job? There *was* no build happening, and even if there was, would hiring Jack be wise?

The questions ping-ponged back and forth, leaving her

slightly dizzy. Keeping her distance from Jack was definitely prudent. And based on the hermit act he'd been pulling since the fires, he wasn't in any mood to be out and about. Losing a workmate in such tragic circumstances was hard enough, but when guilt was involved, it could eat you alive from the inside out. Then again, if that's what was going on with Jack, he needed to get out of his head and start doing something. Swinging a hammer and taking out his frustrations with a saw could be exactly what he needed. Cat's idea wasn't a bad one; he just wouldn't be doing it at Mossy Creek Farm.

Chapter Three

A siren wailed. Eve's eyes sprang open, and she stared into the darkness. Cool night air licked at her cheeks, her heart thundering like a stallion charging across an open field as Banjo's snores rumbled from the end of the bed.

Bit by bit, the dim interior of the caravan crystallised, and her body relaxed. The dream was gone but glimmers of it remained, sending a chill rippling up the back of her neck. The pattern was becoming familiar: bone-wearying fatigue setting in by the end of the day, ravenous hunger satiated only by an overflowing dinner plate, a welcoming bed only to be plagued by disturbing dreams. The same thing every day since she'd left hospital.

Four weeks of wrangling the nightmares: lying awake until late into the night, her entire body wired; stripping off sweat-soaked T-shirts in the early hours after waking herself with a hoarse, soundless scream. Most probably the after-effects of the fires but getting worse when it should be getting better. Come to think of it, the nausea had been getting more severe over the last week, even on the days when she wasn't working, when she lay around doing nothing.

Eve bolted upright in bed like a Jack-in-the-Box springing from its case. She'd had these symptoms once before, twenty years ago.

No!

The dream had unsettled her, got the acid churning in her gut. That was all. Nothing a cup of tea wouldn't fix. Throwing back the covers, she flicked the light switch above the bed and stumbled the few steps it took to reach the kettle. She found the tea bag and grabbed the milk from the fridge. Sniffing it before pouring was a lifelong habit, copied from Nell.

Eve popped open the carton and lifted it to her nose. Bile surged up her throat. Her hand flew to her mouth as she gagged. The kettle switched itself off, but there was no way she was going near that milk. Even the thought of black tea made her want to retch.

Back in bed, she lowered herself down, swallowing a mouthful of spit.

There was no way she could be pregnant. Was there?

She'd only been back in Yarrabee for a few weeks when the fires broke out and there'd been no …

Shit.

Marcus. That hot and heavy farewell when he'd visited trying to patch things up. Weeks since they'd seen each other. Both drunk on Bourbon. Randy as rabbits. How could she have been so reckless?

Sitting up, she shuffled back against the wall of the van. When was her last period? Certainly nothing lately, but she could put her lack of one this month down to her body clock going berserk with the treatment, medication and the stress. PTSD, according to the doctor.

Or it could be something else.

Even without a test, her body was hitting her with a reality stick. The same way it told her when she was seventeen and Bec had just died and the whole fucking world had gone crazy. A world she could never bring a baby into, not when she was a homeless teenager crippled by grief. So long ago. Another lifetime, in a completely different situation.

But what about now?

Was there any way she could contemplate being a mother?

No!

No, no, no, no, no.

Babies needed love and stability and a roof over their heads. None of which she was anywhere near capable of providing. And there was no way she was teaming up with Marcus again – that horse had bolted. Based on his message after that one last time, he was heading back to Italy to 'reconnect with his roots'.

An electrifying shriek rang out from the paddock, setting her teeth on edge. Banjo growled, seemingly in his sleep. That damned plover was making his life a misery even in the dead of night.

She flopped down onto the mattress and did a mental countback, calculating dates. Marcus had visited about two weeks before the fires broke out. Had they used a condom? She lifted a hand to her head and rubbed her forehead, the points of her temples rock hard against her fingertips. It had happened so fast. One minute they'd been in the kitchen, and she'd been telling him to leave, and the next minute they were practically screwing on the kitchen table before taking it to the bedroom. Even the next day, the whole thing had been a blur. But the hollow feeling in the pit of her stomach said they'd used no protection.

What an idiot! She'd been so careful about contraception after what had happened to her as a teenager, but time and booze had lowered her guard.

So, if her instincts were right, she was around six weeks pregnant.

How could she not have known? They'd even asked the question when she was taken into Emergency and of course she'd said no, there was no chance. She hadn't lied. That whole thing was no more than a quick farewell fuck. Over and done with and completely forgotten.

Until now.

Six weeks.

And that meant she had around the same length of time to contemplate the question she'd grappled with as a teenager. Back then, she hadn't had a choice. The decision had been instantaneous and she had no regrets. She'd been in no position to bring a baby into the world. And here she was twenty years later, with not much more to show for herself. Nowhere to live. No money to her name – at least until the insurance claim was processed. No actual plan other than Mel's offer to join her in opening a café in Noosa.

Where would she be in another twenty years if things didn't change? If she didn't *make* a change?

Nell would say this was the universe giving Eve a wake-up call. Telling her to get her bloody act together and grow up. But adding a baby to the load of baggage she was lugging around seemed like more of a burden than she could carry. Just the thought made her limbs ache and her head hurt.

She wriggled back underneath the covers and gazed into the empty black space that suddenly seemed alive and breathing: a shifting, cunning creature, patiently waiting to swallow her whole.

Chapter Four

Morning feed done, Eve drove the trailer back down the hill. Banjo perched beside her taking in the view through the windscreen. With fresh buds of grass pushing through the charred earth, the paddocks were starting to look like they could provide sustenance again. Miraculously, the higher sections had escaped the blaze, as had the shed and equipment. But here, closer to the house where the damage had been the worst, the intensity of the colour was testimony to Mother Nature's powers of regeneration.

Her stomach somersaulted, despite being completely empty. Morning coffee was not an option, unless she wanted it to come straight back up. With the onset of daylight, last night's realisation had faded to a niggling possibility – one she was not yet ready to contemplate. If she kept busy, made sure her mind was always occupied, it could stay that way, at least for a while.

Without any more chores to do, the day stretched ahead of her like the Nullarbor Crossing, stark and endless. Thankfully not as hot. Autumn's arrival had brought a beautiful crispness to the mornings, a frisson against her bare skin that made her feel alive. Leaves turning gold and amber and rust, at least on the deciduous trees in town that were still intact, unlike here at Mossy Creek, where the property was surrounded by an army of incinerated sentinels. But going down that mental road or any of its tangents was way too dangerous – the stuff of nightmares.

A flash of light momentarily blurred Eve's vision, and she turned her head towards a silver car on its way down the drive. Didn't people understand the meaning of a closed gate?

Hang on … was that? Yes … a police car. What were they doing here?

The last time she'd been visited by the police, they'd delivered the news that her mother had died, in what seemed like another lifetime, a world away in Marrickville. Now she had no family left to lose. Even so, a frozen finger worked its way down her spine, scattering a trail of goosebumps in its wake. They wouldn't be calling for a cuppa and friendly chat.

She switched off the motor and stepped down from the Jeep as the police car pulled to a stop. Two uniformed officers climbed out, the driver coming to stand by the passenger door beside his colleague. 'Good morning, Ms Nicholls. I'm Sergeant Adams, and this is Constable Morris.'

Adams? Brent Adams? Her breath snagged in her throat. It couldn't be him, could it? She ran the tip of her tongue across her bottom lip and lifted her gaze to meet the sergeant's. The same hard-set jaw she remembered, the same parasitic stare burrowing into her brain. She clenched her abs, as if preparing for a physical blow, and pushed her weight down into her heels, anchoring herself to the earth.

He'd introduced himself as if they'd never met, so best to pretend the same and not make any waves.

'We were wondering if we could have a quick chat about the fires out this way.'

Oh God, the bloody fires. Hadn't everyone had enough talk about them? All that crap about heroes and sacrifice that had gone on in the local papers straight after it all went down, typical media hype to sell some copies. But a month down the track, what possible reason could the police have to be asking questions? And why did it have to be him here doing the asking?

She shrugged. 'Not sure I can help you with much.'

'As you would know, there were a number of fire fronts, including one believed to have started in this area.' Adams barrelled on despite her disclaimer. 'You may not be aware that a fire investigator was on this property recently, and we have reason to believe that the fire that started out this way was deliberately lit.'

Deliberately lit? Her jaw fell open and she snapped her mouth shut.

People had lost their homes in that fire. Cars had been destroyed. Animals killed. The bush decimated. And Jack's firefighter mate had lost his life. Crimson flames flared behind Eve's eyes. And lurking behind them was a question: why had an investigator been here at Mossy Creek?

The younger guy pulled a notepad from his pocket and waited, pencil in hand, ready to scribe.

She flicked her gaze back to the sergeant, not quite meeting his eyes. 'I'm not sure what that's got to do with me.'

'Are you familiar with a Luke Harris?'

The chill in her spine returned, spreading like an arctic frost across the plains of her back. Why was he asking about Luke? 'Yes, he's a family friend. Did a bit of work for me here at the farm. Helped feed the horses, that sort of thing.'

Pencil-boy scribbled furiously on his pad, leaving the older cop to ask the questions. 'Right. And was he around on the day the fires started?'

Was he? So much had happened in a short space of time. Were they asking because he was a suspect? The idea that Luke could have deliberately started a fire was too bizarre for words. He was Margo and Harry's grandson, for God's sake, living under their roof. Having a few family problems didn't make him an arsonist. But then he'd disappeared almost immediately after the fires and hadn't been seen since. Still, that could be a coincidence. No point incriminating the kid for no good reason.

'To be honest, it's all a bit hazy. I think he was working here that morning, but I can't be sure.'

The sergeant scratched at his temple, nodding his head in the direction of the house. Or at least where it would have been. His eyes moved left to right, like someone watching a tennis match, as he perused the ruins. 'Was this place insured?'

'Yes, it was.' Whatever that had to do with anything.

'And what value would it have been insured for?'

'My mother – my late mother – had it insured for six hundred thousand dollars.' *Not that it's any of your business*. Adams' pointed questions were like hot pokers stabbing at the back of her eyelids.

'Would you say the house, as it was, was worth that much, including its contents?'

Eve shrugged. 'I have no idea. That was my mother's business.'

The sergeant's dark brown eyes zeroed in on hers, like a

cobra trying to hypnotise its prey. Eyes she'd seen before and had hoped never to see again.

He'd mentioned Luke. Now he was onto the house insurance. Where was he going with this?

'People have been known to rig insurance jobs, Ms Nicholls. I'm just wondering if in this case it got out of hand.'

Eve's blood froze in her veins, solid rivers of ice suspended beneath her skin. This cop wasn't just testing the waters, he was pushing her in and seeing if she was going to sink or swim. And judging by the smug look on his face, he'd be more than happy to see her go under. Just as he had when Bec had died, and he'd been hell-bent on trying to prove it had all been her fault.

But she wasn't a teenager anymore, and he couldn't bully her into submission.

She lifted her chin, looked him straight in the eye. 'So, let me join the dots, Sarge ... You think I set Luke up to burn the place down, the fire got out of control, and then I attempted to cover my tracks by almost killing myself trying to save my neighbour's property?' Okay, maybe the killing herself bit was exaggerating but the rest was pretty much what the dickhead was insinuating.

Constable Morris coughed, colour rising in his cheeks.

Adams turned a deep shade of crimson. His brow had more furrows than a freshly ploughed paddock. 'It's *Sergeant*.'

Heat flooded her limbs. 'Well, Ser-geant,' she made sure to emphasise every syllable of the title, 'you're barking up the wrong tree. This place was scheduled to sell the week after the fires, and a sale would have been worth more than any insurance claim hand out.'

'You were intending to sell?' The pitch of his voice rose a note higher.

'Yes.'

'And you can verify that with an agent?'

'Yes.' If he wanted anything more than monosyllabic answers, he could keep digging. She crossed her arms and stared him down.

The right-hand man closed his notebook and stuck it back in his pocket, along with his trusty pencil. He was clearly making a huge effort not to look at his boss.

'And you think Luke Harris was working here the morning of—'

'Yes.' For fuck's sake, hadn't she already answered that question? This was what cops did, bamboozled you with repetition, rewording things the same way those stupid psychological profiles did. Trying to trip you up.

'Did you notice anything strange about his behaviour while he worked for you?'

'No.'

'Nothing at all?'

'No.'

The sergeant pursed his lips, duck-like, and rocked back on his heels. 'Well, if you think of anything that may have been unusual, we'd appreciate it if you could give us a call. Arson is a serious crime, and the community deserves answers.'

A slight twist of her lips was all Eve gave him in reply. He'd just accused her of fraud, potentially arson. He could fuck well and truly off.

'And it might be an idea to stay put while all this is being investigated.'

Was he telling her not to skip town? If it wasn't so bloody cliched, she'd ask him that out loud.

Right on cue, Banjo arrived and dropped a drool-covered ball on the sergeant's boot. It rolled off, leaving a coating of dirt-encrusted slime covering the leather. Adams glared but didn't say a word. As if a film director had called action, the two cops turned in unison.

Banjo sat by Eve's side as they watched the car disappear down the drive. The brief spark of amusement that the tennis ball had ignited died on her lips. Luke was well and truly on their radar. Had they been to see Margo and Harry? Probably not, if they didn't know he'd been living there. But Dean and Michelle would have already been put through the wringer.

What information did the cops have on Luke? Even the suggestion that he could be responsible for the fires and all the grief that came with them made Eve's skin crawl. So much devastation. So much loss. If it turned out that any one individual was responsible, they'd be going away for a very long time and be completely ostracised by the community.

Her chest constricted, as if the sergeant had dumped a ten-kilo kettlebell onto her breastbone. She was definitely on Adams' radar. All his questions about the house, and the insurance, in that same accusatory tone he'd used in the interview room after Bec drowned. Eve had blocked out so many memories from that time, but they were all still there, waiting to rise to the surface like a poisoned fish.

Constable Adams, he'd been in those days. Darker hair and twenty years younger, firing questions at her like bullets at a target, focused and relentless. She'd left the police station convinced of her own guilt, and Adams had done everything he could to smear her name at the inquest and exonerate his arsehole brother Todd, who'd been there at the lake that night too. Adams had practically accused her of being an evil mastermind who'd planned the whole sorry event and deliberately killed her sister, when the whole tragedy had been nothing more than a reckless bunch of teenagers making the biggest mistake of their lives.

He'd looked so disappointed when the coroner handed down a verdict of accidental death. But the mud Adams smeared across Eve's name had stuck. The stench of it followed her wherever she went in town, people scowling and turning up their noses as she passed. Whispering. Condemning. Turning her into an outcast. Even in the eyes of her own mother. Until she couldn't take it anymore, and she left.

Nausea welled inside her, as if she'd crested the peak of a roller coaster. Adams hadn't gone anywhere, and these days he had the authority of being a sergeant rather than a constable. If he was still as big a tool now as he'd been then, he'd be out to find a scapegoat. Someone to lay the blame on so he could big-note himself – Luke, or her. Just when she'd reconnected with Margo, re-established her friendship with Cat, was getting back on solid ground with Jack, and whatever she had with Hugh.

What would they all think of her if Adams started vilifying her again? And what would happen to Luke? He was the same age she'd been when Bec had died. An accusation like this could ruin his life. Turn them both into outcasts.

Banjo nudged at her calf.

'I know, you're hungry.' She pulled open the door and stepped up inside the caravan.

Adams could go screw himself. He could crow all he liked about the insurance money, but he had no proof, and from what he'd said, he didn't have anything concrete on Luke. But that wouldn't stop him investigating, accusing.

She slammed the door shut behind her, and the caravan

shuddered. Banjo dropped to the floor, ears flattened, and rested his head between his paws.

'Sorry boy.' She patted his cheek and sighed as she sank onto the bench seat, collapsing in on herself like a rag doll, limbs loose and shoulders slumped. She looked around the caravan, to the cupboard where her small pile of clothes was stored, the timber box her grandfather had crafted holding the few photographs and knick-knacks she'd managed to rescue before the house went up, her beautiful chocolatey boy waiting so patiently. This was all she had. Everything. It would be so easy to pack it all up and get the hell out of town.

If she could drive anything more complicated than the old farm jeep. The gears on the Kombi were a lot trickier, and her hand wasn't up to them yet.

But that was only a matter of time.

She reached for the exercise ball the physiotherapist had given her, picking it up for the first time in a week. Curling her fingers around the blue rubber, she squeezed it against her palm and released it again. Ten repetitions with a break of a minute between each set. Squeeze, release. Squeeze, release. And with each rep, the idea of leaving blinked like a beacon through the fog on a moonless night. She didn't owe anyone in this town anything. Whether she stayed or went would make no difference to people in Yarrabee. Screw Adams' suggestion she stay put. She could leave all the shit behind her, jump at Mel's offer and follow her dream.

'Give it a week and we'll be on the road again, Banj.'

His eyes brightened at the mention of his name, and he tapped his feet on the lino floor, dancing backwards and forwards. Such love. Such loyalty. The type she could only hope to find in human beings, if she ever got brave enough to really try. She waited for the idea of leaving to trigger an internal jig, but everything inside her remained in stasis.

Chapter Five

'Thanks for the lift, Aunty Marg. I'll meet you out front of *Something Brewing* in an hour.'

'Goodo.'

Eve closed the car door and waved Margo goodbye. She pulled her phone from her pocket. 10.29. Not even time for a pre-torture coffee. Not that she'd keep it down. Pivoting, she took the few steps required to reach the door of the physiotherapist's office and stopped. She tried clenching her hand to activate the muscles in her arm, but it refused to move. Of course the therapy was helping, but the actual session was always agony.

A bell tinkled as she pushed the door open and stepped inside. Simon didn't bother with a receptionist, preferring to handle all the appointments himself, so the waiting room was pleasantly quiet.

'Be with you in five.' A voice filtered through from the next room.

Two white modular chairs filled the small space. Eve dropped into one of them, lifted her arm and placed her hand on her lap, palm down. It lay there like a limp fish. How could a part of your body that had been so integral to your everyday functioning become so defunct, literally good for nothing? It was like carrying around a dead weight attached to her elbow.

The doctor had told her it would take quite a while for all the nerves to regenerate – and some might not – but the reality of living day to day with such a useless appendage was tedious. Having to rely on friends to ferry her around the place. Struggling to do the horse feeds or even wash her hair properly. As challenging as the physiotherapy was, if it gave her back the use of her arm – along with her independence – it was time and money well spent. And then she'd be on the road.

Eve closed her eyes and drew a breath, waiting for the sickening sensation to recede. She stared down at her midline. Since the possibility – the strong possibility – of pregnancy had hit like a lightning strike in the middle of the night, every twinge in her body only added to her suspicions. There was no way she could go into Cat's surgery for confirmation; Cat would have a zillion questions and the whole situation would be way too weird. Seeing one of the other doctors in the practice was a possibility, but there was bound to be someone who knew someone sitting in the waiting room and …

'Eve, come on in.' Simon beckoned from the treatment room doorway. Her other problem would have to wait.

She slid into the chair beside the desk where Simon had taken up his own seat.

'So, how's it going?'

'Not too bad.'

'Is your arm functioning okay?'

'I think so. The graft's taking well, apparently. But I still don't have much feeling in it.'

'Well, that could take a while.' Simon wrinkled his nose. 'Been doing your exercises?'

'Hmm hm.' It wasn't a complete lie. She'd done them on and off, just not the prescribed four times a day, and not quite the number of repetitions.

Simon narrowed his eyes.

'Okay. Some of them.'

'Those nerves need stimulation if they're going to recover, and the tendons were damaged too, remember. We need to keep that blood flow circulating to ensure the graft continues to heal. Let's take a look.'

Eve lifted her hand and rested it on the corner of the desk, and Simon peeled off the thin compression sleeve. Without needing to be told, she rotated her wrist, so her palm faced upwards. There'd been so much talk about 'the arm' it felt separate to the rest of her, almost as if it belonged to somebody else. Like a body part the good doctor Frankenstein had attached to his monster.

'Wow, that is looking good.' Simon nodded as he gently pressed against the graft. The fresh pink skin extended from the heel of her hand to halfway up her forearm. Modern medicine really was nothing short of miraculous. Apart from the dimpling and paler colouring, it looked almost normal. 'Let's do another run through the exercises, shall we?'

Eve sighed but ended it with a grin. 'If we must.'

Simon stood and walked to a cupboard on the other side of the room, returning with a small plastic container. Taking off the lid, he pulled the items from the box one by one and placed them on the desk: a small rubber ball, a set of pincers, wooden rods of various sizes.

Following instructions, using each of the devices in turn, was like a throwback to kindergarten. If someone had told Eve six weeks ago she'd find it hard to hold and squeeze a rubber ball or pinch together the two arms of a set of tweezers, she'd have thought them mad. A light beading of perspiration broke out on her forehead as she focused all her attention on picking up the rods and placing them into their appropriate slots in a wooden tray. Eventually everything was back where it belonged, and she collapsed against the chair.

'Great work, Eve.' Simon packed the equipment away and returned the box to the cupboard. 'You've still got all the stimulus materials I gave you at home?'

'Sure do.' *Still in their boxes*. She wriggled her hand back into the sleeve. More effort than it should be. How could picking up a few toys be so bloody exhausting? 'Do you think I might be able to start driving sometime soon?'

'I wouldn't be able to say that confidently until you have full range of motion in your hand. You have to be able to grip the steering wheel. Remind me, do you drive an automatic?'

She shook her head. 'About as far from one as you can get. A Kombi.'

'Oh, right.' Simon frowned. He was back at the desk, standing beside her while she stood and grabbed her bag. 'A gear stick then.'

'Yeah, not exactly smooth either. More like a crowbar in a bag of marbles.'

'Even more reason to do those exercises.' He gestured towards the door, signalling the end of their session.

'I get the message. Thanks, Simon.' Eve stopped at the desk while he sorted out the bill.

'Might see you at the meeting.'

She handed over her Medicare card, along with her credit card. Giving yourself a serious injury didn't come cheap. 'What meeting?'

'At the community centre, tomorrow night. About the impact of the fires on the town. Councillor Clements is organising it. She's got media coming. Wants to give locals an opportunity to air their grievances and get a list together to present to state parliament.'

'I bet she does.'

With a local election coming up, Kelly Clements would be taking any opportunity she could to make herself look like the town saviour. But a gabfest about the fires was the absolute last thing on Eve's agenda.

'At least we all get to say our bit. You should come. I mean, your place was hit pretty bad, wasn't it?'

'I'm currently living in a caravan, so you could say that.' It came out harsher than she'd expected, and Simon's cheeks turned a distinct shade of peach.

'Anyway, maybe I'll see you there.'

Eve shoved her cards back in her wallet and gave what she hoped was an apologetic smile as she headed out. Bloody typical of Kelly Clements to be big-noting herself to all and sundry. Calling in the press, giving people a chance to 'air their grievances'. All for her own political gain no doubt. It had been the same at school. Kelly had been head of the student representative body, acting like she was divinely anointed. But at least she was doing something with her life. Wasn't pushing thirty-eight with nothing behind her and no prospects for the future.

An old ache washed through Eve's body, sluicing away her bravado. If she sold Mossy Creek, took the money and headed north, she'd be starting from scratch again. Apart from Mel, she didn't know a soul in Noosa, or Queensland for that matter. Anonymity had its pluses, but there was something to be said for neighbours who dropped around with carrot cakes and the warm smiles of friends over a cup of coffee. Or so she was discovering. She'd bolted last time things got ugly – and where had it gotten her?

But this time, she'd have money and a plan. And perhaps a baby. She stopped in her tracks, as if a door had swung back and smacked her in the face. All the signs were there, but she had to know for sure.

She glanced towards *Something Brewing*. No sign of Margo yet, so enough time to pop into the chemist and pick up a test, depending on who was behind the counter. That new girl had started last week: she seemed quiet, not into chatter, not likely to pass comment on what was being shoved into the paper bag. And it would be better to know for sure. Maybe Eve was worrying about nothing. Time to put on her big girl pants and find out exactly what was going on.

Outside the pharmacy, Eve stopped and peered through the window. It seemed pretty quiet: a couple of people at the back counter where the prescriptions were made up; Col Hammond in his white coat, peering over his glasses, talking to an older woman; the new girl shuffling stock around on shelves in the skincare section. Where would the pregnancy tests be?

She lifted her hand to block out the glare and pressed her face closer to the glass.

'Eve?'

She sprang away from the window as if repelled by an invisible force field. 'Hugh. Hi.' A flush of heat fanned across her chest.

Hugh had a wry grin on his face. 'Sorry to disturb your window shopping.'

'Oh, I ... I've just been to the physio and I'm waiting for Margo. She's giving me a lift home.' None of which explained why she'd been acting like a penniless kid outside a lolly shop. 'How're things with you?'

'Busy enough. Always a dog who's swallowed something they shouldn't have, or a cat that needs neutering. You know, same old. You managing okay at the farm?' His gaze fell to her hand, and she pressed her arm against her side. Everything had become about the injury, and it wasn't really something she wanted to discuss ad nauseam.

'Yeah, absolutely fine.'

'That's good.' He nodded. He had such a gentle smile, and kind eyes that looked deep into your soul. Too deep. 'We should catch up. Things are a bit quieter without my star boarder. I miss our chats.'

'Me too.' Hanging out in Hugh's office space after the hospital so she could have the dressings changed daily hadn't been as bad as she'd expected. They'd chewed the fat about all sorts of things in his lunch hours, solving all the world's problems, but never really getting into any of their own. The few times they'd wandered into more personal territory, teetered on the edge of something more, one or the other had pulled back. Usually her.

A buzz sounded from Hugh's pocket. He dug out his phone and squinted at the screen. 'Ah, I have to be getting back.' A sense of resignation laced his tone. 'I'll give you a call and sort out a coffee date.'

'Great. See you.' *Date? Did he just use the word 'date'?*

Eve leant back against the shopfront as he walked away, waiting for that now too-familiar sparking in her veins to settle. Hugh Robertson was so far beyond her comfort zone – town vet, a stalwart of the community, two kids for freak's sake. There was no way she could go there. Was *not* going there because she wouldn't be around for long. But there was no harm in having a coffee with a friend, was there?

Hugh's figure disappeared down the street and around the corner. Eve shot another glance through the window. Now or never. She ran her tongue across the dry skin of her lips and stepped inside.

Dusk. Such a perfect time of day, especially here. Everything soft and pink and mellow. Horses chewing on dinner in the paddocks, noses buried deep in buckets of chaff. Cockatoos screeching in the darkening sky. Even without the comfort of trees and bush and the unnerving lack of wildlife, the air had that special quality of calm that only came with the transition from light to dark. A moment of stillness between the bustle of the day and the thick uncertainty of night.

Everything about this moment was transient. Sitting on an upturned milk-crate outside the caravan, a folded cardigan cushioning her butt, Eve kept her gaze up and outward, anywhere but on the white plastic stick resting on her knee. Any second now the timer on her phone would buzz. The dry crackers she'd scoffed down after feeding the horses stuck in her gullet like fishhooks. Eating before peeing on the stick had been a mistake, but once the big hand on the clock reached five a ravenous hunger drew her towards the fridge, and whatever she could lay her hands on became a pre-dinner snack.

Banjo appeared from nowhere. A squashed tennis ball clamped between his jaws, he sat back on his haunches and whined. A pair of honeyed eyes looked up at her, identical thumbprints of golden hair above them set against the chocolate mask of his face.

'You'd play with that thing all day, wouldn't you?'

He tilted his head to the side, ears pricked to attention in two perfect triangles. With his pink tongue hanging from his open mouth, he jumped forward and nudged the ball closer.

'Luckily for you, you're hard to resist.' She picked up the ball and threw it as far as she could. At least her right arm still worked.

Banjo spun and took chase, legs pumping like a short track sprinter.

She brushed the crumbs of dirt from the slobber-covered ball off her palm, knocking the test stick to the ground – and froze. Banjo was on his way back, ball wedged between his teeth. He'd be dropping it any second, right where the stick had fallen.

This was silly. There was no point taking the damned thing if she wasn't going to check the result. Arching her neck, she leaned forward on her elbows and peered over her knees. It was right there, beside her boot, face down.

Banjo returned, practically tossing the ball at her, and she threw it again. Anything to keep him occupied and out of her hair for a minute. She bent down and curled her fingers around the stick. Her body grew stiff; everything about this moment taking her back to the last time. Just like now, she'd been alone – and just like now, she'd instinctively known the result before checking the window. Her mind dragged her back in time, and like a swimmer caught in a rip, she had no choice but to go with the current.

Seventeen-year-old Eve huddled in the corner of the bus shelter outside the public toilet in Surry Hills, a bitter wind snapping at her cheeks. She pulled the hood of her sweatshirt over her head and hunkered down. Luckily the shelter was empty, for now. She could have waited and done the test at the refuge, but there were too many weirdos there. Too many people crammed into the crowded confines of the converted terrace. Losers like her, who had nowhere to go and no money to support themselves. No one exactly like her though – no one who'd killed her sister and done the bolt on her boyfriend.

Her fractured heart hardened a little more at the thought. That was all behind her now. Jack, too. All of their hopes and dreams shattered. Blown to smithereens like a bunch of dandelion seeds in the wind, all because of one stupid night. A series of stupid decisions. She hunched over and hugged herself tighter. If this test went the way she guessed, it was nothing more than she deserved, the final layer of stinking icing on a very large shit cake.

Drops of rain plopped onto the tin roof overhead, slow at first, then faster and louder. An old dude in a suit sidled past and took a seat at the other end of the bench. Great! No way she could check the test with him sitting there perving. Reaching inside the zipper of her hoodie, she clutched the stick in her hand and shoved it in her pocket. Cars and buses passed by in a never-ending stream, petrol fumes pouring from their exhausts. Nothing like the air in Yarrabee, but she'd have to get used to it if she was going to stay in the city.

Trudging along the pavement, she bent her head into the wind and rain and took a left turn off the main road, passing houses similar to the place she was staying, some renovated, others completely derelict. Some sort of warehouse loomed in her peripheral vision, its walls covered in a chaos of graffiti. The glass doors of its entrance were protected by bars but set back slightly beneath a portico. She ducked inside and pressed her back to the wall. Took a moment to calm herself. It couldn't be put off any longer.

Her hand was still in her pocket, holding the stick. Slowly she drew it out, turned her wrist and opened her palm. A solid pink line. Positive. The overwhelming sensation of being in an elevator going down, one that had come loose from its cables and was hurtling out of control, took hold. Even though she'd known – the missing period, the agonising soreness in her boobs, the out-of-control hunger pangs – a tiny sliver of hope had remained, dashed now by the candy-coloured stripe on the stupid plastic stick.

Not that long ago, news like this would have reduced her to tears, but the well had completely evaporated. Nothing remained but rage. She stepped forward and kicked at the wall opposite, wincing at the sting of her toe inside her boot. Crouching, she dropped her head back against the brick façade at her back and let it take her weight.

What the fuck am I going to do?

One thing she wasn't going to do was have a baby. No way. Still a teenager, alone, homeless and broke. There was only enough money in her bank account to get her to the end of the month. Somehow, she'd have to find a job – waitressing, packing shelves, anything to bring in some cash. Maybe enough to get a shared place: set herself up until she earned enough to hit the road and travel. None of those plans included a child. She was still a kid herself – a messed-up one. Only one option remained. But how the hell did you go about organising that?

She banged the heel of her hand against her forehead.

Someone at the refuge might be able to help. Not one of the other boarders but maybe one of the staff. Marie: she seemed pretty cool. And didn't counsellors have to take some sort of confidentiality oath? Not that it mattered. They didn't have any details about her home address, where she'd come from or why she'd left. And she was over the age of consent, almost an adult. That was it: Marie would help.

Pushing herself upright, she tossed the test stick onto the ground and kicked it against the wall, right next to a used syringe. Some other loser's garbage.

In a split second, Eve's younger self had made the decision. Would it be that easy a second time?

The test stick chaffed at her palm. One flip of her hand and she turned it over. The same solid line, like a sick joke told on repeat. Other than the location, she could be in a time warp. Same careless behaviour. Same predictable outcome. Not Jack this time though. Marcus. Currently off finding himself on the other side of the world. Not that she'd tell him even if he were around. What was the point? They were done. Back then, keeping the baby hadn't been an option, which is exactly why she'd kept it to herself. But what about now?

She stared out across the paddocks. Rain had finished her feed and waited by the other horses, ever hopeful they'd let her share. Bored with the lack of attention, Banjo sniffed at something beneath the burnt-out gum tree beside the house. Tiny leaves were already sprouting from the blistered branches, like green tufts of hair covering its extremities. Life blooming, even in the wake of death.

After Bec's drowning, and all the shit that went down

with the police, the community and with Nell, even contemplating the idea of bringing a child into the world had made Eve's seventeen-year-old-self want to shrivel up and disappear. Afterwards, she'd picked herself up, thrown herself into work and travelled the world. Not with Jack, as they'd once planned, but alone in the bubble she'd created – self-sufficient, needing no one.

Time seemed to have weakened the armour she'd shielded herself inside for all these years. Made her soft.

Cat, Margo, Hugh, Jack.

All of them hurting in their own way after the fires. Could she walk away so easily a second time? Leave them all to deal with their pain and loss without lifting a finger to help? They'd all been so kind to her. Leaving now when they were all floundering would mean the end of those friendships for good.

And could she so easily terminate a pregnancy when there wasn't another soul left in the world who shared her blood?

Last time, when the procedure was over, she'd left the clinic and never given the idea of a baby another thought. Not until she'd confessed to Jack on her return to Yarrabee and accepted his wrath as punishment.

A sob burst from her throat. She pressed a hand to her mouth, but the tears fell anyway. Tears for her broken teenage self, for the mother Bec could never be, for the twenty years of estrangement from Nell, and for all the selfish decisions she'd ever made.

Banjo came and sat quietly beside her, and she rested a hand on his back. She sat until the tears were spent and night fell around them like an invisible cloak. Until the dog nuzzled at her shin.

'Come on, boy, let's get you some dinner.'

Her phone buzzed, and she slid it from her pocket. A text from Mel: *Made a decision yet? Time's ticking girlfriend.*

Time was certainly ticking, and she had more than one choice to make. But not right now. Not when her internal thermostat was rapidly reaching boiling point and her head was about to explode. All of it could wait.

Shoving the test stick into her pocket, she opened the door of the caravan, ushered Banjo inside and shut out the world.

Chapter Six

The hum of an engine roused Eve from sleep. Raising her head was like lifting a bowling ball, every muscle in her neck straining against the weight. Falling asleep in the middle of the day was not one of her habits but yesterday's discovery had kept her awake into the early hours.

Banjo dived off the end of the bed and ran to the door, standing to attention.

She crawled out from under the covers and staggered over to let him out, pulling the door shut again. Grabbing a tie, she swirled her hair into a bun and secured it, turned on the tap and splashed her face. Her reflection stared back at her from the small circular mirror over the sink. Pale. Puffy eyed. Looking every bit of her almost thirty-eight years. In no shape to welcome a visitor.

She lifted the corner of the curtain and snuck a look outside. Banjo bounced around a pair of booted feet, and a man crouched to give him a rub beneath the chin.

Jack.

What was he doing here?

Standing, he stepped up to the door and knocked. 'Hello?'

No point pretending she wasn't home. Letting Banjo out had blown any chance of that ruse.

She dropped the curtain and snagged a cardigan from the end of the bed. Stuck her head back in front of the mirror. God, she looked rough – but not as rough as she felt on the inside. Her body reminding her about her litany of stupid mistakes. She cleared her throat and opened the door, pulling her sleeves down and curling her fingers over the cuffs.

'Hey, Jack. Long time no see.'

Four weeks and two days, to be precise – when he drove past her in the RFS truck, black smoke boiling above them, yelling at her to get out of the place while there was still time. Right before he and his crew mates drove into the inferno that took one of their lives. *How does a person recover from that kind of trauma?* Eve's gut clenched – she knew the answer to that question only too well.

Jack scuffed the toe of his boot into the gravel. Baxters – the same type he'd worn when they were kids. Pushing his sunglasses onto the top of his head, he looked everywhere but at her. Shadows rimmed his eyes, and a three-day stubble darkened his jawline. All those hours in front of the Xbox no doubt, losing himself in another world. He'd lost weight too, his jeans loose around his hips, and his cheeks hollow. No wonder Cat was worried.

He shoved his hands deep into his pockets and squinted at the remains of the house. 'Cat said you're having trouble finding someone to help out with the re-build.'

Good old Cat, ever the fixer, not wasting any time

implementing her plan. 'Well, Cat might have got the wrong end of the stick.' She wrapped her arms across her middle. 'I'm not sure I'm going to rebuild.'

'Why not?'

She shrugged. Now was as good a time as any to test the waters. 'I might sell the place as it is. Whoever buys it can build their own dream home.'

Jack met her gaze for the first time since he'd arrived. 'You're seriously leaving again?' He said it as if she'd announced she was about to sign up for the next mission to Mars.

'Don't see why not. It hasn't been my home for a long time.' Even as she said them, the words tasted bitter. Living here again for that short while, even if it had been precipitated by Nell's death, had been the first time she'd felt anything vaguely near contentment for all her adult life. Albeit short-lived, an illusion, as if she could ever have a normal life – be normal.

Jack shook his head. 'Are you ever going to stop running and just settle down?'

Banjo had ducked under the fence for his morning rounds, checking out the plover nest while the parents were elsewhere, living life on the edge. No wonder the two of them were so well matched.

'Settle down? As in find my soulmate and live happily ever after?' Surely, he knew by now that wasn't her thing. Everybody else seemed to have gotten the memo. 'Fairy tales aren't my kind of story, Jack.'

'No one said anything about fairy tales. But you could have a place of your own right here in Yarrabee if you gave it a chance. There are people here who care about you. Who want to see you happy.'

'People like you?' Why was she poking the bear? What

good was going to come of opening old wounds? They'd cared for each other once upon a time, had so much history between them, but they were different people now.

'Nothing wrong with wanting what's best for a friend.' He swallowed, cleared his throat. 'I know Cat would miss you if you left. Margo and Harry.' He gave her a pointed look. 'And Hugh.'

'Hugh and I are just friends.' *Ouch. Too quick. Too tetchy.*

Jack's mouth quirked. 'I never said you were anything else.' He shook his head. 'Anyway, Eve, whatever you choose to do is completely up to you. I'm just out here following orders to see if you're in need of a builder. But if you're not, then I'll leave you to it.' He spun halfway around towards his ute, ready to leave.

'Hold your horses.' Since he was here, she could use the opportunity to do a bit of digging about his mental health. See if Cat was overreacting. She reached out and grabbed his arm. 'I haven't made any firm decision. I'm ... considering my options. What do you mean following orders?'

'You know Cat. She has to make sure everybody is busy doing something at all times.' There was a snarky note to his voice. 'God forbid a person has any time to sit around and chill out.'

Oh-kay. Definite tone of resentment. Delicate handling required. 'I do know Cat. And I know she's been worried about you.'

'Why? What did she say?'

Oh, shit. Not delicate enough. More care needed. 'Nothing in particular. Only that you were at a loose end and maybe a building project would be good for you.'

'Yeah, right. I'm sure that's not all she said.' His frown lines deepened. 'She's got no right telling everyone our business. My business.'

'Jack. Come on. I'm her oldest friend. *Your* friend.' Eve

let the idea hang. It seemed the only appropriate label for your ex-first boyfriend who was now married to your childhood bestie. 'Cat takes on everyone else's problems day in and day out as part of her job. She has to unload to someone now and then.'

'Not if she's spinning bullshit stories about me.' He spoke through clenched teeth, spitting out each word. His gaze dropped to her hand, still clamped to his forearm, then back to her face.

She pulled away instantly. Jack had always had a bullish streak, like she did. It had made for some great fireworks back in the day. But there was something darker in his voice now, a jagged edge that hadn't been there even in that brief time when she'd seen him again before the fires. He'd only ever spoken about his wife with adoration in his eyes and love in his tone.

'Take it easy, Jack. Cat's not doing anything of the sort. Like I said, I asked after you and she said you could do with some work. She thought it could be a win-win for both of us.'

He let out a long, low sigh. Stared out at the horses at the far end of the paddock and turned to look at the charred foundations, the tension evaporating from him like morning mist burning off after a particularly heavy dew. 'I guess it wouldn't be so bad, working here again. I've always loved this place. Lots of good memories.' He gave her a wistful look.

She folded her arms. 'And not so good.'

'I would like to see the place up and running again, whether it's with you or someone else. And being out here would get me out of the house. Building would add value to the property, even if you do sell.'

He hurtled on, as if he'd thought of the idea himself

and it was gaining momentum with every word he spoke. He'd made the admission that he needed to be doing something. She could provide that something. Still, the urge to pack up and leave gnawed at her insides like a termite chewing through a woodpile. He was so right about her inclination to run but if she fessed up about leaving as soon as the insurance money landed, he'd tell Cat – and those tenuous threads of friendship they'd re-sewn could so easily snap.

She tipped her head in the direction of the caravan. 'If by some remote chance I did decide to rebuild, you'd have to put up with me being your on-site boss.'

The corners of his mouth crinkled. 'Not like I haven't taken orders from you before.'

There it was: that old spark of connection. Maybe they could be friends again. *Real* friends. The kind you've known all your life. Who are there for you no matter what. If you let them be.

She gave a slow nod, warming to the idea, even as it made the words stick in her throat like the sugary coating of a warm doughnut.

'Let me know.' He started towards the car.

'Jack.'

Turning, he slid his glasses back into place, reflective lenses once again hiding his eyes.

'If you need to talk about anything, I'm here.'

'Talking's overrated.' He strode to the car and climbed in, drove past her but didn't bother to wave as he did a u-turn and headed out.

Funny, he'd always been the one who wanted to talk things through when they'd been together as teenagers. She was the one who would shut down, sort things out with silence rather than a discussion. Jack was someone else now.

He'd reacted so badly when he found out she'd terminated her pregnancy without even letting him know about the baby. His baby. Even though it was twenty years later: ancient history. But that was all behind them now and they both had other issues to wrangle.

Thursday afternoon, and Yarrabee was the proverbial ghost town. You could set off a bomb in the middle of the main street and no one would hear a thing. Settling back on the burgundy chaise lounge – one of Fran's aesthetic additions to the cafe – Eve made sure to keep her feet dangling off the velvet upholstery. Banjo, stretched out beside her on the vintage rug, snored softly. She opened the hardcover Dickens she'd plucked from one of the shelves.

'It was the best of times, it was the worst of times,' she read out loud. An absolute cracker of an opening line. Fuzzy images of watching the black-and-white movie as a kid flickered in her head. Rain streaming down the windows, fire burning in the grate, Nell ensconced in her favourite chair patching horse rugs while Eve and Bec sprawled on the floor in front of the television. Tears building at the ending, when the handsome curly-headed hero kissed the young blonde seamstress, comforting her as she was called to the guillotine. And then the sudden fall of the blade.

'Hello?'

Eve jumped and the book tumbled to the floor. Banjo sprang upright, and she clicked her fingers, ordering him to stay.

A tall, blonde woman in jeans and a fitted black t-shirt poked her head around the corner into the library section of the shop.

'Oh, hi.' Eve pushed to her feet and picked up the book.

'*A Tale of Two Cities*.' The woman stuck out her bottom lip. 'Not my favourite Dickens. Have you read *Bleak House*?'

'No. I haven't.'

'I recommend it. Highly underrated IMHO.' She tipped her head towards the counter. 'Any chance of a coffee?'

'Sure.' Taming Clive's beast of a machine into submission had been a feat, but she'd managed it well enough to take orders when he wasn't around.

'Double-shot long black, thanks. Hopefully that will perk me up.'

'No problem.'

Her customer picked up a magazine from the counter and flicked through its pages. There was an air of casual classiness to her. Gold hoop earrings, and pristine, white converse that combined with the jeans and tee screamed *carefully – and expensively –* curated. Definitely not a local. 'You passing through town?'

The woman ran a hand through her long, luscious locks. How did she get it so shiny? 'I'm staying for a bit actually.' She took a step closer to the counter. 'I'm a journalist. Writing a series on the fires. I want to get a feel for how the town is doing, talk to a few people who were impacted, so I've booked a place here to hang out for a couple of weeks. I grabbed a flight from Melbourne this morning and drove straight down from Sydney.'

Eve's inbuilt security system started screeching. A journalist. Snooping around, asking questions when people's wounds were still raw. Exactly what Yarrabee didn't need.

'Were you affected by the fires yourself?'

Eve swallowed and snapped the lid on the cup. Mastering that particular skill, one-handed without spilling a drop, had been the hardest part of the job. She brought the cup to the counter and slid it across to the woman. 'Everyone was affected one way or another.'

'I'm sure. But I'd love to talk to some of those who were more seriously impacted. Lost family members. Or properties.' The journalist bit down on the edge of her bottom lip, as if considering something. 'And I've heard there's talk of arson.'

The skin on the back of Eve's neck prickled. How much did this woman know? Had she been tipped off? Was she zeroing in because she knew the police had been to Mossy Creek? Not a topic Eve wanted to pursue. Better to shut down any ideas of using Yarrabee in general, and herself in particular, as the subject for some melodramatic soap opera.

'I'll give you some advice that might save you some time.' She held the woman's gaze as she edged the EFTPOS machine towards her. 'People around here are still recovering, and they would appreciate being left alone.'

There'd been a national groundswell of support over the last month, most of it well meaning, but people needed to mend in their own time, in their own way, without a stranger with an agenda picking at their still-inflamed wounds.

'Of course. I understand.' No sign of offence taken as the journalist dug into her bag, pulled out a business card and pushed it across the counter, glancing down at the bandage covering Eve's arm and then back up, letting her hazel eyes rest on their target. 'I'd appreciate it if you do think of anyone I might be able to talk to about their experiences.' She tapped her card against the machine and grabbed her cup. 'Thanks for the coffee.'

The screen door banged shut, and a hush echoed through the empty café.

Eve let out a long-held breath. A whirlpool churned

inside her, always there these last few weeks, but worse at any mention of the fires. Why couldn't people leave the past where it belonged and mind their own bloody business? So many people in Yarrabee had been damaged. Not just physically – losing property and livestock – but mentally and emotionally, traumatised by what they'd witnessed and by losing loved ones.

She knew better than anyone how deep that kind of sorrow went, leaching into all the cracks inside you like water filtering into a bore. It needed time to settle before it could be pumped to the surface. And even then, you needed to do the work yourself, not have some ignorant busybody barrelling in and digging away to satisfy her own interests. As much as some people in the town were total pains in the arse, they needed to be protected from prospectors like this one.

The card rested in her hand: *Emily Winters, Investigative Journalist.*

Hopefully that would be their first and last interaction. She crushed the card and tossed it into the wastepaper basket under the bench.

It was 2.57 p.m. according to the quirky wall clock that Fran had stuck above the door, its face a dinner plate and the arms a sculpted knife and fork. Close enough to closing time. She turned the dial on the coffee machine, and a quick shot of steam burst through the pipes. Wiping it over, she rinsed the milk jug and turned it upside down on the sink. Everything was spotless. A small thing but remarkably satisfying given her injury.

Letting her smile bloom, she locked the door and headed up the road to the gallery to meet Clive and cadge a ride home. Banjo followed along beside her, happy to be out and about. A wave of exhaustion rolled over her, a swelling tide seeping into every crevice of her body. Emily Winters had mentioned arson. Where had that information come from? The RFS investigators had already been to Mossy Creek, so no doubt word was spreading. Would the people who had shunned her after Bec's death do the same again once they heard the rumours?

Chapter Seven

The community centre buzzed like an overpopulated beehive. Eve hovered in the doorway. If it was up to her, she'd be tucked up in bed in the caravan with Banjo, reading the copy of the Stephen King she'd plucked from one of the café shelves. Sure to be more riveting than rehashing the events of a day she'd much rather forget. But Margo had insisted she come, that the town had to pull together, and saying no to her godmother was well-nigh impossible after what they'd been through.

Eve did a quick check over her shoulder. Margo was still nattering away to Beverley Fredericks, and they wouldn't be coming up for air anytime soon. The perfect time to duck inside and take a back row seat so she could scroll through her phone and zone out.

Head down, she rounded the corner.

'Angie Flanagan, I heard you were back.' A balding man stood in front of her, blocking her path. The use of her old name suggested he was someone she once knew, but there was nothing familiar about his unshaven face or middle-aged paunch.

'I'm sorry, do we know each other?'

'Huh. Don't tell me you don't remember your old mate, Todd.'

A winter wind sprang from her centre, out through her limbs to the tips of her fingers and she plunged them into her coat pockets. 'We were never friends.'

'Nah. Guess not.' He took a step forward and his rancid breath had her tilting backwards. 'Good thing you skipped town when you did. Your name was mud around here after that night at the lake.'

Dredging up their mutual past was the last thing Eve wanted to do. 'I'm not getting into this with you, Todd.' She attempted to sidestep him, but he moved left, forming a human wall.

'Think you're too good to talk to me now you're a big-time city chick, do ya?'

'Todd.' The sharp snap of his name, like someone calling a dog to heel. 'It's about to start.' Sergeant Brent Adams appeared by his brother's side and took him by the arm. 'Let's take a seat.'

As much as the appearance of Adams senior didn't exactly bring joy, having him intercept his dickhead brother before he made even more of a scene was a welcome relief. Shoving past them, she made a beeline for the back of the hall and found a seat. Of all the ghosts from her past, Todd Adams was the one she'd most wanted to avoid in Yarrabee. Like Jack, he'd been there the night Bec died, but unlike Jack, he'd done everything he could to lay the blame firmly at Eve's feet. Slandered her name in an effort to protect his own.

Someone tapped on the microphone, and the speakers

began to assemble on the stage. Cat was one of them. Long, red coils pulled back into a neat ponytail, sensible shoes with a low heel and a black pantsuit. Elegant as ever, but there was no hiding the bags under her eyes or the forced upturn of her mouth. No sign of Jack in the audience, but then someone would have to be at home with Lilly. And re-living the events of that day would be the last thing he needed.

'Mind if I squeeze in?'

The voice drew her gaze upwards, to a woman pinning her with an expectant smile: the journalist she'd met in the coffee shop. Did she have to sit here? Eve shifted her legs to the side and, despite the fact that there were at least four spare spots along the row, the woman deposited herself in the very next seat.

'Thank you.' The journalist tugged at her navy blazer and crossed her legs. Her black leather ankle boots gleamed. Designer. Probably three times the cost of the scuffed knockoffs on Eve's own feet. 'Eve Nicholls, right?'

She gave a slow nod. How did the woman know her name?

'Emily Winters.' The woman offered her hand. 'We met at the coffee shop.'

'I remember.'

'I was hoping we might be able to have a chat.'

Had she deliberately sat here to stage an interview? A high-pitched whine from the microphone sounded on the stage and the hum in the hall immediately quietened.

Emily's smile turned tight-lipped, and she sat back in her seat, shifting her attention to the front of the hall. Interrogation suspended.

'Right, I think we'll get started.' Kelly Clements stood centre stage, looking exactly as she did in the council election posters: shiny brunette bob, a floral scarf draped around her neck, and impossibly white teeth. 'Thank you, everyone, for coming out tonight…'

Blah blah blah. The woman was a walking press release. Never one to miss an opportunity, Kelly included pretty much every man, woman and child in the district in her introduction as she talked about the impact of the fires, one word melting into the next until she finally got to the point. 'So, the reason for this meeting is to hear from a few people about how they are faring in the aftermath and what we can do as a community to help each other out.'

'Get more bloody government funding.' A shout from the middle of the room set off a chorus of murmurs.

'Find the bastard that started the fire on Mossy Creek Road and lock him away.'

'Hear, hear!'

'We will get to that, thanks, Phil. And Judy.' Kelly shifted from one foot to the other, somehow managing to keep her plasticine smile in place. 'But first, we'll be hearing from a few people about their experiences, starting with Christine Fox.'

The room waited. Not a movement. Not a sound. Eve crossed her arms and sank deeper into the chair.

Chris stepped up to the podium and tucked her short silver hair behind her ears. She cleared her throat, lifting her chin to speak into the microphone. 'When Kelly asked me if I would speak to you today, my first thought was no, I couldn't possibly.' Her shoulders rose, then fell, and she directed her gaze to some invisible spot at the back of the room. 'I'm sure you're all aware of what my family went through. But I know many of you here tonight have experienced something similar. I thought perhaps by sharing what happened to us might help some of you to keep going. I'm sixty-six years old and have seen a few fires in my time but never anything like the blaze that took my grandkiddies.'

Chris's voice cracked. She lifted a hand to her mouth.

Eve's fists clenched against her sides. What was the point of this? Going over the horrific details again in such a public way?

'That day haunts my dreams. It was like a tidal wave of flame …'

Eve closed her eyes, and Chris' voice faded, replaced by images of her own.

Roaring like an avenging dragon, swooping across the treetops, scorching everything in its wake. Black clouds turning light into dark, day into night. Cowering under the blanket in the dam with Margo. Water up to their waists. Arms aching as they formed the poles for the blanket tent, a flimsy wall blocking out the heat. Air so thick it stuck in your throat like a fat wad of cotton wool. Wind booming but no hands to cover your ears. Waiting and hoping and praying.

'Eve, can you hear me?'

A voice came to her as if from the end of a long tunnel. Blinking, she shook her head and sat upright. A vice gripped her chest, compressing her ribcage and hunching her shoulders, making her shirt three sizes too small.

The woman sitting beside her – Emily – stared at her, frowning. On the stage, Chris Fox was still talking, her cheeks wet with tears, every word a sliver of her broken heart. Why? Why was she doing this?

'Do you need some air?' Emily's voice came from far away.

Air. Exactly what she needed. She nodded.

The journalist took her elbow, and they stood together, making their way down the outside aisle and into the cool night. Eve leant against the wall, the rough texture of the bricks scratching her spine. She closed her eyes and took the breath she hadn't managed to find inside. When fire had swirled in her head, and the stench of burning cow-flesh had once again cauterised her nostrils.

One breath … two … then three. She filled her lungs, scanning her body and releasing the tension in her muscles from the neck down.

Inside the hall, a burst of applause erupted. Chris's story must be over. That poor, poor woman. Having to go through it all again to satisfy the curiosity of the local vultures. Eve blinked her eyes open.

'Panic attack?' The journalist was seated directly opposite, on the retaining wall of the garden, hands tucked into the pockets of her jacket.

'Yeah. Out of the blue.' The first since that day she'd gone back to Mossy Creek. If she didn't count the ongoing nightmares.

'Totally understandable, though. After what you must have been through.' If Emily was angling for a story, she wasn't going to get one.

'Thanks – for helping me out.'

'Not a problem.'

A new overwhelming need replaced the one for oxygen, flooding Eve's veins and setting off a sense of urgency. Blocking out any sense of logic. 'You wouldn't happen to have a cigarette, would you?'

'Sorry, I don't smoke.'

Eve shrugged. 'Probably a good thing you don't, or I'd be breaking my abstinence streak.' Pregnancy or no pregnancy, if she had a packet on her they'd be gone in a flash. 'Don't let me keep you. I'm sure you'd like to hear more of what's going on in there.'

'I'm guessing based on what you said when we first met that you're not a fan of journalists.'

'Dredging up people's pain for the enjoyment of others is pointless.' More than that: it's cruel. *Just like the fiasco going on inside.*

'Sounds like you've had some first-hand experience.' Emily angled her head ever so slightly. 'Was that when your sister died?'

Eve felt every drop of blood drain from her face. 'How do you know about that?'

'Your story came up in the research I've been doing on the fires. Like it or not, Google is a wealth of information. I didn't have to dig very deep for your history to appear.'

Eve snorted. 'I'm sure you didn't.'

Even though she'd been a minor at the time, the story had managed to make the national news. Sydney media had descended on Yarrabee, ambushed her and Nell after the inquest, cameras snapping, spitting out questions. They'd even fronted up at the house and climbed over the fences when Nell locked the gates on them, until she got out her shotgun and sent them packing.

It was no different after the fires. Although this time around, it had been the whole town under siege, rather than a few distraught families. Even though Eve had been in hospital, it hadn't stopped the local reporters pestering her for a story.

'I'm sorry that happened to you.' Emily's voice dropped a few tones. The sympathy in her tone seemed genuine. No telling how much information she'd dug up, what she knew or didn't know, but she didn't seem to have the killer streak some other journos thrived on. 'I lost a sibling when I was a kid. Car accident. It stays with you.'

Empathy rather than sympathy. 'Yes. It does.'

'I think it's what made me curious about other people's families. Other people's lives. When you live with grief, you're kind of in this bubble and everyone around you is inside their own. You bump around without ever really knowing what's going on in each other's space.' Emily nodded, as if agreeing with herself. 'It gives you an understanding of other people's suffering.'

She was so right. Emily didn't seem like she was out for blood. Or maybe she was trying to appear onside to get the story.

Someone else started speaking inside the hall. Eve leaned sideways so she could see through the open door.

Cat stood mid-stage at the microphone. Poised and composed, her quiet voice commanding the attention of everyone in the room. Her words were clear, even from outside. 'There's no shame in reaching out for help, even if you weren't directly impacted by the fires. Trauma has a way of creeping up on you when you least expect it. No one is immune …'

'Ain't that the truth.' Had Cat given this same spiel to Jack in the privacy of their own four walls? Based on his attitude when they'd spoken, the answer was probably yes. But based on his belligerence, there was a good chance he wasn't taking his doctor's advice. Eve looked back at Emily. 'You should go in.'

The journo nodded. 'I should. Not coming?'

'I've already heard enough.'

Emily pushed to her feet. 'Will you be alright out here?'

'Yeah, thanks.'

Almost at the door, Emily paused and turned. 'I'd really like to talk to you about your experiences, Eve. I'm trying to get a handle on the scale of these fires, the human impact, and your story would help the wider community understand, give them more insight than what they see in the headlines or the nightly news. All that's over now and they've gone back to their lives. Forgotten it ever happened. But for the town, it's ongoing.'

'No shit.'

'Anyway …' Emily gave a small smile. 'Think about it.' She rounded the corner and disappeared into the hall.

Eve tipped her head back against the wall. Night air frosted her clammy skin. Why had she let Margo talk her into coming? And why did everyone in there want to listen to this stuff? It was enough that she saw it every time she closed her eyes, smelt it, choked over and over again on the roiling clouds of smoke. When it came to sharing the burden, she was with Jack. Carry it yourself, and let others shoulder theirs.

Another round of applause sounded from inside the hall. Kelly introduced the next speaker: Sergeant Brent Adams of the Yarrabee Police. The talk of arson was sure to come up again, and the crowd, quite rightly, would be baying for blood. What if Adams was right and Luke was responsible? What would that mean for his family? For Margo?

And what if Adams pursued his theory that she had been involved?

Too many questions. Too many unthinkable answers. Time to get as far away as possible from all the bullshit.

Chapter Eight

The main street was empty, and Eve's steps echoed on the pavement. A cockroach scurried out from a crack in the cement outside *Something's Brewing*, and she tap-danced around it as it scuttled away. A fog of gnats swarmed in the yellow halos of mist around the streetlights. Shops were cloaked in darkness. Not a soul about.

So different to the noisy streets of Marrickville at this time on a week night: its restaurants filled with chatter, muffled strains of music filtering through bar windows and spilling onto the pavement. It seemed so long since she'd lived in that world and strangely, even though she'd loved her time there, the thought of going back left her cold. Dealing with people who barely lifted their heads from their phones when they ordered their oat-milk iced lattes. People who kept everything superficial and never wanted any lasting connection. People like her.

She snorted. No, if she left here, she'd be going north. Somewhere warm and tropical. Somewhere that wasn't surrounded by an army of dead trees. Where the air didn't perpetually taste of smoke. Or seem like it did.

Mel's proposal seemed a lot more inviting after that ridiculous meeting. The further Eve got from the hall, the more the knots in her shoulders loosened, and the pressure behind her temples eased. So it made sense that the further she got from Yarrabee, the easier life would become.

A splash of light shining from a shopfront onto the footpath ahead caught her eye. She stepped into it and peered through the window. Fran was inside the gallery hanging a painting – on her own. Probably the only person in town not at the community hall.

Eve tried the handle of the door. Unlocked. She opened it and stepped inside.

'Oh.' Fran's hands fell away from the painting she was positioning. She pressed a hand to her chest, a look of relief replacing the startled expression. 'Eve. Hello.'

'Sorry. I didn't mean to creep up on you.'

'That's okay. I was off with the pixies. Come on in.'

Inside, the soft scent of vanilla wafted through the gallery. With its ambient lighting and honey-coloured floorboards, the generous amount of white space on the walls to allow the paintings to be the focus, it could have been a gallery in the inner suburbs of Sydney rather than in a rural backwater.

'Not at the meeting?' Fran turned back to adjust the angle of the painting, making sure it was perfectly square.

'I did go, but…' *But I had a total meltdown and had to be chaperoned outside.* 'Not really my kind of thing.' She strolled over to stand beside Fran. 'Not yours either, I take it?'

Fran pulled a face that suggested she'd rather have her eyeballs poked out with a hot skewer. 'To be honest, I don't really feel I've been here long enough to take part in a community debrief.'

'Clive?'

'He's there. Each to their own.'

Fran and Clive seemed to have a 'you do your thing, I'll do mine' type of relationship. Exactly as it should be.

Fran took a few steps back, folded her arms, and studied the painting she'd just hung. 'What do you think?'

Eve followed her gaze, taking in the artwork in its entirety. A simple unvarnished timber frame, with Fran's initials barely noticeable in the bottom corner. Swirls of paint in varying tones of grey, deepening to black in places, mixed with whorls of red and orange.

The background had a Van Gogh *Starry Night* vibe. In the centre of the chaotic circles, a single bare tree, the colour of charcoal, sprouted from a bed of what looked like ash – tiny dots of paint – standing out from the canvas at its base. The tree was compelling in its starkness, its scorched trunk textured and rough, a few random branches reaching up into the raging sky. A lone leaf grew from the tip of one of the branches, the vibrant green drawing your eye, pulling your focus in to where a vine spiralled through the clouds and back down to the earth.

Eve leant forward, squinting. There in the corner was a … was it a baby? Yes. Or rather an embryo, curled inside what looked like a seedpod, the vine connected to it like an umbilical cord, drawing your eye back up to the tree again, to the boiling smoke and fire suffocating the sky. An unexpected trembling started up in Eve's knees. She shuffled from one foot to the other as she turned back towards Fran.

'Wow.' She nodded. 'Very impressive.'

'Sorry.' Fran shook her head. 'I should have asked how does it make you feel?'

'Feel?'

'Yes. I should have asked you how it makes you feel, not what you thought of it. All art should make you *feel* something, regardless of its form – painting, sculpture, book, dance. It should stir your emotions.'

'Oh, right.' Emotions. Those annoying creatures Eve liked to keep under lock and key. That liked to break out and run rampant when she wasn't looking. She turned back to the painting.

'Out loud, not in your head.'

'Well, my initial reaction was confusion. That mass of swirls and—'

'No need to explain. Just blurt out your feelings.'

'Okay.' She studied the painting once more. The contrasting shapes and colours, patterns and textures, so many elements at war with each other but also a simultaneous sense of unity.

'Confusion. Shock. Desolation. Sadness. Despair. And…' That vine creeping towards the light. That baby nestled against the cool green fronds, evoking a completely different response. 'Yes, that's it … hope.' She let that last one settle in her bones, and an unfamiliar buoyancy infused her limbs.

Fran smiled broadly, her delicately outlined mulberry lips stark against the creamy complexion of her skin, framed by her glossy, crimson fringe. Everything about her appearance was a lesson in contrasts, just like her painting.

'Perfect. That's exactly the kind of reaction I live for. Want a drink?' Without waiting for an answer, Fran spun on her leopard-skin loafers and disappeared behind the partition into the back of the gallery.

At the fridge, she pulled out an already-open bottle of

champagne and filled an empty glass sitting on the bench. She offered it up.

'No, thanks.'

'I've got whisky. Clive's. Don't touch the stuff myself.'

Even the mention of the word had Eve's nostrils flaring and her taste buds preparing for the burn of the Glenfiddich Fran held aloft. But the queasy feeling that seemed to be extending out to the entire day rather than restricting itself to pre-lunch hours dampened the anticipation. 'As much as I'd love to, Margo's driving me home and she has the nose of a bloodhound. I'm not really up for a grilling.' *Not a lie.*

Fran shrugged and returned the bottle to the cupboard. 'How's the arm?'

With the compression bandage now only on at night, long sleeves had become her uniform, but the tightness of the skin and the weird numbness that struck at random moments made it hard to ignore. 'Not much feeling in it yet, but with a bit more therapy I'm hoping I'll be able to drive again soon.'

'Must be shit having to rely on people to get around.'

Eve's lips quivered, as if she'd taken a sip of scalding coffee. Fran's blunt honesty was alarmingly refreshing, but it caught her unawares.

'It is a bit. Margo's been great. And Clive.' She smiled, the thoughts of friends old and new wrapping around her like a warm hug. 'And Hugh. Banjo and I would be eating sardines and tinned soup if it wasn't for the three of them keeping me in food and work.'

'Good to hear. Clive said you're doing brilliantly at the café.'

'Good to hear.' The deliberate echo was probably corny but the compliment – any compliment – made her want to curl into a ball and roll away. Nell had never been one for praise, never wanting her girls to get too big for their boots, so deflection was second nature. 'How's everything going with the exhibition prep? Looks like you're all set up.'

'Pretty much. A few more to hang. I'm calling it "Out of the Ashes".'

'Appropriate.'

'I thought so. I want it to be about hope and renewal. A looking forward rather than a looking back.' Fran took a gulp of her champagne. 'You grew up here, didn't you?'

'Yep. Born and raised.'

'But from what Hugh has said, you only recently moved back?'

The notion that they'd been talking about her made her gut twist. 'That's right. To sell my mother's property after she died, but then the fires and …' No need to fill Fran in on what she already knew.

'So why are you living out there in the sticks in a caravan? Wouldn't it be easier to stay in town? Have a few creature comforts?'

Hugh had asked her the same question. And Cat. She'd claimed it was to check on the horses, make sure they were fed and watered, but there were plenty of people out that way who would have looked after them. And it was more than a desire not to be a burden. There was something about the place. Fire had stripped the trees bare and ravaged the land. It was only after seeing Fran's painting that the feeling she hadn't been able to name seemed to coalesce: connection.

Despite the years she had been away, the farm would always be home. Through the long years in the city, travelling the globe, seeing so many beautiful sights and meeting a carnival of amazing people, something had always been missing. Like a tiny fragment of her soul was waiting for her somewhere. Even though she didn't know it until she returned, that place had been Mossy Creek. The realisation had dawned so gradually, she'd hardly noticed it happening, and yet, she was planning to leave again.

'Eve?' She looked up to see Fran staring at her, waiting for an answer.

'Sorry.' *What was the question again? Oh yeah, why is she staying out there in the caravan?* 'Oh, you know … looking after the horses, getting some space.'

Fran nodded. 'I get that. I'm a big one for personal space myself. So glad I met Clive later in life when we both knew exactly who we were and what we wanted. I couldn't stand it if he was the clingy type. How about you? Partnered up?'

'Happily un-partnered.'

Fran laughed. 'I get that too. I was blissfully single for a long time, scared shitless of being tied down to one person, but there is something to be said for having a sidekick. Someone who really gets you, you know?'

'You don't have any kids?' Clive hadn't mentioned any, but maybe he was keeping his business to himself.

'Nope. Well, Clive does. Three from his first marriage. All adults. And thankfully he didn't want any more. I made up my mind long ago that parenthood wasn't for me. One reason why I didn't bother settling down when I was younger.'

'And you never changed your mind?'

'Never wavered, much to my mother's horror. I've got a few nieces and nephews I worship, and Clive's daughter has a two-year-old who's completely adorable, but I'm not sorry they live six hours away.' A grin stretched across Fran's face, and she looked more like a cheeky kid than a forty-something woman. 'I'm not exactly granny material.' She grabbed the bottle of champers from the fridge and refilled her glass.

'And you never regretted not having children of your own?'

'Not for a minute. I'm too selfish. Too many things I want to do and too many canvases to paint. Kids and the creative life don't mix. Not for me anyway.' Fran sipped her drink and ran the tip of her tongue over her bottom lip. 'Any particular reason you're asking?'

An overwhelming urge to confess her 'condition' simmered in Eve. Fran was deliberately childless: had made the decision and had no regrets. Like her the last time around. But this time, everything was different. Talking it out with an objective acquaintance might help, but could Fran be trusted to keep the information to herself?

'Just curious, really. I'm not getting any younger. Wondering if single parenthood might be an option.' Another not-lie.

Fran stared down into her drink as if she was looking into an oracle, her dark, perfectly shaped brows arching above her turquoise eyes. 'I only considered it briefly. Knew without question that it wasn't for me. But if you're conscious of the clock ticking don't rule out a sperm donor. A gay friend of mine did it a few years back and it all worked out beautifully. Not half the fun, of course, but the end result's the same.'

'Hmmm. Food for thought.' Not the donor – that part was already sorted. So much, in fact, to think about, and not much time to waste. *Time. Shit.* 'What's the time?'

Fran checked her wristwatch. '8.42.'

The meeting was scheduled to finish at 8.30.

Eve stood. 'I'd better head back. It's a long walk home.'

'Thanks for popping in. Nice chat. See you at the exhibition opening?'

'Yeah, of course. Sunday, right?'

Fran winked. 'Four p.m. Champagne and canapes, not to mention scintillating company and brilliant artworks.'

It was impossible not to smile at Fran's haughty charm.

Walking back to the community hall, Eve's mind meandered through their conversation. Hopefully she hadn't been too obvious with her parenting queries.

Fran sounded like she'd been sure all along she didn't want kids and had no misgivings whatsoever. She had a full life, was independent despite her marriage to Clive, and couldn't be happier. But Fran also had siblings and nieces and nephews and stepchildren, even a step grandchild. A whole family.

Something she no longer had.

Something she'd always thought she could live without.

Whirling circles of smoke gathered overhead. A battalion of black trees marched closer and closer bringing with them an overpowering heat. Searing Eve's skin. Branding her flesh. As their branches enveloped her, their dark trunks glowing red, she called out, but her voice caught in her throat.

She woke in a cold sweat, blinking into the darkness, a single remnant image burning in her brain: a solitary green leaf, like the one in Fran's painting, Bec's face smiling out from behind its glistening veins.

Chapter Nine

Eve stepped out of the van into dazzling sunshine. Could the grass get any greener? Hard to fathom that less than five weeks after the fires the paddocks were an ocean of almost fluorescent green. The stark backdrop of charred bush made the brilliant growth even more startling. Little by little, some of the trees were boasting new shoots. Life springing from death, just as it did in Fran's painting.

When she peered toward the spot where the track began at the back of the barn, that small flicker of hope died. The entrance to the riding trail had always been obvious, clearly marked by a gorgeous white gum, limbs arching over the well-ridden path. Now only its ruined trunk remained.

Since coming back to the farm, she had stuck to the area immediately surrounding what was once the house and the centre paddocks containing the horses, venturing down to the barn only at feed times. But now that same feeling the artwork had elicited returned: a connection to the land where she'd grown up, and the joy it had provided in her younger years.

If the love she felt for this place was even a fraction of the kind of kinship indigenous people felt towards their country, how could she abandon it? Her family had lived here for four generations, nowhere near those thousands of years of existence, but perhaps it was possible for white people to form a bond with the land. To feel a sense of guardianship and a desire to help it heal.

'Come on, matey, let's go for a walk.'

Banjo leapt up from his mid-morning sunbake. Smile firmly fixed, he trotted along beside her as she made her way towards the trail. An internal warning siren sounded – walking anywhere near burnt-out trees was potentially hazardous, the chance of them toppling greatly increased without their living root system keeping them grounded. Still, the call from the bush was stronger.

Burnt bark and leaves crunched under her boots as she made her way along the track, Banjo sticking close, sniffing at rocks and gnarled tree roots. None of the usual rustling from sun-lazy lizards making their escape through the undergrowth as the tremor of human footsteps sent them scurrying. No startled wallabies crossing the track to make themselves scarce.

So much wildlife had been lost. Close to seventy percent according to some reports. And with the total annihilation of the bush, there was nothing to sustain any animals that had managed to escape the blaze. Reading about it and seeing it firsthand – being out here in the midst of it – were two completely different things.

Eve's abdomen cramped, the pain sharpening with each step. Some of these trees would never recover, and yet there were infinitesimal signs of life returning. The fuzzy new growth on the gums, the occasional scurry of an ant across a rock, possum scat on a fallen branch – proof that at least one mammal had survived the inferno.

Up ahead, the creek murmured, its sing-song voice a lullaby from Eve's childhood. How many hours had she and Bec spent there, catching tadpoles, poking sticks under rocks in search of yabbies, sailing stick-boats down the 'rapids' and watching them tumble over the edge of the waterfall? How big the world seemed when you were a child. In reality, the rapids were no more than water rippling over the creek bed, and the waterfall was a half a metre drop into what was known as 'the billabong'.

The farm and the bush surrounding it had been their whole world. Yarrabee was part of the wider universe where they'd sometimes ventured, but the two of them were never happier than when they were here with each other and the horses. What would it be like to recreate that world for a child of her own?

The question hit like dry lightning, coming from nowhere, striking right at the centre of her heart, a series of rumbling echoes following in its wake. Of course, there'd been joy in her childhood, and wonder, and love. But there'd also been the loss of her father leaving, and her mother's simmering anger.

Nell's words in the letter she'd left inserted themselves into Eve's consciousness: *Maybe you have children of your own you can bring here to love the way I loved you and your sister when we were all happy together.*

Although she'd sometimes had a strange way of showing it, Nell had loved them. There had been happy times, in the early years, but was it too late for Eve to try and replicate that? Too late to contemplate being a mother herself?

She tripped over a root but managed to right herself without falling. Back in the day, she'd known the trails by memory, but without the usual markers, particular trees and bushes, navigating the path was tricky. Following the sound of the creek, she found her way to its edge. Banjo dipped his head and drank, then splashed through the shallow water, nose down, ears pricked. Kneeling, Eve scooped up a handful of water and wet the back of her neck. Banjo, taking her stance for an invitation to play, grabbed a stick from the far bank and bounced back across the creek, dropping it at her feet.

'You crazy mutt.' Eve bent down to pick up his offering, her gaze snagging on an object in her peripheral vision. An arm's length away, wedged in a crevice between two rocks, was a tin can, the kind used to fill a mower or carry petrol.

Banjo barked, and she jumped.

'No. That's enough.'

He moved a few feet away, dropped to the ground, the stick still balanced between his paws, and sulked.

Eve moved closer to the can. Pulling it out with one hand wasn't easy – it was firmly stuck in place. She grabbed the furthest edge and wiggled the can back and forth, tilting the rim and finally dislodging the thing. The whole can was still intact, but the metal was completely black, and the plastic handle had melted. There was no way it would have found its way here by accident or washed down the creek – it was too high up the bank and too tightly lodged between the rocks. Someone must have placed it here deliberately.

Acid lanced the back of her throat. She covered her mouth with her hand and coughed. When she pulled her hand away, a black coating of soot covered her palm, transferred from the metal. She swiped at her face to remove any stains. Arson, those policemen had said, possibly starting right here on her property, and she'd scoffed. But could this be proof that they were right? Should she take the tin home or leave it? If she reported it to the police, it could confirm their insinuation that she'd hired someone to set fire to the place. Solidify the possibility that the someone was Luke. Or even that she was trying to throw him under the bus and save herself. She sank down into the sand.

Was it Luke? If so, he was responsible for so much destruction. This wasn't some minor teenage prank, but a serious, life-altering, crime.

Eve's breath quickened. She lifted her head and looked around as if the answers could be right there in front of her, could jump out from behind a tree at any minute, like one of the big bad Banksia men in the May Gibbs stories she and Bec had so loved to read. But there was nothing but emptiness.

'Fuck. What do I do?'

Banjo jumped up, tail wagging, and came to her side, burying his head in her lap. Somehow he always knew when she needed comforting. Not that it answered her question, but it most certainly helped to not feel so alone.

She scooped up the jerry can and tucked it under her arm as she stood. This was potentially incriminating evidence – for both her and Luke – so better not to have it out here where someone walking the trails could find it and jump to conclusions. Wrong conclusions. The RFS investigators had somehow missed it on their search but there was always the chance someone else could find it.

She turned and set off towards the house, or at least in the direction she assumed the house was, since the landscape was so barren the path was now impossible to find.

Banjo went ahead, leading the way. He could be teleported to the moon and pick up the scent of home. She followed behind, her arms circling the can. The weight of it pressed against her side, heavier than any load she'd ever carried.

Chapter Ten

'Higher, Evie. Go higher.'

'Oh, I think that's probably high enough for a young lady who has just turned four.'

Lilly's frame was so small against her palms, it didn't take much to keep the swing in motion. Eve wriggled her fingers at the tiny waistline, and a fountain of giggles burst into the air. A smile came unbidden to her lips. That laugh was certainly infectious and went some way to soothe her unease at being here.

A kid's birthday party was the last place she wanted to be right now, when there were so many other things occupying her mind, but she'd promised Cat she'd come.

Besides, the distraction was good — so much better than sitting alone in the caravan thinking about fires and babies, past and future. And this morning's worrying discovery down by the creek.

Not that she'd been much use so far. Cat's perfectionist tendencies had already seen to the decorations. Crepe paper streamers festooned the yard in every shade of purple imaginable, from a delicate mauve to a blinding violet. Glittery balloons hung from the branches of the Chinese maple tree, the gold foil blending with the burnished edges of the leaves, already turning now that autumn had arrived.

Banjo plonked himself on the green stretch of manicured lawn, lolling onto his side and soaking up the afternoon sunshine.

For a kid's party, it was a very adult affair. A cluster of Cat's mother's group friends were positioned under the pergola, sipping wine, kids commandeering the sand pit nearby. The fathers hovered around Jack at the barbecue, beers in hand, but he seemed more intent on turning sausages than joining in any of the conversation. Nothing about his expression said, 'Happy to be here'.

'Liza! Liam!' Lilly squealed, taking one hand off the nylon rope and sending the swing into a wobble.

'Woah.' Eve grabbed the little girl by the arms as she slipped from the seat. 'Be careful, Missy.'

Without a backwards glance, Lilly raced across the yard and threw her arms around Eliza. Hugh, standing behind a disgruntled-looking Liam, smiled down at the trio of kids. Looking up again, he lifted his hand in a wave and grinned.

A zing of electricity zipped through Eve's veins. *Dammit*! What was he doing here?

Lilly carried the gift-wrapped box which Eliza had delivered to the table, and ripped at the paper, squealing with delight when she uncovered a knee-high toy horse complete with flowing lavender mane and tail.

Eve's own memories of birthdays included nothing as lavish. But then there'd never been parties either. Maybe a chocolate cake covered in hundreds and thousands if Nell got time to bake. Green GI cordial, sausage rolls and party pies if she'd managed to get to the shops in between riding lessons. And the present was always something practical – a brush for an actual horse or a new set of reins.

'Can I tempt you with a slice of fairy bread?' Hugh was suddenly beside her, his musky aftershave putting her senses on alert. He held out a paper plate covered in small multi-coloured triangles.

'Oh, thank you.' She downed the offering in two bites – melt-in-your-mouth freshness and the taste of rainbows. 'Nice tie.'

Hugh toyed with the edge of his fuchsia bow tie complete with white polka dots. 'Thank you. Found it in one of the dress-up boxes.' He nodded at the paisley plum-coloured scarf tied around Eve's neck, bandana-style, covering the neckline of her long-sleeved black tee. 'Pretty swish yourself.'

'Why … thank you.' She touched her fingers to the knot of the scarf. 'I found it in the op shop and thought I could make it work.'

'Which you do beautifully.' He gave her a wistful smile, turning her legs to mush.

There was something so soft and gentle about him, so different to the type of guys she normally gravitated towards. Marcus, for instance, all brooding looks and chis-elled edges: eyes dark and smouldering. Would the baby inherit those same Italian features, regardless of gender?

The baby.

She cleared her throat and shook the thought away.

'Come and get it.' Cat's instruction pulled her attention to the here and now.

Sausages sizzled on a huge platter Jack placed on the centre of the table, alongside a steaming dish of honey soy chicken wings, and what looked like a freshly made quiche, all the hot food surrounded by bowls of salad and baskets of bread rolls.

Hustled into order by a couple of the parents, the kids lined up as if they were in a school canteen queue, little ones at the front, with Eliza and Liam playing backstops at the end.

'Shall we?' Hugh waved an arm in the direction of the table, and they made their way towards the feast.

Tongs in hand, Cat doled out food onto paper plates, while a second mother directed the kids into a circle on the grass in the shade of the tree. There was obviously a process here, one based on military precision, which appeared to be secret mother's business. Not a code of which Eve was a member or had ever planned to join.

But she could still make herself useful. 'Can I do anything to help?'

Cat looked up, swiping a loose curl from her face. 'I think we're good, thank you. Grab yourself something to eat.' She shot a look across at Jack, back at the barbecue, alone.

Eve followed her gaze to the can of beer in his hand. Cat frowned as she grabbed a couple of empty plates and dashed back inside.

What was going on? Not that long ago, Jack had mentioned he hadn't had a drink in years; had given up when he married Cat because it had become more than social. He hadn't used the word 'alcoholic', but it was implied. Margo had even mentioned it had been a problem.

Jack lifted the can to his mouth and chugged a few mouthfuls. Should she say something to him – or was it better to mind her own business? Maybe a quick hello would be the way to go while Hugh was occupied with his kids.

Before she could think better of it, she skirted the table and stepped up beside Jack. 'Hey. How's it going?'

'Oh, hi.' He lowered the hand holding the beer. 'Not too bad.' He scraped at the hotplate with a spatula, steel grating against steel, setting her teeth on edge. 'I could do without a tribe of people descending on the place, but apparently every birthday must be publicly celebrated. With excessive amounts of purple glitter.' There was a distinct note of derision in his voice.

She flicked a glance at the beer, still in his hand. 'Didn't you say you'd given up the booze?' Maybe a mistake to mention it, but she'd seen enough addiction over the years to know it thrived on secrecy.

The lock of his jaw was instant. 'I said I didn't drink much these days.' A sharp uplift of his chin. 'Not that it's any of your business.'

'No need to get your knickers in a twist. Only an observation from a friend.'

Cat appeared beside them, a harried look on her face. 'Jack, can I talk to you for a minute?'

'Talk away.'

'Inside.'

He heaved a sigh and dropped the spatula on the tiled countertop, along with the beer can.

'Sorry, Eve.' Cat's expression morphed from contained fury to beseeching apology.

'All good.' Or possibly not.

'Eve, over here.'

She turned towards the excited voice. Eliza, sitting on a bench seat at a table under the maple, waved her fork in the air. Impossible not to smile at the girl's bubbly invitation. For whatever reason, she seemed to have made an impression on Hugh's daughter.

Hugh tilted his head in Eliza's direction. 'I warn you she may chew your ear about a riding lesson, but you're welcome to join us.'

'Thanks. I'll just grab some food.'

Now that morning had become afternoon, she could quite happily gnaw off her own arm. She piled her plate and returned to the table.

Hugh scooted sideways. Eve sat beside him, keeping her focus firmly ahead, across the table.

'Can I come and have a ride soon?' The words gushed out of Eliza like carbonated water, all fizz and motion.

'Eliza, what did I say?' Hugh frowned, but there was no bite in his tone.

'It's okay.' Eve's hand shot out and rested on Hugh's forearm, the fine hairs on his skin soft beneath her palm. Quick as a flash, she whipped her hand back and picked up her knife. Again, she kept her eyes on his daughter. 'Anytime Dad is okay to bring you, Bob will be waiting.'

'Yay! See, I told you, Daddy. Eve is nice, not like some people.' The emphasis on the some and the roll of her eyes was pure diva.

Hugh shook his head but didn't bother with a reprimand. 'If you're sure it's okay—'

'And I told you I'm a grown man who can look after himself.' Jack's voice boomed from somewhere inside the house. 'I don't need you micromanaging every minute of my life.'

Eliza's eyes popped. Liam's hand hovered over his plate; cutlery suspended mid-air. All sound and movement in the yard stopped, as if a spell had been cast, freezing everyone in time and place. A baby squealed, breaking the tension, and noise and activity slowly returned. But a hush had fallen over the gathering, the group hunching its collective shoulders as everyone tentatively returned to their meal.

What the hell was Jack thinking, yelling like that and making a scene at his daughter's birthday party?

Eve scanned the table where the kids were sitting, munching on sausages, party hats strapped to their chins. Lilly was right in the centre, laughing and oblivious to the argument every adult in the place was pretending they hadn't heard. Cat would be mortified. No one had made a move to go inside and check things were okay. Probably all too worried about interfering. But it wasn't like Cat not to be out here playing hostess.

'Excuse me.' Eve shot Hugh a look as she rose from the table.

A few heads turned as she walked towards the back door and pulled it open. A corresponding bang echoed down the hallway as she stepped up beside Cat, bent over at the table, head down.

'You okay?' Her friend's shoulder was steel beneath her hand.

Cat straightened, sniffed and nodded. Her chest rose and fell in a sigh. 'I guess everybody heard.'

'Only a bit.'

'God, how embarrassing.' Cat ran a hand over her face, wiping away a tear from her cheek.

'Where's Jack?'

Cat shrugged. 'He stormed out when he heard someone coming inside.'

Damn! Maybe she should have stayed outside and minded her business. 'Sorry.'

'It's not your fault. He's the one who should be apologising. He did absolutely nothing to help me get ready for the party, just sat in front of the TV playing video games as usual. He's hardly spoken a word to anyone, and then I see him drinking. Like that's a completely normal thing for him to do.'

'I guess he's under a lot of stress.' Even as the words left Eve's mouth, she winced. There was no valid excuse for falling off the wagon, for being such a jerk to Cat.

'Yes, he is, but alcoholics don't get day passes. He knows that as well as I do. And choosing to do it at his daughter's birthday party in front of our friends is the height of selfishness. He can't see past his own nose right now. It's all about him.'

Cat's arms dropped to her side. Tiny wisps of hair had fallen loose from her bun, and a dusting of icing from the cake on the table coated a patch of skin above her right eyebrow. She looked like a beautiful, abandoned rag doll, her body slack.

'I hate hearing myself say that. I know how much he's hurting. I just wanted one day where we could focus on Lilly, be happy, and forget about fires and death and guilt.' Cat looked up, tears welling. 'One day. Surely that's not too much to ask?'

'No. It's not.' Eve shook her head. 'But it's not always that easy either.' Jack was a doting husband and father, but maybe performing for a crowd was too much.

'Could you talk to him, Eve? He knows what you've been through, knows you get it. I'm sure he'll listen to you.'

Really? Did supporting her friends mean playing marriage counsellor? 'Cat, you know I'd do anything I can to help you guys, but I'm the last person who should be giving advice on dealing with grief. It's not like I handled it well.'

'Not back then you didn't, but you were a kid. Now you've got the benefit of hindsight, I'm sure you'd be able to help, or at least be a sounding board. And you've both been through trauma with the fires. He refuses to talk to me about it, or see a counsellor ... I don't know what else to do.'

Cat fixed her with a watery gaze, her pale blue eyes rimmed with red, making it impossible to look away. So much was unspoken in that look – memories of their childhood friendship, the bitterness of the loss each of them felt when that friendship imploded, the strange connection that came from the fact they'd each loved the same man, albeit at different stages of their lives. And as much as playing psychologist to Jack's undoubtedly reluctant patient ground every one of her gears, saying no to Cat was impossible.

'Okay. But it will have to be at the right time. Pushing too hard when he's not in the mood to talk will make things worse.'

Cat straightened, nodding. 'You're right. I trust your judgement. I'll leave it with you.'

An eruption of laughter flowed through the screen door. At the centre of it was Lilly's infectious giggle. Outside the window, a stream of bubbles bounced in the air, buffeted by the gentle breeze, popping one by one, only to be replaced by more.

'Looks like the bubble machine is a hit.' Cat dabbed at her cheeks with the back of her hand. 'Thank you.'

'I suspected she might be a fan.'

A small smile lit Cat's face, watching her daughter through the wire door. 'It never ceases to amaze me how all-consuming my love for her is. I don't think it's the same for men. Don't get me wrong, Jack adores her. But there's something about that biological bond between a mother and a child ... It's there right from the moment you conceive, and it gets even stronger through the pregnancy. Then, once they're born, you're cactus.'

A flutter started up in Eve's belly. Way too early to be any sort of movement; probably a figment of her imagination triggered by Cat's glowing assessment of motherhood. She shrugged the sensation away. 'Some people are born to be mothers, Cat, and you were definitely one.'

The shine faded from Cat's eyes. 'I would have loved to have had a whole brood. Poor Lilly. Being an only child is a blessing and a curse. All that undiluted love showered on her.' She cleared her throat, wiped her hands on the tea towel she was still holding. 'Maybe you'll have one of your own one day, and I can share the love around playing fairy godmother.'

God, could this conversation get any weirder? Did Cat have a crystal ball tucked away in the bottom of her medical bag? Eve kept her attention on the chasing and frolicking happening on the other side of the door.

'You never know, Eve,' Cat continued, perkier now, 'you could meet the love of your life tomorrow, or next week. Or you might have already met him.' She gave her best side-eye, then looked towards the man operating the bubble machine, entertaining all the kids.

Hugh.

'Don't even think about playing matchmaker, Cat. He's got a pretty-full dance card already. And besides, he's not my type.'

Cat snorted. 'I beg to differ, Ms Nicholls. I've seen the way he looks at you. And I'm pretty sure I've seen the same expression on your face when you two are together.'

'We're friends. Nothing more.'

'If you say so.' Cat shot her a side-eye. 'But if you did

decide you wanted to do something about that biological clock, he's a great dad. You could do a lot worse.'

A tiny pang, like a needle in her gut. 'Who says my clock is ticking?'

'Eve, you're a woman, and you're heading for forty. Of course, it's ticking.' Cat moved to the table, picked up the cake and returned to the door. 'I really think you should give it some thought before it's too late. Children can bring so much joy, and I reckon you deserve some of that in your life.'

Tears sprang to Eve's eyes, her traitorous body playing slave to her bloody hormones. She blinked them away, grabbing the matches from Cat's hand. 'Let's get this cake to the birthday girl, shall we?'

Cat held her gaze for a moment. 'Let's.'

Guests gathered around the table, kids at the front, adults forming a scrum at their backs. Lilly was at the centre, her eyes glowing even brighter than the miniature flames dancing on top of the unicorn cake. Cat stood beside her, one arm curled around those small shoulders, all that love she'd talked about shining on her face. What would it be like to be so utterly bonded to another human? To have another human so dependent on you that your lives were forever intertwined.

Someone kicked off the opening bars of 'Happy Birthday' and everyone joined in, Lilly clapping her hands in rough time to the singing.

Hugh's shoulder bumped against Eve's. She turned and he sang louder, exaggerating the enunciation of each word as he nodded along. *Oh, right. Sing!* She joined in the final lines as the rhythm slowed, unable to hide her smile. How did he manage to pull one from her every time he was around?

A 'Hip Hip' on her other side. Jack. Returned from wherever he'd been, standing next to her, right in Lilly's line of vision. His grin widened as he looked across at his daughter, catching her eye as she blew out the candles with Cat's help.

He'd come back, but despite the outward appearance of happiness there was a heaviness about him, in the sag of his shoulders and the lacklustre look in his eyes that told the real story. Knowing Jack, he'd be wracked with remorse over the scene he'd made, about embarrassing Cat. But being here for his daughter was more important, and at least he'd recognised as much.

Cat's request that Eve talk to him loomed like a storm cloud. It needed to be the right time, and that certainly wasn't here or now. Maybe out at Mossy Creek, if she asked him out to discuss the build. If talking to him would make a difference, help these people who had shown her so much kindness over the last couple of months, then why not?

'Cake?' A woman with a blonde pixie cut appeared, holding out a plate filled with pieces of vanilla sponge.

Hugh was already tucking into one. 'Hmmm, good,' he mumbled mid chew, a smear of butter cream coating his top lip. The urge to lift a fingertip to his mouth and stroke it away hit her like a magnetic force.

She clutched the serviette in her hand. Took a huge bite of cake, hoping it would smother the butterflies currently zooming around her insides on overdrive. She needed to get a grip. Get over this ridiculous schoolgirl crush. Follow through on her promise to support her friends and deal with her shit, without adding any more complications to the pile.

Chapter Eleven

Cat and Jack's marriage crisis weighed on Eve's mind all the way home, but there was another, more pressing problem she needed to sort out – within walking distance. Ever since Emily Winters had mentioned her conversation with Sergeant Adams, not to mention finding the jerry can, the whole arson thing had become a knot she couldn't untangle. Sussing her godmother out about Luke would be tricky. Margo was like a mamma bear when it came to her family: she could criticise them as much as she liked, but if anyone else dared to, they would most certainly be subject to her wrath. Similar to the way she herself was with Banjo.

Speaking of …. where was he now?

The bush on either side of the road was as desolate as everywhere else around the place. All the lower levels, vegetation and scrub had been wiped out, leaving only the tall, thin trunks of the gums, once a palette of intriguing greys but now a basic monotone black. Not many places for a dog to hide. No wildlife for him to bail up either, but he had to be snooping around somewhere nearby.

Eve gave a sharp whistle, the volume piercing even to her own ears, making her wince. Stopping, she turned around a full 360 degrees and peered through the trees, up and down the road. Her body tensed, as it always did whenever Banjo was missing or sick, the memory of the snakebite that almost took his life right before the fires still way too fresh.

Sticking the index finger of each hand into her mouth, she whistled again. A movement to her left drew her eye. Bounding over fallen branches and darting around tree trunks, Banjo came screaming through the trees, putting on the brakes to sit by her feet.

Her shoulders fell back into place as she patted him. 'Good boy. At least for coming back when you were called.' She leaned down and cupped his chin in her hand. 'The second time, that is. You stay here with me, okay?'

If anyone had told her years ago she'd be regularly having a conversation with a dog – not to mention having him sleep at the bottom of her bed – she'd have laughed out loud. There'd been a cattle dog cross on the farm when she was small, who'd died from a tick bite, and after that Nell forbade pets, despite having plenty of room. *Too much work and I'd be the one doing it* – her words every time they asked until they didn't bother asking anymore. Now it was hard to imagine life without a dog – and certainly without Banjo.

'Come on, Boofhead. Let's go.'

Margo's place came into view. She started towards it, clenching and unclenching her hand – an automatic reflex now she was following the physiotherapist's instructions – and stopped, her body frozen in place as realisation dawned. She'd just lifted her arm, stuck her fingers in her mouth and whistled – her dud limb had followed her brain's instruction without her even realising. Halle-bloody-ulah! Things were looking up.

Walking down Margo and Harry's driveway was like willingly entering a nightmare. Every muscle in her body tensed, as if she was balancing on a tight rope. No matter how sternly she ordered herself to look straight ahead, concentrate on the house, on getting to the door, her gaze kept shifting: to the incinerated trees and ruined gardens, the obliterated shed. At least the house remained standing. Somehow, she and Margo had managed to save it, filling the gutters with water and soaking the timber before fleeing to the dam, before blackness consumed them.

Now her breath came faster and faster as her legs turned to liquid. Every step was like dragging herself through knee-deep mud. She sucked in a lungful of air, held it and released it again, slower and slower until the rapid racing of her pulse eased. By the time she was at the house, it was almost back to normal. She knocked and waited.

'Oh hello, love. This is a nice surprise.' Margo appeared behind the flyscreen door.

Just in the nick of time, before the temptation to turn towards the place where they both almost died could take hold.

She stepped back slightly as the door opened. 'Thought I'd come and see how you're doing.' *And see if there's any news of Luke.*

'Come on in.' Margo led the way to the kitchen, towards the aroma of fresh baking. 'Have a seat. I'll put the kettle on. Is Banjo okay out there?'

'He'll be fine. A whole new set of smells to explore.' *Hopefully none tempting him to venture away from the house.*

'At least there are no chickens for him to chase.' The slight tremor in Margo's voice belied her attempt at black humour. While the house remained intact, none of the animals had survived, including her beloved hens. And those damned cows – their pained bellowing one of the soundtracks to Eve's long sleepless nights.

'How are you doing? Is Harry okay?' Apart from the humming of the kettle, the house was quiet. No sign of anyone here but Margo.

'He's fine. Dean came and picked him up to take him into The Shed for some supplies.'

'Is he working again?'

Margo huffed. 'When he thinks I'm not taking any notice. Supposedly following doctor's orders, but if I didn't keep a constant eye on him, I reckon he'd be out there digging holes and clearing the yard.' She shook her head as she arranged two cups and saucers on the counter. 'Silly old bugger. He's his own worst enemy. Stubborn as the day is long.'

An image of Harry holding onto the keys to Nell's house, staring her down and practically refusing to hand them over back when she had first arrived home flashed into Eve's mind. Everything had been so cool between them. Harry refusing to forgive her for what he saw as abandoning her mother all those years ago. But he'd never walked in her skin. Never knew what it was like to carry the guilt of your sister's death in your soul and the judgement of the town on your shoulders. Admittedly, he'd softened a little towards her since she'd save this house, and his wife, but there was still that moment of awkwardness between them each time they met.

'There you go.' The cup rattled as Margo delivered the tea, and liquid slopped into the saucer. She'd always had a slight tremor in her hand, but this was more in the realm of a shake. A slice of cake wobbled in the centre of a plate that appeared beside the cup.

'That looks delicious. Lemon syrup?'

Margo nodded.

The citrusy scent took Eve straight back to summer afternoon visits, when she and Bec would be escaping Nell's black mood if a horse had played up during a lesson or if a client had yet again not paid. Picking up the fork, she sliced through the cake and let its lemony tang settle on her tongue as it practically melted in her mouth. 'Ahh, heaven.'

Margo chuckled. 'You always did love that one.'

'Margo, I love everything you cook. I'll end up looking like a beached whale if you keep making those food deliveries.' Her hand flew to her waistline, but a sudden flash of recognition had her dropping it again as if she'd touched an electric hot plate.

Margo nodded towards her arm, now resting against the seat of the chair. 'On the mend?'

'Well, I managed to use my fingers to whistle for Banjo on the walk up, so I think it's getting there. Hoping I'll be able to drive soon, before I wear out everyone's hospitality.'

'Don't you worry about that. Nobody minds. And you don't want to be driving before you're good and ready. There have been enough trips to the hospital around here of late,' Margo sighed into her teacup. She'd always had the hardened skin of a country woman who spent hours outdoors, but now the lines seemed more pronounced, the furrows deeper, and her characteristic spark dimmed. 'Still on for the exhibition opening tomorrow?'

'Wouldn't miss it.' Not quite the truth. The idea of making small talk with a bunch of strangers made her want to stick pins in her eyes. But she'd promised Margo — and Fran — she'd attend.

The cake disappeared in a few delicious mouthfuls. Margo cut another slice and slid it onto her plate. Broaching the subject she'd come here to raise was going to be tricky. If she brought up the question of Luke's whereabouts, Margo might wonder why she was asking after him, and it might alert her to the fact there was something wrong. Better to skirt around the topic and see what comes up.

'How's the family?'

Margo threw her hands up in the air. 'Don't ask me. Dean stomps in and collects his father and stomps out again without so much as a by-your-leave. I haven't sighted Michelle in weeks, barely hear from Douglas and his lot up in Queensland …' Lips pursed, she shook her head. 'Sometimes I wonder what I've raised.'

'Oh, Margo.' Eve hadn't been back long enough to know all the ins and outs of the family dynamics, but it was hard to imagine a more solid bunch. 'I'm sure it's fine. They're probably just busy.'

'I know.' Her sigh was long and deep. 'And worried about Luke no doubt. Little devil. Not a word from him. The police were around here asking about him the other day.'

Shit! If they'd asked Margo the same questions they'd fired at her, it was no wonder the poor woman looked so haggard. 'What did they say?'

Margo flapped her hands about like she was in the middle of a tap dance. She grabbed the handle of the teapot, filling up both their cups. 'Wanted to know what he was doing the day the fires broke out. Pfft! How the bloody hell would I know? He's a chip off the old block when it comes to privacy. Gets up, grunts over his cereal, and then I don't see him for the rest of the day. Or at least I didn't when he was here.'

Her whole body sagged. 'He couldn't get enough of us when he was little. Used to come and curl up in my lap and tell me all about his day. Lick the spatula after I made him a cake and chatter away like a monkey. But he hit high school and turned into a typical teenager. We'd go months on end without seeing him. Used to upset Harry. Then when he was being difficult at home, and he moved in here, I thought it would be such a pleasure to have him around, but he spent most of his time in his room and barely came out for meals. That's when he was home and not off with one of his no-good mates. Harry maintained he needed a firmer hand and he was probably right. I hate to say it, but Dean let him get away with far too much.'

The conversation had taken a tangent. Time for some re-directing. 'So, why are the police asking after him?'

Margo visibly shrank, as if she'd taken a magic pill. Everything about her became smaller. 'It's part of their investigation – arson, would you believe? Of course I told them that was ridiculous. Luke might be a bit on the wild side, but he would never do something like that, something so criminal.'

Eve lowered her cup to the saucer, the image of that jerry can firmly fixed in her mind's eye. 'I'm sure the police were just ticking boxes, nothing to worry about.' She scraped her fork across a blob of icing on her plate. 'Did you tell Dean about it?'

Margo nodded. 'He just laughed and said it was a bloody joke.' She stared into her empty cup, so still that she could be sitting for a portrait. Usually her face was animated, her eyes bright, brows rising and falling as she told a story or staged a friendly interrogation. But today her features were drawn, and she looked every day of her seventy-five years. 'You know, as much as I love my boys, sometimes I wish I had a daughter.'

She looked up and that moment they'd had in the dam passed between them.

'Having a child of the same gender doesn't necessarily make you closer.'

'No, it doesn't. But men can be so obtuse. So bloody ignorant. Harry, Dean, Luke, they're all the same. Too wrapped up in their own worries to think about anybody else. And Michelle keeps to herself. At least a daughter might want to have a conversation from time to time.'

'You know I'm always here if you want to talk.'

'I know that, love.' She patted Eve's hand. 'And I appreciate it. It's just ... ever since that day, when we were under the blanket together, and I told you about ...' She shook her head and bit down on her bottom lip.

'The baby you gave up?'

A nod. Wisps of silver-white hair fell across her forehead as she quietly cleared her throat. 'It's like telling you about her has opened up a box I'd locked the memory away in a long time ago. And now I can't stop thinking about her. She'd be going on fifty-eight. Hard to imagine when all you knew of your child was the newborn baby.'

'You haven't told Harry?'

Margo straightened, and her head shot up. 'No. And I don't intend to.'

'Don't worry, Margo. I promise I won't tell a soul.'

'To be honest, I was relieved when I had a boy the first time, with Douglas. Then I had Dean and I was happy, but something in me wanted a girl. I had two miscarriages after I had Dean. The doctor told me it wasn't a good idea to try again, that it could be dangerous. A little part of me always wondered if it was payback for giving away my child.'

'Oh, no. Of course, it's not.' Eve shifted her chair closer, lowering her head to try and catch her godmother's eye. Margo was such a rock – seeing her beating herself up like this was completely disconcerting. 'You know you could try to find her. It's much easier to track down adopted children these days.'

'No.' Margo shook her head way too vehemently. 'Best to leave the past in the past. Besides, what would I say to Harry and the boys? And she might not even want to see me.'

Eve shrugged. 'Or she might.'

'Nope. Forget I mentioned it.' Margo picked up the teapot in one hand, the milk jug in the other and stood. 'Urgh.' She winced, doubling over. The jug slipped from her grip and fell to the floor, milk splattering across the lino tiles.

'Margo!' Rushing to her godmother's side, Eve slid an arm around her shoulder, took the teapot and placed it back on the table.

'I'm fine. Don't fuss. Only this damned back of mine. Been giving me hell at night. I'll be good in a minute.' Slowly, Margo righted herself, one vertebra at a time, hand resting on the base of her spine. Her face was ashen, and a thin sheen of perspiration beaded her top lip.

'How about you sit down and let me clean this up?'

'No!' Margo batted Eve's hands away as she continued to clear the table, cups clattering on their saucers en-route to the sink. She returned the teapot to its spot on the bench with a deliberate thud and grabbed a cloth to mop up the spilt milk.

All of it was so unlike Margo: at least not any version Eve had ever met. Her godmother's mouth was a thin, flat line and her scowl would frighten a snail out of its shell. What was going on?

'Are you sure you're okay?'

Margo dropped the dishcloth into the sink and gripped the edges of the bench with both hands. Her arms shook and her shoulders shuddered. Her head dropped, and a sob echoed through the kitchen.

With each reverberation, the ache in Eve's diaphragm sharpened. Her hands met in a double fist, and she squeezed them together using the pressure to steady herself and regain her own composure before she spoke. Margo was everybody's rock. It was a shock to see her crumbling. Eve took one step and then another, then a third until she was by Margo's side.

'What is it, Aunty Marg?'

Margo sniffed and shook her head, swiping at her cheeks with the heel of one hand, the other still gripping the bench. 'Nothing. It's nothing. I'm just a silly old galoot. Feeling sorry for myself. I'll be alright once I get a good night's sleep.' She let out a hoarse laugh. 'Might mean I'll be sleeping in the spare room to get away from Harry's snoring, but if that's what I have to do, then so be it.'

'Sounds like a plan.' Not a convincing one, but much more reassuring than seeing Margo in pieces. 'Do you have any medication you can take for your back, or maybe some sleeping pills?'

'Don't believe in them. But I've got some of that strong ibuprofen there, that'll sort me out.' Margo wiped her hands on the red checks of her apron and looked up, her smile forced rather than genuine. 'Don't give it another thought. You get back home to whatever you were planning on doing next. I've got a few things to do, so I'd better get on with them.' As she spoke, she sliced off a chunk of cake, wrapped it in plastic and handed it across.

'Thank you. You're sure you don't want—'

'Yes. Now off you go.'

'Call me if you need anything. I'll see you tomorrow.'

The door banged shut behind her as Eve stepped outside. Banjo jumped to attention with a stick clamped between his teeth as they started off on their walk home.

All the way back, bits of the kitchen table conversation bounced around in her head like a pinball ricocheting off bumpers: the questions from the police, Dean's belligerence, the weight of Harry's recovery, and that strange mention of the baby given up for adoption so many years ago. No wonder Margo wasn't sleeping with all that on her mind. Did she know more about Luke than she was letting on?

Eve's phone buzzed in her pocket and she pulled it out. Another text message from Mel: *You still alive? Real estate agent is on my case. He's not going to give us much more time. I need an answer girlfriend.*

That same prickling sensation appeared every time Eve thought about saying yes to Mel's offer. Nothing to do with the pregnancy nausea and everything to do with something else: excitement or trepidation? There was so much going on inside her body, it was hard to decipher. And the conversation with Margo hadn't helped. Everything here was so complicated. The temptation to march back to the caravan, pack up her few pathetic belongings and drive away caught her like an ocean current dragging her north.

But didn't she owe it to Margo to hang around until this whole mess with Luke was sorted out? The two of them had cheated death together, and Margo had looked out for her from the day she'd arrived back in town. Making sure her godmother was okay before disappearing again was the least she could do.

A few paces ahead, Banjo turned right into the driveway without any instruction, already knowing the way home. In the paddock, fat, healthy horses picked at the remains of their hay. A salmon-pink light threaded its way through wisps of cloud – late afternoon whispering across the farm. Perhaps there were other reasons to stay.

She typed a hurried message into her phone: *A few things to sort out. Will let you know soon. Promise. x*

It was the weekend. The agent wouldn't get back to Mel until Monday.

Chapter Twelve

The car driving towards her wasn't a silver Mazda, and the person sitting behind the wheel wasn't Margo. It was most definitely Hugh. What was he doing here?

He pulled to a stop outside the caravan where she was waiting, wound down the window and poked his head out. 'I know I'm not as pretty as Margo, but you don't have to look so disappointed.'

He couldn't be more wrong. Willing away the trembling between her thighs, she pushed herself to her feet. Last time she'd seen him, outside the chemist, the sensation was more dread than pleasure, given what she was up to at the time. But that had been an aberration, and given his crisply pressed shirt and freshly shaven face, his appearance today was more of a … pleasure?

'Margo called to say Harry's not feeling well and asked if I could pick you up.' He narrowed his eyes. 'I take it from the look on your face that she didn't call you.'

'No, she didn't.' What the hell was going on with

Margo? Was her back pain worse? Had yesterday's conversation upset her? The fizz in her stomach soured.

'Eve?' Hugh's voice pulled her out of her reverie. 'I promise I'll have you home before you turn into a pumpkin.'

That boyish grin was impossible to resist. 'Why thank you, Prince Charming. How can I refuse an offer like that?'

Banjo ran towards the passenger side of the car.

She gave a sharp whistle and he returned to her side, looked up at her imploringly. 'Sorry, matey. You stay here, and I'll be back soon.'

She blew him a kiss as she climbed in beside Hugh. Never any need to worry about Banjo wandering off when she was out; he was such a good boy.

'You look ... great.' Hugh faltered, as if struggling for the right word.

'No need to sound so surprised.'

'Oh no, I ...'

'All good.' She laughed. 'I even washed my hair for the occasion. And threw on a clean top and jeans.' In truth, she'd gone as far as to swipe on some mascara and apply a coat of lipstick. 'You look pretty dapper yourself.'

Dapper? Where did that come from? These antiquated phrases that seemed to appear out of nowhere were pure Nell, of course. Was she getting more like her mother as she got older? Would she be the same kind of mother if—

'So, how's it all going?'

'Not too bad.' If you didn't count the unexpected pregnancy and the police accusing her of arson. 'How about you?'

'Work's good. Not too busy.' The stiffness of his jaw and the creases around his eyes belied the light tone of voice. He had his sunnies on and kept his gaze on the road. 'The horses all okay?'

She turned from the window. 'Yeah, seem to be. I was worried about them ingesting too much crap, but the grass is going wild, and I'm making up feeds for them.'

'Are you going to keep them all?'

'Not sure yet.' Saying goodbye to the herd would be hard. They'd all come through so much. They were survivors, like her. 'You thinking about one for Eliza? There's a nice little pony.'

'Well, I wasn't thinking of that, but I'm sure she'd love to come and see them. She hasn't stopped yabbering on about it since you gave the okay. Liam too. Some animal therapy might be good for him.'

'Why? What's wrong?'

Hugh let out a long sigh. 'He's anxious. Has been having night terrors, wetting the bed. Poor kid. He gets so embarrassed. I'm at a bit of a loss really.'

'Have you talked to a doctor?'

'Yeah. Cat says this sort of thing is common with kids who've experienced trauma. He was in the car when his mother died.' The quick breath was almost undetectable. 'They both were. He was doing better, but the stress of the fires may have triggered something.'

'Must be hard when you don't know how to help them.'

'You're not wrong. Parenting is the toughest gig in the world. At least with animals, you can generally work out the source of the problem and treat it.'

'I'm sure you're doing a brilliant job, Hugh. You're welcome to bring the kids out anytime to muck around with the horses, give them a brush. They can have a ride if they want.'

'That'd be great, Eve. They'd like that.' The smile he gave suggested he might like it too. And her own duplicitous heart may have done a little happy dance, overriding the worries of prospective parenting. 'Just don't go giving Eliza any ideas about getting one of her own.'

'Hugh, she's a ten-year-old girl. She already has the idea.'

He turned slightly, raising his eyebrows. 'The voice of experience, I'm guessing.'

'It was a little different for me and Bec. We grew up with them all around us. Could pretty much ride as soon as we walked. Had our own ponies from when we were two years old, so we didn't know any different.'

The smile fell from his face, replaced with an expression of contemplation. 'Bec was your sister?'

'Yeah.' Her name had slipped out naturally. Coming back and finally facing her death had loosened the shackles. It still stung a little to think of her, but there was joy there too, a genuine happiness that came with remembering their early years together.

'I've never heard you talk about her before.'

Eve shrugged. 'I suppose I haven't. But she's always on my mind. I don't think there's a day that's gone by in the last twenty years that I haven't thought of her.'

'I know what you mean.' Hugh's Adam's apple bobbed. Losing his wife must have been so hard, and the children were daily reminders. The clicking of the indicator filled the interior of the car as they turned onto the road into town. 'The grief never leaves you, does it?'

'No. It doesn't.' She touched a hand to where her shirt sleeve covered the tattoo she'd had done on the first anniversary of Bec's death. A horse running in the wind,

Bec's initials flowing from its mane. 'It becomes part of who you are.'

'It does.' There was a wistfulness to his tone, bordering on melancholy. Maybe not the direction they should be heading in right now.

'So …' She made sure her voice was upbeat, breezy. 'Today should be … fun.'

Hugh laughed. 'Art soirees not your thing?' Mission accomplished, even if hiding her apprehension about the afternoon was a complete fail.

'God, no. But I really like Fran, and her art is amazing. How long have you known her and Clive?'

'I've known Clive for about ten years. Fran for much longer. She was matron of honour at our wedding.'

'So, she was a friend of …' Eve winced.

'Corinne, my wife. She and Fran met at uni.'

'Was your wife an artist?'

'She was, but she went into teaching. And then when the kids came along, she took some time off. Wanted to do the stay-at-home mum thing. She did get back into painting though. She loved painting flowers, trees … anything in nature really. I think she would have continued with it if she'd lived.'

'Do you still have any of her work?'

Hugh nodded, slowly. 'I do. It's in the shed with a lot of her other things I never had the courage to get rid of, packed up in boxes and locked away.'

Not just physically, based on the strain in his voice.

Not having to look at the evidence Bec had once lived had been one of the benefits of taking off, made it easier to pretend that the night at the lake had never happened. And after twenty years away from the farm, all that was left of

Bec was the heart-shaped necklace now permanently secured to the chain hanging around her neck. She rubbed her fingers over the engraving, and a burst of warmth radiated through her chest.

'You should do it – get the paintings out, I mean. It would be nice for the kids to see what their mum did. To have that piece of her to claim as theirs.'

'I should.' Hugh cleared his throat. 'And I should clear her things out too.'

'Has to feel right.' How long had Nell left it before removing Bec's belongings?

Even the idea of it made Eve's throat burn.

Another nod from Hugh. The two of them seemed to be good at the whole tangent thing but had probably strayed far enough from their original topic of conversation.

'So … Fran?'

'Oh, yeah. She was amazing when Corinne passed. Came down straight away and helped me look after the kids. Looked after me, for that matter. She fell in love with the place, and then when Clive sold his business in Sydney, this was the first place they looked. Just so happened there was a café for sale and a space that was great for a gallery. Win win. Are you enjoying the work?'

'Yeah, it's great. Clive's so easy to get along with. And the whole book-coffee combo is perfect.'

'I'm glad.' His smile was broad and genuine. This was a man who really got a kick out of helping people.

Her mind drifted back to the day of the fires. His appearance at Margo's place, the three of them bundling into his car and racing back through the smoke to Nell's, trying but failing to douse the flames as they consumed the house. A phantom pain needled her arm.

She glanced down at the ugly scar and pulled the sleeve

of her linen blouse closer to her wrist, falling quiet as Hugh parked the car.

The place was already buzzing when they stepped inside, with people milling about sipping champagne. Locals in cotton dresses and clean jeans; out-of-towners in pant suits and chunky heels. She followed Hugh through the crowd to the back of the gallery, where Fran was deep in conversation with an older couple who looked like they'd stepped straight out of the society pages of a Sydney newspaper. Good chance they had.

As soon as Fran saw them coming, she broke away. 'Thank the lord.' She leant forward conspiratorially and whispered into the space between the two of them. 'Those old geezers were boring me stupid.'

Hugh kissed Fran's cheek. 'Who are they?' He mimicked her stage-whisper tone.

'A couple from Woollahra. Patrons of the Arts.' Fran gave the title in a deliberately faux English gentry accent, emphasising it with air quotes. 'Apparently I've come to their attention.'

'In that case, I hope you didn't call them old geezers to their face.' Hugh rested a hand on Fran's shoulder.

'You know me, darls – charm personified.' Fran turned slightly. 'Eve, you look fabulous. Love the hair out. I've only ever seen you wear it up.'

Eve pulled a face she hoped was appreciative. First Hugh and now Fran with the compliments. Did she really look that different to her day-to-day self? 'Well, you know, posh gallery exhibition and all. Thought I'd go all out. I even pulled on a clean pair of jeans.'

Fran narrowed her gaze and waved a finger, drawing an invisible line between them. 'Did you two come together?'

'Yes, we did.' Hugh jumped in to answer the question, almost too eagerly.

'Margo was going to give me a lift but couldn't make it, so Hugh very kindly picked me up.'

'Right.' Fran looked slightly deflated, and it seemed Hugh did too, if the downturn of his mouth was anything to go by. 'Well, grab a drink, eat some cheese, mingle. Oh, and feel free to sing my praises to anyone who looks cashed up.'

'We will.' Hugh stuck his hands in his pockets. 'Where's Clive?'

'He's somewhere about.' Fran glanced around, then waved at someone at the other end of the room. 'Sorry, must go and schmooze.' And like a sharp gust of wind on a summer's afternoon, she was gone.

'Drink?' Hugh gestured towards the makeshift bar set up along the side wall.

'Yeah, that'd be great. Just a Coke or something, please.'

'No champers?'

'No, thanks.' *Think fast, Eve.* 'I'm off alcohol right now. On a health kick.'

That sounded so pathetic, but Hugh didn't seem to notice. She scanned the walls, taking in the various artworks. Some of the paintings were by other artists. Fran's brief had been a single word: Hope. It was there in the splashes of green, the flocks of birds soaring across the horizon, the bursts of flowers exploding from a stretch of black earth. And inside that larger image, her gaze kept returning to Fran's major contribution, still mesmerising even though she'd already seen it: the single tree wrapped in a green vine – as if it was a gift and the vine was the ribbon – and that floating baby so weirdly intertwined with the whole, all the separate elements of the painting so intricately – even intimately – connected.

'Pretty impressive.' Hugh returned and handed her a glass of Coke, ice tinkling against the edges of the glass.

'I can't take my eyes off it. I couldn't paint to save myself.'

'Well, we all have our strengths.'

'True.' Even though her own were a mystery. 'What are yours?'

Hugh pointed at himself. 'My talents? Is that a trick question?'

'No.' She smiled. 'It's not. Three things you're good at. Go.'

'Okay, well, I'm good with animals, hence the job.' He squinted, as if he was trying to see something in the distance, then lifted his head slightly as if it had come into focus. 'I make a mean margarita. Oh, and I'm a pretty good cook.'

'Well, I can attest to that. Those meals you whipped up and delivered while I was staying at your surgery were to die for.' Not an exaggeration. The guy had even cooked curries and casseroles she didn't have to cut, since she'd only had one working hand. So thoughtful. A personality trait rather than a talent but a very admirable one.

'How about you?'

'Me?'

'Your talents. Three.' He grinned. 'Share and share alike.'

What had she got herself into? 'Umm…'

'Oh, come on, Eve, off the top of your head. Don't think too hard.'

'Horses. I'm good with horses.'

'That you are.' He kept his gaze fixed, clearly determined to wheedle another two confessions out of her.

'I make a mean cappuccino.' If he could claim a cocktail, she could include a coffee. 'And if I have to go for a third ...'

'Which you do.'

'I can sing. I mean, I used to sing a bit.'

'Really? What type of singing?'

'Country-style, I guess. Acoustic guitar stuff.'

'So, you sing professionally?'

'I wouldn't say professionally.' Oh no. Hugh looked way too excited. She'd dug herself a deep hole and jumped right in. Any minute now, he'd be making a song request. 'Just the odd gig in some small pubs.'

Hugh's eyes brightened. 'I'd love to hear you play some time.'

Even the possibility of getting up on a stage seemed so far away. A gathering of people standing around, looking at her in anticipation as she fumbled to find the chords.

She looked down at her left arm, the one that would have to hold the neck of the guitar, and the fingers that would work the frets. Or not. 'A bit tricky right now.'

He winked. 'I'm sure it won't be too long until you have full use of it again. Playing might be good therapy.'

'Possibly.' She'd always found singing and playing therapeutic. Maybe it was time to give it another try? But where was her ... *Oh, no!* Why hadn't she realised?

'Eve, is everything okay? You've gone a hideous shade of pale.'

'I only just remembered – my guitar was in the house. It's gone.'

'I'm sorry to hear that.' There was a genuine sympathy

in Hugh's tone. He leaned in. Was he going to put his arm around her?

She tossed her hair back over her shoulder and shifted slightly to the left. 'It can be replaced. Others have had it much worse.' But the lump in her throat stuck like glue. That guitar had travelled all around the country with her and Banjo. Been a constant and faithful companion. The thought of playing a different one left her literally cold, goosebumps rising on her skin.

'Still, I'm sure it carried a lot of memories for you.'

She gave a slight nod.

'Hey, there.' Eve turned towards the voice. Emily, the journalist. Perfect timing. 'You feeling better? After the other night?'

Hugh looked at Emily then back at Eve, a frown forming.

'Oh, yeah. I'm fine. Thanks again for your help.' *Not that you needed to mention it here.*

Around them, the noise in the completely packed gallery seemed to crescendo to an almost deafening level.

'Great crowd,' Emily observed through the din. 'Nice vibe.'

'Hi.' Hugh reached across the centre of the small circle formed by the three of them. 'Hugh Robertson.'

'Emily Winters.' The two shook hands. 'You a local?'

Clearly a standard question in the journalist's quest to find people to interrogate.

'Yes. I'm the vet in town.'

'Must be an interesting job.'

'It has its moments. And you?'

Neither of them seemed put out about having to introduce themselves. Fortunate since the best Eve could do right now was steel herself against the ringing in her ears.

'Journalist.' Emily looked at Hugh as if he was the centre of the universe. Another of her professional skills no doubt. 'I'm doing a series on the impact of the fires, so I'm in town for some reconnaissance.'

Hugh nodded. No indication on his face that he thought dredging up painful memories was a bad idea.

'I hear police suspect arson, possibly a local. Must be hard for the town to think one of its own is responsible.'

If blood really could run cold, then Eve's froze solid at the memory of the policeman's steely gaze as he questioned her.

She shook the vision away and took a long guzzle of Coke. 'Hearsay and gossip run rampant around here, so I wouldn't put too much weight into accusations like that.'

'It's more than hearsay,' Emily continued, the proverbial dog with a very juicy bone. 'Sergeant Adams told me they were investigating a particular suspect and had a few serious leads.'

Did he now?

Emily turned her head towards the back of the room. 'Excuse me. There's someone I need to see. It was lovely to meet you, Hugh. And to see you again, Eve.' She'd dropped the bone and left, all smiles as she edged her way through the crowd.

'Seems nice.' Hugh downed a mouthful of beer as he looked over to where the journalist was cosying up to the Thompsons. Another family who had lost their whole property out on the Cataract Road. More fodder for her story.

'Lots of people are nice when they want something from you.'

Hugh frowned. 'Meaning?'

'I've had experience with the media before, when my

sister died. The press are like the dementors in Harry Potter. They like to feast on people's misery.'

Hugh considered her for a moment, a soft sheen glazing his eyes. Had he had a similar experience after his wife's car accident? 'They have a job to do, I guess, like everyone else.'

'More like they have stories to sell. This one told me she wants to shine a light on the aftermath of the fires, so the rest of the country has a better understanding of what it's been like.' *Shine a light, my arse.*

'That's not a bad thing.'

'As long as she doesn't try digging deeper than people want her to go.' Surely that was something Hugh would understand.

The chiming of metal against glass quieted all conversation in the room, including their own.

Fran stepped up onto a podium. 'Thank you all for coming to this ground-breaking exhibition of work by local artists who have been kind enough to donate their work to raise money for the bush fire recovery fundraiser.'

Eve scanned the crowded room as Fran continued. That was one good thing about living in a small community. When the chips were down, everyone helped out. Every single local in this room had been impacted in one way or another by the fires. There'd been more than one fire that week – a whole string of them joining up to create a monstrous inferno. But if the one at Mossy Creek had been started by someone, didn't the people who lived there deserve justice? Even if that someone was Luke.

Fran's voice faded as Eve took herself back in time to that hideous day. Had Luke been there that morning? He'd worked random days, and with everything else that had happened it really was hard to remember. She let her eyes fall closed, willing the memory to solidify, but nothing came.

She had to be sure of the facts before she said anything about the jerry can. It could be the nail in Luke's coffin once the police found out. And maybe even her own.

A burst of applause broke out as Fran introduced the various artists who had contributed paintings to the exhibition. From the other side of the room, Emily caught Eve's eye and smiled. She forced a smile in return. It sounded like Emily Winters might have some inside information. Meeting up with her might not be such a bad idea after all.

Chapter Thirteen

Standing on the very edge of the rubble, she shoved her hands into the pockets of her hoodie as Jack walked the perimeter of the space that used to be a house, Lilly mimicking him as she followed along behind.

A fresh wind blew across the paddocks, nipping at Eve's cheeks. This was the closest she had come to the site since the day of the fires, and the proximity made her gut churn. Everything that had once been inside the walls no longer existed. Even the people were ghosts, excluding herself, although she was only a blurred reflection of the girl who once lived here.

'So, what are you thinking?' Jack stopped a metre away and kicked at a charred piece of brick.

He looked haggard, as if he hadn't slept. No mention of his outburst at Lilly's party, although he did look a little sheepish when he first arrived. Making the call to get him to Mossy Creek to discuss the house had been a ploy to fulfill Cat's request of a friendly chat. Not easy to do when he had his sidekick.

'What I'm thinking is this is a fucking mess.'

'Evie said a bad word, Daddy.' Lilly fixed shining eyes on her father.

Ouch! 'Sorry.' She gave an exaggerated cringe. 'I'm not used to being around little people.'

She was saying it more to Jack by way of apology. A nugget of warmth glowed inside her at the name Lilly had used: Evie. Jack was the only one who ever used that abbreviation, a throwback to her younger name, Angie.

'You're not wrong about it being a … mess.' He scratched the side of his forehead. 'But I meant about the new place. What style of house are you thinking?'

'I don't really know.' *Something that has good sales potential?* 'Nothing fancy. Something simple. Easy to build.'

'Well, if we go with the same footprint, it will make it easier from an approval perspective. Council is expediting permissions for residents who were completely burnt out.'

'Sounds good.' If she did go ahead with the build, the sooner Jack started, the quicker he'd be occupied and the sooner the tension with Cat would ease. Hard to believe things were less than perfect in their household, with Lilly standing there at his side: a miniature version of both her parents.

'So maybe a three-bedroom weatherboard with a veranda out front. Similar layout to the old place.'

She jerked her head back up to meet Jack's gaze. 'That'll work.'

He pointed into the centre of the space. 'We could do the living area more open plan than the original, separate the kitchen from the dining area with an island bench, and have the lounge area flowing on from that. French doors at the front would look good too. You could open them up to get the view and air flow happening.'

He looked skyward. 'Perfect angle to catch the sun, so we can have solar panels on the roof. Save a heap in electricity bills down the track.'

Well, it would save *someone* a heap. 'Great.'

'You don't sound that keen. Would you prefer something else?'

'Oh no, I am. It's just … I don't know. The whole thing is strange. This place held so many memories, and now it's … gone.'

Her throat thickened. Maybe the pregnancy hormones were kicking in, turning her into a sook, or maybe the possibility that someone wanted to deliberately burn it down and pin the blame on her was at the bottom of her unexpected emotion.

She shrugged.

Jack let out a sigh. 'Yeah. I know what you mean.'

Of course, he did. He'd seen it first-hand. She shook the thought away. This whole thing was about giving him a purpose. 'Anyway, this will be a fresh start. And that layout sounds perfect. Thank you, Jack.

'Daddy.' Lilly took her father's hand and gave it a tug.

'I can sketch something out and get a draftsman mate of mine to draw up the plans. Quicker and cheaper than an architect. The sooner we get them into council, the better.'

'Perfect. How long will that take?'

Lilly gave another yank, dragging Jack's arm sidewards. 'Daaaaddy.'

'Hang on a minute, Lil. I'm talking.' He held up his hand, speaking firmly but patiently to his daughter, before turning his attention back to the adult conversation. 'Hopefully we can get it submitted in a couple of weeks.'

'And the build?'

He angled his head from side to side. 'If I can get the

right tradies on board, it should only take about four months, six months tops, and then you'll be in.'

Six months? By then her baby would be the size of a piece of fruit. Wasn't that how they measured them these days? She pressed a hand against her belly. How big was it now? Peanut size? Grape? Was it really possible that in such a short space of time she'd have her own home, and a place to raise her child? They'd be their own compact little family, and she'd have the support network she'd been lacking ever since she left. And yet, something niggled. Scratched at the soft tissue under her skin, every time the possibility of staying solidified. Every time the idea of actually keeping the baby coalesced.

'You okay, Eve?'

She blinked at the sound of Jack's voice. All this zoning out was ridiculous. 'Just a bit hungry. Haven't had breakfast yet.'

'I'm hearing you.'

'Want some toast? Coffee?' Even the thought of the latter made her want to heave, but vegemite toast usually stayed put if she ate it late enough.

He looked down at his watch. 'Yeah. Why not?'

'You said I could see the ponies.' Lilly stood, arms folded across her chest as if she was giving herself a hug, her bottom lip well and truly pouting.

Jack crouched and rested his hands on his daughter's shoulders. 'I said if Eve had time she might be able to take you over to see the horses. Sooo ...' He looked up, gave his best pretty-please smile, 'maybe if you ask nicely, Eve might think about it.'

He was so gentle with his daughter. Seeing him with a kid of his own was weird. Even though it was decades since they'd been together, she still thought of him as that teenage boy she'd lost her virginity to – the same boy who could have been a father to her own child.

'Can I pat a horsie? Please, Evie?'

How could anyone resist those big blue eyes? 'Since you asked so nicely, of course you can.'

Lilly clasped her hands together and jumped up and down on the spot, strawberry curls dancing on her shoulders. Her resemblance to her mother was almost scary. If clones were a thing, Lilly would certainly be one.

'She's the spit out of Cat's mouth.'

Jack pushed to his feet and shrugged, a grin emerging through his stubble. 'She sure is.'

'Urgh, gross.' Lilly pulled a face.

'She doesn't miss much, does she?'

Jack laughed. 'Nope. Got her mother's smarts too.' His phone buzzed, and he pulled it out of his pocket and studied the screen. 'Mind if I grab this?'

'All good. We'll head over to the paddock and do some horse whispering.'

Lilly took her hand, the small palm fitting snuggly as they headed out through what used to be the front gate of the yard and made their way towards the paddock. Kids were so trusting. Lilly seemed to have no qualms about holding hands or leaving Jack to his phone call despite the fact Eve had only met her a few times. She clearly had no idea the woman she was currently walking beside was a complete novice when it came to children.

Lilly looked up briefly. 'Mummy said you and her were best friends when you were little.'

Were. Meaning in the past, not the present. Things had been going so well between Eve and Cat, but that youthful camaraderie they'd shared was long gone. At least she'd spoken to Lilly about their friendship.

Eve forced a smile. 'We sure were. All the way through school.'

'And she said you used to have a sister, but she died.'

Wow. No punches pulled. 'Yes. A long time ago.'

'Were you sad?'

'Yes. Very sad.' Stupidly, her eyes burned. She couldn't cry in front of Lilly and freak her out. 'But now I have lots of great memories about her that make me smile.'

'What was her name?'

'Rebecca. But I called her Bec.'

'That's like me. My name's Lilly, but Mummy and Daddy call me Lil.'

A smile chased away the threatened tears. How could anyone be sad around this little ray of sunshine? She really was the sweetest thing.

'I want a sister too, but Mummy says I'm her special only girl.'

Getting into the details of Cat's fertility issues was a little weird, but thankfully they'd arrived at the paddock and the horses were ambling towards them. A single air kiss put Rain into a trot, always happy to come for a pat and scratch. Eve lifted Lilly up and the mare stuck her nose through the railings of the gate, her whiskers brushing the little girl's cheek.

Lilly giggled. 'That tickles.'

'She likes you.' Eve took Lilly's hand and guided it towards Rain's face, and together they stroked the horse's muzzle. The mare dipped her head a little lower.

'She's very soft.'

'Yes, she is.'

'Can I ride her?'

'Well, she's a little big for you, but there's a smaller one over there by the tree.' Bob was too busy eating leftover hay to bother with the pint-sized visitor. 'Maybe we could get a crate for you to stand on and you can help me groom him sometime.'

'Can we do it now?' Lilly's voice was high pitched, her eyes wide.

Eve glanced over to where Jack was standing, returning his phone to his pocket. 'How about we talk to your dad and see if he can bring you back soon, and I'll have all the grooming gear ready. We might even give her a bath.' Between Hugh's kids and Jack's, the place would turn into a regular petting zoo.

'Ooh, yes please.' Lilly clasped her little hands together as she bounced up and down.

'Okay, it's a date.'

'What's a date?' Jack stepped up beside them and gave Rain a rub on the neck.

'Evie said I can come back soon and help her wash and broom the horsie.'

'Wow.' He gave a considered nod, ignoring the grammatical faux pas, leant down and scooped Lilly into his arms. 'That's exciting.'

She lifted her hands and sandwiched his face between them, making sure he was looking directly at her. 'Can I come tomorrow?'

'Slow down, Princess. We have to check with Mummy that it's okay, and we have to see what's a good time for Eve.' The two of them turned to face her.

'I have to work the next few days, but we'll make it happen soon.'

Lilly's face fell. She rested her head against her father's cheek.

With his arms wrapped around her, Jack squeezed her to him and pressed a kiss against her forehead. So gentle.

His love for his daughter tangible in that one small action. Was this parenthood? This unfathomable, unconditional love everyone raved on about?

Eve's bruised heart ached a little at the possibility.

'That coffee still on offer?' Jack looked hopeful.

'Yeah, of course.'

'Can I have a shoulder ride, Daddy?'

'Sure can.' Jack lifted Lilly up, swung her around, settled her on his shoulders and took hold of her hands.

The sound of her own childish laughter echoed down the years as Eve walked beside them. Riding on her father's shoulders. The spicy scent of his favourite aftershave. The roughness of his beard, and the sure, solid feel of him as he carried her along. Something she hadn't thought about for a long time. How she'd loved him. Missed him when he travelled to Sydney for work. Thought her world would end when he left for good. Perhaps it did. But not in the way it had when she lost Bec. Loving someone so completely meant taking the risk of one day having to live without them. Could she do that again?

At the van, Jack swung Lilly through the air and deposited her on the ground. Banjo licked her cheek, and she wiped at the spot where he'd planted the kiss, bursting into a fit of giggles.

Such a contagious sound.

Inside the van, Lilly sat at the table beside Jack, her head tilted to one side like a dashboard puppy. 'Do you have any Milo, Evie?'

'No, sweetie, I don't.' She opened the cupboard and pulled out a packet of Tim Tams. 'But I have milk. And these.'

Lilly looked up at Jack, with a grin from ear to ear;

matching dimples dotted their cheeks. 'Daddy's a chocolate monster.'

'Hmm, I remember.'

Jack met her gaze, and his eyes shone. All those blocks of chocolate he'd demolished single-handed. That time he'd taken up her challenge to scoff a whole family-sized block in one sitting and done it in less than two minutes. His mouth had been stuffed so full he could barely chew. Right now, he sat munching on one biscuit, another in his hand. Nothing much had changed. Everything had changed.

Eve went about making the coffee, which they drank over small talk, the conversation directed by Lilly and centred around her rabbit Flopsy but thankfully nothing about former best friends or departed sisters or past relationships. By the time they finished and stepped outside, the sun had inched higher and the sky was an even more electric shade of blue.

Jack opened the car door and Lilly climbed into her seat. 'I'll get onto those plans today and be in touch about approval. You might want to start thinking about things like windows and flooring. I'll send you through a few ideas.'

Flooring and windows were the last things Eve wanted to think about, but if they were going to keep Jack busy and focused, she'd better get her head around them. There was already an ease about him that hadn't been there when he arrived.

'Thanks, Jack, that'd be great.' Somehow she'd decided to build a house. What did that mean for her potential move north?

'Bye, Evie.' Lilly leaned forward and peered around her father.

'Bye, Lil.'

A sigh came from nowhere as they drove away. Mission

accomplished as far as giving Jack a job to do. He'd been lukewarm to start with. But the more they talked, the more animated he became. By the time he left, it was almost as if he was his old, easy-going self. But appearances could be deceptive, and things might be completely different when he was back at home.

At least she could call Cat and tell her the good news. Jack had a project now. Something to keep him busy, physically and mentally. Having him around more would no doubt mean seeing more of Lilly since Jack was the primary caregiver.

Staring out at the paddocks, she waited for the tingling sensation bubbling up from the depths of her body to subside. It wasn't the same kind of feverish feeling she'd had towards lovers in the past, and different to the attraction she had towards Hugh. That was like waiting on the platform right before a bungy jump, trying not to look down.

No, this one came from being around Lilly rather than Jack. It was more like a warm, rising tide of tenderness. One in which she could very possibly drown if she didn't hold her breath. If she didn't keep moving.

Chapter Fourteen

The ringing in Eve's ears was like a flock of lorikeets shrieking in the top of a coral tree. Probably the result of too many drunken nights standing too close to speakers on crowded pub dance floors, and worse whenever she was anxious, but she'd never bothered having it checked out. She squeezed her hand around the top of the gearstick, tightening her grip as she pushed it down and to the left, before jerking it back towards where she sat in the driver's seat.

Clunk. She'd hit reverse. Her arm was working. She was doing this. She could do this!

'Woohoo!' She let out a shriek as she edged the Kombi backwards, pushed the gearstick into first and did a U-turn.

Banjo joined in from the passenger seat with a high-pitched yap, puncturing her elation and dragging her back to earth. Silly to be so excited about such a small thing as driving a car, but it was about being independent, not having to rely on anyone but herself. And this car trip needed to be solo.

Finding the address in the White Pages online had been a coup and meant not having to ask Margo and field any questions. This would be a private chat between two people with a mutual interest.

Sunlight flickered through the remains of the bush, flashing beneath the rims of her sunglasses, along with snapshots of other times she'd been behind the wheel on this stretch: being run off the road and Jack coming to her rescue by towing the car into town; racing Banjo in to see Hugh when that bloody snake struck; the CWA morning tea with Margo where she reconnected with Cat.

The Eve who'd made those drives only a couple of months ago seemed like someone else, a shadow she'd left behind. One who'd known where she was going. Her newer, untethered self had no idea which direction she should take, or how she would reach her ultimate destination. And yet she could almost see it in her mind's eye, feel it in the buzz inside her every time the idea of staying surfaced.

On the outskirts of town, her phone directed to the address: 37 Corella Road. A spear of pain shot through her hand as she shifted gears. Not quite back to normal, but then it might never be. She groaned, and Banjo turned towards her, clearly jittery.

'I know. I might have got ahead of myself.' She pulled up and turned off the ignition. Maybe she'd overdone it for a first outing, but pain was better than numbness. The conversation with Dean would give her arm time to rest.

She and Banj hopped out together and approached the front door. Luckily there was a footpath because the grass was almost knee-high. By the porch steps, a garbage bin overflowed with rubbish, the smell hitting her like a wet fish to the face, prompting yet another wave of queasiness. Every time she managed to forget, even for just a short time, that there was an alien invading the space between her hips, her body found some not-so-subtle way of sending her a reminder. She swallowed back the saliva pooling beneath her tongue, stepped up to the door and rang the bell.

A tinny rendition of ACDC's 'Long Way to the Top' chimed through the speaker. Footsteps sounded, and the lock clicked. A face appeared behind the fly screen, unshaven, hair mussed.

'Dean?' It came out as a question, even though it was obviously him. The last time they'd met, at the hospital when she and Margo went to find Harry after the fires, he'd been so neat and well groomed. It was hard to believe this was the same person.

'Hi.' He rubbed a hand across his eyes as if trying to adjust his focus.

'Sorry, did I wake you?' It was the middle of the day but maybe he'd been napping.

'It's okay. I sat down for a rest and must have nodded off.'

Fair enough. 'Can I come in for a minute?'

'Is this about Mum?'

'No. I wanted to talk to you about Luke.'

His brow furrowed. 'What about him?'

'I um ... look, can we talk inside?'

Dean shoved the door open and led the way down the hall and into the living room. A pile of clothes sat on the rug by the TV, and based on the odour wafting from them, they were waiting to be washed. He grabbed a couple of dirty plates from the lounge and stacked them on the coffee table in the centre of the room alongside three empty mugs, a handful of used cutlery and half a dozen empty beer cans already littering its surface.

He gestured for her to take a seat on the lounge and lowered himself into the recliner opposite.

'Is everything okay, Dean?'

The growth covering his jaw and the multiple stains on his sweatshirt suggested otherwise. Dean was swarthy, like his dad, but with Margo's grey-blue eyes. Right now, they were bleary and bloodshot. He clenched his right hand, punched it softly into his left palm and tapped his fingers against his knuckles. His mouth opened, then closed again, his body caving in like a punctured tyre.

'Dean?'

'No,' he huffed, 'everything is not okay.'

Was he talking about Luke?

He stared off into the distance, eyes fixed on the giant TV screen where a daytime soap couple were having some kind of Mexican standoff. 'Michelle's shot through.' He spat the words out, suddenly fiery. 'Apparently she's been seeing some bloke on all those supposed work trips she's been taking. Left me high and dry.'

'Oh, Dean, I'm so sorry. Margo never mentioned anything.'

'She doesn't know.' He shook his head. 'She's got enough on her plate.'

He was right about that. Keeping Harry on a short leash wasn't easy, and Margo had been strangely secretive of late. But given Dean had spilled the beans on Michelle, he might be open to another question.

'Have you heard from Luke at all?'

He folded his arms, unfolded them and tucked them against his chest just below his armpits. 'He's gone fruit picking with his mates, apparently. Still a bloody kid and he thinks he can run his own life. Got in with the wrong crowd at school, that was the problem. Might have helped if his mother had been around a bit more to keep him on the straight and narrow.' He gave a loud huff. 'Too busy putting it around, as it turns out.'

A sour taste coated the back of Eve's throat. Discussing Dean's marital problems wasn't exactly the direction she'd wanted the conversation to go. Bringing up the police accusations directly was awkward when the guy was clearly not in the best of places, but it wasn't only Luke whose reputation was on the line. Finding him was the best way of clearing both their names.

'I'm guessing the police have asked you about the fires?'

Cold burned in his eyes. 'What about them?'

'I'm not sure exactly, but they were out at Mossy Creek, asking questions. Like was Luke working there the day the fire started.'

Another huff. More like a growl. 'What did you tell them?'

Something wet and viscous settled beneath Eve's skin. If the guy who'd greeted her in the hospital waiting room, who'd thrown his arms around his mother and been nothing but kind was Dr Jekyll, then this one talking right now was definitely Mr Hyde.

'Nothing. Only that he was working for me and he kept to himself. But Margo did say he was in a pretty bad mood that day.'

'Doesn't mean he started a bloody fire.' Dean's voice boomed into the cluttered room, drowning out the voices of the couple still arguing on the screen. Straightening, he sat forward. 'He's not a bad kid, and he's not a criminal. The cops have got nothing on him other than …' He stopped short, as if he'd been running and hit a wall he hadn't seen.

'Other than?'

He heaved a sigh and stuffed his hands into his pockets. 'Forget it.'

Whatever it was he'd omitted to say didn't seem like nothing. It was enough to make him bite his tongue and rattle his head as if shaking the thought far, far away. What was he hiding? Luke was Margo's grandson, and as much as the thought he could have started the fires was hard to swallow, if he had been responsible, he needed to be brought to account. Now was not the time to let Dean off the hook. Maybe he needed a little more bait.

'I went for a walk the other day, along the trails out the back of the farm.'

Dean only had eyes for the TV screen, but the slight angle of his head suggested he was listening.

'I found an empty jerry can. It had been shoved in between a couple of rocks. Clearly deliberate.'

Dean's head snapped upright.

He was biting, so best to throw out a bit more berley. 'If someone did start the fires, maybe they hid the can there, so no one would find it.'

'What sort of idiot would do that? Leave it there in plain sight for someone to find?'

'It was well hidden. Took a bit of getting out. The only reason I saw it was because there's no vegetation left to keep it covered.'

Dean rubbed a hand across his mouth. 'Have you told the cops?'

'No. I wanted to talk to you first. Maybe find out where Luke is so I can ask him about it.'

'Well, there's no need. It wasn't him.' Any flicker of doubt Dean might have had about his son vanished.

'Dean, I know it's hard to fathom but sometimes kids do inexplicable things.'

He fixed her with a hard stare. 'Like take their younger sister out to a lake in the middle of the night and let her drown.'

All the air left her lungs, as if he had landed a physical blow right to her middle and not a lower-than-the-gutter insult that didn't deserve a response.

She gritted her teeth and shot him a glare. 'The reason I haven't told the police about the jerry can is because I wanted to give Luke a chance to explain himself. So, if you know where he is, it might be in his best interests to let him know.'

He stood and took a few steps forward, signalling the end of their conversation. Could this man really be Margo's offspring? He certainly wasn't the big brother figure she remembered from her childhood.

Eve pushed herself to her feet. 'And it *is* my business, Dean. The cops insinuated I paid Luke to set fire to the place so I could collect the insurance money, so I'd like to be able to clear my name.'

'Finding that can seems pretty convenient. Funny that you knew exactly where it was. If it was even hidden.'

'Why would I suddenly produce a scorched jerry can as evidence if I'd done it?'

'To take the spotlight off yourself. Blame some poor kid who isn't here to defend himself.'

'And what would I have to gain by doing that?' Her voice was too loud, way too screechy, any modicum of civility right out the window.

'Oh, I don't know …' Dean waved his hands around, floundering, 'maybe the cops were right about that insurance payout.'

'When I already had the house on the market? Buyers lining up to sign on the dotted line?'

'No more ridiculous than Luke doing it.'

This conversation was going nowhere. She heaved out a sigh. 'Look, all I'm saying is, if you can get in touch with Luke, it might be a good idea to convince him to come back and talk to the police.'

'Since he's my son, I'll decide what's good for him and what's not.' Dean rocked forward on the balls of his feet. The sour scent of stale beer wafted from him, making her insides reel. He placed his hand against her arm, not tight, but enough to let her know her time was up. His jaw hardened. 'I don't think there's anything else to discuss.'

He was so right. But he definitely knew more about Luke and his whereabouts than he was letting on.

She followed him towards the doorway. 'I understand you're worried about your son, so I won't go to the police with the information about the jerry can yet. But Luke needs to get back here and sort this out asap. If he's innocent, he should have nothing to hide.'

Dean banged his hand against the wire door and shoved it open. 'Enough.'

His shout startled her into action. She rushed past him, tripping over the raised sill of the doorframe, which she hadn't noticed when she entered the house, and tumbling to the ground. The slam of the door punctuated the screaming chorus in her ears.

Banjo barked and appeared by her side, licked her face and whined.

'It's okay matey.' She lay still for a few seconds, sucked in a lungful of air. The fall had winded her. 'I'm alright.'

Could a fall like that do any damage if you were pregnant?

She scanned her body. Nothing obvious, but perhaps that would come later if there was a problem. The wrist she'd fallen on throbbed. Easing herself upright, she winced at the stab of pain. And damn it, the skin was grazed, right along the seam of the graft. She brushed away the coating of dirt, and crimson beads dimpled the still-pink flesh.

A thud sounded from inside the house. Was Dean coming back? Did he know she'd fallen? No approaching footsteps. The place was shrouded in silence.

Banjo licked her arm, his tongue rough against the tender skin. Blood oozed from the freshly opened seam close to her wrist. Even though it had grafted well, the doctor had stressed the importance of avoiding any kind of infection. That would mean more grafts, another operation, more time in hospital. And could she even go under anaesthetic if she went ahead with the pregnancy?

Those two pink lines in the window of the test stick flashed into her mind. Why had she even bothered to vacillate. There was no 'if', only a 'when'. Every protective movement of her hand towards her belly, every scattered thought about holding the hand of her own child, helping her – or him – onto a horse, of the two of them walking together down a winding bush trail as whip birds called from the tops of banksia trees – all of it answered the truth she'd been too afraid to voice.

And yet hadn't she known all along?

She wanted this baby. She wanted to be a mother. To build a home and a family of her own. In the place where she belonged and couldn't leave again – unless she was forced out.

She glanced up to the white wisps of clouds moving across the sky, to the flock of cockatoos swooping and swirling through the soft afternoon light. If she was going to be a mother, her future lay at Mossy Creek, where her child could grow up with the same love of the land that ran through her veins; the same connection to people and place. Where they could sit together on the veranda and watch the bush come back to life.

But none of that was possible if the arson accusation stuck. Adams had it in for her and based on their 'conversation', Dean would not hesitate to throw her under the bus if it meant protecting Luke. It was up to her to clear her own name. In order to do that, she'd have to find out who – if anyone – started that fire. And she couldn't do that from a hospital bed.

She climbed into the Kombi and took out her phone. There was no delaying the inevitable any longer. Not now she'd made a final decision. Calling Mel would be the right thing to do but dealing with the fallout in real time was more than she could handle right now.

Sorry my friend, but I have to decline your offer. Will be in touch. x

She inhaled and pressed send. Once she knew the full story Mel would understand but that explanation would have to wait.

Turning the key in the ignition, she made a left turn at the end of the street and headed towards town to pay a visit to her doctor.

Chapter Fifteen

'Eve, what are you doing here?' Cat, standing at the reception counter, gave a wooden smile, as if she'd been caught reading someone else's mail.

The figure standing behind her stepped to one side – Margo, her face ashen.

'Hello, dear. Sorry I can't stop to chat. I have to get home to fix Harry's lunch.' Clutching her bag in one hand and an envelope in the other, she rushed out the door, cutting short any possibility of conversation.

Eve turned back to Cat. 'Is it her back?'

'She came in for a check-up. You know I can't tell you more than that.' Cat stuck a pen in her top pocket, as an underscore to that part of the conversation. Cat had always been a stickler for rules and would never break patient confidentiality. 'So, is this a social call or a medical visit?'

She held out her arm, wrist side up, where a smear of blood had congealed along the graft line. 'Thought I'd better get this checked out.'

Cat bent over, inspecting the wound, her hand soft as

silk. 'Hmm, good idea. How did you do it?' She looked up, her gentle blue eyes simultaneously comforting and concerned.

Lying to Cat wasn't ideal, especially when their friendship was starting to blossom again, but telling her what had happened with Dean would open a whole can of worms that might not be easy to contain. If she hadn't already heard the arson rumours, it was better things stayed that way.

'I, um, tripped when I was putting the horse feeds out, and that was the arm that hit the ground first.'

'Okay. Well, it doesn't look deep, but I'll take a closer look and clean it up. Come on in.'

Ambient music filtered through an invisible speaker, and the faint scent of cinnamon wafted from a candle of the mantelpiece, almost like walking into the comfort of a bakery. Doctor's waiting rooms were never the most soothing places, given that stepping across the threshold meant you had a problem, but somehow Cat had made hers as relaxed and welcoming as possible. Even in her office, the pastel walls and vases of flowers made the mood calm rather than daunting.

'How's everything out at Mossy Creek?' Cat gestured to a chair and pulled on a pair of disposable gloves. Taking a sterile pad and a bottle of antiseptic, she dabbed at the site of the wound.

Eve braced herself against the sting. 'All going okay.'

'You're managing out there without any help?'

'Hmm hmm.'

Cat peered down at the wound, prodded the skin around the graft with the pads of her thumbs. The movement of the wrist bone sent a fresh spear of pain shooting up Eve's arm. She curled her right hand into a fist.

Cat looked up. 'That hurt?'

'A little.'

'Or a lot.' A line formed between Cat's brows. 'Sorry, I need to see how extensive the damage is.' She pressed her fingers against the back of Eve's hand and gently moved the wrist backwards and forwards. Rotated it slightly to the left and right. 'That hurt?'

'Surprisingly, no.'

'Good. Nothing fractured then. Bruised, I'd say, so it might be sore for a few days. The cut isn't bad, but given the graft is fairly fresh we don't want to risk infection, so I might give you a prescription for antibiotics to be on the safe side.'

'Okay, great.'

Cat rolled her chair back to the desk and started typing into her computer. She was so smart, so efficient, so together. Maybe some of that would rub off if they continued hanging out. Not that it had when they were younger. Cat had been way too sensible to put up with Eve's crap when she went off the rails. All ancient history now. But the baby subject had to be broached. Somehow.

She bit down on her lip. 'How's everything going with you?'

'Oh, you know, it's going.' Cat's mouth flattened and she gave a slight shrug. 'Jack's been talking to the drafstman and the council about your plans, so that's positive. Still spending way too much time on the Xbox and not really engaging much with me or Lilly. But any progress is good progress.'

'So they say.' Asking about the drinking was perhaps a step too far.

The printer whirred to life and spat out a piece of paper. Cat handed it across. 'Take one morning and night until they're gone and if you notice any reddening around the graft line or anything at all that doesn't feel normal, let me know. I might put a small dressing on that cut to keep it clean.'

She pulled a pad of gauze from a container on a shelf above her desk, peeled the backing off and laid it gently across the wound.

Antibiotics and a plaster. Good outcome. But was it safe to take antibiotics?

A labelled diagram of a foetus in utero caught Eve's eye from the opposite wall. Cat's surgery was also a shared-care facility for women who elected not to travel further to see an obstetrician. She'd be able to answer any questions but …

'Eve, is everything alright? You've gone as white as a sheet.'

Now or never. 'I'm pregnant.'

'What?'

The urge to share her secret bubbled up inside her like water spewing from a drinking fountain, lifting the corners of her lips into a tentative smile. When she'd kept it to herself, it didn't seem real, but now any sense of pretence evaporated.

'I did a test last week. It turned positive straight away, and I've been having the worst nausea. Not to mention eating everything I can get my hands on.'

Cat lowered herself back into her chair. She laid a hand against the base of her throat and straightened her shoulders. 'Any idea how far along you are?'

'I'm guessing about eight weeks. It was just after I came back to Yarrabee, so …'

'After you came back?' Cat's eyes were the size of dinner plates, the noise of the cogs spinning inside her head almost audible. She didn't think it was Jack, did she?

'My ex, Marcus, arrived from Sydney trying to patch things up. We didn't, but we did have one last ... you know.'

'Right.' Cat gave a small sigh and leaned back into her chair. 'I can do a blood test, or I can pull out that scanner over there and do an ultrasound to see where things are at.' She pointed to a small portable machine on a stand, similar to the one they'd used to X-ray Eve's ankle when she'd sprained it all those weeks ago. In another lifetime.

'Let's do it.'

Cat stood and organised the machine. 'This ultrasound should give us accurate dates. Given that this is your first pregnancy and you're of advanced maternal age, we advise doing antenatal testing at around eleven weeks to check for any genetic ...'

'It's not my first pregnancy. Does that matter?' The question came out of nowhere, unfiltered, as if her body itself needed to know the answer.

Cat's face paled. 'You have a child?'

And just like that Eve had dumped herself in the quicksand of her past. 'No. But I've been pregnant before.' *To your husband.*

Jack's words when she'd told him she'd aborted their baby replayed themselves in her head. *Cat must never know.* She looked towards the chart on the wall, at the image of an eight-week-old foetus, then forced her attention back on Cat.

'I had a termination. It was a long time ago.'

'I see.' Cat gave an almost imperceptible shake of her head. 'Makes no difference. I'll need you to lie up on the bed and lower the waistband on your jeans.' With her back turned, it was impossible to read the expression on Cat's face but there was a distinct coolness in her tone. Had the mention of a termination put her offside? As a GP, she must have conversations like this with women on a regular basis, but as a woman who'd had multiple miscarriages and desperately wanted more children, maintaining that professional manner would mean pulling on a mask, being firmly in doctor mode, separating herself from the patient – and her emotions. Not always an easy call.

The machine burst to life with a loud beep. Icy cold gel on her stomach took her breath away. Everything about this scenario was at once familiar and strange, sweet and sour. Last time there'd been no question about a termination. She had lain like a statue on the bed as the nurse did the examination and discussed the procedure as if they were talking about someone else. Another teenage girl, who had been stupid enough to have sex in the back of the car with her first boyfriend without using any protection. Not knowing that less than an hour later her sister would be dead, and it would be her fault. That everything would change.

This time couldn't be more different. Laying on the bed, jeans shuffled down to her hips, all her nerve endings ignited at once. That same rush she'd experienced when Lilly took her hand, when she watched Hugh hugging his son, when she saw the expression on Jack's face as he carried his daughter on his shoulders, swelled as she turned her gaze to the screen.

Cat moved the head of the scanner, pressing it harder in places, stopping and watching the monitor before moving it around again. Shifting it lower, she stopped, pressed a couple of keys on the computer and pushed the device a fraction deeper.

Whoosh. Whoosh. Whoosh.

There it was: the unmistakeable sound of a tiny living being buried deep inside her body, reliant on her for nourishment, for growth – for life. The rhythm repeated itself in her brain as she stared, lips parted, throat dry, at the blurry shape on the monitor.

'You're spot on with your dates. Just under eight weeks, I'd say.' Cat remained focused on the machine. 'You can't see much at this size, but that's the foetus there.' She pointed to the grainy image: a round head at one end, attached to a longer oval-shaped body. Alive and growing. Completely dependent – on her.

'And that's its heartbeat?' Of course, it was. Why ask such dumb questions?

'Hmm hm.' Cat punched at a few more keys. 'Did you want me to print off the image?'

Eve stared at the screen and her vision clouded. That wasn't just a picture on a monitor: it was a baby, a chance at a different future to the one she'd envisaged. One that would give her life purpose and meaning and, as unreliable as it sometimes was, love. She drew in a single lung-expanding breath and let it go again.

'Yes.'

Chapter Sixteen

A grinder buzzed behind the counter of the coffee shop, and the aroma of freshly ground beans spilled into the ether. Seated at the back of the café, away from the window, Eve waited for the rush of nausea. Nothing. That was new. Things did seem to be settling down in that department, as if committing to the pregnancy had given her body the green light to be more cooperative.

The pregnancy.

Such a distancing phrase, but she still couldn't quite believe the creature growing inside of her was *a baby*.

Her baby.

It was all too surreal.

Flipping open her phone case, she slipped the folded piece of paper from the pocket and spread it on the table. She'd only had the image for a few days and the edges were already tattered from too much handling. There it was – a blob of white suspended in a pixelated dark grey pool, round head and oval body, stumpy bits that could be arms and legs, floating like a tiny astronaut joined to its mothership by a single lifeline.

A strange sense of lightness filled her. At some stage, she'd have to come to grips with the fact that she was going to be responsible for another human being, but right now all she could do was try to process the fact that she was carrying this … baby … and that they were already connected.

'Anything interesting?' Emily Winters hooked her bag over the back of the chair opposite and peeled her arms out of her coat.

Fingers flying, Eve folded the printout as if it was one of those kid's paper chatterbox games and poked it back into her phone case. 'Nothing exciting.' She coughed to clear the white lie. 'Just a boring "to do" list.'

Emily slid into her seat, lithe and luminous, collected her long blonde hair and pulled it to one side where it sat over her shoulder mermaid-style. 'I was surprised we didn't meet at the coffee shop where you work.'

'Thought it might be easier to talk here. More private.'

'Good point.' Emily nodded. 'Have you ordered?'

'Not yet.'

'Great. Let me grab you something.'

'Just a peppermint tea, thanks.'

'Very healthy. I'm a caffeine tragic myself. I'll be back.'

Eve quirked a smile as Emily headed to the counter. It had taken some time to rustle up the courage to set up the meeting. There was no way of knowing how this conversation was going to go, but hopefully by giving Emily something she wanted – a profile story on the fires – she might be able to get some information in return.

'On its way.' Emily clasped her hands together on the table, her pale pink nails like pearlescent shells imprinted on the tips of her elegantly long fingers. 'So, why the change of mind?'

'Sorry?'

'About agreeing to talk to me. You seemed dead against it the first couple of times we met. I can't help wondering what changed your mind.'

Emily was a smart cookie, and it wouldn't be easy – or prudent – to lie to her. Better to be upfront from the start. Not something she'd always had the courage to do.

'I'm hoping we might be able to help each other by sharing some information.'

A series of fine lines appeared on Emily's brow. 'About?'

'The fires. You want a story about a local's experience …'

'And you want?'

Eve ran the tip of her tongue over her bottom lip. There was no way of knowing how much Emily knew already and revealing too much could send her running to the police. Sharing anything was a risk but there was so much at stake: Eve's reputation, and maybe her freedom, Margo's friendship, and possibly justice for those who were impacted by the fire on Mossy Creek Road. People like Jack's mate, who had lost his life trying to save others.

'I'd like you to help me get some information in return for my interview.'

Another frown, deeper this time, marring the perfectly smooth plane of Emily's forehead. 'What sort of information?'

'You intimated at the gallery opening that you were privy to some information from the police about an arson suspect.' *How much to say?*

Emily gave a small nod, as if waiting for more information. Hopefully the empathy she'd displayed at the community hall was genuine.

'Look, to be completely honest, they've questioned me about arson. Suggested I might have set fire to my place to collect the insurance money, or that I got a kid who worked for me to do my dirty work.'

'Luke Harris.'

So she knew. 'Yes.'

The waiter placed their orders on the table.

Emily stared down into the depths of her long black. 'I get why the police suspect Luke. He fits the profile of a teenage arsonist to a tee: left school early, conflict with his parents, no job to speak of, hanging out with an older crowd which butt heads with the law from time to time. Not to mention the fact that he's disappeared.' She looked up, her eyes almost navy in the dim café light. 'But I'm curious as to why they would have you on their radar.'

'Once an outsider, always an outsider, I guess.' She made an effort to keep her voice steady.

'But you're a local. Home-grown.'

'I might have been born here, but I left for good reason.'

'Your sister.'

Eve took a sip of tea and let the minty tang settle before gulping it down. They were entering dangerous territory. Now that she'd finally accepted Bec's death for what it was – a horrible tragedy – she had enough compassion for her younger self to be able to go there. But the taunts of her peers and the condemnation she'd received at the hands of some people who should have known better still cut deep.

'More what happened afterwards. I couldn't walk down the street without someone making a comment about how out of control I was, about how it must feel to have killed your sister.'

'That's appalling. You were a kid.'

She shrugged. 'In my mind, they were right. But now I realise how cruel they were. And the cops were no exception. Brent Adams' brother, Todd, was with us at the lake when it happened. He spouted a whole lot of shit to make sure he didn't wear any of the blame. The mud stuck, and Brent was fresh out of the police academy and high on the power his uniform provided.'

'As in Sergeant Adams?'

'The very one.' A shudder rippled through her ribcage. 'You'd think he might have mellowed over the years, but apparently hindsight hasn't changed his perspective. He's still champing at the bit to make me the scapegoat.'

'Interesting that he's never moved on, that he's stayed in Yarrabee. But then, it's easier to be a big fish in a small pond, so maybe small-town policing suits him.' Emily drained her coffee cup and deposited it back onto the saucer. 'So, are you looking to clear your name or Luke's?'

Eve gave a soft snort. Emily didn't mince her words. 'Margo Harris, Luke's grandmother, is my godmother. Our families have known each other for years. The Harris's are good people. Salt of the earth.' The memory of Dean's enraged scowl as he shouted her out of his house made her throat constrict. But whatever was going on with him didn't diminish her love for his mother, the need for Margo's support and respect. 'I know what it's like to be accused of doing something horrible; to be ostracised by the community. And I don't want that to happen to Luke. Or anyone in his family.'

'Or a repeat version for yourself.' Emily had gotten to the essence of her motivation.

'When Bec died, I was a kid, drowning in grief and guilt. It was easier to leave than deal with my emotions, without seeing the turned heads and whispering behind raised hands.' *Without shouldering the blame from my own mother.* 'It was the only way I could cope.'

'What's different now?'

The heat of the liquid seeped through the ceramic cup and into Eve's palms. She sipped at the tea, let the bite of the peppermint soothe the ache in her chest and the longing in her heart.

'I want to be believed. I don't want to feel like a criminal again.' A gnarly laugh erupted from deep inside of her. 'It sounds ridiculous, but I want the people I care about to believe me, and to believe *in* me.' *And to love me. And help me raise my child.* Not a desire she was yet willing to voice.

'Not so ridiculous. Look, Eve. I like you. You're a straight shooter, and you had a shit deal handed out to you by some people in this town. From what I've heard of how you handled yourself in the fires, you were nothing short of a hero. And that's a story I want to tell. If I can get an extra story about an arsonist, even better.'

Eve's fingers burned hot as if she was holding that jerry can instead of a pottery mug. Should she play that card yet? Expose Luke to more scrutiny and risk Margo finding out? No. Not until it was absolutely necessary. Until Luke's involvement was certain.

'So, if you do find anything out about the arson investigation, you'd be willing to let me know?'

Emily looked her directly in the eye and nodded.

'Okay.' She sat back, releasing the trapped air from her lungs in a long exhale. 'So, what do you want to know?'

Emily gave a soft smile. 'I'm not doing a tick-the-box "what, when, who, why, how" story, Eve. I like to take the time to get to know the people I'm interviewing. Watch them go about their day. See what makes them tick.'

'You'd be following me around every day?'

'Not all the time, only a few hours here and there.'

'But aren't you writing about the fires?'

'Yes, I am. But this would be a profile on you and your experiences – before, during and after.'

'Right.' That meant her story would be broadcast for everyone in the world to judge. She slumped against the cushion at her back, one arm folded across her middle.

'I'll only include what you're comfortable with, Eve. And you'll have final say on what goes in and what gets edited out.' Emily leaned forward, her voice low and deliberate, 'And anything I find out in my research on the fires that helps you clear your name, I'm more than willing to share.'

Exactly what she needed to hear. 'When do we start?'

Chapter Seventeen

'Sign here.' Jack pointed to the dotted line beneath a whole lot of gobbledegook Eve hadn't bothered to read. 'And here.'

Scrawling her signature, the similarity to her mother's handwriting was scarily obvious. As long as the likeness ended there.

Nell hadn't been a bad mother, but she was never an affectionate one. Never hands on. Too busy teaching riding lessons and making enough money to keep their heads above water. But that hadn't been her fault, had it? She'd done the best she could under the circumstances, and wasn't that all you could ask of a person? The idea of taking on that role herself, of being solely responsible for the well-being and life of another human, was terrifying. No matter how good your intentions were, shit happened, and it could steer the parenting ship way off course, smash it against the rocks and leave you both floundering.

'Hello?' Jack waved his hand in front of her face, and she snapped to attention.

'Sorry. Miles away.'

'I noticed.'

'How did you get all this happening so quickly?'

It was only a bit over a week since she'd given the green light for the build. When Jack had called to say he had the draftsman lined up and ready to go, she'd almost choked on her dry toast.

'I'm at a loose end, and my mate is between projects. It's a simple design, and he had similar plans from another job so …' He gave a no-big-deal shrug, slid the papers off the table and slipped them into an envelope. 'I'll drop this in to him on my way home. Once the plans are drawn up we'll put in the council application. I know a guy who works there who'll be able to fast-track it, so it shouldn't take long. We'll have to apply for a construction certificate too, and—'

'You know a guy?'

Jack smirked. 'Sure do.'

Looking after the development application and taking charge of the rebuild seemed to be doing him some good. And there was also that request Cat had made: talking to him about where his head was at and making sure he was okay. Maybe now was a good time to check in, while he seemed chirpy, and there were no little ears around to tune in to their conversation.

'Feel like a walk?'

Jack raised his eyebrows. 'A walk?'

'Yeah, just around to the back of paddocks. Want to pick your brain about fixing some fencing.' As good an excuse as any to get him walking and possibly talking. More chance of him spilling his beans if they were outdoors and mobile, than closeted in the four walls of the caravan.

He shrugged. 'Okay.'

Stepping out of Daisy, they meandered up the access

road that led to the rear of the property. In the main paddock, Rain lay in a patch of dirt, soaking up the cool autumn sunshine, flecks of gold glinting in her chestnut coat. Not far away, a black mare stood still as stone, taking her turn guarding against predators. Funny how those primal instincts remained, despite thousands of years of domestication. Once a prey animal always a prey animal. Was it the same with humans? Or was it really possible to change? To reinvent yourself?

'A good thing most of the fences survived.' Jack nodded at the metal fencing, which had withstood the heat of the blaze.

'Thankfully Nell had it all redone a few years back. Otherwise, this lot would have been running wild, and who knows where they would have ended up?'

'Hard to believe all this infrastructure is still standing and the house is gone.' Jack sighed. He shoved his hands into the pockets of his jeans and gazed off into the distance. No one knew better than him how unpredictable and ferocious the flames had been. Refusing to talk about it was a form of self-protection, of keeping the demons at bay. But sooner or later, they would break out and run rampant.

Eve stopped, rested a hand lightly on his forearm. 'I'm happy to listen if you want to talk about anything.'

'Aren't we talking about fences?' He narrowed his eyes, gave a slow deliberate nod. 'Ah, right. Did Cat put you up to this?'

A small white lie wouldn't hurt. 'You don't have to be Einstein to see that you're hurting, Jack. I was there at Lilly's party, remember? Bottling things up makes them worse. Take it from me. I'm the expert.'

She squinted into the sunlight. Sharing her experiences wasn't top of her playlist, but it had gotten easier and that old wives' tale about a problem shared being a problem halved did hold some truth. 'All the years of keeping my guilt and shame about Bec's death to myself may have helped me deal with the pain, but it paralysed me emotionally. Stopped me feeling. Stopped me building any meaningful relationships with anyone. I'd hate to see that happen to you.'

'I already have meaningful relationships, Eve.' There was an edge to his voice. A warning not to go in too hard with the advice. 'But I don't want to burden the people I love with my misery. Not when I can't even process it myself.' There was a lost – no, haunted – look about him that spoke of everything he couldn't say. But at least he'd admitted he was struggling.

A weathered bench seat rested against the fence behind them. Eve took the two steps towards it and sat down, leaving enough room for him to join her if he chose. He glanced from the paddock to the seat, heaved out a sigh and flopped down next to her. Hunched forward, elbows on his thighs, he stared at the ground between his feet.

'I think about it 24/7. Go over and over it in my head. The flames. The heat. Even from inside the truck.' He raised his chin and gave the slightest shake of his head. 'Embers were flying everywhere and the fire … it was like a monster devouring the bush. I had this weird moment, like a nanosecond, where I thought how beautiful it looked. Crazy, hey?'

'Not so crazy. I remember thinking the same thing, just before Margo and I pulled the rug over our heads in that dam.'

'The sky kept changing colour, but then it got darker … and darker. Like we'd been catapulted into the middle of the night or something.' His voice was quiet, almost a whisper, as if he was sitting in a room alone talking to himself. 'The fire had already hit the house, and the owner was standing there with a garden hose trying to douse the flames. He started shaking, told us he wasn't sure, but he thought his dog was still inside. Matt didn't even hesitate. He pulled his shield over his face and ran straight towards the front door. I shouted at him to stop, but there was no way he would have heard me over the noise. He just kept going, and he was swallowed up by the flames, then there was this ear-splitting noise and the rafters collapsed and …' Jack dropped his head into his hands, his shoulders trembling as he cracked.

Eve's eyes had fallen closed as he spoke, the heat of the fire and the smell of the smoke once again scorching her skin, pulling all the air from her lungs. She shifted closer, rested her arm across Jack's back and leaned into him, his whole frame shaking beneath her touch. What they'd experienced wasn't the same, but they'd both come close enough to death to have it seared into their memory banks.

A cool breeze stroked her cheek, and the mournful cry of a black cockatoo broke the quiet. Breath by uneven breath, Jack's body stilled, and her own tension eased.

'We managed to hose everything down enough that we could go in and get him. But it was too late. He was gone.' He let out a ragged laugh. 'The dog came out from behind the shed half an hour later. He wasn't even in the fucking house.'

'Oh, Jack.'

The story she'd heard in hospital was that the truck had been surrounded by fire, but misinformation was always rife in the midst of a crisis. Either way, it must have been horrible.

Jack thumped his fists on his knees and sprang to his

feet, stalked a few paces along the fence line and then back again. 'It's in here,' he tapped his finger against his temple, 'every minute of every day. Have you any idea what a person looks like when they've been burnt to death?'

The pungent stench of the charred cows in Margo's front paddock returned, making Eve's head spin, as it had that day. She shook the memory away.

'And I'm supposed to swan around at a kid's birthday party and blow up balloons and act like everything's normal?' Jack paced like a caged tiger. 'Like there isn't some arsehole arsonist running around town who's responsible for the fire that killed my mate. I swear if they catch that bastard his life won't be worth living in this town.'

Rumours must be flying if Jack had heard them – he'd practically been a hermit since the fires. Maybe Cat had passed on the gossip. There'd been nothing in the papers about it yet, but people were clearly talking. Better to turn the conversation back to Jack's issues than go down that rock-strewn path.

'Life never goes back to normal, Jack. But it does go on. It has to. And it wouldn't have been fair to Lilly not to have the party.'

He started walking again. Slowly, head down, arms stiff. She followed his lead, and they walked side by side, loose stones slipping under their boots. He stopped again, and the headstones she'd seen for the first time on her return to Mossy Creek were in full view. One for Bec and one for Nell, beside the graves of Nell's parents, all their ashes scattered in the place they'd called home. It hadn't been her intention to end up here but maybe seeing them, being reminded that she and Jack were alive, wasn't such a bad thing.

'I know you think it's like what happened with you and

Bec, but this is different.' Jack wiped a hand across his mouth, and let his arm drop again. 'I was in charge that day. It should have been me checking the house. Not ...'

There was no point telling him he was wrong. That he and Matt were both doing their jobs and that taking risks was part of being a firie. That was an understanding he'd have to come to in his own time. She looked over at the headstones, and he followed her gaze.

'I know it's not the same. But I have been there with the guilt trip, Jack. If there's one thing I've learned from Bec's death, it's that life goes on. And we have a duty – an obligation – to those we've lost to make the most of it.' She brandished a knowing smile. 'I'm pretty sure it was you who reminded me of that. If I remember correctly, your exact words were, "Bec's not here to enjoy her life but you can and you owe it to her to do it."'

'Did I say that?'

'Verbatim. I committed it to memory.' His life advice had struck a chord. One that played over and over in her mind until it became a mantra. Helped pull her out of the fog of self-blame she'd stumbled around in for way too long. 'I'm not saying it's easy, but you have to let the people who love you in. Locking Cat out, wasting your time on those stupid video games, drinking ...' She bit down on her lip but let it go again. 'None of that is going to help you deal with what you've been through. I never had any counselling after Bec died, but I should have. It's helped me a bit this time around, after the fires, when I was in hospital. I reckon it would do you good to talk to someone.'

Jack bristled. 'So, Cat really has been filling you in?'

Shit. Why did she mention the video games? Major blooper. She lifted her hand in a stop-right-there gesture.

'She's your wife. She's worried about you. Don't rule out going to see someone, okay?'

He gave a hell-will-freeze-over-before-I-see-a-shrink glare. 'Are we done?'

Were they? She scrunched her nose and threw her hands up in shrug. 'I guess we are if you don't want to talk anymore.'

'Good.' He turned back in the direction they'd come.

So much for the intervention. He hadn't exactly been forthcoming about changing his ways but at least he'd talked about what happened and that was a start.

They walked together back along the road to where Jack's ute was parked beside the van. Banjo lay spreadeagled on the gravel, mouth open, tongue lolling. The thing Jack had said about the dog appearing too late jabbed at her insides, like a blade scoring the cage of her ribs. He was right about one thing: once the locals found out who was responsible for starting the fire, the culprit would be blacklisted for life, and their family along with them.

She couldn't let that happen to Margo, and she certainly wasn't going down that road ever again.

Chapter Eighteen

Taking kids on a pony ride was the last thing Eve felt like doing but there was really no excuse now she'd agreed, and Hugh had sounded so hopeful when he asked if he could bring the kids after school. Luckily there'd been no change in her physique just yet– if anything, the nausea had put her off food, and her jeans were looser rather than tighter. But the blotchy state of her skin and the bags under her eyes were testimony to the long sleepless nights that left her feeling wrung out most days. And that had nothing to do with the pregnancy.

Reaching the gate, she clicked her tongue and the horses stood to attention, heads upright, ears pricked. Bob was notorious for not wanting to be caught – typical bloody pony – but he could never resist her secret weapon. Digging into her pocket, she whipped out a few pieces of liquorice and opened the gate, sure to keep the lead-rope and halter tucked under her arm out of sight.

She pointed a finger at Banjo. 'You stay here. The last

thing I need is you trying to round him up.' Banjo whimpered but sat as instructed.

'Bob, come on. Come and get it.' She massaged the soft treat between her fingers and the pony lifted his head, his Tina Turner mane standing upright in the air, as if he'd had an electric shock.

At thirteen hands, Bob was bigger than a purebred Shetland, the Welsh riding pony in him giving him the height, but he had the hairstyle and attitude of the smaller breed. Nell had probably taken him in when someone no longer wanted him, her compassion for horses a whole lot stronger than for people. He was a likeable little man, just not overly cooperative.

Flattening her palm, she held out the bait and Bob took it hook, line and sinker, while she grabbed a handful of mane and wrangled him into the halter. 'There we go, that wasn't so bad.'

The little guy snorted as she tugged on the lead-rope. He wasn't great on the ground, but fortunately once he was saddled he was a lot more compliant.

The other horses sniffed the air, and Rain nudged at her arm.

'Here you go, girl.'

The mare gently took a piece of liquorice between her teeth and rolled it around her gums with a faint slapping sound. Hard not to play favourites after she'd been at death's door and recovered so beautifully.

Banjo barked and ran around in circles as they walked back towards the barn. Interesting how those herding instincts remained, even though he'd never been trained to round anything up. Maybe it was the same for humans. Maybe our behaviour was part of our DNA, and no matter how hard we tried to change it our wiring couldn't be altered.

Hugh's car pulled up just as she reached the van. The passenger door opened, and Eliza jumped out, immediately breaking into a run.

'Eliza, what did I say? Take it slowly,' Hugh called out as he climbed from the car, shaking his head with an apologetic smile. 'Sorry, Eve.'

'All good. Bob's pretty bombproof.'

'Can I pat him?' Eliza looked up, her dark brown eyes glittering. They must have come from her mother, but she had Hugh's fair hair, pulled back in a braid, and freckles smattering her cheeks and nose.

'Of course, you can. You can brush him if you like, then help me saddle up.'

'Really?' The kid was bursting out of her skin. 'Is that okay, Daddy?'

'If Eve says so.'

There was no sign of any other movement from the car. 'What about Liam?'

'Liam's being a baby.' Eliza's expression was snark personified. Ten going on twenty-five.

'Eliza, what have I told you about that?'

'Sorry, Daddy.'

Hugh pursed his lips. 'Liam might take a while to warm up.'

'That's okay.' Supervising one kid at a time would definitely be easier.

Taking a piece of bailing twine, Eve tied it to a hook on the fence, then looped the lead rope through it, securing the pony. She pulled another bit of liquorice from her pocket and handed it to Eliza.

'Do you want to give him this? He'll be your friend for life.'

Placing the treat in Eliza's palm, she guided it towards Bob's mouth. 'We don't want you to lose any fingers, so keep your hand nice and flat.'

Bob snuffled at the treat and devoured it in one go.

Eliza giggled. 'His whiskers tickle.'

'Okay, so here's the brush. Give him a good once-over and get all the dirt out of his coat. Then we can saddle him up and lunge him.'

'And then can I ride him?'

'On a lead for today. You need to get used to sitting in the saddle and get a feel for the movement.'

'But I want to ride him on my own.'

'All in good time, Missy.' Hugh flashed his daughter a frown. 'Eve's the boss, so do what she says.'

'O-kay.' Eliza drew out the last syllable of her reply, as if she was dealing with total numbskulls, and began the grooming process. Bob lowered his head and licked his lips as she lavished him with love.

'Argh, I forgot something.' Hugh turned and headed back to the car.

'Daddy bought you a coffee. He said you're a caffeine nut.'

'That I am.' A smile sprang to Eve's lips, more at Hugh's kindness than at the prospect of caffeine.

Hugh returned, handing the cup across. 'Double shot espresso, if I remember rightly.' He gave an oh-so-pleased-with-himself smile and liquid sunshine trickled though her veins.

The strong aroma made her want to heave the same way those pot-loads of tripe her mother used to cook made her practically puke when she was a kid. Breathing through it, she forced her mouth into the appropriate position. 'Thank you.'

Whether or not she could drink it was another matter. She sank into one of the folding chairs set up beside the van and gestured to Hugh to take the other. 'So, how are things?'

'Let's just say thank God it's Friday.' He glanced towards the car. No movement from Liam. 'It's been a long week. And for once I'm not on call this weekend.'

'That's good. You work too hard, you know.' In the two weeks Eve had stayed at the vet surgery, Hugh had been called out more times than she could count.

'Yeah, well, that's the life of a country vet, I guess. Good thing Darcy Houghton is on board to do a few shifts now. Takes the pressure off.' He sipped at his coffee, licking the residue from his lips, a gesture that shouldn't have drawn her attention. A tender spot tingled and she crossed her legs. 'How about you? How's van life?'

'Apart from the lukewarm showers and the limited space in which to do expressive dance, it's actually pretty good.'

Hugh looked startled. Then the penny dropped. 'Oh right. So, no dancing then.' He laughed. 'How's the arm?'

She lifted her left hand and turned it over – still tender around the wrist and a freshly applied patch covering the graft. 'It's fine. I grazed it while I was doing the feeds, but it's nothing.' She flexed her fingers as the story rolled off her tongue. 'And the movement is coming back. I drove the Kombi the other day.'

'Great news. On both counts.'

'Eve, is this right?'

She turned towards Eliza, who was stroking the brush

ever so gently down Bob's forehead. The pony stood with his eyes shut, lapping up the attention. If he was a cat, he'd be purring. 'He's loving it. Good job. Don't forget his tail and mane. But stand to the side. He doesn't kick but you should always be careful.'

'Okay.' The smile on Eliza's face was watermelon-wide.

It was like watching herself and Bec as kids, loving every minute. Grooming horses together before a ride, running their hands over the sleek warm coats, completely absorbed in the process. So many beautiful moments she'd forced from her mind to avoid the pain. But remembering them brought Bec back in some small way, just as it brought her back to herself.

'Would Liam like a turn?'

Hugh shook his head. 'Who knows?' He threw up his hands. 'Honestly, I have no idea what to do with him right now. He's so withdrawn. I've talked to his teacher, and he's no different at school. She says he hangs out on his own at breaktime, and he just sits in his room reading most of the time at home. I can't get a peep out of him.'

'Do you think it's got to do with the fires?'

Hugh angled his head but kept his attention on Eliza. 'Possibly. It's certainly been getting worse.' He lowered his voice almost to a whisper. 'I don't know. They say time mends all things, but maybe in some cases it doesn't.'

Being a single parent must be tough. Was she really up to the task? Maybe it was only a matter of applying common sense, of drawing on your own experiences, and asking for help when it was needed. But that was something she'd never been good at doing. Asking for help meant you were vulnerable and admitting that usually meant inviting people into your life, letting them see all the mess and ugliness you'd so carefully compartmentalised. Like Hugh was doing right now.

'It must be hard to lose your mum at such a young age.' So different to her own mixed-up grief for the mother she had as a child but never knew as an adult. But maybe not so different to having a father walk out the door and never come back. 'I guess we all handle things differently. Have you thought of getting some help?'

First Jack and now Hugh. She was becoming a regular agony aunt.

Hugh gave a resigned nod. 'He talks about anything and everything with the school counsellor. Except his mother.'

'Maybe some of that equine therapy we talked about could work.'

'It could. If there was anyone around here who did it.' He raised an eyebrow and fixed his gaze on her, the suggestion clear.

'Don't look at me.'

'Why not? You have the horses here. And you already have the instinctual horse knowledge.'

She looked towards the herd, standing under the scorched old gum tree as if it still had the power to provide shade. Survivors, all of them. Kindred spirits. What would she do with them all if something forced her to leave? So much was dependent on clearing her name, on being able to start afresh with a clean slate. And that wouldn't happen until the culprit was found.

'There's more to it than knowing a bit about horses, Hugh. But I'll keep it in mind.'

'You absolutely should.'

If he knew the full version of her own chaotic story, he would know she was the last person who should be responsible for the mental health of children. But that was not a place they needed to go. It was so tempting to ask about parenthood: how was it possible to always think of someone else before yourself, to give up every scrap of independence, to be so connected to them that the possibility that one day you could lose them didn't stop you loving them with your whole being? But putting those thoughts into words was like trying to make a sandcastle out of clay. Too sticky, too slippery to grasp.

The car door closed, and they turned in unison. Liam walked sheepishly towards them. He had darker hair than his sister, a soft chocolate brown, perhaps more like his mother's, but the same green eyes as Hugh.

'Hey, my boy.' Despite the upbeat greeting, Hugh's voice held a note of caution, the same voice she'd heard him use when he was coaxing a frightened animal out of its enclosure at the surgery.

'Do you want to groom the pony?' Eliza held the brush out. 'He's friendly. And he loves liquorice, doesn't he, Eve?'

'He sure does. Here you go.' She reached into the cup holder on the chair and pulled out the almost empty packet. Bob's ears pricked at the rustle of the bag. 'One piece left. Would you like to give it to him?'

Liam looked from Eve to Bob to Hugh. Eliza moved toward her brother and took his hand. 'Come on, Li. I'll help you.' She took the treat and placed it in her palm, demonstrating how to hold it as she led Liam towards the pony. 'It's easy. You can pat him first.'

Liam raised his hand and pressed it against Bob's shoulder. Hugh's hands gripped the edge of the armrests on his chair, as if he was ready to spring from his seat at any moment. Eliza stood beside her brother, still holding the liquorice. Slowly, Liam moved his hand in a patting motion, stroking the fur in a steady rhythm.

Phew. Tension had spread through all four of them like a contagious disease, and now they could relax. Liam took the liquorice Eliza offered, pinching it between his fingers in a pencil grip, and held it out to Bob.

Eve stood. 'Ah, maybe…'

Bob didn't even bother sniffing the offering. He opened his mouth and chomped. An ear-piercing scream burst from Liam. Hugh dived forward, wrapping his arms around the boy's waist and lifting him into the air.

'I told you to put it out flat, Liam.' Eliza scowled and shook her head.

'It's alright, mate, the finger is still attached. Let me take a look at it.'

Liam lifted his arm skyward. 'No, don't touch it, don't touch it.' He waved his already swelling index finger in reprimand.

'I need to see if the skin is broken.'

Liam arched his back like a gymnast doing a walkover, stretching his arm out further, but Hugh managed to grab his wrist and reel it in. How he was managing to keep hold of the human cyclone writhing against him was a miracle.

Holding the hand, Hugh peered down at the finger, red and swollen but not bleeding. 'I think you'll live. But there'll be a bit of bruising. You wouldn't happen to have any ice, would you, Eve?'

'I think so.' Shit, why hadn't she thought of that straight away instead of standing there gawking.

Pulling open the door of the van, she dived inside and grabbed the tray of ice cubes from the freezer section inside the small fridge. Prepped for quiet-evening bourbons, but untouched. Once the ice cubes were wrapped in a clean cloth, she headed back outside.

'Sorry.' It hadn't been her own teeth clamping down on

Liam's finger, but a surge of guilt swamped her nevertheless. She should have supervised more closely.

'Not your fault.' Keeping a firm hold on the patient, Hugh jiggled the ice cubes inside the cloth and held them against the injured digit, resulting in an even louder squeal, punctuated by snotty sobbing.

Could it really hurt that much? A similar thing had happened to her as a kid when she'd offered a finger covered in icing from a pink bun to one of the school horses. Not surprisingly, it had bitten rather than licked, and Nell hadn't bothered with the ice. Or the sympathy.

'You need this on it, matey, or it will be even worse.'

Liam sniffed multiple times, finally giving in. While Eliza seemed years older than the ten she'd been on earth, there was something fragile about her twin that made him seem much younger.

Eliza had returned to the grooming session, with a look of complete disdain etched onto her face. 'He's such a baby.'

'Eliza. That's enough.' Hugh's saintly patience seemed to be wearing thin.

'I want to go home.' Liam's shoulders rose and fell in a shudder.

'But I haven't had my ride yet.'

'Well, your brother is hurt, Eliza, so that might have to wait.' Hugh's saintly patience seemed to be wearing thin.

Eliza stomped her foot, but the pony didn't even flinch. Good old Bob, solid as a rock. 'You said I could have a ride today. You promised.' Eliza directed her complaint at her father but then looked to Eve, eyes stormy with accusation.

Wow, things were escalating fast. 'You can come back any time. Bob's not going anywhere. And he's really enjoyed his brush.'

'It's not fair.' Tears welled in Eliza's eyes. She was clearly a justice freak.

Life's not fair. The words rang loudly in Eve's ears, as if Nell was standing right there reciting one of her favourite sayings. How right she'd been.

Hugh's sigh was tsunami-strength as he scooted Liam off his lap and rose to his feet. 'I'm sorry, my girl, but you'll have to wait until next time.'

Eliza swept past them all, marched to the car and climbed in, slamming the door as if channelling Scarlett O'Hara.

Hugh was in for a very unpleasant car ride home.

With one hand on Liam's shoulder, he screwed up his face. 'Thanks, Eve. Maybe we can reschedule the ride?'

'Anytime.' She glanced towards the car. 'Good luck.'

'Thanks. The joys of parenthood.' Hugh gave a small smile and shook his head. 'Come on, mate.'

Liam leaned into his father as they walked to the car.

'I'll see you on Saturday?' Hugh called through the car window as he did a u-turn.

'Saturday?'

'The fundraiser for the fire victims.'

'Oh, yeah.' The one Fran had roped her into, despite her protests that she was crap at trivia. 'You're going?'

'Sure am. The babysitter's all lined up. Would you like a lift?'

A lift from Hugh would mean him driving all the way out here to pick her up and then driving her all the way home, at night, the two of them alone in the car. Her heartbeat picked up pace, but she slowed it down with a long exhale. Things had to stay platonic with Hugh. She wasn't stepmother material, and the last thing Hugh needed was another kid to worry about. There was too much going on to let this become anything but friendship, wasn't there?

'Nah, all good, thanks. I need the driving practice.'

Was that a look of disappointment on his face? He gave a wave and drove away, and she took a slow breath. If that was part of 'the joy of parenthood', as Hugh coined it, the whole idea scared her senseless. So much pressure. If you said the wrong thing – or did the wrong thing – it could all go arse up in a second. And if you got it wrong too many times it would be the kid you'd be screwing up and not just your schedule.

A noise behind her. Bob pawing at the ground, impatient to be untied and put back in the paddock now the grooming session was over. Kids and animals. No wonder there was that old show business saying about never working with either. At least the animals didn't talk back, or scream, or demand you do their bidding.

She untied the lead rope and started on the uphill walk to return Bob to his mates. Never wanting to miss out, Banjo sprang to attention, and strolled along at her side.

Yep, even if they were dependent on you, animals were a whole lot easier than kids. How the hell was she going to cope with one of her own – *on* her own?

Ever since the positive test, she'd put the whole baby issue on the backburner. As daunting as impending motherhood was, dealing with the Luke situation was more pressing. What was the point of planning for the future when it was obscured by such a dark cloud? Despite her pledge to share information, Emily Winters had gone very quiet. Had, in fact, seemed to vanish off the face of the earth: no texts and no phone calls. Was that a good sign, or bad? She'd promised to help but could the journalist be trusted?

Eve opened the gate and let Bob loose, a heaviness

weighing down her limbs as she started back towards the caravan. A soft purple haze had fallen over the paddocks, everything still and quiet. Not a sound or movement other than the horses picking at remnants of hay, leftovers from their earlier feed.

Limbo.

The same feeling she'd had all week: waiting for something to happen.

Chapter Nineteen

Considering it was a 1960s building with a blonde-brick exterior and pine flooring, the community centre didn't scrub up too badly. It certainly looked different to the night of the post-fire gee-up. The rows of black plastic chairs had been arranged around circular tables, all of them decorated with strands of fairy lights and strategically placed vases of brightly coloured dahlias.

Standing in the doorway, Eve watched the guests mingle.

Despite the wild days of her youth, she was essentially a solitary being, and small talk didn't come naturally. But if she was going to make a home in Yarrabee being sociable was probably a good move. Besides, Fran had begged her to take up the spare seat on her table, determined to form a formidable team, and would not take no for an answer.

All good. It was a trivia night, nothing more. Smile and nod, attempt to answer a few questions and then she'd be home to bed, having done her civic duty.

'Eve, so glad you're here. Come and meet the other

members of the A team.' Fran took her arm and led her towards a group of people drinking and chatting. Her hair, pulled up into what was almost a beehive – apart from the blunt fringe – was an even deeper shade of cherry than the last time they'd met, and she was a vision in silver sequins.

Eve glanced down at her black jeans and bottle-green silk shirt, the dressiest thing she could find at the local Vinnies. 'I feel a little underdressed.'

'Don't be silly.' Fran squeezed her arm. 'I always frock up. Can't help myself.'

They stepped into the circle, and six heads turned towards them in unison. Fran made the introductions to the people she didn't know, and they greeted her with a mixture of polite nods and handshakes. 'And you know these two reprobates.'

Hugh stood beside Clive, one hand holding a beer, the other stuck in the pocket of his caramel chinos. His pale blue shirt brought out the mossy hue of his eyes.

A tiny whirlpool started deep in Eve's belly at the sight of him. But in that direction lay danger.

She nodded at them both. 'Looking very dapper, gentlemen.'

'We do our best.' Clive looked to his friend for confirmation, and Hugh nodded without wiping the smile from his face or taking his eyes from hers. 'Can I get you a drink, Eve?'

'Just a mineral water, thanks.'

'Still on your health kick?' Hugh flashed his brows, as if he knew her well enough to be surprised that she'd have enough self-control to stick to a regime.

'Yep. Don't want to spoil all my good work so far.'

'I have great admiration for anyone who has the discipline not to partake of the finer things in life.' Fran took a glass of champagne from Clive, who passed Eve her drink. 'Sadly, I'm not one of them.'

Me neither. How she was going to abstain from both alcohol and coffee was a question she'd been turning over in her mind like the proverbial Rubik's Cube. A puzzle she wasn't likely to solve any time soon.

She smiled and sipped while the conversation continued around her. The hall filled with background music and happy chatter, and it almost felt normal to be out at a social event having a pleasant time, until the banner above the stage caught her eye: *Yarrabee Fire Victims Trivia Fundraiser.* A stark reminder of the homes and lives lost. Of the person who might have started one of the fires responsible for that loss.

A vision of Luke standing in the bush holding the jerry can forced its way into Eve's brain: the sense of power he experienced as he poured the petrol, struck the flame and watched the embers spark. His too-long fringe hanging across his face as he peered down at the burgeoning flames, as the drought-dry scrub started to crackle, the fierce scent of the fuel-induced smoke swirling around him.

The vision was so clear in her mind's eye; no voice telling her the notion was ludicrous. Luke was a brooder – said barely a word to anyone. It didn't automatically make him a criminal, but there was something anti-social about him. Then, wasn't there about most teenagers? Hadn't she been all too happy to give the bird to almost everyone and everything at the same age?

'Earth to Eve.' Hugh waved a hand in front of her face. 'We're about to start.'

Behind them, the rest of the group had taken their seats at the table.

'Oh, sorry.'

'Are you sure you're okay? You look a little peaky.' Hugh seemed genuinely concerned, a definite furrow between his brows.

'Just a little tired. Not sleeping too well.'

He gave a brief nod but didn't look convinced.

'Come on, you two, enough of the *tete a tete*. We need you focused on the task at hand.' Fran directed them towards the two vacant seats at the table which were, of course, side by side. She tilted her head and gave a sardonic smirk. She was playing Cupid and was going to be so disappointed when her scheming didn't work.

A shock of red hair flashed by, as Cat, flustered and pale, slid into an empty seat on the table opposite, joining a few of the women from Lilly's party – the yummy playgroup mummies, dressed to the nines and sipping on glasses of Prosecco.

Something sharp pierced Eve's chest: a reminder that she hadn't been a part of Cat's life for the last two decades, that it would take more than a few coffees and an invitation to a four-year-old's party for them to re-establish their relationship. If they ever did. She kept her gaze on Cat, and when their eyes finally met there was a small nod of acknowledgement. But Cat's mouth remained decidedly straight before turning to chat to her immediate neighbour when it lifted into a so-good-to-see-you smile.

What was that all about? The last time they'd spoken had been in the surgery, when Cat had printed off the ultrasound photo and advised her about taking folate and following a diet of fresh fruit and vegetables. She'd seemed okay at the time, maybe a little surprised. Had she reflected on it afterwards and been reminded of her own inability to have any more kids? Or had something else happened with Jack?

'Okay, let's get this trivia night started.' The Master of Ceremonies, a swarthy man wearing a three-piece suit and a not very subtle toupee, boomed into the microphone, which gave off a high-pitched squeal. Hands flew to ears, and disapproving glances shot across tables. Apologising profusely, he dived into the first series of questions on the topic of geography. Simple things like the capital of Morocco and the name of the mountain range running along the east side of the USA.

Given the extent of Eve's travels in her twenties, most of the questions were a piece of cake, but she sat back and let the more eager members of the table provide the answers, jumping in only when it was clear they had no idea.

'You're quite the dark horse when it comes to trivia.' Hugh leant in and spoke quietly in her ear. Way too close.

Eve shifted in her seat to quell the vibration beneath her skin. He'd drunk a few beers, so clearly wasn't driving, and was loosening up. All the more reason for her to stay tightly zipped.

She gave a light shrug. 'I travelled a lot when I was younger. Kind of nomadic really, and I spent a lot of time looking at maps and guidebooks. Things stick, I guess.'

'Planning on doing any more jaunts overseas?'

'Not for the time being.'

'So, you're definitely staying on in Yarrabee?'

Was there a hopeful note in his voice? She let her eyes rest on the gentle green of his irises, the slightly dilated black of his pupils that almost masked the underlying sheen of sadness he carried around. Losing his wife and having to be a single parent to two grieving children must have taken its toll, and yet he was one of the kindest, most generous men she'd ever met. And he was right here, in the middle of a crowded room, looking at her like she was a goddess.

'And the winners of Round One are The Terminators.'

'Yes!' At the MC's announcement, Fran leapt from her seat, hands in the air, stomping her feet as if she was demanding an encore at a concert.

Heads turned in her direction, some laughing at her exuberance, others shooting her looks of disapproval. Having a big personality in a small town was hard, but based on what Fran had communicated so far, she had no plans to shrink herself to fit any ready-made expectations.

Fran was a take-me or leave-me type. The type of person Eve had always pretended to be. She'd managed to maintain the bravado until her only living relative in the world died, and the need to belong trampled on her sense of self.

At the next table, Cat rose and headed to the bathrooms.

The need to be around her oldest friend, someone who knew who she was deep in her core, washed over Eve and pulled her to her feet. 'Excuse me.'

Hugh had been mid-sentence, but what he was saying was a mystery. Her mind was somewhere else entirely. In her peripheral vision, a man in jeans and a checked navy shirt stopped what he was saying and looked in her direction. Dean Harris. Drunk as a skunk. Seven sets of eyes followed his gaze, all the faces wearing looks of disgust. Were they talking about her? Was Dean …? No, surely not. If word got out that Luke was suspected of arson his family would be blacklisted.

The soupy sensation in her legs said otherwise. Moving forward was an effort but she pushed open the door of the women's bathroom. Inside, one cubicle was occupied. She made use of the visit to relieve her swollen bladder and returned to the basin. Cat's head shot up and their eyes met in the mirror.

'Hey, I didn't know you were coming tonight.' Eve washed her hands, keeping her focus fixed on Cat's reflection.

'I'm the town doctor. Wouldn't look good if I didn't attend the fundraiser.' Not even the glimmer of a smile.

'Jack at home with Lilly?'

Cat swiped a piece of paper towel from the dispenser and wiped her hands. 'Well, he's certainly not here.' Her tone was distinctly salty. The vulnerability Cat had shown at Lilly's party was gone, replaced with an air of wintry animosity. She shoved the used paper towel in the bin, left the lid swinging, and turned towards the door. Something was definitely wrong.

'Cat, is everything okay?'

Her friend's sudden pivot startled Eve, and she took a step backwards. Cat gave a stony-faced glare, raising her arms from her sides to fold them firmly across her middle. 'Funny you should ask, Eve.' She exaggerated the name as if sounding it out for a pre-schooler. 'Or should I say – Angie?'

'What are you talking about?'

'I'm talking about the person you used to be, the one you still are underneath the cool inner-city facade and the selfless heroine who rescues old women from fires at her own peril. You remember that person, I'm sure: the one who shoplifted and snuck out of her house late at night and basically fooled everyone in her life into thinking she was just a bit of a larrikin?' She gave a huff and a quick shake of her head. 'Deceit has always been your strong suit. Looks like nothing's changed.'

The closed space of the washroom was suddenly cloying, the air trapped in Eve's lungs as surely as if the room had filled with smoke. Cat hadn't mentioned Bec, but she was there in the charged personality profile of Eve's younger self, in the thing Cat stopped short of saying.

Cat scoffed. 'Don't pretend you don't know what I'm talking about.'

There it was again, that word 'pretend', as if everything about Eve was a sham, as if none of the in-roads they'd made in rebuilding their friendship mattered.

She reached out a hand, but Cat pulled away, and she let it drop. 'Cat, I'm not pretending. If I've done something to upset you, please tell me what it is and we can fix it, here and now.'

Cat pulled her bottom lip between her teeth as if contemplating. 'Fine.' She tossed her head like a mare trying to get rid of an annoying insect. 'But it's nothing that can be fixed.'

A sinking sensation enveloped Eve's body, everything inside her dissolving, as if her organs had liquified.

'Jack came home from your place all chirpy the other day. He seemed calmer, more like his usual self. He even sat on the lounge with Lilly and read a book, and he hasn't done that since before the fires. He told me he was working on the plans for the house, so I figured doing that was taking his mind off everything else, giving him a sense of purpose.'

So far, nothing Cat had said was a negative. What was the problem? 'We did talk about that, and he's happy to be taking on the job.'

'Yes, he is. And I'm guessing he's happy to be back out there with you at good old Mossy Creek Farm too.'

'Cat …'

'When I got home from work yesterday, he was in the spare room, the room we'd always planned to use for our second child but has now turned into a storage room. He was sitting on the sofa bed going through a box of old photos. And do you know which photo he had in his hand when I walked in?' Cat paused for a beat but nowhere near long enough for her question to be answered. 'You, *Angie*, laying on a picnic blanket, topless, leaning on one arm giving what could only be described as a seductive look, right into the camera. Or rather, at the person holding it.'

The space they were in became claustrophobically hot. *What the hell was Jack doing?* 'I have no idea why he'd be looking at that photo, Cat. But I ...'

'Funny,' she spat. 'When I asked him what he was doing, he turned the same colour you're turning now. Said he was reminiscing. Reminiscing! Not once have I ever had to worry about Jack straying or being attracted to another woman. It just wasn't in his playbook. We've been through a lot together with his drinking, then all the miscarriages, and we have Lilly and things were good. Even when you came back, I wasn't worried.'

That wasn't quite true but better to let it slide. 'So what's changed?'

'You tell me. What did you two talk about the other day, Eve? Old times? Lost love?'

Blood whooshed through Eve's ears like wind through the treetops. Cat was way out of line. 'You asked me to talk to him to see if he was okay, and that's what I did.'

'Oh, I'm sure you did. I'm sure you talked about the baby you aborted when you disappeared into thin air. The baby that was Jack's.'

Despite Cat's scarily controlled volume, her words bounced off the tiled floor and walls, turning them both mute. Staring at each other, jaws clenched, arms crossed, as if mirroring the other's stance, neither willing to budge.

Every cell in Eve's body contracted. *Cat must never know about that baby.* Jack's warning. And yet he'd told her himself. Why? 'It's ancient history, Cat. I can't see any point in digging up the past.'

'When you told me in the surgery you'd had a termination, I did wonder about the circumstances, but never in a million years did I think the father was Jack. You know why? Because a friend would have told me the truth, and I thought we were becoming friends again. Jack only told me out of spite. We argued when I caught him red-handed with the photo. He started carrying on about how the history between two people couldn't be erased, about how much you went through when you left town and how if I'd been a better friend to you back then, you mightn't have gone and you mightn't have got rid of his child.' Tears trickled down Cat's cheeks. She lifted a hand and swiped them away, faint rivers of mascara staining her cheeks.

Cold seeped through Eve's shirt as she slumped back against the tiles. What the hell had Jack been thinking? Nothing rational, that was for sure. He was acting on pure emotion, tapping into the vein of hurt and anger and grief he'd shut off long ago, just as she had. Wounds that had been opened and mined afresh by the fires. Taking his pain out on the one person in the world who had his back, as people do when they're hurting. And in the process dumping Eve – and her friendship with Cat – on the slag heap.

'Was that story you told me about the one-night stand with your ex true?'

'What?' Eve's mouth fell open.

'Or is this baby Jack's too?'

'You are so far off base it's not funny.' And yet a rough

laugh worked its way up her throat and burst into the space between them.

Cat stared at her with a watery gaze and shook her head. 'You're right. It's not funny.'

The door swung open, and a woman staggered into the bathroom, holding the wall for balance. 'Oh, sorry, Doc.' She hiccupped and lifted a hand to her mouth. 'I think I've had one too many glasses of bubbles.'

Cat looked at the woman sternly. 'Maybe a glass of water or two when you get back to the table.' Without a backward glance, she grabbed the handle of the partly opened door and stepped back into the hall.

The tipsy woman stumbled into a cubicle and turned the lock, leaving only a silent echo where Eve and Cat had stood.

Chapter Twenty

Eve took a breath and stepped back into the hall; the next round of questions had started, and Cat had resumed her seat. Continuing their conversation out here was out of the question. Did Cat really believe her capable of coming back to Yarrabee and carrying on an affair with a man who was now married to her oldest friend?

But were they friends? Or had the hurt they'd inflicted on each other all that time ago caused too thick a scar? And then there was the issue of Jack: caught red-handed with a semi-nude photo of Eve's younger self, that should have been relegated to the bin.

The moment it was taken was timestamped on her brain, as clear as if it had been yesterday, not over twenty years ago. The middle of summer, cicadas singing high in the treetops, beads of sweat trickling down her chest and pooling in the gap between her boobs, barely covered by her skimpy bikini top. Jack had finished feeding the horses early – with her help – and they'd disappeared down to the creek for a dip, in the deepest section where you could just about get yourself wet. They ripped off their clothes and splashed into the water together, desperate to cool off.

She lay on her back, floating, wary of eels that might be cruising the bottom of the creek bed. Tendrils of cloud hung in the sky like freshly woven cobwebs. A water dragon skittered across the top of a rock and slid into a hollow. Jack swam towards her, wrapping his arms around her waist, and in an instant he'd undone her bikini top. Swinging it in the air like a stripper might spin discarded underwear, he let go and tossed it onto the grass.

'Jack, go get it,' she squealed, batting her hands against his chest but giving in to the pressure of his body against hers, kissing his wet lips, tingling all over at the sensation of his hard-on pressing against her.

'I can take the bottoms off too, if you like.' His smirk was wicked. Dangerous. Tempting. They hadn't gone the whole way yet, but it was going to happen soon. It was just a matter of when and where.

'Nah. First one out gets the bikini top.' She wriggled out of his hold and stumbled through the water, but he raced ahead, grabbing the bikini top first. He held her at arm's length and ran his eyes down her body and back up again. 'Hey, how about you pose for me?'

'Pose?'

Reaching down, Jack pulled a camera from his backpack: a present from his parents for his eighteenth birthday. He'd been snapping photos of the horses and the farm – and her – for the last three weeks.

'Only if you give me back my top.'

His grin stretched. 'I'll give it back after the photo session.'

She narrowed her eyes. 'The bottoms stay on.'

'Deal.'

For some reason, she'd chosen to stretch herself out on the blanket, leaning on one elbow, head resting in her hand. She stared straight at the lens, warm air dancing across her naked breasts, loving the feeling of being appreciated. Of being wanted.

'You've got a nerve showing yourself here.' A sharp voice pulled Eve from her reverie. An older woman she vaguely recognised stood in front of her, hands on hips, like she was lining up for a square-dance.

Damn. She should have made a beeline straight to the table and not loitered outside the bathrooms, lost in the past. Now she'd have to deal with whatever was on the woman's mind. 'Pardon?'

The woman huffed. 'Don't pretend you don't know what I'm talking about.'

Pretend. That damned word again. 'I'm sorry, I don't.'

The woman waved a hand in the direction of Dean's table, where all heads were once again turned towards her. In the middle, sat Kelly Clements, a vacant seat beside her. The penny dropped with a clang: this was Kelly's mother, Rita. They had the same high forehead and ability to mould their expressions, chameleon-like, to suit their audiences. Right now, the mother's face was fashioned into a sneer.

'I suppose it's a good ruse coming along here tonight. As if you're just as traumatised as the rest of the town by the fires. But don't think you're fooling anyone for one minute.' Rita shot a glance toward Dean. 'You didn't even have the good grace to come back here and bury your mother, but you've got the hide to stay after setting fire to her house.'

The trembling of Eve's knees threatened to knock her off her feet. For a brief moment, she was transported back in time to another accusation, another public place, outside the courthouse when the coroner deemed Bec's death an accident, but some of the town criers had expressed their opinions regardless.

She wasn't that girl anymore.

Squaring her shoulders, she looked her accuser directly in the face. 'I don't know what you've heard, but whatever it is I don't appreciate being blamed for a crime I did not commit. I'm just as upset about the fires as the rest of the community.' She pulled back her sleeve, holding her injured arm up as if it was a trophy. 'And I'm just as eager to see the person who started the blaze out at Mossy Creek brought to justice.'

Eve turned her head in Dean's direction and gave him a glare that did nothing to wipe the smug look off his face. 'Now if you'll excuse me …'

Before she could sidestep Rita Clements, Hugh appeared, coming to stand by her side, their shoulders touching. 'Is everything alright here?'

'It's fine.' The lie slipped out through gritted teeth. She didn't need a knight in shining armour coming to her rescue, and she didn't need to be in this hall for one second longer. She strode to the table and collected her bag from the back of her chair.

Her teammates eyed her with a mix of surprise, curiosity and concern, none of which put a dent in her anger. 'I'm sorry, Fran, I have to go.'

Aiming straight for the door, she made her way through the tables and out into the coolness of the night air. Down the street, a fuzzy image of the Kombi came into view. What the fuck? Why was she crying? She'd left narrow-minded small-town busy bodies like Rita Clements behind long ago. Why did they still had the power to get under her skin?

'Eve, wait up.' Hugh's voice penetrated the buzzing in her ears.

No, not now. Couldn't they all leave her alone?

She slowed to a stop by the Kombi door just as Hugh caught up, puffing slightly from the exertion of chasing her down the street.

'You'd better work on your fitness levels.' Diversion was such a useful tool when you didn't want to address the real issue.

Hugh rested his hands on his waist and gave her a soft smile. 'You might be right.'

It would be so easy to reach out and touch his face, feel the smoothness of his freshly shaven cheek, fall against him and let him pull her into an embrace. But that would be stepping over a border into a territory she could never inhabit.

He jerked a thumb over his shoulder. 'What happened in there?'

Where would she start? With the side eyes from Dean's table? Cat's revelations and suspicions about Jack? Or should she begin with Rita Clements' blatant accusations, and work backwards? She shook her head and snorted out a laugh. 'It doesn't matter.'

'Well, if it upset you enough to make you leave, I beg to differ.' Hugh gestured towards the Kombi. 'We can hop in and have a chat if you don't want to go back inside.'

How tempting that offer was, and how pointless. She couldn't drag Hugh into her fucked-up life. He had enough complications of his own to manage. Cold spiralled through her body from the ground up, a whirling tornado of emotion she needed to outrun. She rummaged in her bag for the keys, pulled them out and let the cold jangle of metal against metal spur her into action.

'I don't want to talk about it, Hugh.'

'Eve, please, I …' He ran a hand through his hair. 'I know you're dealing with a lot after the fire, and you're recovering from the burn, and I'm going to be completely honest with you. I haven't even looked at a woman since my wife passed, but I think there's something here between us, and I'd like to explore that.'

Oh God. She should have nipped this in the bud weeks ago.

He stepped forward and held her forearms gently but firmly. 'I'm not doing a very good job of this, but what I mean is, I'd like to be more than friends. I know I come with baggage and kids and—'

'I'm pregnant.' It spurted out just as it had in Cat's surgery.

Hugh's eyes were hidden in the dim light. His hands fell away, releasing her from his grip.

And that was as far as this conversation was going. 'Go back inside to your friends, Hugh. Enjoy your night.'

Blood pounding behind her temples, she rounded the van and opened the door, climbing into the driver's seat without a backwards glance. But the reflection of Hugh's silhouette hovered in the passenger sideview mirror as she drove away and headed home alone.

Chapter Twenty-One

Each time Eve pulled into the carpark at the lake, the sensation of a spider crawling up the bare skin of her spine lessened. She'd been back a few times since that first day, when she'd made her peace with the past, and each visit became more and more about being in a place she loved than about Bec's death. Banjo loved it too. The grief was always there, of course. A cocktail of guilt and regret she would never quite digest. But now there was an acceptance too, along with the better memories of the times she and Bec had spent here together as kids.

She cracked open the door, and Banjo leapt out, charged to the grass and started his usual inspection. A figure waved from the nearby bench seat: Emily, blonde tresses wound up into a bun that should look messy but was remarkably elegant for someone sitting by a lake alone on a cloudy Monday afternoon. A tan blazer and knee-length matching boots topped off the outfit. The woman was all style.

A crisp wind skipped across the water, and Eve reached across to the passenger seat for her own coat before closing the door. Slipping her arms into the faux sheepskin, she pulled the collar up to block out the cold. Even though Emily had instigated the meeting to chat more and dig a little deeper into her story, Eve had an agenda of her own and would not be leaving until all the boxes were ticked.

'Nice coat.' Emily nodded at the jacket she'd picked up only last week.

'Thank you. I might actually be getting used to op shopping.'

Emily grinned. 'You mean collecting vintage pieces.'

'Yes, that sounds a lot more sophisticated.' She sat down, leaving a gap between them.

'Thanks for coming.'

'All part of the deal.' Hopefully a mutually beneficial one. 'Why here?'

'I'm surprised you didn't ask when I texted you.' Long legs crossed, Emily swivelled slightly and placed one elbow on the back of the seat, so they were almost face to face. 'In fact, I was expecting an emphatic no.'

'But you asked anyway.'

'I wanted a bit more insight into how you've dealt with your past. It speaks to the courage you've shown in coming back to Yarrabee, to the farm, and here.' She waved a hand in the direction of the lake. 'To face your demons. It's an important part of who you are. I knew if you really objected to coming, you'd say so.'

Eve stared out across the water, her gaze drifting, as it always did, to the centre. To the spot where the boat tipped. To where Bec drowned and the world tilted on its axis. She'd kept that chapter of her life locked away for all these years, hadn't spoken about it to a soul – but secrecy didn't negate the pain. It only numbed it; kept it dormant until she returned, when it burst from her past with a frightening, but cleansing, vengeance.

Maybe if she'd shared all those complex emotions with someone earlier, she would have healed sooner.

She swallowed to ease the strain in her throat. 'There's still a part of me that relives that night each time I come here, but now it's more like a series of snapshots than a movie, like I'm flicking through a viewfinder and there's a fresh stab of pain as each image appears, but then the photos run out and it dissipates. It took me a long time to face it, but I did. And now I want to move on.'

Without raising her fingers, she touched the necklace she'd found in Bec's old room before the house went up in flames. A nurse had taken it off in the hospital after the fires, and she'd gone ballistic, demanded it be returned and hadn't removed it since. There would always be memories, always be hurt, but she knew deep down that Bec, wherever she was, had forgiven her.

'And you want to move on at Mossy Creek, despite the trauma you must have experienced after the fires?'

'Strangely enough, yes I do.' Saying it wasn't quite as easy as thinking it but did make it more real. 'When I first came back, all I wanted was to see the place again and get the hell out, but even before the fires hit I was having second thoughts. I don't know if I would have acted on them at that point. It sounds stupid, but I'd never expected it to feel like coming home. All of it: being at the farm, seeing old friends, everything so familiar. Then, it all went up in smoke. Literally…' Eve's breath hitched. 'Weirdly, the threat of losing it has made me want it back.'

Emily lifted an eyebrow. 'I'd say it's more than a threat. There's not much left.'

'There's the land, and the horses. The bush is already regenerating. And I'm having plans drawn up for the rebuild.' Was there any point, when things were once again starting to unravel? She shook her head, glancing around to make sure Banjo hadn't roamed too far. 'But none of that is going to matter if Brent Adams has his way. Correction, if half the bloody town has its way. Did you know Dean Harris has been spreading rumours about me? Letting it be known that I'm the number one suspect in the arson investigation. Rita Clements –mother of Kelly Clements who spoke at the information night – bailed me up outside the women's bathroom at the trivia fundraiser last night and demanded to know how I could show my face in public.'

'What?' Emily looked incredulous.

'Yep. Didn't do it quietly either and Dean was there at the table watching his handiwork, looking completely self-satisfied. It was all I could do not to slap him as I walked past.'

'What did you say?'

'To him? Nothing. I told Rita she could shove her opinions up her arse, and then I walked out.'

Emily spluttered out a laugh. 'I bet that caused a stir.'

'I'm sure it did. I didn't stick around to find out.'

A shame she hadn't skedaddled quicker, and then Hugh might not have had time to catch up with her. And initiate that awkward conversation. Unsurprisingly he had sent no follow up texts. But then why would he? She'd made her position – and her condition – perfectly clear.

A sigh emptied her lungs. 'The thing is, if Rita knew then Dean has filled her in ... and if he's filled her in, then a whole bunch of other people in town know.'

Emily stared out at the lake but narrowed her gaze. 'It might not have been Dean.'

'What do you mean?'

'Adams has been asking around about you.' Emily lowered the volume of her voice even though there was no one around to hear. 'Trying to work out your movements the day the fire started, digging into your history.'

'He's well acquainted with my past, believe me.' Why the hell was Adams holding such a grudge? 'How do you know all this anyway?'

Emily tilted her head from side to side, as if inspecting her reflection in a mirror before a big night out. 'I may have the ear of a certain young constable.'

'Morris?'

'The one and only. Ran into him last night at the pub. He was off duty, and we got talking about the town, the fires, and I may have led him down the let's-talk-about-the-investigation-path.'

'And he told you they're seriously looking into me?'

'Well, he didn't name you initially, but when I mentioned you as a possible suspect he didn't deny it. And he did raise his eyebrows in a you-might-be-right gesture.'

Unbelievable. Emily was good, no doubt about it. 'What did you have to do to get him talking?'

'Not a lot. He'd already had a couple of beers. When his mate left, I sidled up to the bar and re-made his acquaintance. We got chatting. I get the feeling he's not the biggest fan of his boss.'

Interesting. Not that it made any real difference. 'Any news on Luke?'

'A little. Did you know he'd been in trouble at school?'

Eve snorted. 'I knew he'd had a few problems. That's why he left early. Why I gave him the job.'

'He didn't leave. He was expelled.'

'Really?'

Emily widened her eyes and gave a slow nod. 'For starting a fire in a locker.'

Shit. Margo would be beside herself if she knew. 'Why the hell would he do something like that?'

'Pissed off with the kid who owned it? Rebelling? Attention? Maybe all of the above.'

'Did Morris tell you all this?'

'No. I managed to track down Luke's mother, Michelle, when I was back in Sydney last week.'

'And she openly told you all this?'

Emily tipped her head from side to side. 'She was a little reticent at first.'

'You didn't buy her a drink too?'

'A coffee.' A small smile curved the corners of Emily's mouth. 'And I used my journalistic charms. Started talking about Dean and how scrappy he'd been with you, and she put the knife straight in. Blamed him for Luke going off the rails, for shipping him off to his parent's place rather than dealing with his issues, and she let slip about the expulsion. She was quite upset. Even more so when I told her the police are interested in Luke's whereabouts.'

'She didn't know?' This story was getting stranger by the minute.

'She's had no contact with either him or Dean since she left. They've both refused her calls. The first she knew about any of it was when we had the conversation.'

Not surprising, given Dean's spitfire determination to blame all their marital problems on his wife. 'According to Dean, *she* wasn't interested in having any contact with *them*. I had no reason to disbelieve him at first, but after our chat I'll take Michelle's word over his.' She grasped her still aching wrist.

A gust of wind lifted the dry grass fringing the verge of

the shoreline. Clouds had gathered while they'd sat talking, casting a shadow over the surface of the lake, turning the far channel a vibrant shade of turquoise beneath the sliver of remaining sunshine. Banjo had given up scurrying after lizards and, resigning himself to never catching a seagull, flopped down at the base of a nearby banksia tree.

Eve pulled her attention back to the conversation. There was a lot to process, none of it good. 'So, both Luke and I are still on the police radar?'

'Looks that way.'

'Shit.' The whole situation was getting worse. Once rumours started in this place, there was no stopping them. They flew thicker and faster than a throng of bats at twilight, fed by the gossipmongers of the town, swirling in an ever-growing cauldron. And with every tasty morsel, the dream of staying put and settling in at Mossy Creek faded that little bit more.

'How do we know Luke has left town?' Emily's question interrupted the staccato beating of her heart.

'What do you mean?'

'Well, who told you he had?' Emily was in full interview mode.

'Margo.'

Emily nodded deliberately, as if she was weighing up the information.

The more details she had the better. 'Plus, when I was at his place Dean told me that he'd had a call from Luke saying he was on a fruit-picking trip with some mates.'

'The same thing Dean told the police.' The journo's tone was getting more and more emphatic. 'But he didn't say who the mates were or where they were doing the work.'

'No. Only that it was somewhere south.'

'So the story could be a cover.' Emily lifted a finger and

pointed it in the air, as if testing the temperature. 'Made up either by Dean or Luke, to get the police off his case.'

Eve let the possibility settle. She'd never had any reason to question the story, but if Dean was hell-bent on protecting Luke, he might not be beyond bending the truth. 'True. He could have gone in any direction.'

'But the police have tracked down all his known mates, and they're all here in town. None of them know anything about his whereabouts. They haven't heard from him. Or if they have, they're not saying.'

'And I suppose they have put out a search on his car?'

'Exactly!' Emily reinforced her point with a sharp nod. 'In which case, you'd think they would have found him if he was fruit picking.'

'What are you getting at?'

'I haven't put all the pieces together yet. But the fact that Luke disappeared straight after the fires has to be more than coincidence. Especially given he was a firebug at school.' Emily's gaze fell on an oystercatcher wading through the shallows, his bright orange beak dipping in and out of the water as he searched for brunch. As if a lightbulb had flicked on inside her head she turned back, her face animated. 'How old is Dean Harris?'

Eve did the mental arithmetic. 'He'd be eight years older than me.'

'And he was born and bred here,' Emily said, obviously thinking aloud. 'Would he be the same age as Brent Adams?'

'Possibly. Todd was a couple of years older than me, and Brent was older by a fair bit than him, so yeah – Brent and Dean would be around forty-six.'

'And they probably went to school together?'

'I guess so.' Why does that matter?' Keeping a lid on her

frustration was becoming difficult. Emily was asking more questions than a TV courtroom attorney.

'Well, from what you've said about the way Adams acted when your sister died, he might not always have a straight-and-narrow perspective on law enforcement. Which means he might not be averse to sharing details of a case with one of his old schoolmates. And he might be keen to pin the blame on someone other than that mate's son.'

A bell rang inside Eve's head. 'I wouldn't put anything past Adams. But it's all assumption. We can't prove any of it.'

'Not yet,' Emily agreed, 'but it gives me another angle to investigate. Have you had any more conversations about this with your friend, Luke's grandmother?'

'No. She's been strangely MIA.' The last time they'd seen each other was at Cat's surgery when Margo had looked decidedly pale and shaken. And it seemed like she'd been laying low ever since. Hadn't even made an appearance at the trivia fundraiser which was completely out of character. 'Why?'

'You said she was cagey about Luke when you last brought up the subject. Could she know more than she's letting on?'

'No way. Margo is as straight as an arrow. She wouldn't lie about anything.'

'Not even to protect her grandson?'

The memory of Margo's reaction when Eve had mentioned the police were asking about Luke reverberated inside her brain like the snap of a billiard ball against a cue stick. But surely that was only the worry of a concerned grandmother, nothing more? 'No. Margo is my godmother. She wouldn't dump me in it to protect Luke if she thought he really was guilty of a crime.'

Emily gave an emphatic shake of her head. 'Blood is thicker than water, Eve. I really think you should have another conversation with her about her grandson. See if you can glean anymore about his character, and if she knows where he might be. Finding Luke is the key to getting Adams off your back. Or at least getting closer to the truth.'

'Only if Luke comes forward and confesses.'

'At the moment, Adams is suggesting you paid Luke to start the fire in order to get the insurance money for the property. Luke is the only one who can confirm or refute that argument.'

'And if he confirms it?'

Emily shrugged. 'Then it's your word against his. The law says you're innocent until proven guilty, and they have not one scrap of evidence.'

A wavery image of the jerry can quivered at the back of Eve's brain. Why had she told Dean about it? He was sure to tell his son she'd divulged the information and there was every chance Luke could lie and say he'd seen her with it on the day of the fire. She should have got rid of it instead of stashing it in the barn; driven it somewhere and dumped it. Or, more sensibly, fronted up to the police station with it – but then Adams might have twisted her story, and she would have been placing the noose around her own neck and giving him an invitation to yank it tight. Telling Emily about the jerry can now might make her look like she really did have something to hide.

The fly in the ointment was Dean. But surely he'd keep his mouth shut about it if there was a chance saying something could implicate Luke?

One thing was certain: that bloody jerry can had to go. And something else: she had to have a frank talk with

Margo and get to the bottom of what her godmother was hiding. The sooner the better.

Eve's stomach flipped. She'd already alienated Cat and Hugh, and God knows what her status was with Jack. Right now, Margo was the only friend she had, and it was a friendship too important to lose.

Chapter Twenty-Two

Seeing Harry's car in the driveway always made Eve's pulse quicken. Now he'd been given the all-clear to drive, the fact that his four-wheel drive was here meant he was home, so she'd have to suck up her jitters, pull on her big girl pants and knock on the door.

Back in the day, there'd been no knocking. Having neighbours who were more like family had been a godsend, and over the years the distinction between the two had blurred so much that there'd been times when the Aunty and Uncle titles had been more fact than fancy. So much had changed.

'Hello, Angie …' Harry shook his head as if a bug had zipped into his ear. 'Sorry, *Eve*. I'll get used to the new name one day.'

She forced a smile. He probably wouldn't but at least he was trying. 'That's okay. How are you feeling?'

'Getting there. Much better now I can drive. There's a lot I'd like to be doing around here that's a bit beyond me, according to the doctor at any rate. Caravan going okay?'

This was the most civil he'd been to her in two months and the change was disconcerting. No point looking a gift horse in the mouth though – she could use all the friends she could get right now, considering the way they were dwindling. 'Yeah, it's great. Thanks so much for lending it to me. She's very cosy.'

'Daisy.' He huffed. 'The wife's idea, that name. Can't see how a bloody caravan can have a name, or how you'd know it was a female. Anyhow I suppose you didn't come here to pass the time of day with me.'

He wasn't wrong. 'Is Margo home?'

Harry pointed in the direction of the newly constructed greenhouse. 'She's down there faffing around with some seedlings. Not in much of a mood. Back's been giving her grief. But I'm sure she'll be pleased to see you. I'll get back to me sudoku.' He turned and ambled down the hallway.

Banjo sniffed at the ground, darting in one direction and then the next as they made their way towards the greenhouse. His scent radar had gone onto overdrive since arriving at the farm – maybe making up for all those years in the city, when the only smells he could follow were imprinted on cement or wafting from a takeaway restaurant. The fact he was sniffing anything was a good sign: maybe some of the wildlife that had survived was returning.

'Bugger it.' The sharp sound of Margo's cursing pierced the polycarbonate walls of the greenhouse.

'You stay out here, Banj. I won't be long.'

Pulling open the door, she stepped inside to find Margo crouching, scooping handfuls of soil from the floor into a pot. 'Can I give you a hand?'

Margo sprang upright and let out a clipped scream, as if the hand pressed to her chest had forced it from her diaphragm. 'Oh goodness, you frightened me.'

'Sorry, Aunty Margo, I thought you would have heard me come in.' Eve took a step closer. Margo's face was flushed but the dark circles were even more pronounced than the last time they'd met. 'Here, let me get that. You shouldn't be bending over with a bad back.'

One knee cracked as Eve knelt and swiped the dirt back into the pot, pinching a seedling lying on the ground between her thumb and forefinger. Standing, she handed the lot over to Margo, who placed it on the bench beside a pile of other small plastic pots and a bag of potting mix.

'Don't you start. It's bad enough having Harry on my case. I've come down here for some peace.'

'I'm sure he's just worried about you.'

'Well, he can find someone else to worry about.' Margo tipped a cupful of the mix into the pot around the rescued seedling and pushed her fingers around the base of the plant. 'And that goes for you too.'

Okay. Not the ideal way to start a tricky conversation. Better tread carefully. Whatever was bothering Margo would only be exacerbated by casting aspersions on her son or grandson. But things were getting far too serious to pussyfoot around.

'We missed you at the trivia dinner.'

'Yes, well, I was busy.'

'Busy?' Margo had never been one to miss a community event. In fact, she generally organised half the things that went on in Yarrabee. 'Doing what?'

'Minding my own business.' Could she get any snippier? 'And it might be an idea for you to mind yours. Based on what I've heard, it might have been a good thing if you'd stayed home yourself.'

Oh God. The peppermint tea Eve had drunk with her lunch backwashed through her system, threatening to defy gravity. News always travelled fast in Yarrabee. But which version had Margo heard, and from whom? In times gone by, this would be the point where Eve did a fast about-face and hightailed it home. But she'd learnt from experience avoiding judgement never lessened it.

'I'm guessing you're talking about Rita Clements.'

Margo snapped off the green gardening gloves and tossed them onto the bench. Hand on hip, she turned, eyes blazing. 'What were you thinking, making a spectacle of yourself like that in front of the whole town, or at least a good number of them? I thought you wanted to fit back in around here?'

'I do.' Had she actually voiced that longing to Margo, or had her godmother joined the dots?

'Well, causing a scene is not the way to go about it.'

'I don't know who you've heard the story from …' Although she had a pretty good idea. 'But Rita was the one who bailed me up and went on the attack.'

If Margo had heard the post-trivia night gossip, she'd also know about the arson accusation. Surely that would make her realise how ridiculous the whole thing was?

'I don't have a lot of time for Rita Clements, and I don't know where she'd be getting her information but fronting up to her like that is not going to win you any brownie points.'

A rush of heat flooded her veins, just as it had when Rita went on the attack. What was she supposed to do? Stand there and take the hits like a human punching bag? 'Maybe not, but I've done my time running from the people in this town who need a scapegoat. If I hadn't been made to feel such a pariah twenty years ago, I mightn't have left. This time I'm staying, and I won't stand for Rita – or anyone else – spreading lies about me.'

Margo pursed her lips and stared at the freshly potted seedling as if considering her options. 'It works both ways, you know. Dean said you were out at his place harassing him about Luke.'

Harassing? Eve glanced down at her arm, at the fresh gauze she'd applied only a few hours ago, and her inner combustion engine exploded. If Dean wanted to play dirty, she could meet him and match him.

'See this?' Holding up her arm, she pointed to the bandaged graft. 'This is here because Dean didn't like what I had to say and bullied me out his front door. In my hurry to leave I tripped over and fell on my arm.' Should she mention he was the one starting the rumours? Her chest rose and fell as she built up steam. 'Do you know what's going on with him, Margo? Did you know Michelle has left him?'

Margo blinked but kept her focus on the pot in her hand. 'You had no right to go there accusing Luke of starting the fire.'

'I went there to see if Dean knew where Luke is, so we can find him and sort this mess out. Luke is implicated in this arson business as much as me.'

'Huh! Just like Dean said, trying to save your own backside.' Margo shook her head. 'I trusted you, Eve. I was so happy to have you home. And then after the fires … I can't believe you would try to make Luke look like the guilty party. Not when you know what that feels like yourself. Not after everything we've been through.'

'I'm not trying to make Luke look guilty. But there are people in this town who want to pin the blame on me – like, seriously pin – and I'm not wearing it.' Margo's rose-coloured glasses were firmly in place when it came to both Dean and Luke, and it was time she took them off and had a good hard look at reality. 'Did you know Luke was expelled from school for lighting a fire in a locker?'

'What a lot of rubbish. Who told you that?'

'Michelle told Emily Winters, the journalist doing the story about the fires.'

Margo's jaw hardened and her eyes narrowed. 'You let a journalist poke around in my family business?'

'She's helping me try to clear my name.'

'Helping you put the blame on an innocent young man, more like it, to take the heat off yourself.'

What the fuck was going on? Who was this woman – the closest person in the world Eve had to a relative – accusing her of being a criminal?

'Margo, you're not listening to me. Brent Adams has it in for me. He's determined to smear my name and either run me out of town or have me locked up. I know Luke is your grandson, and I know how much you love him, but you have to face facts: he was working on my property, which is where they say the local fire started; he has a criminal history and he disappeared into thin air as soon as the fires broke out. It doesn't take a genius to put it all together. I'm sorry, but I am not going to take the wrap for something I didn't do. I know he's your family but—'

'Don't you talk to me about family. You have no idea what the word means. Family sticks together. It doesn't up and leave when the going gets tough. And it doesn't turn its back on someone because they've made a mistake or two. We look out for each other, and we look after each other. That's just the way it is.'

A sharp pain stabbed at Eve's chest. It couldn't have hurt more if Margo had pulled a knife from her garden toolbox and stuck it between her ribs.

'Do you honestly think I started that fire?' Her voice was

as wobbly as her insides. 'That I would burn down the house I grew up in to get insurance money I would get anyway when I sold the house? Think about it, Margo. It doesn't make any sense. The whole scenario is ridiculous.'

Margo's chin quivered. Tears filled her eyes, but her mouth was set firm, and she didn't let them fall. 'I don't know what makes sense and what doesn't anymore. But I do know I will not have you running around disparaging my grandson. I've stood by you, Eve, and I've stuck up for you, but if it comes down to me choosing between you and Luke …' She pressed her lips together and shook her head.

'It's fine. You don't have to say it. I get the message.' Eve swallowed against the razor blade slicing through her vocal cords. Emily's words echoed in her head. 'Blood's thicker than water, right? I'll leave you to your planting. I hope your back feels better.'

Walking away was an effort, as if her feet were encased in concrete not her dusty farm boots. As if this could be the very last time she and Margo would speak. She let the greenhouse door swing shut behind her.

Giving a whistle, she started down the driveway. Banjo heeled like the faithful boy he was, the one being who had her back no matter what. Her hand drifted to her abdomen, to where her blood pumped through a tiny being. A child she would never want to let down or doubt the way her own mother had doubted her twenty years ago. The way Margo doubted her now.

Chapter Twenty-Three

Banjo stopped before the driveway, ears pricked, one leg bent at the elbow, paw lifted.

'What is it matey?'

Eve tracked to where he was looking. Parked beside the caravan were three cars: a white covered-in utility with red-and-yellow branding – a Rural Fire Service vehicle – and two police cars. Three uniformed policemen hovered nearby, one of them on his phone: Brent Adams. A shiver shook her frame, as if she'd just stepped under an ice-cold shower.

'Oh shit.' *What now?*

She was still a fair distance away and no one had spotted her yet. She could easily turn around and go back the way she'd come, keep walking past Margo's as if she was out for a Sunday stroll and wait for them to track her down. But what was the point? Sooner or later, she'd have to deal with Adams and his bullshit. It might as well be now.

'Come on, Banj, let's get this over and done.'

The closer she got to the gate of the farm, the more violently her knees trembled. The fact the police were back, with the RFS in tow, probably meant they were onto something. Considering what she'd already been accused of, it wasn't hard to put two and two together. But if they wanted to search her property, didn't they need a warrant? And wouldn't they have to wait for her to be present to search her premises? Then again, what they were supposed to do and what Adams did could very well be two different things.

Banjo picked up his pace as they turned into the gate of the property.

'Heel.' She clicked her fingers and he returned to her side, on alert, eyes trained on the strangers they were now walking towards, head and ears upright. There was no way he'd bite a soul, but he had a mean bark, and it would only take one short instruction to send him on his way and have him bailing up the visitors. Tempting. But not advisable given the shit she was already in. Better to keep him close, for moral support if nothing else.

With every step she took towards the cars, Eve's internal alarm system rang louder. Two men she'd never seen before stood beside the ruins of the house, deep in conversation. One of the policemen – the constable who had accompanied Adams when he'd first questioned her, the same one Emily had cosied up to in the pub – turned to his boss and pointed in Eve's direction. The look on Brent Adam's face couldn't be haughtier.

No matter what happened, no matter what was said, she had to keep her cool. If she let them see she was rattled, it would only play into their hands. Every atom in her body jostled like a sprinter at the starting line, urging her to run.

None of the visitors said a word as she approached.

Keep it casual, Eve. Meet Adams head on. 'Anything I can help you with, Sergeant?'

'Pretty sure you won't be so polite when you find out why we're here.' Adams, arms folded, leant against the car. Strands of grey peppered his hair – or what was left of it – slightly gelled and brushed forward in the traditional combover of a middle-aged man gone prematurely bald. 'We have a search warrant for this premises, Ms Nicholls. You've met Constable Morris. This is Constable Treloar. And the two gentlemen over there …,' he pointed to the men perusing the ashes, 'are RFS Bushfire Investigators.'

Morris stepped forward with a brief nod and handed across a piece of paper. The policewoman, Treloar, stood to his side, eyes fixed on the ground.

The document shook in Eve's hand. She squeezed it between her fingers. **Police Search Warrant.** Right there in bold at the top of the page, her name and address typed below it in smaller print. 'What exactly are you looking for?'

'You'll see when we find it.' At Adams' wave, Morris and the two investigators turned and headed in the direction of the barn. 'Although I'm sure you've got a fair idea.'

There was zero point denying it, given that in a minute or two the constable would be returning with the jerry can. But she wasn't going to give Adams the satisfaction of admitting to anything until push came to shove. It was clear they knew what they were after and exactly where to find it.

'I gather you've been talking to Dean Harris.' Nothing ventured, nothing gained. 'Or rather he's been talking to you.'

Adams sneered. 'And what makes you think that?'

'A hunch.' Emily's pondering about the relationship between the two men filtered through the screeching in

Eve's ears and solidified in her brain. 'Not that it would be ethical to discuss a police case with an old schoolmate, especially one whose son is under suspicion of arson.'

Adams blinked, a cloud darkening his expression before he shut it down again. 'I'd be careful what you say, Ms Nicholls. It won't help your case to throw aspersions at others. Or the police.'

She shrugged. 'Wouldn't dream of it, Sergeant.' She kept her tone nonchalant, despite the rabble of butterflies pummelling around in her gut. Letting Adams see she was nervous would only feed into his power trip. In the distance, Morris emerged from the barn holding the jerry can in his gloved hands, flanked by the two investigators.

Her stomach hollowed out. Laying at her feet, Banjo whimpered, and Eve let out an silent whine of her own. How was this going to play out? Having the jerry can wasn't proof she'd done anything wrong. But if she lied about where it came from, things would only get worse. For her and for Luke.

At the sound of footsteps, Adams turned his head, looking back again with a smirk. 'Well, what have we here?'

'Funny you knew exactly where to look.'

'Well, when you go bragging about your exploits it's not much of a challenge to find the evidence.' He nodded towards the other car, the one he wasn't using as a sun lounge. Morris placed the jerry can on the back seat, grabbed a notepad and pen and started writing. Constable Treloar had apparently been brought as a prop.

One of the investigators, a stocky man with a mop of curly hair and a neutral expression, appeared in her peripheral vision. 'We're here to investigate the origins of the fire, Ms Nicholls.' He unfolded a map and pointed to the outline of the farm. 'This is an enlarged photograph of the property. Can you give us some idea of where you ... found ... the petrol can?' He shot a glance at Adams and then a conciliatory look back in her direction.

How was this happening? A man standing here with a map asking her to pinpoint exactly where she'd supposedly started a fire.

'We don't have all day, Ms Nicholls.' Adams' voice barely made a dent in the disorienting aural orchestra playing in her ears.

She peered at the map, tracing her finger along the trail she'd walked that day, and located the outcrop of rock where she'd found the jerry can. 'Here. Wedged under a boulder. About five metres from the creek.'

'Thank you. We'll head down there and take a look.' The man followed his colleague, each of them hauling a canvas backpack onto their shoulders.

'I notice you're not denying anything.' Adams zeroed back in on her with his beady eyes, a hawk cornering its prey.

'There's nothing to deny. I found that jerry can when I was out walking on the property.'

'And when would that have been?'

'A few days after you were here asking me about the house and the insurance.'

'So, you either *found it*, as you say, or decided you'd better get rid of the evidence in case someone came looking.'

The laugh escaped of its own accord, let loose from the prison of her throat. 'If I was hiding it, why would I put it in my own barn?' Adams wasn't making any sense. 'Admittedly I should have come straight to you, but I was trying to protect Luke. I was worried he might have done something stupid and wanted to give him the chance to defend himself before I told anyone what I'd found.'

Adams straightened, finally uncrossing his arms and hooking his thumbs through the belt tabs of his trousers. If he was any more of a caricature, he might actually be funny. 'That's not the information we've received, Ms Nicholls.'

'Information? What are you talking about?' The now obvious tremor in her voice was in direct contrast to Adams' own cocksure manner.

'Luke Harris. He came to the station last night and told us the whole story.'

The skin on her scalp shrank. Luke was back in town? And he'd been to the police? Spun a story that would no doubt implicate her and take the pressure off himself.

Now it was her turn to fold her arms, lower than Adams, across her middle, protection against the next blow. 'What story?'

'That you put him up to starting the fire. Said you'd pay him fifty thousand dollars when the insurance money came through, and when he refused to do it you threatened to report him to the police for theft. Apparently he was tempted by your offer but thought better of it. Then, when the fires broke out, he was worried he'd be implicated so he took off. After having some time to think about it, he decided to come back and tell the truth, particularly after you went to his father with your own fabricated version of events.'

What the fuck? 'This is absolute bullshit. Why would I want to burn down my own house when I was about to sell it?'

'Oh, I don't know.' Adams pursed his lips in an exaggerated pout. 'Maybe revenge against your dead mother – we all know there was no love lost between the two of you. Or a way of destroying the house so you'd have the money to rebuild once the excessive payout came in. Any number of reasons, which we'll explore at the station.'

He gestured towards his lackey, who stepped forward once again, this time with a set of handcuffs. 'Eve Nicholls, you're under arrest for withholding evidence in a criminal investigation and suspicion of arson. You will be taken to Yarrabee police station for questioning. You do not have to say anything but anything you do say may be used as evidence against you. Do you understand?' Morris held the cuffs towards her, as if waiting for her to put them on herself.

'Is that really necessary?' Surely this was a joke. Some weird dream she would wake up from any minute, to find Banjo curled up on her bed in the folds of the doona. The ground beneath her feet turned cold, as if she was standing on a rapidly thinning biscuit of ice that could disintegrate any second. She flicked her gaze from the constable to Adams to Treloar, clenching her hand, the action second nature now after all the exercises, but on this occasion a reminder to keep her cool.

'As officers of the NSW police force, we have the authority to use handcuffs when arresting a suspect.' Adams' monotone statement said it all: he was the one with the power and she was nothing. He dropped his arms by his side and came to stand directly in front of her. 'This is an extremely serious matter, and it would be in your best interests to cooperate. Given that we have a witness statement and a piece of evidence you deliberately hid, we have enough to arrest you on the offence you've admitted to already: concealing evidence in a criminal investigation. But you should know that pending the results of the investigation you could be charged with arson. And given a firefighter lost his life in the blaze that started in this vicinity, possibly manslaughter.'

He nodded to Morris, who took her by the wrist and turned her around, pulling both her arms behind her back. The handcuffs locked with a click. Bit into the tender skin of the graft.

The repeated call of a wattle bird chimed, vibrating against the inside of her skull like an iron bell in a clock tower. Sounding out the seconds. One, two, three …

There'd been hardly any birds around since the fires – funny that one would appear now.

Everything around Eve turned hazy. She yawned deliberately, cracking the fog in her brain, dislodging the rock in her throat.

A whimper floated up from beside her feet.

'It's okay, matey.' The quiver in her voice said otherwise and Banjo moved closer, head tilted, looking up at her with his beautiful honey-coloured eyes.

'Can he come?' It was a stupid question, but she seemed to have lost any sense of logic. Any ability to think straight.

'No. We'll have him taken to the vet.' Adams stood firm.

Oh God, Hugh. The memory of his face as she'd dropped the pregnancy bombshell before leaving him standing on the street corner made her insides shrivel. What would he think of her when the police rocked up with her dog and told him she'd been arrested?

Only a few steps to the police car and yet it felt like kilometres, every footfall taking her further away from the life she'd envisaged – setting up home with her own flesh and blood – and rocketing her back into the uncertainty of the past. To an end, instead of a beginning. The same sense of dread she'd had in the dam that day with Margo as the flames surrounded them and they pulled the blanket over their heads, smothering themselves in darkness.

She stopped and waited while Morris opened the door, hazarded a glance at Daisy, where all her possessions were stored. A handful of clothes, a wooden box, and a few photos summarising everything that had gone before. Everyone who had left. Would it be here when she got back or would Margo, in her anger, have Harry come and collect it and dump all her belongings?

And what would happen to Banjo?

Eve's bones loosened. Her muscles melted. Everything in her wanted to crumble to the ground, collapse in a heap and bury her face in Banjo's soft brown fur. The last time she'd been ushered into the back of a police vehicle was the night Bec had died. Cold and wet, bare skin prickling inside the woollen blanket they'd thrown around her shoulders. The lake, a black expanse of glass under a moonless sky. Somewhere out there her sister lay tangled in the weed. Eyes open without seeing. Staring into the dark.

Adams had driven her into town for questioning then too, but with a few less stripes on his arm. A questioning that had been more of an interrogation after Todd had accused her of orchestrating the whole thing. Made sure his big-shot policeman brother knew the score. And she'd been happy to take the blame. Craved it even. Her punishment. Maybe this was karma after all: a final reckoning for her adolescent stupidity, for spending her life avoiding anything and everyone who would even remotely remind her of that night. For not making things right with Nell.

'Ms Nicholls?'

She looked up into the eyes of Constable Morris, who gestured towards the still-open door of the car. Climbing in, she slumped against the back of the seat, watched Treloar clip a lead to Banjo's collar and lead him into the second police car, as if he too was being taken in for questioning. As the car pulled away, she rested her elbow on the window frame, knuckles wedged against her cheekbone, gaze fixed on Banjo, her right arm folded against her belly. Holding on tight.

Chapter Twenty-Four

Riding through the mountains on Rain, wind ruffling her hair, the rhythmical beat of hooves beneath her body and the warm thud of the mare's blood pumping beneath her hands. Spring sunshine. Lemon-scented eucalypts. Water gurgling in a creek bed.

The bang of a door.

Eve's eyes flew open and weak sunlight flooded the back of the car. She blinked back to the here and now. Someone reached in and took her arm, pulling her out, as if she couldn't manage the movement herself. Not sweet alpine grass under her feet but the mottled concrete of a footpath. A group of people milling out the front of the police station. Hard faces turning towards her as Adams, gripping her elbow, led her towards the entrance.

Why had they parked out the front on the street? Surely there was a car park out back?

'Is there anything you can tell us about the arson investigation, Sergeant Adams?' A voice emerged from the murmuring crowd, and a thirty-something man stepped forward, flicking his shaggy fringe from his face. He stretched an arm out, phone nestled in his palm.

'Is she the one who did it?' A round woman in an oversized cardigan stood beside a balding man, hands in his pockets.

'Apparently.'

'You should be ashamed of yourself,' the woman hissed, and a globule of spit landed at Eve's feet.

Adams stopped, jerking her to a standstill beside him.

'Anything you can tell us about the arrest?' The man with the phone again. Closer now. More familiar. Ellis Harding, the reporter who had tried to interview her after the fires when she was still recovering in hospital. What was he doing here? What were any of them doing here?

'As you know, Mr Harding, this is an ongoing investigation so I'm unable to divulge any information about the case. Ms Nicholls is assisting us with our enquiries. As soon as we know any more, I'll certainly inform you.' Adams was in his element, chest puffed out, shoulders square, an air of pride in the upward jut of his chin. Playing to an audience.

Reality sparked like an old fashioned camera flash. He'd orchestrated this whole scene – let a few key people know he was bringing in Eve Nicholls, even tipped off the local paper. Hence the handcuffs and parking out the front in full public view. He was dragging her into the bear pit and feeding her to the dogs.

She yanked her arm away, but Adams reacted instantly, digging his fingers into her skin, letting her know he was the one calling the shots. 'Now, if you'll excuse us.' He moved forward once more, and the automatic doors of the station slid open, closing again with a hush and leaving the mob outside to gloat, to gossip, to spread the word that Nell Flanagan's daughter had been arrested for arson.

On the other end of the line, the ring tone sounded for the fifth time. 'Come on, pick up.'

The one phone call allowance scripted in all the television crime shows was apparently based in fact. Luckily, she'd had her phone in the pocket of her jeans and the number of the one person left in town who might actually be speaking to her was in her contacts list. Constable Treloar had dialled the number on the police station landline and now stood awkwardly by her side.

'Hello?' Finally, an answer.

'Hi Emily. It's Eve.

A short beat of silence. 'You sound a bit shaky. Is everything alright?'

Shaky was an understatement. 'I'm at the police station. I've been arrested.'

'What?'

'I could only make one call and you were the first person I thought of.' In fact, she'd thought of numerous people before Emily – Margo, Cat, Jack and Hugh – but telling them what was happening wasn't something she could even consider. Not when there was a chance they would assume her guilt. Emily was an outsider, objective enough to look at things without the emotional lens a local would have about the fires, without assumptions based on the past, but invested enough in what was happening to want to – hopefully – help.

'What are they charging you with?'

In the glass cabinet on the wall, an assortment of fabric badges from all over Australia and the world – NYPD, Halifax, Canada – were pinned like dead butterflies in a lepidopterist's cabinet, like in that John Fowles book about the creep who abducted the woman and added her to his collection.

'Eve? Are you there?'

Her stomach clenched. She ran a hand over the graftline on her arm, where the graze now looked a little angrier after its altercation with the handcuffs. She could hang up now and forget involving Emily. Answer the questions and accept her fate. But that would mean giving up any hope of staying on at Mossy Creek.

One deep breath. *Go.* 'They found a jerry can on my property. Luke Harris is claiming I set him up to light the fire so I could claim the insurance money and give him a cut.'

'A jerry can? Sorry, where did they find it?'

'In my barn.'

'That's where Luke left it?'

'No.' Eve coughed to clear her throat. Time to come clean. 'I found it and stored it there so Luke wouldn't be implicated if someone came across it in the bush. I wanted to talk to him first. Make sure he didn't know anything about it before I went to the police.'

'How long ago was that?'

Fuck. Just say it. 'A couple of weeks ago.'

A sigh sounded on the other end of the line. Eve's mouth tasted like sandpaper: dry and coarse. Waiting for Emily's response was like waiting for the verdict from the school principal after she'd been caught jigging class so she could spend the afternoon with Jack. Like waiting for Nell to blow a gasket when the truancy had once again been reported.

'Why didn't you tell me about this, Eve?' That neversurprising tone of disappointment.

'I'm sorry. I should have. I just ...' *Didn't want to look like an idiot so I pretended it wasn't there? Lame.* 'I don't know.' Her initial motivation of protecting Luke had well and truly backfired and now seemed like a pathetic excuse from a person with something to hide. 'I guess I was worried it would make me look guilty.'

'You thought I'd believe that of you? That your friends would believe it?'

'You don't know me from a bar of soap, Emily. From where you're standing, the police could be right. I could be spinning you a whole lot of lies to keep you onside. Or so you'd track Luke down and then I could pin it on him.'

'Sounds like you're starting to believe all that shit they're accusing you of, Eve. It's called paranoia.'

'Time's up.' Constable Morris appeared, tapping the face of his watch. Adams' mannerisms were rubbing off on the poor guy, but there was a hint of kindness in the way he averted his gaze, the grace he had to not quite meet her eye.

Eve looked up at him and then back to the phone. 'I have to go. They're going to interview me now. Look, I don't really know why I called you.' *Lie.* 'I'm not sure what will happen, so I wanted to let someone know. Banjo is being taken the vet's – to Hugh's place. Could you …'

A shard of glass inserted itself in her throat and her voice splintered. The thought she could be locked up within the next few hours was nothing compared to the idea of not seeing Banj again. Of what would happen to him if … no, it didn't bear thinking about.

'Don't say a word to the police without legal representation. I'm on my way.'

Emily ended the call before there was any chance to say thank you, any chance to confess she didn't have a clue who to call to arrange a lawyer.

The constable held out his hand and nodded at the

phone. She let him take it, her palm clammy in its absence. Pushing herself to her feet was like trying to stand upright under a mountain of sludge.

A wave of exhaustion washed over her as Morris's outline blurred and wavered, as two of him appeared before her. The room began to spin, the badges in the cabinet taking flight, butterflies suddenly released from their cage. Eve tried to steady herself against the wall, but it too was on the move, shifting sidewards.

Her vision swam. Her knees buckled. Her head hit the floor with a loud crack.

Chapter Twenty-Five

Memories of her last visit to Casualty were hazy: a kaleidoscope of squeaking trolleys, hurried voices and concerned faces – one of them Cat's – but not much else other than the excruciating pain from the burn before her meds were topped up.

This time, it was all perfectly clear: an unfamiliar nurse at her bedside, getting her details and asking questions about her pregnancy, all without a single reference to the circumstances of her collapse. Not that she wouldn't be wondering, dying to know why her patient had been delivered to the hospital door in a police car, and why Constable Morris had taken up a chair in the waiting room.

There was a dull throb above Eve's temple. She ran her hand over the dressing.

'Not too bad. About six stitches, so it shouldn't be much of a scar. You must have hit that floor hard.' The red-haired nurse unwrapped the cuff of the blood pressure machine and gave a concerned half-smile. 'Still a bit low. Have you been drinking much?'

'Drinking?' The three-quarter full bottle of bourbon in the cabinet above the caravan sink had been a temptation more than once, but in highly uncharacteristic fashion she had resisted.

'Water. You need to keep hydrated.'

Of course, the nurse wasn't talking about alcohol. Maybe that knock on the head had done more damage than a cut.

'Drink double the amount of water you usually do.' Despite her youth, the nurse had a do-as-I-say-or-else manner. 'What about diet? Eaten anything much today?'

Had she? The shakiness of her insides suggested not. But the whole day had been such a blur, it was hard to remember. 'I don't think so.'

'Okay, well I know that whole eating-for-two thing is a cliché, but you really are. You need to eat regular healthy meals.'

'So, that's why I passed out, not eating and drinking enough?'

'Fainting is a sign of low blood pressure. In pregnancy, your blood flow is rerouted to the foetus, and your hormones are all over the place. Could be low blood sugar or iron levels. Or all of the above. You need to look after yourself, eat well, and see your doctor for regular check-ups. We'll send the details of what happened today on to Doctor Woods. She's busy at the surgery, otherwise she would have been attending to you.'

'Okay. Thanks.' Thank the lord Cat hadn't been available.

'Doctor Zhang advised you stay for a couple of hours, until your blood pressure is stable. 'It's up to you but …' The nurse turned her head towards the door and then back again, shifting closer to the bed. 'The policeman who brought you in was called out on a job. He asked us to let him know when you were ready to leave and he'd come and collect you.'

Back to the station for questioning.

By now, half the town would know she'd been taken in, thanks to the greeting committee Adams orchestrated outside the police station. He probably thought she'd faked the collapse to get out of being questioned. Not that the delay was a bad thing, but she may as well face the inevitable. Sooner rather than later. Staying and making a home at Mossy Creek had been pie in the sky, a ridiculous daydream, one that was rapidly turning into a nightmare. And there was only one way out of a nightmare: wake up and face reality.

'I can stay here until the police come and pick me up?'

'That won't be happening.' Emily strode into the room in her usual uniform of jeans, crisp white shirt and perfectly fitted blazer.

One glance at the look of stark determination on the journalist's face and the nurse pushed the blood pressure machine against the wall. 'I'll arrange some sandwiches to be brought in. Let me know if you need anything else.' She pointed to the full glass of water sitting on the cabinet by the bed. 'And make sure you drink all that.'

Emily deposited her bag on the end of the bed and perched beside it as the nurse made herself scarce. 'How are you feeling?'

'Head's a bit sore. Apparently I'm dehydrated and have low blood pressure.'

'Being man-handled by the local constabulary wouldn't have helped.' It had been Emily who insisted Eve was brought into hospital when she'd arrived to find her semi-conscious and bleeding on the floor of the police station. Being completely honest with her was only right.

'I'm pregnant.' Those same two words that didn't seem to want to be contained.

Emily gave a couple of slow, considered nods. 'So, that explains the peppermint tea. And the soda water at the gallery opening.'

'Yup.'

'Not that there's anything wrong with either, although getting through the day without caffeine would be anathema to me.'

'Me too, believe me.' The conversation was surprisingly cheery considering the news Eve had just delivered. Emily had taken it in her stride. 'I'm sorry I didn't say anything. It's early days and …'

'Not my business, Eve.'

'I appreciate that, but you may as well know. After today, everybody else will.'

'I guess it complicates your situation. But at least it's bought you some time.'

'Time?'

'When Adams wouldn't let me ride along with you down here to the hospital, we had a little chat. I got my friend Brook on Facetime. She's a hotshot criminal lawyer and she reminded him that the presumption of innocence is a fundamental principle of Australian law, and that he'd overstepped in handcuffing you and dragging you in for questioning in such an aggressive manner.'

The invisible weight of the handcuffs chafed at Eve's wrists. Emily had some balls confronting Adams. 'How did he take it?'

'He got stroppy at first, but when Brook told him she

was representing you and had a background in dealing with police misconduct, he backed right off.'

A smile ruptured the banging in her head. If only she'd been there to see Adams get his comeuppance. 'How did she get away with that?'

'Because it's the truth.' Emily pulled a business card from her bag and handed it across, the same way she had that day in *Something Brewing* when they'd first met. Only this card had a different name and title. *Brook Perry. Criminal Defence Lawyer.* 'I did a double degree in law and journalism. That's where I met Brook, and we've been friends ever since. Initially I decided on law because it paid better, but after a few years of defending criminals and listening to their bullshit stories – which I had to pretend to believe – I'd had enough. I decided I'm more interested in what makes people tick, why they do what they do, so I switched back to journalism. But Ms Perry has gone from strength to strength. She's a partner in one of the top law firms in Sydney, and she's happy to take on your case – pro-bono – as a favour to me.'

Taking in everything Emily was saying was like trying to do complicated algorithms without a calculator, especially with the jackhammer operating behind Eve's eyes. All she could do was shake her head.

'*If* there ends up being a case. Brook reminded the sergeant that until the bushfire investigators have completed their assessment and come up with conclusive evidence that you in particular had deliberately started the fire, that it was the word of a seventeen-year-old – who already has a record of fire-lighting – against someone who has no police record and little if any motive to torch her own property. She may also have hinted that the case smacks of a witch hunt and that she'd be happy to pass on the details to her father, who is a barrister with a brilliant record of exposing police corruption.'

The story kept getting better. 'Holy hell. I can imagine how well that went down.'

An orderly arrived with the promised plate of sandwiches and placed them on the tray beside the bed. A sudden pang of hunger had Eve downing a triangle in an instant. She swallowed quickly, processing the information. 'So where does that leave things?'

'You are officially a person of interest in the case, but until they have actual proof that you were responsible, you will not be taken into custody and are free to go home on the provision that you stay in the area.'

'What about the concealing evidence charge?' Surely she couldn't be off the hook on that count.

'Currently no proof it's connected to the bushfires.'

All the tension Eve's body had been holding evaporated and she sank back into the pillows. 'I notice Adams isn't here to inform me of this himself.'

Emily laughed. 'I think he's still at the station licking his wounds.'

'Or trying to rustle up more crap to pin on me.'

'Well, at least he knows now that he can't pull any more stunts.' Emily's brow furrowed. 'I've been wondering exactly why the good sergeant has it in for you, so I started doing a bit of digging. Adams is married. No kids. But a bizarrely symbiotic relationship with his younger brother.'

'Todd?'

'Hmm hmm. Apparently after your sister died, Adams junior went completely off the rails. Brent had a hard time reining him in, and then he was transferred up the coast. While he was gone, Todd was picked up for a few things – car theft and joyriding, a few minor assaults, drug possession

– but always managed to avoid being incarcerated. Then when Adams came back, all the wrongdoing seemed to stop.'

'Todd was pulled into line by his big brother?'

'Maybe.' Emily raised her eyebrows. 'Or maybe big brother made the charges go away.'

'I wouldn't put it past Adams to sweep things under the carpet. He wouldn't want his reputation tarnished.'

'From what I gather,' Emily said, 'he's very protective of his younger sibling. Both their parents died when Todd was in his early teens and Brent took on responsibility for him.'

Once again Emily was leading her down a path to an unknown destination. 'Where are you going with all this?'

'Remember I told you Luke Harris was expelled for lighting the fire?' Emily waited for her nod of recognition. 'Well, he'd previously been caught smoking dope behind the toilets. One of Luke's mates has a very loose tongue. He let slip that Luke sold the stuff too, and that he had this weird friendship with his supplier. An older guy he'd started hanging out with who lived alone. They played video games, got wasted and occasionally lit fires just for kicks.'

Each individual bone in Eve's skull contracted, as if her head had been placed inside an invisible vice and the handle turned too many times. Heat burned her cheeks. All this time she'd been trying to protect Luke, seen him as a maligned misguided teenager, but now everything pointed to that being a total lie.

'Guess who his supplier is?'

The way Emily phrased the question made it sound like it could be someone she knew, but there was only a handful of people she'd reconnected with since her return, and it certainly wouldn't be any of them. She let out a sigh. 'Honestly, my brain hurts thinking about all this. I have no idea.'

'Todd Adams.' Emily announced the name with a sense of triumph.

'Todd?!' He'd always been a loser. It wasn't a surprise that he was into drugs – using or pushing. As desperate as she'd been in those first few months after losing herself in the city, she'd never let herself go down that path. Maybe Nell had succeeded in knocking some common sense into her, after all. But hearing Todd was a firebug and had a relationship with Luke was the opposite of satisfying: it made the egg sandwich she'd just eaten turn to rubble.

'So, there's a connection between Luke and Todd.' Emily kept talking, briskly now, as if this new information meant something important. 'And of course, there's a link between Todd and his brother the sergeant, and between Luke's father and the sergeant.'

'But what exactly does that all mean?'

Emily slumped back in her chair. 'That's what we need to find out. Todd's actual whereabouts is a mystery. He's a recluse. Lived with his brother until the wife had enough and kicked him out. He's seen around town occasionally but doesn't seem to be employed anywhere or have any meaningful relationships with anyone outside his family other than Luke. Is there anyone you can think of who might know anything about him?'

'I haven't lived here for twenty years, remember.'

'I know, but still. Small town, and all that.'

Catching up with Todd Adams hadn't exactly been Eve's top priority on her return. Nor had checking in on his wellbeing. But … 'Jack did mention a while back that he's in the RFS. Maybe he knows something more about him.'

'Worth a shot. Could you find out?'

The idea of talking to Jack, who had been caught red-handed looking at a photo of her semi-clad younger self was not appealing. But the conversation might be crucial in securing her freedom. 'I'll see what I can do.'

'And I'll keep asking questions too. Might try and ingratiate myself with Dean Harris.'

'Good luck with that.'

Emily arched one perfectly groomed eyebrow. 'He might be happy to spill some dirt on the woman who is suspected of arson and trying to pin it on his son, maybe give away a few other things in the process. Now, how about I break you out of here. I can drop you home.'

The prospect of getting away from the glaring white walls and disinfectant-coated floors of the hospital was enticing. 'The hospital is supposed to notify Morris when I'm ready to leave.'

'No need for that now Adams has backed off.' Emily gave a wicked schoolgirl grin. She was a rebel at heart, probably what made her so good at her job, and why they got on so well.

'Well, the nurse did say I could leave once I'd rested.'

'Great. Let's go.' Emily picked up her handbag. 'But promise me there'll be no more fainting or splitting open parts of your body. I don't deal well with blood.'

'I promise.' Eve swung her legs over the edge of the bed, touched her feet to the floor and stood. No spinning walls, no weird sensations, the ground solid and sure beneath her feet. 'Ah, my phone. It's still at the police station.'

'Nope, it's right here.' Emily pulled it from her coat pocket and handed it across. 'A few missed calls. Sorry, I couldn't help but notice.'

Eve glanced down at the screen. Five missed calls, all from Hugh. Not so long ago seeing his name on the text messages had made her insides bubble. Now it turned them completely flat. Probably the same way he'd felt when she told him they would never be any more than friends and then threw in the pregnancy hand grenade for good measure. Still, he had Banjo, and the sooner she collected him the better. 'Okay if we make a pitstop?'

'Sure.'

Chapter Twenty-Six

'I'll go grab some petrol and come back.'

'Thanks.' Eve closed the door of Emily's hatchback and turned to face the vet surgery. A wave of nausea rolled deep in the pit of her belly. Maybe if she gave a loud whistle Banj would hear it and come running. Then they could bolt together, and she wouldn't have to face Hugh. If only it were that easy. Life had a way of making you face your fuckups, sometimes sooner, sometimes later, and right now it was shoving them in her face and making her deal with them one by excruciating one.

Okay. Do it. Start walking.

At least, being early afternoon, the surgery was officially closed for operations and home visits. Which meant Hugh might not even be there. Only one way to find out. She zipped up her jacket and ran her hands over her middle. Flat. Normal. At least on the outside.

Stop dithering. Get it over and done with.

Another three torturous paces and she was at the door. A figure appeared on the other side, and a tall woman, wavy blonde bob tucked behind her ears, pushed it open and joined her at the entrance. 'Hi. Eve, right? We haven't officially met, but I've seen you around. I'm Darcy. I help Hugh out occasionally.' She thrust her hand forward and surprised Eve into shaking it.

'Nice to meet you.' Her voice sounded robotic, as if the response had been programmed in advance, but it was all she could manage.

'I just met your kelpie. What a gorgeous boy. He's been watching the door the whole time, so I'll leave you to it. Off to do a house call. Hope to see you again sometime.'

Darcy breezed away, leaving Eve standing at the open door. *Now or never*. Emily would be back before too long.

She stepped into the reception room and a flood of memories washed through the shallows of her brain: Banj limp in her arms, his gums a scary shade of white when she carried him in after the snake bite; Hugh showing her into the small living room out back where he'd already made up the sofa bed and placed a vase of orange gerberas on the table; the minty aroma of the leftover roast dinner he'd warmed and cut up for her when she could only use one hand. Tiny pieces of glitter floating in the snow globe of her mind, then sinking to the bottom and taking with them any illusions her body might have harboured about her relationship with Hugh being more than platonic.

'Eve.' The man himself, coat in hand. 'I was just closing up to come to the police station.'

'Beat you to it.' She tried for jovial, but the levity fell flat. The smile she attempted was no more than a twist of her lips, and Hugh's expression remained blank. Maybe not the right time for humour. 'I came to pick up Banj. Thanks for looking after him.'

Hugh did a doubletake. 'That's it? That's all you have to

say?' He gave a brief shake of his head. 'You're unbelievable.'

Better this way, having him pissed off with her, than the look of longing in his eyes the last time they'd spoken. Easier to make the break. 'Well, I am who I am, Hugh. I'm sorry if that upsets you.'

He moved forward and past her, flipped the 'Closed' sign of the door and pushed it shut.

'What are you doing?'

'Can we talk about the fact that you were arrested? What's going on?' He pointed to her temple where the stitches were hidden beneath a dressing – another one!

Even the thought of telling Hugh the whole sordid story drained what was left of her rapidly dwindling energy supply. Walking, talking, thinking – all of it was an effort. Her head pounded and her arms and legs were more like the hinged appendages of a marionette than those of a living, functioning human. Judging by the steely look in Hugh's gaze, he wasn't going to let her get away without some kind of answer, but she could keep it brief. Basic facts.

'I fainted at the police station. Low blood pressure. Hit my head on the way down and ended up with a couple of stitches.' That wasn't all he'd asked about. 'The arrest thing … it's being sorted. A misunderstanding.'

Hugh pointed to the bench seat beneath the window. 'Eve, can we sit for a minute and have a talk?'

'I can't. A friend – Emily – is picking me up. I just need to grab Banjo.' A whine started up from behind the reception room wall, followed by a high-pitched yelp.

'Is that right? A friend? I thought I was your friend, Eve.' He gestured to the space between them, gesticulating from himself to her and back. 'I thought we were friends. But apparently not. You dump your baby bombshell on me and drive off into the night. You didn't think to call me when you were taken to the police station?'

'No, I …'

'No. Of course not.' He was on a roll. Hands flying. Brow collapsed into a frown. 'Why would you call me? I'm only the sucker who tried to help save your house when it burnt down, visited you in hospital – while minding your dog – invited you to stay, cooked you meals and generally tried to make your life a little easier.'

'I know that, Hugh, and I appreciate it. I do. But …'

'I'm not saying all this because I want you to feel obligated, Eve. That's not my point.'

'Then what is?'

'Friends look out for each other. They take care of each other. When the chips are down, they ask for help. It's not a one-way street. There has to be an element of reciprocity. Of trust. Why couldn't you trust in our friendship enough to call me, and not some random journalist you barely know?'

Trust. There was the crux of the matter. Ever since Bec's death, she had mastered the skill of keeping people at arm's length. Of relying on no one but herself, because in the end everybody let you down. Because it was safer to bury your battered heart beneath a layer of permafrost than let it thaw. But that meant isolating yourself. Pushing people away, even when you needed them most. Hurting them instead of being hurt.

Hugh didn't deserve it, but he'd thank her for it in the end. Be glad he'd dodged the bullet.

'You made it clear that you wanted to be more than friends, Hugh, and that isn't possible.'

He opened his mouth, only to close it again. Shoulders dropping, he caved in on himself and gave a slow shake of his head. The coolness of her tone seemed to have done the trick. 'Well, considering the fact that you're pregnant there's obviously someone else.'

Should she explain? Try to help him understand why getting involved with her would be a mistake? Or better to go with his assumption that she was with the father of the child she was carrying? As hurtful as it seemed, it would make it easier for them both to walk away.

Yes. One syllable, and that would be it. The lie would do its trick. But the word stuck to her tongue like a piece of hot ice, jamming itself behind her teeth and refusing to be uttered.

'It's complicated.'

'I'm sure it is.' This time there was resignation in Hugh's words, flavoured with a sprinkling of bitterness. 'I'll get your dog.'

Turning away, he disappeared into the back of the surgery.

Eve's heartbeat may have slowed when she fainted, but it had ramped up again now, knocking away inside her ribs like a wild animal caught in a trap. Her tactic had worked. And yet, there was no sense of victory.

Banjo skittered around the corner and bounced up and down at her feet, eyes bright, tail whirring like a propeller. Hugh followed and handed across the lead the police had attached when they'd put the dog in the car. All that was left to do now was leave.

'Thanks, Hugh.' *Nowhere near enough.* 'Look, I …'

'It's fine, Eve. You've made things perfectly clear. No need to explain further.' He glanced down at his watch. 'I have a procedure to do, so—'

'Of course. I'll leave you to it.' She clipped the lead to Banjo's collar and stepped through the door Hugh had opened. It shut behind her before she had a chance to turn around, his shadow disappearing through the frosted glass into the bowels of the surgery.

CLOSED. The red sign, printed neatly in capital letters said it all.

A spot of rain hit her forehead. She swiped it away as another splatted against the paving at her feet, fat drops plopping onto the faux suede of her jacket. Out on the street Emily's car waited. She made her way towards it, Banjo making a pitstop en route. She lowered her head against the rapidly falling rain, forcing her weary legs to move, cold gripping her limbs and a sharp ache burning behind her eyes.

Chapter Twenty-Seven

Sitting alone, book in hand, wind battering the sides of the caravan and rain hammering onto the roof, wasn't an ideal way to be spending the night but it suited Eve's current mood. Declining Emily's invitation to stay at her Air B&B – despite its 'no dogs allowed' rule, or for her to stay on for some company – had been the right move. She needed time to process everything that had happened in the last twenty-four hours, and that meant she needed time alone.

Apart from Banj, of course. He'd been an A-grade cling-on since they'd been reunited, and now lay curled into a ball on her bed, eyes closed, deep in slumber. Despite total exhaustion, sleep was impossible, a beguiling prankster luring her into dreamland only to mock her as she stood on the brink waiting to fall. Reading was a waste of time, her concentration not even lasting for a paragraph before lapsing, instead revisiting every ridiculous minute of the day, tormenting her with the incomprehensible facts.

Fact: Brent Adams, for some nefarious reason, was hell-bent on charging her with arson.

Fact: Luke Harris, for some unknown reason, had lied about her to the police.

Fact: Hugh Robertson, for reasons completely of her own doing, would most likely never speak to her again.

A tingling started in the back of her neck, spreading across her shoulders and down into her chest. Creeping through her body like a winter fog, numbing every cell as it filled the empty spaces inside. There was no point dwelling on the final fact. It had been done out of necessity. He was better off without her – not that they'd even been a 'thing'. Only a glimmering possibility she'd hardly let herself consider.

The book wasn't cutting it. *Thanks for nothing, Stephen King.*

Tossing the book on the bed, she stood and reached into the cupboard, rummaging about behind the small rack of shirts and jeans and the single dress that made up her entire wardrobe. Her hands landed on Grandpa's timber box. She pulled it out and placed it on the table, ran her palm over its time-smooth lid and flipped open the lock.

Here it was, her whole family history contained in one handmade heirloom. Thank God she'd had the smarts to keep at least some of the old photos from Nell's collection, and the foresight to grab it when she left the house. Nell's letter sat right on the top. No need to re-read it – it was already committed to memory and had gone some way to mending the torn fabric of their mother-daughter relationship. Albeit too late.

She dug down and pulled out a handful of photos, laid them on the table like a set of tarot cards, and chose one at random.

'Hmph, that'd be right. No letting me out of your clutches.'

Out of the Ashes

A black-and-white photo of Nell, clad in a one-piece swimsuit, her hair windswept, wearing a faint smile as she reclined in the back of a rowboat. She was young. Probably in her early twenties, way before she'd had children. Before life had taken the twists and turns that left her a single mother, doing everything she could to keep food on the table and her children safe and happy.

Eve stared into the young woman's eyes. 'Would you have done it all again despite the way things turned out?'

Yes I would have. No question. But I might have done a few things differently.

The voice startled her. It was Nell's, without question. Low and throaty. Each word slow and deliberate.

Eve straightened, looked around the caravan. No one there and yet the voice had been clear as a church bell, drowning out the cacophony outside. She shook it away and stuck the photo back in the box. There'd been a few times before the fires when she'd been in the house and thought she'd seen a woman standing in the doorway. Always at night, when she was tired and overwrought. Like now.

Another photo. This one of her holding a newborn Bec, looking down with an expression of pure wonder. They'd had their moments growing up, fought on occasions as all siblings do, but that sense of reverence Eve had felt for her baby sister had never disappeared. If only she'd listened when Bec said she didn't want to go to the lake. They'd have stayed home watching TV, snuggled up beside each other on the lounge, legs tangled together beneath a crocheted blanket.

It's ancient history, Sis. Let it go.

This time, the soft, whispery tones of her sister's voice echoed through the inside of the caravan. What the—

A flash of white light electrified the night through the

curtained windows. A rolling boom. An ear-splitting crack. The van fell into darkness.

Synapses crackling, Eve grabbed her phone, flicked on the light and stood up. Found the candle on the bench and struck a match. The wick sizzled and caught, the aromatic scent of vanilla wafting into the air.

Through the gloom, Banjo sat up and gave a low moan. He was generally okay with storms, but the lightning bolt that had taken out the power was a doozy.

'You're alright, my man.' Eve gave him a pat, and he dropped his head back between his paws. Sliding onto the bench seat behind the table, her gaze fell once more to the photo of Bec. She shoved it to one side and turned to the next in the pile. Her: sitting on a buckskin horse, bare legs astride its barrel of a belly, holding a tussock of mane and grinning into the camera like a warrior queen.

You can't hide inside this caravan forever, you know?

Oh God, her own voice now. Or at least that of her thirteen-year-old self. Should she shut it down like she had the others, or let it speak? Goosebumps prickled the skin on the back of her neck. She clenched her teeth and leaned in, closer to the image of her younger self.

Hugh was right. Relationships are a two-way street. You can't push people away and then be miserable when they go.

'That's not—'

Do not dare use the word 'fair'. Life. Is. Not. Fair. You already know that. You might have made a few mistakes but nothing that can't be fixed.

The flare of the candle caught Eve's eye, glowing warm and orange in the darkness, but she flicked her attention back to Angie in the photograph, willing her to continue.

Fact: You're having this baby.

Fact: You want to make a home and a life here at Mossy Creek.

Fact: You need to clear your name once and for all.
Nothing new there.
Fact: You need to do it fast, and you can't do it alone.
You've got a chance to make a life for yourself here, Eve. Now get out there and do it.

She blinked at the photo, and the vibrancy it held faded. The conversation was over. So much wisdom for a girl who'd never seen life beyond the small town where she'd been raised. But of course, that was the point: her childhood-self saw the world simply, with all the crappy layers life had added over the years stripped away.

A strange feeling whirred at the back of her throat, vibrating through her chest and deep inside the chambers of her heart. It was time she listened to her younger, wiser self. Let go of all the crippling beliefs she'd clung to for the last two decades. Yes, she was independent and didn't need anyone to survive. But wasn't life about more than survival? Wasn't it better shared? Filled with joy and laughter and love and trust.

Friends look out for each other. They take care of each other. When the chips are down, they ask for help.

Hugh's voice this time, the words he'd said only this afternoon. Words she'd known at the time were so right but was unable to fully hear. The facts were all there. And now was the time for action.

Chapter Twenty-Eight

Driving along Mossy Creek Road, hands wrapped around the steering wheel, Eve leant forward and peered into the inky blackness. The wipers swished as they traversed the windscreen, clunked as they met the rubber and returned with a faint screech. Forward and back, forward and back. Rain pelting on the glass. Wind buffeting the van, forcing her fingers to tighten their grip.

Banjo lay on the floor between the two front seats, safer there in the walk-through space than perched on the passenger seat – if she had to jam the brakes on, he'd go flying, and neither of them needed more injuries. Focusing on the driving meant she didn't have to think about where she was going or whether a visit was prudent. The series of thoughts which had triggered the crazy idea had moved her up and out of the caravan within minutes, pumping more than adrenaline through her veins. Every muscle in her body was on alert; her vision tunnelled to the mental map she'd drawn of her route. The sooner she got there, the sooner she'd be able to piece together the puzzle.

She drove on, blocking distractions as they rose their hands for attention inside her brain, nothing but the destination in mind. Right onto the road into town, right again before the main drag, a final left-hand turn before she pulled into the kerb. It was 9.52 according to the blue digits glowing on the dashboard. Not exactly the best time for a visit, but then this wasn't a popping-in-for-a-cuppa kind of call.

'Wait here, Banj.'

He looked up at the click of the door and groaned.

Pulling the hood of her jacket over her head, she dashed down the front path before shoving it off under the shelter of the bullnose veranda. A light sprang on as her feet traversed the timber decking.

Her chest heaved and she took a long slow breath. Who would open the door? Only one way to find out.

Raising her hand, she rapped against the weatherboard panels. Would they even hear it above the din? Gusts of wind battered the limbs of the deciduous trees in the front yard, whipping leaves from their branches and sending them somersaulting through the air. Water pooled at her feet beside the sodden door mat where a set of olive-green spotted gumboots lay on their side, toppled against a smaller purple pair covered in miniature rainbows.

No sound from inside the house. Maybe they hadn't heard? Eve knocked again, a faster rhythm this time, the action infused with the same sense of urgency that had brought her here.

A lock clunked. The door cracked open. Not fully, but enough to reveal Cat bunching the collar of her dressing gown to her neck. 'Eve. What are you doing here?'

'I need to talk to Jack.' No point pussyfooting around.

'That's not possible.'

'Cat, I know you're mad. And I don't blame you. But you have to believe me there is nothing going on between Jack and me. Whatever there was, it's long gone. I don't know why he was looking at that photo – probably just taking a jaunt down memory lane.' Even as she said it, the thought made her cringe. 'Please, Cat, I would never compromise our friendship that way. I only want the best for both of you.'

'What's so urgent that you need to speak with him at this time of night?' Cat leant forward, squinting through the wire. 'What's that on your head?'

Instinct lifted her hand to her temple, touched her fingers to the plaster. So, Cat hadn't heard about any of today's events? 'I fainted in the police station this afternoon, after being arrested. Banged my head and cut it open. Six stitches.'

'Arrested?' Cat unlocked the screen door. 'You'd better come in.'

Finally! She followed Cat from the foyer into the lounge room and out to the kitchen. Water dripped from her jacket onto the polished wood floor. She unzipped it and slipped it off. 'Sorry.'

Cat took it and ducked into the adjacent laundry, tying the cord of her dressing gown into a knot as she returned. 'She gestured towards the stool at the island bench. 'I've popped it in the dryer. Take a seat.'

Taking the weight off her feet was a relief, but the weird quiet filling the room set Eve's teeth on edge. She'd come to see Jack, not to review the events of the day, but Cat slid a glass of water across the bench and stood behind it, like a bartender ready for the story.

Where to start? So far Cat knew nothing about the arson accusations, unless she'd heard them on the grapevine, so that was probably the spot. Recounting the strange details of the last few weeks was like giving a summary of a movie, one that was still playing since the ending was yet to be revealed.

Arms crossed, Cat listened intently, her expression growing increasingly bewildered as the most recent plot points were detailed. No attempts to interrupt or comment, but perhaps a slight softening of the hard corners she'd had at the start of the conversation.

'From what Emily found out, there's a link between Todd Adams and Luke that could be the key to sorting out this whole mess. That's why I wanted to see Jack. He mentioned Todd was in the RFS. I thought he might know a bit more about him or be able to tell me where he lives.'

'Todd Adams. Urgh.' A visible shudder rippled through Cat's body as she repeated the name. 'He's a piece of work.'

'Always was.'

'You're not planning on going to see him, are you?'

'No, I …' Her plan hadn't gone beyond seeing Jack. 'Why?'

Cat shook her head. 'Like I said, he's a creep. Keeps to himself most of the time from what I gather, but back in the day he was well known for being on the other side of the law. And never getting charged with anything.'

'Helps to have big brother protecting you.' A shiver skittered across the back of Eve's neck at the memory of Brent pulling his younger sibling away when he'd bailed her up at the community meeting.

'Haven't heard much about him lately. I assumed he'd moved, or at least mended his ways.'

'At the very minimum, he's a drug supplier, and Emily's source said he and Luke lit fires together.'

'Right.' Cat's mouth twitched. She stared into the distance. 'Hence your interest in finding him.'

'Yes.' They'd been carrying on an almost normal conversation for a good fifteen minutes despite the arctic greeting at the front door, but it was time to get back to the purpose of the visit. 'Hence me disturbing you at such a ridiculous hour.'

'I'm sorry, Eve, Jack's not here.'

'Oh, where is he?'

Cat swallowed. She bit down on her bottom lip as she inhaled. 'He's moved into the granny flat behind his brother's house.'

'Moved in? As in, moved out?'

'Yes, Eve, he's no longer living here.'

Shit. Things were worse than she'd expected. 'Was that his idea or yours?'

'Mine.' Tears pooled in Cat's eyes. 'I can't do it anymore. The mood swings, the anger he's bottling up. I know he's going through a lot, but I've pleaded with him to get help and he flat out refuses. We've been fighting. All the time. It's not good for Lilly. Then …' Cat looked up and a tear trickled from the corner of her eye. 'Finding him with that photo was the last straw. He wouldn't explain himself, just shoved past me and refused to talk about it so I jumped to the wrong conclusion. About you, at least. I'm sorry.'

'That's okay. I probably would have done the same.'

'No, it's not okay. I should have known you wouldn't do anything like that. I should have trusted you.'

'It's not like we know each other that well these days, Cat.'

'No, we're not. But I know you're a good person. Just like I knew it twenty years ago and still acted like an idiot, turned my back on you when I should have supported you.

That won't happen again, Eve. This whole arson scenario is a farce.'

'Agreed.' Eve choked out the word. Were they friends again?

'Oh, Eve.' Cat rounded the bench and in a second they were in each other's arms.

She inhaled the scent of musky soap perfuming Cat's skin and closed her eyes against the silky auburn curls. Having Cat back on side was like slipping into a rose-scented bath, warm and comforting. But there was still a long way to go before she was in the clear. Adams would be on the case, doing whatever he could to find more evidence against her. He already had one dodgy witness statement — there was a chance he could drum up more.

'Do you think it would be okay if I went to see Jack?'

Cat's mouth curled into an almost evil grin. 'Absolutely. With a bit of luck, you'll wake him up.'

'I'll do my best.'

'Grant's address is 24 Turiel Lane. Keep going down this road to the end and turn right. It's in the new housing estate. Granny flat is out the back.'

'Great.' Eve slid off the stool. 'I'll get going.'

'Wait a tick!'

Cat disappeared back into the laundry, returning with the rain jacket, and held it up. Eve slid her arms into the now-dry nylon sleeves, the lingering warmth seeping through her skin. Her eyes watered and stung. She lowered her head and latched the zip.

'Are you sure you're okay?' Cat's frown was back.

'Yeah. All good.' She sniffed away the emotional epilogue to their conversation. No time for sooking. 'Probably the bloody hormones.'

A gentle smile lit Cat's eyes. 'There's a lot more of that

to come.' She led the way to the front door and pushed it open. 'Let me know how it goes. But promise me you will not go chasing Todd Adams on your own. Find out where he lives and pass the information on.'

'To who? His police sergeant brother?'

Cat's shoulders slumped. 'Maybe your journalist friend has some ideas about the next step?'

'I'm sure she will.' Not completely sure, but Cat had enough to worry about without adding to her load. 'Thank you, Cat. I'll keep you in the loop.'

One last warm, fuzzy hug, and Eve headed back to the van, to the usual where-have-you-been-all-this-time greeting from Banj. She started the ignition and took one last look through the rain-streaked window; Cat, dressing gown firmly tied, still stood at the open door.

Chapter Twenty-Nine

By the time Eve pulled up outside Grant Mitchell's house, the rain had eased to a light sprinkle. The house was shrouded in darkness. She unlatched the side gate and crept down the path towards the small building at the back of the yard, where a dim light bled around the edges of a shuttered window. Hopefully that meant Jack was awake.

One sharp knock was all it took for the door to fly open.

'Hi, can I come in?' Her voice was surprisingly upbeat. The conversation with Cat had bolstered her courage, given her a much-needed boost of optimism, and there was no way Jack was going to drag her back down.

He looked haggard, wearing worn tracky pants, his usually tanned face pale and his eyes bloodshot. He gave a half shrug, pushed the door open and deposited himself on the sofa, flicking off the TV with a remote, before sticking his hands in the pockets of his hoodie.

His actions were more like those of a belligerent teenager than a grown man. A canvas duffle bag sat at his feet, clothes spilling out onto the floor. On the end of the kitchen bench sat an opened bottle of whisky. He glanced up, then followed Eve's gaze to the half full glass on the coffee table.

'Don't bother saying anything.' More of a growl than coherent words. 'It's none of—'

'None of my business?' Why couldn't he join the dots? 'I'd say the fact that you're here is very much my business. Cat told me about the bullshit you've been carrying on with, and since it included ogling a picture of a semi-naked me, then it's very much my business.'

'I wasn't ogling.'

Whatever he had to say, he could damn well listen first. It wasn't why she'd come, but they may as well get it sorted.

'Whatever you were doing, it almost wrecked my friendship with your wife, which I have been making inroads on re-establishing. So thanks very much for that.' She threw her arms out, gesturing to the room. 'And it doesn't look like it's done much for you either. What were you thinking?'

'I was going through an old box of photos.'

'Why?'

He looked at her, his mouth thin and flat. 'I don't know, alright? Maybe I was looking for the person I used to be. Before life turned into a complete shitshow.'

He was well and truly wallowing

'Your life with Cat and Lilly is a shitshow, is it? I'm sure your daughter would love to hear that when she's old enough to understand.'

'She's better off without me.'

A chill rolled across Eve's scalp like a slowly falling shadow. 'What's that supposed to mean?'

'It means she doesn't need a father who can't be there

for her. Not when she has a mother who is so bloody competent. At everything.'

'That's bullshit, Jack. Lilly loves you and needs you, as does Cat. Don't you dare even think about taking off and leaving them in the lurch.' Whatever he was considering, that was as close as she could come to giving it voice. 'My father left when I wasn't much older than Lilly, and I can tell you I would have given anything – anything – to have him in my life as I was growing up. Maybe you and Cat are having a rough patch right now, but you can get through it if you work at it.'

'Listen to you, the big marriage expert. I don't see you hand in hand with your Prince Charming.'

'No, you don't. But I've had enough failed relationships to know why they haven't worked, and a lot of that is down to me. Never letting anybody in. Walking away the minute things got hard because I didn't want to have to deal with the truth: that it was as much my fault as it was theirs, probably more. If I'd sorted out my own issues, there would have been a lot better chance of everything else falling into place.'

'Is that it?'

'What?'

'Is the lecture over?'

He was clearly in no mood to listen to her life advice, so she might as well get what she came for and leave. 'I didn't come here to haul you over the coals, Jack. I came to see what you know about Todd Adams.'

'He's a dropkick. End of story'

'You and Todd were pretty good mates back in the day.'

'Not after Bec.' He looked straight at her for the first time since she'd arrived, underlining his words with a glare. 'Why do you want to know about him?'

'Because Luke Harris has told the police that I set him up to light the fire, and I think Todd has something to do with it. Did you know he has a fire fetish?'

'As in lighting them?'

'Yes.'

Jack wiped a hand across his chin. 'He's in our local brigade. What makes you think he could be connected to Luke?'

'He's his drug supplier, and Luke has been hanging out with him apparently. But I'm not sure where.'

Pushing to his feet, Jack walked to the kitchenette and stood behind the bench, placed his hands on it, fingers splayed, arms straight, as if stretching out the muscles in his neck. 'Do you think he started the fire out behind your place?'

'Maybe. I found a jerry can stuck inside a rock. The police have it and want to use it as evidence to charge me. And Luke is saying I put him up to it.'

'They want to charge you?'

'Yeah. They already would have if I hadn't fainted and done this.' She pulled her hands from the pocket of her jacket and pointed to her latest wound — she really was turning into a walking disaster zone.

Jack's eyes softened. 'Shit. Are you okay?'

'Yes.' Recounting the whole story about the arrest, the pregnancy and the visit to the hospital could wait. That baby issue would be a sore spot for Jack.

'So, you think it was Luke who started the fire?'

'I don't know.' She shook her head. 'Possibly. On his own or in tandem with Todd. But I'm up against it with Adams senior. There's no way I can go to him with a theory that it was his brother.'

'Have you tried talking to Luke?'

'No. I'm a "person of interest" in the investigation, so talking to him won't do my case any good.'

'This is crazy, Eve.'

'I know.' She had to keep reminding herself this was real life and not a ridiculous nightmare. 'The only thing I can think of is to track down Todd.'

'I could talk to him,' Jack offered.

'Uh-uh. I don't want you to get involved. You have enough of your own shit going on.' To be fair, she hadn't thought beyond getting Todd's address.

Jack raked a hand through his hair. 'This is my shit, Eve. My mate died in that fire, remember? And I want to see whoever was responsible brought to justice.' There was a fervour in his voice, the dull monotone completely gone.

'Do you even know where he lives?'

'Not off the top of my head. But I can find out. Check the RFS files. He's a member so he would have had to fill in forms with all his details. I don't have my laptop here to access the database, but I can do it first thing in the morning when I pick Lilly up to take her to preschool.'

So, he was still helping out with his daughter. That was a good sign. Maybe getting closure on the fire would help him too.

'Okay. Once we know where he lives, we can work out the next step.' Her earlier tiredness returned, as if getting what she came for – or almost – had rewound her body clock. She lifted her hand to her mouth to hide a yawn. 'I'd better get going.'

'Drive safely.' Jack remained where he was as she turned towards the door. Standing right in front of that damned whisky. In for a penny …

In one swift move, she spun around, grabbed the bottle and stuck it under her arm.

'Don't drink it all at once,' he called out as she started up the path, the cool night air making her shiver. Without answering, she opened the bottle and tipped it upside down, showering Grant's lawn with Tennessee's finest.

Chapter Thirty

Eve lay in the half-light, staring at the ceiling of the caravan, every part of her body wired after a long sleepless night. Maybe if she closed her eyes one more time, she could drift off, get an hour or two's sleep to see her through the day. Weirdly, dawn was always the time she slept best, as if she was some strange nocturnal creature who could only rest at the first hint of sunlight.

Closing her eyes, she focused on the flow of air in and out of her nostrils. In and out, in and …

A key turning in the lock. Footsteps fading away. Wherever she was, it was dark and dank, water dripping from a crack in the ceiling and pooling onto the floor, forming a fetid puddle at her feet. Every part of her body was cold. Huddling into herself. A bone-numbing quiet filling the gloom. If she spent one second longer in this miserable place, she would surely die. Scrambling from her cross-legged position on the floor, she launched herself at the door. Only it wasn't a door, but iron bars locking her into a tiny cell. Wrapping her fingers around them; shaking them until her whole being trembled. But the bars wouldn't budge. Quiet pierced her eardrums. Cried out to be broken. 'Let me out.'

Flattening her hand, she banged it against the stone wall. 'Let me out. Let me out.' But even as she screamed, the silence swelled. Somehow, she had to make someone hear. She banged, and banged again, louder and louder and finally someone called her name.

'Eve, Eve, are you there?'

She jolted upright. Her dream had morphed into a strange reality. She glanced at the clock: 6:32. Thin light outside the van.

'Eve, please.' More banging. A man's voice.

'Alright, hold your freakin' horses, I'm coming.'

Banjo beat her to it, jumping out when she threw the door open and bolting past their visitor.

'Luke?' What the hell was he doing here?

Pacing up and down outside the van, he lifted his arm and wiped a snotty nose on his sleeve. Gave a low moan. He was clearly distraught, but after the stunt he'd pulled, dredging up sympathy for the kid was a challenge.

She pulled on her boots and stepped into the pre-dawn air, shrugged her arms into her coat, and her hands into the pockets. 'What are you doing here?'

'He's going to kill him. He made me tell him where he lives, and I'm pretty sure he's going to kill him.' He spoke in a wheezy voice, his words running together, barely coherent. 'But he's got a gun. It won't work. He's got a gun.'

Her ribs constricted, as if someone had wrapped a girth around them and yanked tight. Whatever Luke was talking about, someone was in danger. Somehow, she had to calm him down and make him talk sense.

He gave a violent shake of his head. 'We have to do something. Now.'

Moving closer, she grabbed his arm. 'Luke, take a second.'

He bent forward, hands on his knees, and she released

her grip. His shoulders heaved chaotically, then settled in a more rhythmic pattern. Now they were getting somewhere. Slowly, he righted himself and they were face to face. As much as she wanted to hate him for the lies he'd told, all she could see was a frightened boy. Margo's grandson.

'Right. Now tell me who you're talking about.'

His hands rose to his temples, and he held his head between his palms. 'Jack Mitchell. He came to our place. My dad answered the door, but Jack punched him and came bursting into my room. He ... he pulled me out of bed and started screaming.' An animal cry punctuated his story. 'He said he'd beat me to a pulp if I didn't admit I'd lied about you and tell him where Todd lived. So I did. I told him, and then Dad came in and they had a punch up and then Jack left.'

The gist of Luke's garbled explanation made Eve's legs turn to porridge. Jack had said he'd check the RFS database for Todd's address, so why had he gone to Luke's?

'Had Jack been drinking?'

'I don't know. But he was really mad.'

Maybe the bottle of whisky she'd disposed of hadn't been the only one. Could Jack have been drinking all night, got himself riled up and decided to tackle the whole thing himself? He was generally placid, but since the fires his moods were all over the place, and if he'd downed more booze anything was possible.

'What about your father? Is he okay?'

Luke nodded. Now he'd blurted out the details, he had calmed a little. 'He told me to stay in the house, got in his car and drove off.'

'Do you know where he went?'

'No, he didn't say. I only told the police you started the fire because Todd threatened me. I owe him money – a lot –

and he said if I tell the police it was you, he'd let me off the hook.'

Eve's jaw hardened. A white-hot ball of fire swirled in her chest. 'You lied about me because you owe that dickhead money? Do you have any idea what you've done? How serious this is?'

'Yes.' He sobbed out the answer. 'That's why I'm here. I'm sorry, alright? I shouldn't have done what I did. But Todd said it would all be okay because his brother is a cop. That we wouldn't get caught.'

Get caught? The step Eve took into his space put them almost nose to nose. She grabbed the collar of his sweatshirt, her knuckles clenched. 'Luke, did you start that fire with Todd?'

He closed his eyes, and sniffled.

'Look at me. Look at me and tell me the truth. Is that why you bolted? Because you started the fire?'

'No.' Eyes open, wide and wet. 'It wasn't me. It was Todd. But he told me about it. He thought it was funny. Said he'd started it on your property so your house would go first. Said you deserved it after the way you'd wrecked everything when you were teenagers. I promise you it wasn't me. But I took off because he said if I told anyone, he'd dob me in. Make out I'd done it. And after I was caught for that locker fire, everyone would believe him.'

Dubious, given Todd's own history, but clearly what Luke believed. 'Jesus.' Eve shrugged him away.

The kid was scared shitless, but he seemed to be telling the truth. The trick was to get him to admit the truth to the police, when Todd's brother was running the show at the local station and seemed to be more than happy to turn a blind eye to his sibling's misdoings.

Right now, there was a more urgent issue to deal with – the reason Luke had come here in the first place.

'You told Jack where Todd is living?'

'Yes. It's just up the road.'

What? 'From here?'

'He's been squatting at the Macintosh place. The old guy went into a nursing home last year, and Todd's been living there.'

'Macintosh's? That land backs onto here.' All the time she'd been living at Mossy Creek Farm that moron had been no more than a stone's throw away. 'And Jack was going there?'

'I don't know. But he made me give him the address, and if Todd finds out I told him—'

'For fuck's sake, Luke, enough. Stop whining and worrying about yourself. Don't you think you've caused enough trouble?'

If Jack had been drinking and was as furious as Luke said, he only had one reason to go after Todd: he had a score to settle. He was out to avenge the death of his colleague, and he could get himself hurt in the process.

'How long ago did all this happen?'

'I came straight here after Jack and Dad left.'

So, if Jack had gone to see Todd, he'd already be at the Macintosh place. There was no time to waste.

'Get in the car.'

'Where are we going?'

'You're taking me to Todd's.'

Luke cowered, as if she was about to take to him with a baseball bat. 'I can't. He can't know I've told you all this. You don't know what he's like.'

He was way out of his depth. Taking him with her was probably pointless. There was no telling if he'd do a backflip when he got there and side with Todd. Better to leave him out of it.

'Fine. Stay put. And make sure you're here when I get back.'

She made a run for the Kombi, and Banjo jumped in beside her. She shot off a message to Emily, then shoved it into gear, did a u-turn and turned left onto Mossy Creek Road. The Macintosh place was a rundown old shack on the back road into town. By some miracle, that stretch of bush had survived the fires, provided the escape route she, Margo and Hugh had negotiated after Nell's place had disappeared. And all the while, Todd Adams had been living there, scheming and plotting and using Luke as a pawn in his sick games.

He'd made Eve's skin crawl that night at the community centre, the way he'd used his size to block her path, but right now she was too fucking angry to be afraid.

It was what Jack might do to Todd that made everything inside her petrify.

Sure enough, Jack's ute was parked in the front yard. Another car, a battered old Ford station wagon, sat under a rusted carport. Weeds smothered the remains of a garden at the entrance, and a wall of bamboo bordered both sides of the property.

Eve eased the Kombi to a stop a few metres before the driveway and hopped out.

'Heel.' A click of her fingers, and Banjo did as he was told. Having him at her side helped calm the choppy sea sloshing around in her belly. A showdown between Jack and

Todd would be ugly at best – particularly if Luke's description of Jack's mental state was accurate.

Every step she took towards the house dialled up the tension in her muscles. The bush surrounding the house was eerily quiet. Not even the call of a bird. No voices coming from inside. Rain damp leaves slid beneath the soles of her boots, slowing her pace.

One footstep at a time brought her to the front door of the shack. The windows were boarded up, and the screen door hung on a single hinge against the fibro. The main door was open.

Heart pounding, she stepped over the threshold. The squelch of rubber on linoleum pulled her up short. Her own boots but still no other noise. The living room she stood in was sparsely furnished. A stained lounge sat against the far wall, a small television on a table perched directly in front. Straight ahead, a doorway led into the kitchen and a further door out into the yard.

Something brushed against her leg. She froze. At her calf, a pure-white cat meowed and looked up at her through pink eyes. Behind her, Banjo let out a brief whine but didn't move. As much as he'd love to make the cat's acquaintance, he'd be reading her cues and knew better.

'Jack?' Her tentative call echoed slightly through the apparently empty cabin. 'Todd? Are you here?'

Nothing.

Where the hell were they? Not that she had any idea what she was going to say to them when they were found. Hopefully something would come to mind.

She moved through the kitchen, taking in the chaos of unwashed saucepans, empty cans of baked beans and dirty plates. Flies hovered around an open tin of cat food, and a rancid smell made her gag. Covering her mouth, she made a beeline for the back step and gulped down a lungful of fresh air. The small yard sloped into bushland a short distance from the house. Nothing but scrub and gums for as far as the eye could see. Dull morning light filtered through a heavy bank of clouds.

She squinted into the glare, towards the opening of a track immediately opposite.

Could they have gone for a walk to talk things out?

Weird as it sounded, it was a possibility.

'Come on, Banj.'

Being outside, away from the claustrophobic space of the house, gave her a much-needed boost of adrenaline. She marched towards the trail. Last night's rain had left puddles of water pooling on the ground, and in between trodden-down tufts of grass, fresh footprints patterned the muddy track. Large footprints. Man-sized. Someone had come this way very recently.

Eve picked up her pace, tea trees and gums and gnarled old banksias flicking past the edges of her vision. The wind direction had kept this part of the bush safe from the fires, so it was all still green and alive. A vibration in her back pocket made her flinch. Only her phone. She pulled it out and tapped on the screen as she kept walking.

A blue dot on the message list. Three missed calls. All from Emily. Why was she—

Eve hit the ground with a thud, pain radiating through her toe, and lay sprawled out face down in the mud, an exposed tree root cushioning her left foot. Banjo licked her face. Her phone had gone flying. Pushing herself upright, she scanned the area. Nothing but crumpled grass, sodden leaves and dirt. It had to be here somewhere. Standing, she scoured the edges of the trail. On the righthand side, it fell away into a deep fissure where the rock had eroded, forming a knee-deep pool.

She crouched, looked closer.

Fuck!

Of course, her bloody phone had landed in the ditch by the side of the track and of course it was covered in water. She pulled her arm from her sleeve and plucked it out.

'Please still be working.' She turned it over. The screen was black.

Shit.

She wiped it on the wool lining of her jacket and gave it a shake. Nothing. Whatever Emily wanted would have to wait.

A shout sounded from up ahead. Nothing comprehensible, but definitely a man's voice, almost a growl.

Eve shoved the phone in her pocket. 'Let's go, Banj.'

Keeping an eye open for obstacles on the path, she raced towards the noise. The closer she got, the louder the voice became, but still only snatches of words. More primal caveman than human male. Urgency spiked in her veins, pushing her forward, blood pumping, chest heaving. A deafening blast ruptured the quiet. She jerked to a standstill. Ears ringing, she peered through the thinning bush to the clearing ahead. A tall figure in a dark sweater stood over a second man in a light grey sweatshirt spread-eagled on the ground. From behind, it was hard to tell who was who, but Jack had been wearing a navy hoodie last night. She inched closer: the man standing upright was holding a gun.

He's got a gun. He's going to kill him.

Luke's words chimed in over the top of the ringing. She'd assumed he'd meant Todd. A cold sweat broke out on her temples as she inched closer. The upright figure was Jack's body shape: tall, broad-shouldered, stocky and fit. He lowered himself over Todd Adams, knee to his groin, gun pointed at his chest.

'Jack. Stop.'

In a few long strides, she was standing to the side of the two men, but even from a couple of metres away the trembling of Jack's hand as it held the gun was clear. On the ground, Todd wore the terrified look of a fox caught in a trap.

Jack's other hand was at his throat, pinning him in place. 'Stay out of this, Eve.' Without turning his head, he spoke though gritted teeth. 'This is between me and Todd.'

'No, it's not. I'm the one whose property he torched. I'm the one he's set up to take the wrap.'

'And I'm the one who saw his mate burned alive. Do you know what that's like?' Jack rammed the barrel of the gun closer to Todd's face. 'Hearing a man scream as he's consumed by fire. Answer me. Do you?'

'No.' Todd's chin quivered. He gave a low moan.

'This isn't the answer, Jack.' She had to find some way of getting through to him. 'I know how much you're hurting but pulling that trigger will only make things worse. Think about what it will do to Cat. To Lilly. They need you.'

For one tiny millisecond of time, the rigid line of Jack's shoulders slackened. And that was all it took. Todd lifted his head and smacked his forehead against Jack's, knocking him off balance and onto his side. Enough time to push himself upright, wrench the gun from Jack's grip and stagger backwards.

Banjo barked, his ears pricked, his tail straight as a flagpole.

'Get over there with lover boy.' Todd waved the gun in the air. 'Now.'

Fuck.

Eve's chest rose and fell, rose and fell. Reaching down, she grabbed Banjo's collar and moved towards Jack lying on the ground, leaning on one elbow, the other holding his head.

'Get up,' Todd shouted, using the gun like a pointer, directing Jack to his feet.

Jack winced as he righted himself, a golf ball-sized bump already forming on his hairline. Standing so close, the odour of stale sweat and even staler whisky confirmed Eve's suspicions. An all-night bender on top of PTSD was making him act like a total lunatic. Jack swayed, like a sapling bending in the wind. She grabbed his arm and his body stilled.

'Aw, so sweet.' Todd's saccharine voice was as sickening as his smartarse expression. 'Bet your doctor wife isn't too happy your old screw is back in town, Jackie boy. You two were hot for each other back in the day.'

Beneath her palm, Jack's bicep tensed. Eve curled her fingers tighter around the rigid muscle. *Don't bite.* Hopefully he'd get the message.

Todd had the gun trained on them, but would he actually use it? By all accounts, he was a mad bastard, so anything was possible. Was there any hope of appealing to his sense of humanity?

'Todd, can you put the gun down so we can talk?'

His cackle sent a shiver galloping down her spine. 'Why would I want to do that?'

She shrugged. Better to feign indifference than let him think he had the upper hand. Perhaps even rattle him back to some sense of reality. 'Oh, I don't know. Maybe so you don't get arrested for holding people at gunpoint. On top of everything else you'll be going to prison for.'

'I'm not the one going to prison, bitch.' Globules of

spittle sprayed into the air as Todd's face turned a violent shade of scarlet. 'That'll be you. You come back here thinking everything is forgiven and forgotten. Well, you're wrong. If it wasn't for you, I would have left this shithole town by now. But everything turned to crap after that night at the lake. And that's on you.'

'For fuck's sake, get your head out of the past.' Jack sprang to life, throwing his retort at Todd like a gauntlet. 'No one shoved those drugs down your throat or forced you to do all the stupid shit you've done over the years, just like no one forced me to down all the booze. But you've gone a step too far with the fire and you're going to pay.'

'And who's going to make me?' Todd approached, stopping only an arm's length away. He held the gun in both hands, arms straight out, training it first on one of them and then the other. It would only take one jerk of his finger to pull the trigger and—

Banjo let out a high-pitched bark.

Todd swung in his direction.

'No!' A spike of energy shot from the balls of Eve's feet up through her body. She sprang forward and threw herself at Todd, forcing him backwards. Everything was a blur of noise and movement. A sharp pain radiated through her scalp as Todd grabbed a fistful of her hair and jerked her upright. Hot, putrid air washed over her face as the barrel of the gun jammed hard against her cheekbone.

Chapter Thirty-One

Breathing fast and hard. Her face aching. Scalp on fire.

A movement in the bush at their backs.

Todd spun around, dragging her with him, but the glare and the pain blurred her vision.

'Put the gun down, Todd.' A different voice. Light years away, yet close by.

Head at an angle, Eve blinked her eyes open, pushed through the burning in her skull.

Constable Morris stood a few metres away, and behind him was a woman: tall, honey hair in a high ponytail. Emily?

Morris held a raised gun. A tremor vibrated through Todd's body, but he didn't loosen his grip. Eve's neck spasmed and a cramp pinched her shoulder but moving was impossible.

'Fuck off.' Todd kept up the bravado, 'Take another step, and she gets it. Throw your gun on the ground or I'll pull the trigger.'

'I can't do that, Todd. You need to let her go.' The

constable's voice was sure and steady, as if he'd done this dozens of times, as if he was one hundred percent used to coming across crazed gunmen in the middle of the bush on a weekday morning.

'Drop it or she gets it.' Nothing but venom from Todd.

Would he actually pull the trigger? The thought came like a butterfly dancing into Eve's field of vision, black and white and orange flitting past, leaving no answer in its wake.

'I said drop it.' An order this time; a brutish growl that ricocheted through Todd's body and echoed in her own. Echoed too through the other-worldly hush that had descended on the clearing.

Morris's shoulders fell. 'This isn't going to help your cause.' He tossed the gun on the ground a short distance away from where he stood. Gave a slow shake of his head as he raised his hands.

'I don't give a shit.' Todd waved his gun in the air, gesturing to the right and back. 'Move.'

Morris glanced in the direction indicated but didn't budge.

'Move!'

Eve's body jolted again as Todd yelled. She bit down on her lip, the metallic taste of blood coating her tongue.

Slowly, Morris took a couple of steps sidewards, away from the entrance to the clearing. Arms behind him, he sheltered Emily with his frame.

Todd moved forward, dragging Eve with him, every footfall tugging on her skull, sending arrows of pain spearing through her head.

Stop. Please Stop. She kept her mouth closed; her plea silent.

Behind them, Banjo whined. Was Jack holding him? Otherwise, he'd be here by her side, exactly where she didn't want him. If Todd pulled the trigger, would Jack and Cat look after him? Would he be okay without her? Her eyes stung, but she swallowed back the tears. She was not going to let this monster see her cry.

Please be okay, Banj. Please be safe.

She let the thought go out into the ether. Surely someone up there would hear and make it happen – Bec, or Nell perhaps. If Todd did go through with it, the baby would never be born, her dream of starting again, of having a family of her own, would never have a chance of becoming reality. She would never have the life she'd always wanted but had been too afraid to claim. Never get to share it with her child.

A noise from up ahead. Todd stopped dead in his tracks. All eyes flicked towards the sound as Brent Adams materialised out of the scrub, chest heaving. He saw his brother and pulled up short. For a few long agonising seconds, there wasn't a sound, only the thundering of blood through her ears. All around them, the bush held its breath.

Adams reached out a hand. 'Give me the gun, Todd.'

'No. I can't.' Todd's voice trembled. 'I'm getting out of here. With her. You can cover for me.'

'Not this time.'

She couldn't see the look on Todd's face, but she could picture the disappointment, his incredulity that his big brother wouldn't clean up his mess as he'd always done.

'Spud, let me have the gun and we can sort this out.' Adams spoke softly but Todd didn't budge, not even at the family nickname.

Todd had her by the hair, and her head was starting to spin. Tree and sky. Sky and tree. Round and round on rotation like a playground merry-go-round. Someone had to do something.

A sharp yap broke the cycle. The pressure on her head ceased. A scream. Todd leant sidewards, to where Banjo ravaged his ankle.

Now! Raising her arm, she angled it up and swung it backwards, elbow first, delivering a sharp blow to Todd's ribs. Everything happened simultaneously in fast and slow motion. A raucous grunt as Todd hunched over. A deafening blast cracking the air. The pungent smell of sulphur. Jack diving forward and grabbing Banjo by the collar. The two of them a knot of writhing arms and legs.

Until everything stopped and fell silent.

Brent Adams lay on the ground, hands to his middle, blood seeping across his knuckles.

On his hands and knees, Todd scrambled towards his brother. 'Nooooooo.'

His scream rang out as the bush and the people and the world went black.

Chapter Thirty-Two

'How are you doing?'

Now the ear-ringing had faded, Emily's voice was coming through loud and clear. Sitting on the floor of the Kombi, where someone had opened the side door and directed her to stay, Eve gulped another mouthful of water and let it wash over her tongue and soothe her parched throat.

'Apart from my head feeling like it's been squeezed through a mangle, I'm perfectly alright.' She touched the tender spot on her scalp where Todd had grabbed the handful of hair and held her in place. Ouch. Nothing some ibuprofen wouldn't fix – but could pregnant women take that?

'You do seem to be making a habit of this fainting business.' Emily gave a feeble smile, which she attempted to return.

'Well, I'm not planning on running any marathons.'

The series of knots that Eve's organs had twisted themselves into were still loosening, but now that it was all over the whole scenario seemed like nothing more than a horrible nightmare. Strangely unreal and yet vividly tangible. Hard to reconcile with the bright morning sunshine coating the shimmering leaves of the gum trees, and the aquamarine sky forming their backdrop.

From where she sat, looking out across the dirt road to the stretch of bush sloping up to the escarpment, there was nothing to indicate what a shitshow the last hour had been. One small turn of her head towards the Macintosh shack told a completely different story: ambulance doors closing on a trolley carrying Brent Adams; Constable Morris questioning a dishevelled-looking Jack; Todd, cowed and handcuffed, being bundled into the back of one of the three police cars that had arrived in fast succession. The crime show reel kept on rolling.

'Tell me again how you ended up being here with Constable Morris?' Emily had outlined the vague details as they'd walked back along the track, but at that point the pounding in Eve's head had turned the journo's words into white noise.

'When I got your text, I may have been in the same bed as Tim—'

'Tim, as in Constable Morris?'

'Yes, the exact one.' Emily's cheeks flushed.

'Okay, interesting.'

'Anyway ... I told him I was concerned when I couldn't get onto you, and he suggested we head to your place to make sure you were okay. We were almost there when he got a call from the station. Dean Harris was in there screaming bloody murder about Jack breaking into his house and assaulting him and his son. While he was there, Luke called him to say Jack was going after Todd and that things could get nasty. Dean told the officer on duty who passed on this address and asked Tim to check it out. When we got here and saw the cars but found no one here, we knew there was something wrong.'

'And Constable Tim was perfectly okay about you traipsing into the bush with him?'

A second, brighter blush coloured Emily's whole face. 'No. He told me to stay in the car. And I did. For a minute or two. But the suspense was too much. I went into the house right as he disappeared down the track, so I followed him. He didn't even know I was there until he got to the clearing, and then Banjo barked, and I may have let out a small yelp myself.'

Laughter rumbled deep in Eve's belly, rising up and out through her nose in a snort. The image of Banj latching onto Todd's ankle and chewing on it like a discarded brisket bone would be one she would treasure for the rest of her days.

Emily gave her a gentle shoulder shove. 'Fast thinking with that elbow action, too. You and your dog are regular superheroes. God knows what would have happened if you hadn't slogged it to Todd.'

Any remaining shimmer of frivolity evaporated. Eve looked up at Emily and nodded. What could very well have happened was that she could have been the one being carted off to hospital instead of Brent Adams. Or Jack or …

She traced her fingertips over the waistline of her pyjama pants. 'What's the prognosis for the sergeant?'

'He's lost a fair bit of blood but according to the medics he'll probably pull through, depending on what damage the bullet's done on the inside. And he won't have a hope in hell of covering up his brother's crime this time.'

'The shooting or the arson?'

'Both. Dean has taken Luke into the station to make a

full statement about Todd. The drugs, the fires, his bragging about blaming it all on you. There'll be no getting out of it.'

Despite the unreality of it all, the seriousness of the situation was sobering. Todd Adams was responsible, and now he would pay for his crimes; go to prison for a very long time. And yet there was no surge of excitement, no celebratory party poppers bursting in Eve's belly. A father of three had died in those fires. His family's lives forever altered.

Behind them, the murmuring of voices ceased. Constable Morris appeared from around the front of the van, his gaze fixed on Emily, a smile playing on his lips.

'I think we're all done here.' He dragged his gaze away from his lover. 'We'll need a full statement from you, Ms Nicholls, but it can wait, if you're up to coming into the station sometime today?' He spoke in the same kind tone he'd used when he'd arrested her at his boss's orders, a tone that suggested he wasn't likely to go down the same rocky path as his superior.

'Sure.' She glanced down at her black-and-white horse-print PJs, poking out from beneath her jacket. 'I might head home and freshen up first.'

'No hurry.'

'I'm really not sure you should be driving.' Emily's concern was sweet but unwarranted.

'I'm fine.' Eve stood slowly, making sure her body agreed with her assessment. All good. No head spinning.

She turned towards the house where Jack sat motionless on the front step. He'd come to confront Todd and was thankfully leaving in one piece, but there were still so many issues he needed to face and one particular demon he needed to vanquish before his life – and Cat's, and Lilly's – could get back to any kind of normal.

Eve nodded at Emily and the constable. 'You guys get going. I'll see you soon.'

In a second, Emily's arms were around her shoulders, pulling her close. 'You were so brave out there.' The journalist pulled back, tears glistening in her eyes. 'Definite superwoman material, Eve Nicholls.'

Heroic was the absolute last thing she felt. Confused, shocked, surprised – any and all of them – but not brave, or courageous or fearless. She'd acted purely on impulse, like she'd done so many times before in her life, but for once it had worked in her favour.

Walking towards Jack, with car doors banging behind her and Banjo glued to her side, her entire body felt like one giant bruise. The way Todd had wrenched her head around at such an awkward angle had contorted her body into an unnatural shape, leaving her shoulders throbbing and her back rigid. Jack didn't so much as twitch as she approached. He stared ahead and down, seemingly transfixed by a bare patch of dirt on the ground by his feet. Not lifting his eyes until she stood directly in front of him.

Eve caught his gaze. His eyes filled. He dropped his head into his hands and sobbed.

Oh, Jack.

She stepped forward and let him bury his face against her chest, draped her arms around his shoulders as his body shuddered. All the pain he'd squashed down inside himself, all the stress of the fires, of losing a mate, of thinking it was all his fault, coursed through his body, needing release. So, she held him until every tear was spent, until he sat dry-eyed and shaking, looking up at her. Something in his expression told her he was ready to hear whatever she had to say.

'That was some crazy-arse stunt you pulled, Jack Mitchell.'

The edges of his mouth contracted but he didn't speak.

'You had more booze after I left you last night, didn't you?'

An agonisingly slow nod. There was no point berating him for his actions. As foolhardy as they'd been, he'd already been through enough. And after the amount of alcohol he'd consumed, his head was no doubt hurting as much as her own.

'Does it feel better, knowing the person who started the fires has been caught?'

'No.' He gave a small shake of his head. 'I thought it would, but it doesn't. It doesn't bring Matt back and it won't help his family. But landing that first punch felt so fucking good.'

'Please tell me that wasn't your gun.'

He shook his head. 'It was Todd's. We had a tussle when I first got here. He pulled the gun on me, but I managed to knock it out of his hand and then he ran. I'd just caught up with him when you found us.'

'As in, I found you with the barrel pointed right at him.' The memory sent a shiver lancing through Eve's insides. The possibility it raised was one she wasn't sure she wanted an answer to, and yet she was compelled to ask. 'Would you have pulled the trigger if I hadn't interrupted?'

'I think I would have.' Again, Jack's voice trembled, but he sucked in a draft of air and settled himself. 'Something else to add to my therapy sessions when they start.'

She widened her eyes in a question.

'I should have listened to you a while back when you

told me I needed to get help. Then I might not be sitting here.'

'No, you mightn't. And Todd Adams might not be at the police station getting charged with arson and manslaughter like he deserves. None of us are perfect, Jack. We all make mistakes. This was one of yours, but the outcome wasn't bad, so don't beat yourself up too much.'

He let out a soft sigh. 'Not sure Cat will be so understanding.'

'Yeah, well, she has to live with you – I don't.' Even as the words left her lips, she wanted to bite them back. The last thing Jack needed was a reminder of his shaky marital status. Or maybe that was exactly what he needed.

Hands on knees, he pushed himself to his feet. 'She's the reason I'll be getting counselling. And going to rehab. She and Lilly. I'm nothing without them.'

Eve wanted to argue, to tell him he was someone of worth in his own right, someone who deserved to live a happy life because he was a good man, but if his wife and daughter were giving him the motivation to ask for the help he needed, that was a start.

'Constable Morris was pretty understanding about the whole thing. Said that given the outcome they would overlook me confronting Todd. But I still have the outburst with Dean and Luke to deal with, if they decide to press charges.' Jack gave a resigned sigh. 'I have to go into the police station and give a statement. May as well get it over and done with. Are you okay to drive, or can I give you a lift back to the farm?'

'Shouldn't I be driving you?' She raised an eyebrow.

'It's all good.' His sheepish look said he knew exactly what she was referring to. 'They breath tested me, and the booze has worn off.

They walked together and stood by their respective cars, hovering as if there was more to say. Banjo looked up hopefully, and Eve opened the Kombi door so he could jump in.

Jack caught her eye then dropped his gaze to her legs. 'Nice pyjamas. A shame you didn't dress for the occasion.'

'Thanks.' She grinned back, a soft heat suffusing her veins. The fact that they could still see the funny side of things was a comfort after all the weird shit they'd been through over the last few hours. 'See you.'

She hopped in and started up the Kombi, turned it around and headed back to Mossy Creek Farm.

Chapter Thirty-Three

The invitation to morning tea had come after numerous apologetic phone calls and check-ins to make sure Eve was alright. They were from the 'old' Margo, not the bitter woman in the greenhouse whose words had cut so deep and left her shell-shocked. Her godmother's easy acceptance of the lies that others had spread about her was an open wound, one that would hopefully heal with time. For now, taking Margo at her word would have to do.

A crisp breeze ruffled the newly green branches of the trees bordering Margo and Harry's place. Banjo, familiar with the drill, plonked himself on the bottom step, stretching out like a furry welcome mat. Totally at ease.

If only she felt the same. Re-hashing yesterday's unbelievable events was sure to be on the agenda, and as two of the minor players were related to Margo, emotions were bound to run high. And Margo still didn't know Eve was pregnant, so there was another revelation to throw into the mix. Getting everything out in the open would mean a fresh start for their friendship, and they could both use a friend right now.

Stop dithering and get on with things.

'Thanks for the life advice, Nell.' Eve raised her hand to ping the doorbell, but Margo appeared before she had the chance.

'No need to stand on ceremony. Come on in.' The door was flung open, and Eve joined Margo in the hallway. Had her godmother shrunk since the last time they'd seen each other? In contrast to the chirpy greeting, her skin was pale and her eyes bleary.

For a few seconds neither of them spoke. Eve's lungs contracted at the sight of the clearly pained expression on her friend's face. She pulled Margo into her arms, breathed in the comforting scent of lavender, felt the frail thinness of an old woman's frame as they hugged. Without a word, Margo took Eve's hand and led her to the kitchen, where the table was set with a crocheted lace cloth, china teacups and a plate of scones. As always, Margo's solution to a problem was food. But there were things to be said first.

'Margo, I—'

'Not a word.' Margo raised a finger. 'Sit and eat. I'll do the talking.'

Comforting to know the bossiness hadn't disappeared. Following orders, Eve halved and jammed a scone, smothering it with cream while Margo poured the tea. Not peppermint but maybe she'd be able to have a second scone for ballast.

Margo sat and clasped her hands. 'Now, I want to explain myself.'

'Please ...' She managed to interject just as Margo opened her mouth to argue. 'You don't have to explain anything. Dean and Luke are your flesh and blood. I understand.'

Tears welled in Margo's eyes. She pulled a tissue from her pocket and dabbed them away. 'That they are. But you're as good as, and I had no right to speak to you the way I did. I should have listened to what you had to say, and not latched on to gossip and hearsay. I should have known you had good reason for suspecting Luke. And I shouldn't have been such an old fool when you tried to open my eyes to what he'd been up to.'

'It's hard to believe anything but the best of those we love.'

'Be that as it may, based on the boy's track record alone I should have had more sense.' Margo shook her head roughly. 'And I might have known better if Dean had bothered to tell me about what was going on with him and Michelle. It's no wonder Luke's off the rails, but there's no excuse for what he's done. Or his father. That's why I'm making Dean come here to see you.'

'Dean's coming here today?'

'Yes, Harry's gone to collect him. Just in case he decided he had something better to do.'

A knot formed in Eve's gut. The last time she'd seen Dean, hadn't exactly been a picnic. But based on the glint in Margo's eye, arguing the point was a waste of time.

'Before they both get here, there's something I want to tell you.' Margo's voice dropped to a hush. 'Two things, actually.'

'Okay.'

'Do you remember that day we bumped into each other when I was coming out of Catriona's surgery?'

The same day Dean had bullied Eve out the door. The same day she'd heard her baby's heartbeat. 'Yes, I do.'

'She'd given me the results of a scan I'd had done, because my back was giving me grief. Well,' Margo worried the edges of the tissue she was holding, working her thumbs against it as if she was pressing pastry into a pie plate, 'the scan showed some dark spots on my spine, and in a few other places including my liver.'

An icy hand grabbed Eve by the shoulder and a chill trailed down her spine. 'Dark spots?'

A small nod. 'Cancer.' Margo gave a raspy snort. 'I was almost up to my five years. Positive I was going to get the all-clear. But it wasn't to be.'

The air of resignation in Margo's tone sent Eve's blood whizzing through her temples. 'But they can treat it, can't they? Operate? Or chemo or whatever they do?'

'They can. But the prognosis isn't good. The cancer has spread through my organs, but the radiation might give me more time.'

Eve's body hollowed out, as if her organs had been removed and only her aching heart left in place. Margo couldn't die. Not when they'd so recently reconnected. Not when she was the closest thing Eve had to family. Not when her baby was on the way. Her eyes filled. Stung. She hung her head and let the tears fall. As much as she wanted to be strong for Margo, the idea of losing her was too much.

But she had to put her own needs aside. Focus on what Margo needed. She swiped at her cheeks. 'I'm so sorry, Margo.'

'I'm not dead yet so don't go acting as if I am.' There was a shakiness to Margo's voice despite the remonstration. 'I've got a lot to live for, so I'll take whatever help the doctors can give me and see how we go.'

'Yes. You do have a lot to live for. You're going to be a great godmother in about six months' time, and I have no idea what to do with a baby so don't even think about going anywhere.'

Margo's mouth fell open. 'Well, I never! Who is the lucky fella? I didn't know you were seeing anyone.'

'I'm not.' How many times would she be telling this story over the coming months? 'My ex visited, before the fires, and we ...' Explaining her final one-night fling to her godmother actually made her blush. She took another bite of her scone, savouring the doughy cake, the combo of sweet and creamy.

'Yes, I do know.' Margo's expression softened, a broad smile lighting up her face. 'And I think it's wonderful. You'll make a wonderful mother. There's nothing like the feeling of holding your little one in your arms when they're born. Especially your first.'

Margo's smile faded. She glanced at the clock above the sink and then back. 'I want to hear all about your plans, but before Harry and Dean get here, there's something else I want to discuss.'

So far their conversation had covered death and birth and by the serious look on Margo's face, the next topic would be equally significant. Eve took another sip of tea and let the warm brew soothe the rawness in her throat.

'I want to find my daughter. And as you're the only other person who knows she exists, I'd like your help.'

For a long second, Eve forgot to breathe. Wow. Margo's baby had been adopted out when she was sixteen – would now be a woman in her fifties. She'd made no attempt to track down her birth mother so would she want to be found? If she was even alive?

'I know what you're thinking, and I've had the same thoughts myself. I've been around long enough to know these sorts of things don't always work out well. But like I told you, not a day goes by when I don't think about her, where she is and what her life has been, and I don't want to be going to my grave wondering. She might not be my daughter in name or family, but she's my flesh and blood, and you'll know what that's like soon enough.' Margo's cup rattled as she lowered it to the saucer. 'Will you help me?'

'Of course I will.' Not that she had any idea where to start, but they'd work it out together. 'Are you going to tell Harry?'

'Not just yet. No point rocking the boat if our search is fruitless. I'll see how things pan out.'

'Does he know about your … about the cancer?'

'He knows what he needs to know: that there's something there and they're treating it to clear it up. He'll find out the rest in due course, as will the boys. There's enough going on at the moment without adding to everyone's load.'

As much as Eve wanted to argue, make Margo see she needed to tell her family the truth, that she'd need their support, it wasn't her call to make. And her aunt's dogged determination would get her through the difficult days to come. All Eve could do was be there for her.

'Whatever you need, I'm—'

Heavy footsteps sounded in the hallway. They had been so engrossed in their chat, they hadn't heard the car pull up, or the door open and close. Two large figures stepped into the kitchen: Harry, holding his battered old farm hat in his hands, and beside him a clean-shaven Dean, dressed in jeans and a button-down shirt.

Eve caught his eye, and he turned a distinct shade of crimson. This was going to be so awkward.

Tea poured and scones deposited onto plates, Harry took a seat at the end of the table, leaving the one directly opposite free for his son. Dean lowered himself into the chair, keeping his focus on the cosy-topped teapot. Silence bristled. It was unlike Harry to keep his opinion to himself: perhaps he'd been instructed not to say a word. To leave the onus on his son.

Margo flashed Dean a pointed glare. He shifted in his seat but didn't seem to take the hint.

Someone had to get the ball rolling. Time was, Eve would have run a mile before deliberately starting a hard conversation, but it was rapidly becoming her signature move. 'Is Luke doing okay?'

Dean frowned. 'He's been charged with providing a false statement to the police. They said he'll probably get community service, and it will go on his record.'

'Won't hurt the little coot. He might think twice before doing something stupid again.' Harry practically growled his assessment of his grandson.

'Might be a wakeup call.' Eve offered her own thoughts to Dean in a much softer tone. As much as Luke's behaviour had caused her a huge amount of trouble, in the end he was a misguided kid. He'd screwed up big-time, but he had a great family to keep him on the straight and narrow now they were aware of what had been happening.

'He's very sorry for what he's done. For the lies he's told.' Dean looked directly at her for the first time – and despite his neat and tidy appearance, the toll his son's antics had caused was written in the deep lines creasing his forehead. 'Michelle and I have to take some of the blame. We've been too caught up in our own problems to take notice of what he's been doing. He's not a bad kid, but he needs more guidance. And I should have given him that. I should have known better than to believe him when he told me he was covering for you, Eve. And I shouldn't have spread those rumours. It was wrong.' Dean's chin dropped. He looked like a chastened little boy caught with a permanent marker in front of a freshly painted wall. 'I'm sorry.'

The memories of her argument with Dean, and the way Rita Clements had bailed her up outside the women's toilets marched hand-in-hand into her brain, but there was no accompanying reaction, no ire or indignation, only a sense of them passing and then fading into the distance. Life is life. Shit happens. Then you move on. Holding grudges was as harmful as holding onto grief. And there was so little time to do either.

'That's okay. I'm just glad the person who caused all this has been caught.' And did Dean have something to do with that? 'By the way, where did you go when you left Luke at home, after Jack had been there?'

'I went to see Brent Adams, at his house. After Luke told me he'd lied, and exactly what happened, I knew things would get nasty if Jack tracked Todd down.'

'Ah, right.' So Dean had been the one to force Adams to see the light about his brother. 'I'm surprised he believed you, given he's spent half his life covering up for Todd.'

'It was actually his wife who tipped the scales. She heard us talking, came to the door and started shouting at Brent, told him to wake up and do something about Todd before someone got killed. He got straight in the car and drove off.'

'Good for Mrs Adams. She saved a life.' Hers, or Jack's. Or both. A shiver skittered across Eve's scalp, the hard press of the revolver a ghostly pressure against her cheek.

'And Dean's decided not to press charges against Jack.' Margo piped up for the first time since the men had entered the room.

Her son's face darkened for a moment. Jack's drunken outburst would be a lot to forgive but considering the consequences of the lies Luke had told, the fact that he'd known Todd had started the fire and said nothing, letting Jack off the hook seemed only fair.

Dean lathered a layer of cream onto a second scone. Harry glanced across at his wife and gave a small nod. After the news Margo had delivered in private – was it only half an hour ago? – they would all have plenty more to deal with, but for now, at least, things seemed to be getting back to normal.

'Well, thank you so much for the deliciousness, Aunty Marg, but I'd better be getting back.' There was nothing in particular calling Eve, only a desire for her own company after all the kerfuffle, a need to be alone and ponder her next move. She cast her gaze across all three of them. 'Is it okay if I stay on in the caravan for a while?'

'Stay as long as you want.' Surprisingly it was Harry who provided the answer.

'Thank you. I'm hoping Jack will still be able to get the house built in the next six months.'

Margo flicked her a secret smile. 'That would be absolutely perfect.'

'Fingers crossed.'

Chapter Thirty-Four

'Okay, Banj, are we ready?'

Banjo looked up with an obvious smile. Probably hoping that he'd soon be scoring some of the food laid out on the thrift store card table. Fresh bread rolls, slices of Jarlsberg, leg ham, strawberries, tomatoes and cucumber. Not exactly a gourmet meal, but a healthy, simple lunch, perfect for someone taking a bit of time out from their busy day. Midday sunshine showered the farm in short-sleeved happiness, a nice reprieve from the last few days of rain and cold. All Eve needed now was the guest of honour to arrive.

The hamster wheel spinning inside her brain went into overdrive. Would he actually come? They'd only exchanged a couple of short texts after the 'Todd' incident, and his replies had been on the brief side – even though he'd been the one to initiate the conversation, checking in to make sure she was alright. Nothing since then; no reply to her invitation. But she'd taken a leap of faith and gone ahead with her plan. If worse came to worst, she and Banj would have plenty to eat for the next couple of days.

If he was coming, he should be here by now. Eve pulled her phone out of her pocket: 1.09 p.m. A message binged.

Mel: *All systems go up here, girlfriend. Let me know when you're coming for a visit.*

A photo of the cafe followed, a selfie of Mel, standing behind two shirtless surfy-looking types seated out the front.

The smile it elicited made Eve's cheeks ache.

In your natural habitat, I see? Congrats. Can't wait to see the place. x

She pressed send. Stopped to consider. Not even a twinge of regret, only pure happiness for Mel and a genuine desire to see the café sometime soon.

Banjo jumped to his feet, tail wagging. She stuck her phone in her pocket and looked up. The sight of the approaching white van sent her pulse into overdrive.

She pulled her hair out from where it was tucked behind her ear and touched her fingers to the spot on her temple where the cut had now healed. She ran her tongue over the not-quite-cherry red lipstick Fran had given her from her stash with the accompanying comment, 'I'm hoping this is for seduction purposes.' Not exactly, but maybe a step in that direction.

Hugh stepped out of the car, held onto the door and took off his sunnies as he spied the food-laden table. His smile started slowly, before stretching all the way up to his eyes. With his thinning fair hair, a stature almost equal in height to her own, and his crooked gait, he was completely ordinary, and yet everything inside her glowed at the sight of him.

'Hi.' *Great start, Eve.* 'I wasn't sure you'd come.'

Hugh leaned in through the car window and retrieved an envelope, slipped the card out and held it up. 'I could hardly refuse an invitation that says, *Please join me for lunch so*

I can grovel and explain myself. Especially since it's a school day and it was timed for my usual lunch hour.'

Eve gave a shrug. 'I had to make sure there were as few excuses as possible for you not to accept. Not that you did accept, just showed up.'

He grinned. 'Keeping you on your toes.'

'Rude, if you ask me.'

'Payback, if you ask me.'

There was no malice in his comeback just as there'd been no bite in hers. So far, so good. 'Fair enough.' She waved a hand towards the folding chairs set up at the table, and Hugh took a seat.

Now that he was here, the words she wanted to say seemed to have papier-mâchéd themselves to the bottom of her tongue. No matter. There was plenty of time. She poured them both a glass of mineral water, the bubbles sparkling in the tumblers, tickling her nose as she raised hers to her lips. It had been weeks since she'd last had a drink of anything heavier, and amazingly she no longer missed it. Some things in life were simply a mystery.

She sat opposite Hugh and raised her glass. 'Cheers.'

'Cheers to you.'

'Dig in. It's not much of a feast, but since I'm currently without an oven to whip up a roast, it was the best I could do.'

'Looks perfectly fine to me.' Hugh helped himself to a roll and layered on the fillings.

Suddenly ravenous, Eve did the same, glancing across the table every now and then, painfully aware of the superficial small talk about the horses and the weather. When would be the best time to start the real conversation?

There's no time like the present.

As usual, her mother was right.

'So, feel free to start grovelling whenever you like.' Hugh had beaten her to it. 'And explaining.'

Where to start? She laid her partially eaten roll on the plate and dabbed at the corners of her mouth with the piece of paper towel she'd torn from the roll. Tiny petals of lipstick left an imprint on the makeshift serviette. She took a sip of water, loosening the apology she so desperately wanted to give. A lot was riding on this: Hugh's friendship had come to mean so much, and it was something she wanted to preserve and nurture. At the very least.

'I'm sorry I dumped my pregnancy news on you the way I did. It must have been a shock.'

He raised his eyebrows. 'That's one way of putting it. Certainly didn't see it coming.'

'That makes two of us.' She tried for frivolity, but Hugh's expression remained blank. *Just get on with it, Eve.* 'Like I said, my ex arrived out of the blue only a few days after I arrived back here. He wanted to reconcile, but I was done.'

'Not quite, it would seem.'

'No.' She gave a weak smile. 'Not quite. We had a few drinks, and one thing led to another.' This honesty business was like pulling out a stubborn splinter buried beneath layers of toughened skin. But leaving them in only allowed them to fester. 'He left the next morning. Then the bushfires happened, and the skin graft. It wasn't until I'd left your place and was back here in the van that my body started giving me the signals.'

'They didn't pick it up at the hospital?'

'Apparently not. They asked me if there was any chance I was pregnant, and I automatically said no, so they wouldn't have tested for it.'

'And the father?'

'Marcus.'

'Right, Marcus. What does he think about it all?'

She looked out across the farm, to where one of the plovers was dive-bombing Rain as she walked past the nest. Hugh really was asking all the questions. Rightly so. 'He doesn't know.'

'You haven't told him?' Hugh's voice took on a distinctly higher pitch.

'He's in Italy. He made it clear a while back that he wasn't interested in having children. I'll have to tell him at some point. I'm not sure how he'll react, but I'm doing this on my own.'

'I see.'

The need to explain further, to make him understand where she was coming from swept through her like a river breaking its banks. 'I never wanted kids. Not after what happened with Bec, probably not after what happened with my parents. My father left when I was five, and I still remember how distraught I was when I realised he wasn't coming back. Made me wary of the whole "happy families" story we're led to believe we all want. Motherhood was never on my agenda.'

Should she go further, tell him the whole ugly truth about her teenage pregnancy? No point muddying the waters, especially since those waters involved Jack. Better to stick to the here and now.

'But coming back here, and then losing the house … it triggered something in me I think has lain dormant all these years. I want a family. Even if it's a small one, just me and whatever this is.' She pointed to her belly, a trickle of something warm and gooey coursing through her veins. 'And I want to do that here, at Mossy Creek, where I have history and memories and friends. I'm hoping you're still one of them.'

She held his gaze across the cluttered table, and he held hers, neither of them moving, neither of them speaking for what seemed like minutes but was probably only a few short seconds.

The buzz of his phone broke the spell.

'Sorry, occupational hazard.' He reached into his back pocket and stood as he took the call. Walked away a little as he continued the conversation with whoever was on the other end of the line.

Had she said enough? Explained herself clearly? Would he understand that she wanted him to be part of her life?

'I'm sorry, Eve.' Hugh's shoulders slumped. 'There's an emergency at the surgery. I have to go.'

'That's okay.' It wasn't, not according to the chunk of cement that had just dumped itself in her belly.

'I appreciate all this.' He waved a hand in the direction of the table. 'And your honesty. Of course, we're still friends.'

Their friendship was intact. Her lunch – and her candour – had worked their magic. He was about to leave, and that was okay.

Pushing to her feet, Eve shortened the distance between them and pulled him into a hug. His heart pulsed against her chest, the loss of it as he pulled away like a wayward cloud blocking out the sun on a winter's morning. Their eyes locked, and without even knowing who moved first, their lips met, the kiss soft and brief.

His phone buzzed again, and he lifted his head. 'I have to go.'

'I know.'

He took a slight step backwards, grabbed hold of her

hand and ran his thumb over the rapidly fading scar. 'It's looking so much better.'

'Practically healed.' What was going on here? Eve raised herself onto her toes so she could look straight into those forest green eyes. 'I really value your friendship, Hugh.'

'I know. And if things were different ...' His smile dimmed. 'But you've got a baby on the way. And I've got my hands full with work and the kids.'

He gave another squeeze of her fingers and let his hand fall away.

She offered a small smile. 'See you soon, my friend.'

'Not if I see you first.' Hugh climbed into the car, doffing an imaginary hat as he drove away.

How lucky she was to have him in her life. To have Margo and Cat and Jack. Fran and Clive and Emily. All of them, and all of this – Mossy Creek Farm – in her future. And more. Her hand rested on the imaginary curve of her belly.

A small white butterfly floated by, circling Banjo's head and flitting off in the direction of the house remains. Eve followed its trajectory as it skimmed the rubble and disappeared into the trees.

Home.

The word echoed around her, humming through her body like an old familiar song, one she'd known all her life and yet had somehow forgotten. She closed her eyes, let the afternoon sun dance across her cheeks, the soft breeze skip through the ends of her hair, held a tiny invisible bundle against her chest and let the wonder of it all settle into her bones.

Next in the Blackwattle Lake Series

vinci-books.com/placeofherown

Home is finally within reach… if she's brave enough to hold on.

Eve Nicholls has spent years escaping the wreckage of her past. Now, with a baby on the way and a new love on the horizon, she's ready to put down roots at Mossy Creek Farm. But when her ex threatens to take it all away, she must decide—will she fight for the life she's built, or let her fears chase her away once more?

Turn the page for a free preview…

A Place of Her Own: Prologue

Saying no to her dream life had been the best decision Eve Nicholls had ever made. Gazing out at the pristine stretch of Noosa sand, inhaling a cocktail of salt air, sunscreen and aromatic coffee that was making her head spin, was exactly the confirmation she needed. Especially when all she could think about, could not wait to get back to, was an elixir of a completely different kind: a heady mix of bush mint, eucalyptus and horse manure. Scents that represented the one thing she'd pretended for so long not to crave: home.

She snorted softly and rested a hand on her belly. Gave the small being growing inside her a pat. Even at fourteen weeks, the whole idea of it was still hard to get her head around. 'You and me, kid. We've got this.' No more than a whisper, her lips barely moving, and yet saying it out loud almost convinced her it was true. She could be a mother.

'Oh. My. God.' Mel flopped into the mint-green timber chair opposite. 'I honestly thought things would calm down this month after the post-summer rush, but we're busier than ever.' She took a sip from the monogrammed drink bottle, the café name, Driftwood, written in flowing script beside a pastel transfer of a beach umbrella. Perfectly branded. She really had thought of everything.

Eve raised her glass of lime and soda. 'All money in the till.' Not that she would be sharing in the profits as originally planned, but some things in life couldn't be measured in dollars and cents.

'You betcha, baby.' Mel's grin stretched from ear to ear. She slipped the elastic from her blonde ponytail, gathered her hair into a bun and bundled it onto her head. Her blue eyes shone: a startling lavender against the sun-kissed bronze of her cheeks. A born beach babe, even in the midst of winter. Everything about her buzzed.

'This place really agrees with you, Mel. Good decision.'

'It could have agreed with you too.' No malice in the statement; a simple observation. One hundred percent true.

Could have. But doesn't.

Eve drew in a fresh draft of sea air. Overhead, gelato-coloured bunting flapped and snapped in the mid-morning breeze. Buffed bodies sauntered by: a bikini-bottomed twenty-something walking her dachshund; a shirtless jogger, his butt barely covered by a tiny pair of nylon shorts; a couple of sun-worshipping women waddling in their one-pieces, towels thrown lazily around their necks. And beyond them, nothing but a ribbon of white and a blanket of turquoise stretching all the way to the horizon. Yes, she could definitely have been happy here, if she'd never returned to Mossy Creek.

'Not having second thoughts by any chance?' A hopeful tone to Mel's question this time.

'Absolutely not.' Eve shook her head. 'Like I said, this place is perfect for you. But, as you know, things have changed for me.'

'You can say that again. Honestly, Eve, when you told me you were pregnant and staying on at your old place, I thought you'd had a menty B. No offence, but I just could not picture you as a mother *or* a cowgirl. Especially when your house burnt down and you literally had nowhere to live. *Still* have nowhere to live, might I add.'

A too-loud laugh spilled from Eve's lips. 'Believe me, I had trouble picturing it myself for a while.' They'd skirted around this conversation over the last few days, ever since she'd arrived for what would be her last holiday for the foreseeable future, at least solo. But her imminent departure was forcing them to deal with unfinished business. 'And I really am sorry for letting you down after we'd talked about taking on a place like this for so long.'

Mel gave a one-shouldered shrug. 'No hard feelings, my friend. Fate stepped in and led us in different directions. Having my brother as a silent partner isn't turning out so bad. All he's interested in are the profits so I can run the place the way I want.'

'Well, you're doing a brilliant job.'

'I'm so glad you came up to see it.'

'Me too.' Eve reached out and squeezed Mel's hand. Even though they were chalk and cheese when it came to pretty much everything, somehow their friendship had lasted beyond their days working together at the Marrickville bar. 'You've worked so hard to get this place up and running. I'm really proud of you.'

'Thanks, chick.' A light sheen glazed Mel's eyes. She took another sip from her drink bottle. 'So, what's next for you? I mean ... apart from being a mumma.'

'Ah, now there's a question.' Eve gulped back a mouthful of her drink, letting the cool bubbles soothe the chafing in her throat. Between surviving catastrophic fires, fending off arson accusations, and discovering she was pregnant, there hadn't been much time to regroup. Now she finally had a plan, but it was a little too soon to spill the beans. She squinted into the distance, peering between the scratches on her sunnies. 'I have something in the pipeline, and in the meantime I've got the job at the café.'

Mel dropped her gaze to the tips of her French-polished nails. Whatever she wasn't saying formed an invisible wall between them. One that needed to be scaled. Who knew when they'd see each other again?

'You can say it, Mel.' Once upon a time, Eve would have run a mile from tough-love conversations. Maybe she really was growing up. About time at thirty-eight.

'Okay.' Mel shifted the bottle to one side and leaned into the edge of the table, hands loosely folded. 'I know you said you want to do this whole baby thing on your own, but I think you should reconsider not telling Marcus.'

Eve stiffened, as if she was standing with her back to the wall being measured. And in a metaphorical sense she was. Hugh had also questioned her decision, then Margo, and now Mel. This baby was the last shot she had at creating a family, her own family, one she would not be sharing with a man who had turned out to be a liar and a cheat. Just like her father.

'We've talked about this already.' Try as she might, it was impossible to explain exactly why she didn't want to tell Marcus. Even to herself. 'He never wanted kids – he made that more than clear.' Not that she'd wanted them herself at that point. 'Besides, he doesn't even live in the country anymore.'

'Mobile phones do work internationally.' Mel punctuated her deliberate sarcasm with a single raised eyebrow.

'And this isn't just about what you want, Eve. Surely the kid deserves to know its father.'

Eve took in a breath and waited for her galloping heartbeat to slow. Yes, every child had the right to have a relationship with its father but not when there's a good chance that parent will up and leave. Better to avoid any possibility of that happening by not having them around in the first place.

'Believe me, I've thought long and hard about this.' It hadn't taken long at all to decide on single motherhood, but Mel didn't need to know the specifics. 'At some point down the road, if the *bambino* wants to know about his or her father, I'll cross that bridge, but until then it's just the two of us.'

'See what you did then?'

'What?'

'*Bambino*. Italiano for baby. It's a sign that subconsciously you know you should get in touch with Marcus.'

Where *had* that word come from? So far, Eve had labelled the baby 'alien', 'peanut', 'creature' and every fruit and vegetable specified by the baby websites. *Bambino* was certainly new, but it was definitely not one of Mel's signs from the universe.

Eve batted her hand in the air. 'It's because you mentioned Italy. Nothing more, nothing less.'

'Whatever. But apart from anything else, he could be good for some child support.'

'I don't need his money. And I won't be asking him for anything.' Her mother had survived just fine on her own, and she could do the same. But if it was going to get her friend off her case, stretching the truth a little wouldn't hurt. 'It's early days. I'm not even halfway through the pregnancy yet. I'll tell him at some point. Promise.'

Mel clapped her hands together. 'Okay.' She adjusted her face into a smile in an obvious attempt to lighten the mood. 'One thing's for sure. That gene combo is going to make one adorable baby. You two would look right at home on the red carpet. I always thought you were the hottest couple.'

A gentle flush heated Eve's cheeks. Marcus was certainly handsome, with his dark waves, brooding bedroom eyes, and permanent three-day growth. But she'd never thought of herself as anything more than ordinary and didn't take compliments well. She picked her phone up from the table, checking the time. The Uber would be here any minute. A new message notification caught her eye and she flicked it open. Hugh.

When are you back? I have some news about the grant.

A frisson of excitement bubbled through her veins. Or was it nerves? Starting her own business was such a huge step, especially when she was single and pregnant. But the idea of working with horses again made something deep inside her glow. Not to mention her business partner.

Heading back today. Her thumbs tapped away on her phone. Even the one on her left hand had healed enough from the burn to work. *Will call when I'm home.*

She glanced up from her phone to meet Mel's quizzical gaze. 'What?'

'That smile. Your whole face lit up when you read that message.'

'Pfft.' Eve stuck her phone back in her pocket. 'Just replying to a text from a friend.'

'Uh huh. And that *friend* wouldn't be a certain veterinarian by any chance?'

'How did you—?'

'Oh, Eve, come on. Every time you talk about him, you

get this glint in your eye and a dreamy look on your face. You're totally lovestruck.'

'Oh, fuck off. I am not.' Had she even mentioned Hugh since she'd been here? Surely only once. Or twice. 'There's nothing in it. He's a widower with two kids, and I'm having another man's baby. Hardly a recipe for a happily ever after, which I am not in the market for anyway.'

'You keep telling yourself that, girlfriend.' Mel didn't even attempt to hide her laugh. 'But keep me posted. I want to know all the details when and as they happen.'

A white SUV pulled in beside the kerb. Eve checked the number plate and rose to her feet. 'That's my ride.'

Mel pulled her in for a hug in a cloud of florally scent. 'Sorry if I overstepped, about the whole Marcus thing.'

'Don't be silly. I know you're looking out for me. And I will tell him. Soon.' She could almost feel her nose growing, Pinocchio-style.

Wheeling her suitcase to the car, she gave a final wave and climbed into the back seat. The driver pulled away, and before they rounded the bend she twisted to look out the rear window. Even as they grew smaller in the distance, the summery colours of the café and the soft blues of the sea merged into one sparkling possibility: a life she could have had but definitely did not regret forfeiting. But as it faded into the distance and she turned back around, all she could see in front of her was a murky fog she couldn't quite bring into focus.

One she would hopefully be able to navigate. Solo.

A Place of Her Own: Chapter One

24 WEEKS

Squeezing the curve of her belly behind the steering wheel of the Kombi was not something Eve had ever thought would be a problem. But then she'd never anticipated driving to an obstetrician's appointment. Or being pregnant. Or having a business partner.

A rabble of butterflies jostled around in her stomach. She contracted her abs, willing them into submission before they could take flight. Her relationship with Hugh was purely work. And friendship. Would never be anything more. Could never be.

She needed to focus on building her house, setting up the equine centre, and having her baby – and right now, getting to the obstetrician on time. The café meeting had already made her late, and she needed to get her arse into gear.

Shuffling back in the seat, she turned the key in the ignition. Nothing but a click.

'What the…?'

Another turn. Another click. Even fainter than the first.

'Shit. Really?'

She slumped against the back of the seat and thumped her hands on the sheepskin wheel cover. As much as she loved driving a vintage van, there were moments when she could quite happily put a bomb under it and blow it to smithereens.

A tapping on the passenger window dulled that thought. She turned her head, not even bothering to disguise what must be a look of pure contempt.

'Everything okay?' Hugh's forest-green eyes peered in at her, his question muffled by the moth-stained glass.

Why was he still hovering? Didn't he have a cat to spay or a dog to neuter?

She shook her head. *No, everything was definitely not okay.*

The door clunked open.

'Bloody thing won't start. Sounds like the battery.' She exhaled a heavy sigh. 'How can it possibly be dead when I just drove it into town?'

Hugh gave one of his trademark shrugs. 'Might be on its last legs. Want me to have a try?'

'No.' What was it with men thinking they could fix every broken thing on the planet? 'Thank you.' No point taking it out on Hugh when he was only trying to help.

'Are you in the NRMA?'

'Yes, but I don't have time to wait for them. I have an appointment.' While the topic of her pregnancy wasn't exactly off limits, she never volunteered information about it in case it made Hugh feel awkward. Not that it should. They'd sorted that issue out long ago, hadn't they?

'I can drop you off wherever you need to go, and we can sort the battery out later.' Hugh would make someone a wonderful—

Eve Nicholls, do not go there!

'It's fine. It's only a check-up. I can reschedule.'

'At your OB?'

She gave a small nod. Cancelling would mean waiting who knew how long for another appointment, and there were those blood test results to discuss. Supposedly routine, but the Googling she'd done had put her on edge. She could hardly ask Hugh to drive her forty minutes there and back, could she?

'Darcy is covering for me this morning, so I'll see if she can stay a bit longer.'

'No, Hugh—'

He'd already dialled and had the phone pressed to his ear. He took a few steps away from the van, smiling and nodding. Honestly, the guy could not be any nicer. Her heart sank.

'All good.' Hugh reappeared at the still-open door. 'Darcy is fine to hold the fort. I'm parked down the road.'

Technically she hadn't asked for his help, and accepting the offer didn't mean anything more than allowing a friend to do a favour. Grabbing her bag, she climbed out and locked the van. At least they had plenty of business talk to keep them occupied on the drive.

Leaving Hugh sitting in his car in the pouring rain while she attended her appointment seemed rude. Eve directed him to the café and headed along the corridor to the prenatal clinic. Being a public patient meant making the trip north to the hospital for each visit, but being a friend of a doctor meant snagging a highly sought-after obstetrician, one of the many advantages of re-connecting with Cat after so many years of estrangement.

The wet soles of her boots squelched against the linoleum floor. She kept her breathing shallow, trying not to take in the cloying smell that always seemed to cling to hospital walls. Bec had been brought here after the lake accident, but thankfully Nell had identified the body on her own. No doubt the morgue had been drenched with nostril-burning disinfectant.

Her stomach gave a slow roll. She quickened her pace and pushed through the plastic doors that led to the clinic, hovering at the entrance to the waiting room. A few pregnant women occupied the seats, along with a couple of men who were probably their partners.

'Hello.' The receptionist flashed a smile. She glanced at her computer screen and then back up. 'Doctor is running a little behind I'm afraid, Ms Nicholls. Take a seat.'

Maybe she would have had time to call for roadside assistance after all. Poor Hugh was going to be stuck here for a while. He could go for a drive. In the rain. Or grab another cup of coffee. She pulled out her phone and sent him an apologetic text.

Of course, he replied that it wasn't a problem. Of course, he asked if he could get her anything.

A peppermint tea would be great. She typed the text and grabbed a magazine from the pile, keeping her gaze down. She'd never been one for small talk, and on her last couple of visits the woman now sitting directly opposite her had tried desperately to engage. Flipping the conversation back to The Talker had worked a treat, and Eve had heard all about how horrendous the woman's last labour had been, how she'd needed a blood transfusion and almost died, and how wonderful her husband had been caring for both her and the baby when they'd finally been able to go home.

The same woman, her toddler asleep in its pram, was

currently singing the praises of reusable nappies to the woman sitting beside her, who gave the occasional polite nod. Why anyone would willingly go back into the birthing suite for more after 'almost dying' the first time was a complete mystery. But then accidents did happen, as Eve knew only too well.

Keeping her head down, she flicked through a pile of magazines until the door opened and Hugh appeared, wearing his trademark grin and carrying two takeaway cups. Everyone turned at once as the enticing aroma of coffee wafted through the space. Was she imagining it or did the room collectively salivate? Probably just her own body responding to what used to be a staple. Being off both caffeine and booze so soon after quitting smoking had certainly created more than a few cravings. Thankfully, herbal teas and oranges had recently taken precedence.

She took the cup and cradled it between her hands, letting the minty warmth seep through the cardboard into her palms. 'Thank you.' She smiled at Hugh. 'Over and above.'

'All part of the service.' He pointed to the empty seat beside her. 'Okay if I—?'

'Be my guest.' She made a theatrical gesture. Even though they'd made a pact to keep their relationship platonic, there was still that lovely sense of banter in their interactions. Hugh's Scottish humour blended well with her Australian sardonic wit. It was almost like they had their own private comedy act going on.

'Anything interesting?' He nodded in the direction of the magazine she was mindlessly skimming through.

'Only if you think Kylie Minogue's apparent weight gain or David Hasselhoff's run-in with paparazzi is essential reading.'

'Oh my God, I love the Hoff.'

Oh great. The chatterbox from across the room had jumped into the conversation.

Hugh's attempted smile was more like a wince.

'My hubby couldn't make it today,' The Talker continued as everyone simultaneously looked down at their laps. Except Hugh's. 'He's actually away at the moment. For work. Normally he never misses an appointment. He gets such a kick out of seeing the ultrasounds and hearing the heartbeat. I swear, if it was humanly possible he'd carry the baby and give birth himself.'

Oh God. Any minute now, that woman would be engaging Hugh in conversation.

The door to the surgery opened and a heavily pregnant patient waddled out. How was it possible to be that round and remain upright?

Forty minutes and a dozen magazines later, Dr Walker finally ushered her into the surgery. 'Your partner can come in too if he likes.'

Eve's face heated as she stood. 'Oh, he's not—'

'It's fine. I'll wait here.' Hugh, his cheeks a shade rosier, gave a tight smile.

Eve had filled the doctor in on her single status on her first visit, but with the number of women who passed through the clinic doors, it was probably hard to keep track.

The Talker shifted forward in her chair, as if she was watching a particularly riveting twist in a movie. No doubt she would grill Hugh any minute.

Eve shot him a wink as she left the room. 'Have fun.'

The obstetrician started talking as soon as they stepped inside the surgery. 'Good timing having an appointment today. I need to talk to you about your recent screening test.'

Cherie Walker was the best kind of doctor. Firstly, she was a woman, and secondly she was a no-nonsense, straight-talker who didn't muck around with preliminaries.

'The blood sugar one?' The foul orange liquid Eve had drunk had almost made her heave, and the waiting around for multiple blood tests had been more than tedious.

'Yes.' Cherie pressed her lips together as she scrolled through a document on her computer screen. 'It's positive for gestational diabetes. Do you know if there's a history of it in your family?'

Gestational diabetes … family…

'Eve?'

'Sorry. No, I don't.'

'Any idea if your mother had it?'

'If she did, she never mentioned it.'

'And she's—?'

'Dead.' It came out in a rush and hovered like a cartoon caption.

'Ah, I'm sorry.' Cherie gave an appropriate pause. 'Well, there isn't always a family connection. Geriatric mothers are more prone to it. Have you been thirstier than usual? Peeing more?'

Apparently being over thirty-five and pregnant for the first time made you a geriatric. Had she been thirstier? She'd never been a huge water drinker, but she had been filling her bottle more often lately and waking up parched in the middle of the night. 'Yeah, I have. I thought it was a normal pregnancy thing.'

'I'm afraid not.'

'Is it bad?'

'Not if it's managed properly. But there is a slightly

higher chance of pre-eclampsia, excess amniotic fluid around the baby, and pre-term delivery. There's also an increased chance of the baby...'

Cherie's voice faded into the background, with only the occasional word piercing through the cloud filling Eve's brain.

Jaundice ... macrosomia ... trouble breathing...

Which was exactly what she was currently experiencing. Her diaphragm tightened, as if she'd been breath-tested and exhaled too much air. The idea of motherhood – of being responsible for another human being for the rest of her life – had taken some getting used to. But slowly the vision of creating her own special family of two had taken hold. Now the thought of something being wrong with her baby made her whole body quiver.

She forced her lungs to expand and recalibrated.

'We'll make some dietary changes, but given your age and the fact you're a primigravida, I'll refer you to an endocrinologist, who will no doubt get you onto an insulin program.'

'Insulin?' Was she now officially a diabetic?

Cherie nodded while she typed. 'You'll need to test daily and give yourself injections. It's all about monitoring the levels and adjusting the dosage accordingly.' She said it so matter of factly, as if jabbing yourself with a needle was as everyday as brushing your teeth.

The rest of the examination passed in a whirlwind of blood pressure testing, dietary advice and exercise guidelines, and finally a referral to see the specialist. Eve feigned a smile as she said goodbye and stepped out into the waiting room.

The Talker had changed seats; positioned herself in the

chair beside Hugh, who looked up, glassy-eyed, and practically leapt to his feet.

He couldn't get out the door quick enough. That made two of them. 'Everything okay?'

'Yes, all good.' She accentuated her words with a breezy smile. Nothing Cherie said had sunk in as yet. She needed to find out more about the diabetes thing before she shared the news. Make sure it wasn't going to put a spanner in the works of the equine assisted therapy business Hugh was helping her set up and had become so invested in – literally and otherwise. That he'd managed to secure a grant to get up and running.

Cherie hadn't mentioned anything about additional rest or having to give up work, but better to know what she was dealing with before telling Hugh or anyone else. As soon as Margo got even a whisper of a complication with the pregnancy, she'd pull the godmother card and start nagging about taking it easy. And Margo had enough of her own medical problems right now.

All the way to the car, Hugh filled her in on The Talker's stories. Eve managed to pay enough attention to smile at the appropriate times and give what she hoped were sufficiently sympathetic comments.

But all the while, her mind was racing.

What did this diabetes thing really mean for her pregnancy? What if she had to stop working? What if the baby she'd never planned but now so desperately wanted was…?

No. She couldn't go there. Everything would be fine.

A Place of Her Own: Chapter Two

'Did the mechanic say how long it would take to fix the starter motor?'

Through the passenger window of Fran's Tesla, scorched patches of bush flashed between fingers of fresh, green sprouts. The recent week-long deluge had been a pain in the arse on the building front, but at least it had encouraged new growth.

'Eve?' A single brow arched beneath Fran's heavy fringe – an even darker shade of mulberry than it had been a week ago.

'Sorry?' She rattled her head, shaking herself out of the daze she'd been in ever since she'd left the obstetrician's office.

'The Kombi. How long until it will be good to go?'

'Could be a while. He needs to get parts.' She let out a sigh. 'At least this time it didn't have to be towed far.' Normally this sort of inconvenience would have her ranting, but she had more important things on her mind.

'It might be time to start thinking about some new

wheels. You don't want to be stuck somewhere with a screaming baby. And those things are worth serious money now the whole van life thing has taken off.'

The Kombi was as much a part of Eve as her Kelpie, and the idea of driving a sensible sedan was as outrageous as swapping Banjo for a miniature poodle. 'We'll see.'

'Hmm.' Fran pressed her lips into a thin line. 'At least you're not living in that dreadful caravan anymore. How are you liking the Tiny House?'

'It's fantastic.' She needed to stay focused, at least until she was alone, and Fran's choice of topic was the perfect diversion. Living in the caravan for a short time hadn't been so bad, but the extra space was blissful. 'Are you sure your friend is okay for me to use it? I can pay rent. I mean, I'd like to.'

Fran gave an almost violent shake of her head. 'Nope. Pete wouldn't hear of it. He had it on his property for his daughter to live in, but she's moved to South Australia. He's happy to wait to sell it, and he's already said he doesn't want any payment in the meantime.'

Accepting kindnesses from anybody, let alone a complete stranger, wasn't exactly part of Eve's DNA, but she was trying to be more community-minded now she'd decided to stay. Kicking a neighbourly gift-bearing horse was not exactly in line with her new philosophy.

'I'm so grateful to you and Clive for setting it all up, although I think Margo is still a bit snippy that I've traded up.' Her godmother could get a little touchy if she thought she wasn't being appreciated.

'She'll have to get over it. Your comfort is more important. I know it's still a small space, but at least you can wash your hair in the shower without dislocating your elbows.'

'So true.' Fran had a point. 'I won't know what to do with myself when I get back into a real house.'

A real house.

A place that was completely her own.

Fran turned the final corner, and Mossy Creek Farm shimmered in mid-afternoon sunlight. Warmth filled Eve's veins, as if that single ray of light beaming across the front paddock had somehow suffused her skin. Horses grazed behind the post and rail fences, or at least the fire-resistant version her mother had the good sense to install a few years back. Otherwise, they'd have been burnt to the ground, just like the house.

As always, her gaze went straight to Rain, the gorgeous chestnut mare she'd managed to nurse back to health when she'd first arrived. She tracked along the fence line to the end of the drive, to where the timber frame of the new build was starting to take shape. It was a simple design, so hopefully it would be done in the next few months. Weather permitting. As much as losing her childhood home had hurt, the idea of her own brand-new cottage was a bright beacon shining on the horizon.

But for now, the small cabin on the hill was home.

'...won't know yourself.' Again, the sound of Fran's voice brought Eve back to the real world.

Whatever she'd said, a vague smile seemed to be an acceptable response.

'Did everything go okay with your check up? I totally forgot to ask when I picked you up from the repair shop.'

Her stomach cartwheeled. She'd never been one for sharing, especially if it was going to mean a fuss. And there was a lot to get her head around before she told anyone about the diabetes. 'Yeah, all good.'

Fortunately, the drive was over. Fran pulled up outside

the Tiny House, its colour scheme blending in beautifully – and weirdly – with the ashen hues of the bush forming its backdrop.

Banjo sprang from his spot on the small porch and leapt around the car like a gazelle, all four feet leaving the ground at once, before zeroing in for where-have-you-been pats.

She leaned down and inhaled his soft, familiar scent. Always such a comfort. 'I've missed you too, matey.'

He yapped, as if in agreement, his mouth splitting into an ear-to-ear grin.

Fran rounded the car. 'I think someone might be a tad put out when there's competition for your affections.'

'Possibly.' Eve hadn't thought as far ahead as to what sort of adjustment Banj would have to make when the baby arrived. Had barely got her head around the fact that it would be here before the end of the year. And now there was a whole new set of medical facts to absorb.

Hand on hip, Fran narrowed her gaze. 'I know you're hellbent on doing this whole baby thing on your own, Eve, and I totally admire your independence, but don't forget there are people here who are more than happy to help you out anytime. I'm no expert but pregnancy and parenthood aren't walks in the park.'

Where had that come from? Had Fran picked up something in her non-response about the appointment?

'Of course.' She made sure to sound agreeable. 'Thank you so much for the lift home. You're a life saver.'

Fran pulled her into a musk-scented hug. 'No problem at all. I know it would have been much pleasanter to have Hugh at the wheel.' She leaned back, quirking her cherry-red lips. 'Hopefully he's managed to extract the gut full of rubber from that poor retriever.'

'Hopefully.' Best to ignore the suggestive tone Fran used

whenever Hugh was the subject of the conversation. Eventually she – and everyone else – would get the message: they were not, and never would be, an item.

Fran opened the driver's door. 'Well, I have a date with a bottle of champers. Might even share it with Clive. And you look like you could do with a rest.' She winked and climbed into the car, gliding away with a quiet hum. So different to the guttural growl of the Kombi.

Not that it had made any noise at all today as it was towed away.

She breathed in the blissful quiet. Fran had confused her distraction for exhaustion, which was probably a good thing. And she was feeling more tired than usual. Was that the diabetes? Doctor Google would be able to answer that question.

'Right, matey, let's get you fed.'

Banjo raced to his empty bowl by the door. Stopping on the porch, Eve glanced across the paddocks to where the horses were nibbling the newly installed round hay bales. So much easier than doing twice-daily feeds. The soft mauve glow of approaching twilight had turned them all into silhouettes, thrown long shadows across the grass, and darkened what remained of the day to a deep indigo sky. She had visited so many beautiful places in her travels, but there was nowhere she'd rather be than here.

The thought hummed through her like a cloud of bees in a lavender patch. Stepping inside, she paused to revel in the buzz. It had been only a couple of weeks and it was still hard to believe this Tiny House was home. For now, at least.

Honey-coloured floorboards creaked gently beneath her feet as she stepped across the threshold. A grey velvet lounge begged to be occupied. The country-style kitchenette, with its soft-white timber walls, two clear glass lampshades dangling from a cathedral ceiling, was straight off a Pinterest corkboard. Making a dash for the small but adequate bathroom, she sent up a prayer for the flushing toilet. As grateful as she'd been for Margo's caravan, the composting loo had been a little too basic.

She scaled the ladder to the loft bedroom and swapped her jeans and coat for trackies and a dressing gown before climbing down again. Navigating them with a watermelon belly would be interesting, but there was always the downstairs sofa bed. At the door, Banjo gave his please-feed-me whine. She filled his bowl with kibble, flicked on the heaven-sent reverse cycle air con and opened her laptop.

Fingers poised above the keys, she drew in a sharp breath. Ever since she'd been exonerated from the arson accusations, made the decision to keep the baby and to start life again here at the farm, things had been falling into place. Hugh's enthusiasm for the equine therapy centre had been contagious and persuaded her into a partnership. Her morning sickness had vanished, only to be replaced by a vibrant energy. Even being drawn into the web of friendships she'd so studiously avoided on her return to Yarrabee hadn't been so bad. Everything had gone so smoothly for the last few months, it had sucked her into a false sense of security, wrapped her in a fuzzy blanket of hope.

But the GD diagnosis had ripped her right back out again. She'd been so focused on the decision to keep the baby and raise it on her own, she hadn't stopped to consider something could go wrong with the pregnancy. Now she had a new diet and exercise regimen to follow. And the endocrinologist would start her on insulin, but what did that really mean? How would it impact her day-to-day life? The reading material Cherie had given her was a starting point, but there would be plenty of information on the internet. If she was doing this, she'd do it right. Be the best damned geriatric pre-term mother ever to grace the doors of her OB's surgery.

She rolled her shoulders, pressed the space bar on her computer and typed in the question that had been burning like a grassfire at the back of her mind all afternoon.

How do you manage gestational diabetes?

A Place of Her Own: Chapter Three

25 WEEKS

Eve jolted awake to the sound of an engine and Banjo's ear-piercing bark. A fine thread of drool laced her chin. Swiping it away, she sat upright on the couch momentarily disoriented. Her laptop was still open on the table beside the GD pamphlets. Trawling the internet for more information had literally put her to sleep.

A knock sounded, and Banjo kept up his alert, turning to her for acknowledgement.

'That's enough. Drop.'

While his bark was generally worse than his bite – apart from that one time when he quite rightly dug his teeth into Todd Adams's ankle – it had a way of sharpening every bone in her skull.

Dog sorted, she opened the door.

'Don't you ever collect your mail?' Beneath the glaring automatic porch light, Margo held up a handful of envelopes. The grouchy tone was a cover. Her godmother was like a toasted marshmallow: a crusty exterior, but inside soft and gooey.

Ushering Margo inside, Eve pulled her into a hug, snuggling against the feathery pillow of silver hair. Not so thick and lush anymore, after multiple rounds of radiation and chemo. She hadn't been around when Margo went through the breast cancer, but now it had spread, the treatment was sure to be harsher.

A sharp pain stabbed at the back of her throat, but she swallowed it away. 'You're not still grumpy about my new accommodation, I hope.'

'Don't be ridiculous.' Margo tutted and shook her head, but the way she avoided eye contact suggested otherwise. Shifting from one foot to the other, she motioned towards the small table. 'Got time for a quick chat?' She rubbed the pads of her fingers together, and they made a papery sound.

Strange for Margo to be here after dark.

'Of course.' Closing the lid on the computer, Eve gathered up all the pamphlets and shoved the pile on the bench, face down.

'What's all that?' Nothing escaped Margo's eagle eyes.

'Just reading up on pregnancy bits and pieces.'

They sat opposite each other, Margo's gaze resting on the purple African violet decorating the centre of the table. Her face was pale, and dark circles ringed her eyes. She'd lost so much weight. No surprise, given what she was going through. But hopefully the treatment would perform a miracle. The alternative didn't bear thinking about.

Had Margo received bad news on the health front? Was that why she was here? As difficult as it was to raise the subject, maybe she needed a prod to get her talking. 'How's the treatment going?'

'Oh, it's going.' Margo sighed. 'Harry's been taking me to the radiation sessions. Drops me off and goes to wander the aisles at Bunnings, buy supplies he doesn't really want.

Better than having him mope about in the hospital. The last thing I need is him sitting there looking miserable. Thank God I haven't told him the whole story.'

Keeping the truth from Harry about the aggressive nature of the cancer was a well-worn argument. Margo would tell him in her own time. Everyone had their own way of dealing with things, as Eve knew only too well. 'And you're feeling okay?'

'Better than I expected.' She worried at the bottom of her flecked cardigan, shuffling the wool between her fingers, the way a small child might do with a comforter.

A heavy silence filled the small space. Banjo stretched out under the table, hiding as if he'd read the room. Above the fridge, a wall clock ticked way too loudly, the monotonous sound setting Eve's teeth on edge. Finally, Margo shuffled through the envelopes she'd laid in front of her on the table, moving aside the few she'd collected on her way in and opening the one in her hand. She pulled out a folded piece of paper, her hands shaking as she smoothed it out flat. As she pushed it across the table, she lifted her chin. Tears swam in her eyes.

A screw turned in Eve's chest. Hopefully this wasn't a will. Or a doctor's report confirming the worst. Was she going to be forced to confront Margo's mortality right now?

'What is it?' The question came out in a whisper.

Margo tipped her head towards the document in a gesture that clearly meant *see for yourself*.

Eve picked it up, her hands trembling as she read.

Dear Mrs Harris

I have been contacted by the Adoption Information Unit of the Department of Justice and Community Services to say that you have recently registered your details in an attempt to find the child you gave up for adoption. According to the Reunion and Information Register, I am your daughter.

My adoptive parents christened me Wendy.

Holy fuck! Margo had added her name to the register well over two months ago, but hadn't mentioned a word since about trying to locate her daughter. It was as if they'd made a silent agreement never to mention the subject again.

Across the table, Margo swiped at her cheek and waved her hand towards the print-out, sending a clear message: keep reading.

I added my name to the register twenty-five years ago when I gave birth to my first child, eager to know more about my history, genetic and otherwise. Since so long has passed, I had given up any hope of finding you, so it was a shock to receive a notification that you are now looking for me. I actually received your details some time ago, but it has taken me a while to consider whether or not I should contact you, particularly given how long it took you to seek me out.

I thought long and hard about whether there is any point dredging up the past. But curiosity has gotten the better of me, so I am reaching out to see if we might be able to have some sort of contact. Perhaps it would be best to talk on the phone initially, with a view to meeting in person if we both feel it would be the next best step.

It feels very strange to be writing this email to a woman whose blood I share, but who I could pass in the street and not recognise.

Let me know your thoughts, and we can proceed from there.
Kind regards,
Wendy Pike

Grab your copy...
vinci-books.com/placeofherown

About the Author

Pamela Cook is an author, podcaster, writing teacher and mentor. Her debut novel *Blackwattle Lake* (2012) was published by Hachette Australia in 2012 followed by three rural fiction titles. She subsequently published two independent titles (*Cross My Heart* and *All We Dream*) and is now publishing with Bolinda Audio and Vinci Books.

Pamela writes stories of longing and belonging, delving deep into the psychology of her characters and the complexity of relationships in all their forms. She explores the impact of trauma, grief and generational conflict, drawing on the resilience and courage she finds in inspirational women. Her writing is imbued with a deep love of the natural world and its power to heal.

Producing and hosting *Writes4Women*, a weekly podcast that supports women writers and celebrates women's writing, is one of Pamela's not-so-guilty pleasures. She is also a Writer Ambassador for Room to Read, a not-for-profit organisation promoting literacy and gender equality in developing countries.

An experienced teacher, Pamela loves to mentor emerging authors. When she's not writing or reading, she wastes as much time as possible riding her handsome quarter horse Baloo, hanging out with her family and menagerie of animals on her dream-come-true rural property in the beautiful Illawarra region of NSW, and dreaming of a road trip in Virginia, her vintage caravan.

Acknowledgments

When I wrote *Blackwattle Lake*, the first story in this series, I had only a vague thought that I might write a follow-on book, so continuing Eve's journey more than a decade after dreaming her to life, has been both a surprise and a joy. As always it would never have happened without the support of my wonderful writing buddies in The Inkwell: Angella Whitton, Terri Green, Rae Cairns, Penelope Janu, Laura Boon, Joanna Nell and Michelle Barraclough. Particular thanks to Rae, Pen and Laura for your input into this manuscript — your feedback was invaluable.

A huge thank you to my agents at Key People Management, Jeanne Ryckmans and Lou Johnson. Your belief in me and your guidance is truly appreciated and I'm so glad to be riding this rollercoaster with you both.

Thank you to my daughters Freya, Amelia and Georgia for your constant belief in me and for allowing me to lock myself away when deadlines loom! And to my husband John, for your unwavering love and support, and for holding my hand and putting up with the tears when things haven't gone according to plan.

Finally thank you to everyone who has read one of my books over the years. Knowing that my readers have connected to something in my stories is the absolute best part of being an author. If you read *Blackwattle Lake* I hope you enjoy this continuation of Eve's story. Stay tuned for the third and final instalment!